D1085770

Confessions after dark

by

Kahlen Aymes

TELEMACHUS PRESS

This book is a work of fiction. Names, characters, places and incidents are either the product of the author's imagination or are used fictitiously. Any resemblance to actual persons, living or dead, or to actual events or locales is entirely coincidental.

CONFESSIONS AFTER DARK

The publisher does not have any control over and does not assume any responsibility for author or third-party websites or their content.

CoverArt:
Designed by: Kristen Karwan
Cover photo by: Scott Hoover Photography
Cover model: Colby Lefebvre

Published by Telemachus Press, LLC
http://www.telemachuspress.com

Visit the author website:
http://www.kahlen-aymes.blogspot.com

ISBN: 978-1-940745-83-1 (eBook)
ISBN: 978-1-940745-84-8 (Paperback)

Version 2014.05.16

Printed in the United States of America

10 9 8 7 6 5 4 3 2 1

Dedication

This is for my readers... I adore you and you are my inspiration.

Acknowledgements

Thank you to Kendall Ryan and Kelly Elliott for their endorsement of this series. I fan-girl just a bit when you contact me and tell me that you love my books! I'm so grateful for your support! I'm in awe of you.

Thanks to my new friends Ilsa Madden-Mills, T.K. Rapp, Ella Fox, Julie Richman, Sandi Lynn, & Aleatha Romig. It's been a pleasure getting to know you and I'm thankful for your support and friendship. Liv Morris... thanks for always being there. I love you all.

To Olivia, I love you. Thanks for being understanding of all of my time in front of the evil laptop.

Many thanks to the bloggers and the street team who toil endlessly to pimp me out, and to the many of you who sponsor and organize the signing events!

Kathryn Voskuil, Elizabeth Desmond, Sally Hopkinson (my editing team)... I couldn't do this without you!! <3

Thank you to Elizabeth Winick-Rubinstein (my agent) & Shira Hoffman (my foreign rights agent) at McIntosh & Otis Literary. I sincerely appreciate all of your support and dedication to introducing me to the world. xo

Table of Contents

Confessions after dark

1
Light of Day

DR. ANGEL HEMMING sat in the leather chair across from one of her regular patients, listening to her drone on about her abusive ex-husband. Impatience filled her despite the desperateness of the situation. Her mind was filled with other things; more important things. The rape case she was working on and her new relationship with Alexander Avery, the most fascinating man she'd ever met occupied her mind. It'd only been a few weeks since he'd bulldozed his way into her life, but he had taken a strong hold on her mind and body. She sighed, trying to concentrate on her patient's words.

"Megan, we've gone over this." *Over and over this*, her mind complained. Her frustration welled up inside her chest until it ached. "You know what you need to do."

"But—" Angel's patient wiped at her face with an already soggy Kleenex. "He says he loves me, Dr. Hemming."

Angel's eyes wanted to roll toward the heavens. This woman didn't want to hear what she had to say, and although Angel had done her damnedest to get Megan to take control of her life and get herself and her children out of the situation, she only had more excuses for the bastard who beat her. There was nothing to be done. If abuse of the woman's two children had come to light in their conversations, Angel would have no choice but to contact child protective services. Megan was an adult and had to take action to protect herself.

"Megan, may I be frank?" Angel's plum-colored Prada stiletto pump bounced along with the foot of her right leg, neatly crossed over her left knee. She pulled off her glasses, clicked off the recorder, and leaned forward in her chair.

The woman sniffled and pushed back her sleek black hair from her face. She was slightly plump, but pretty. Her husband had money, she didn't have to work, and he justified his treatment of her with his bank account. On the other hand, Megan made the choice to remain where she was.

"Please. That's what I'm paying you for." She nodded and her thick hair brushed her chin as it bobbed with her head.

"I'd like you to stop paying me."

"Wha-what?" Shock registered on her face.

Angel shrugged. "There's nothing more I can do for you. We've rehashed the situation for over a year and nothing's changed. You know what you need to do. So do it." Her tone was authoritative. "You know he's a bastard, so get the hell away from him or stop whining about a situation you refuse to change. Either that or convince him to come to your sessions with you. I'd like to talk to him."

The other woman's eyes widened in surprise.

"But—"

"No buts. If all you want to do is complain about him, you can do so with a friend. I'm here to validate your decisions, but when you refuse to do anything to help yourself, there is nothing here that I can affirm or condone. My time is far too valuable. I'm very sorry, but I have other patients and serious court matters to attend to, and my conscience demands that I devote the bulk of my time to those cases." She glanced down at her sleek Gucci watch before she stood and moved from behind her desk to walk her out. The woman slowly rose and moved in stunned silence toward the door where Angel offered her a hand. "Good luck. Take care of yourself and your children."

Megan left without a word, and a few minutes later Angel's professional secretary, Elizabeth, entered briskly and placed a package on Angel's desk. It was wrapped in white linen and had a beautiful organza ribbon in lavender tied around one of the dark purple lilies. Angel flushed as pleasure flooded through her and her mouth widened in a secret smile.

"Wow. You need to spill, missy." Liz cocked her neatly waxed brow.

"Not *wow*. It's just a cell phone charger."

"How do you know?" Surprise laced Liz's voice.

"I just know." One shoulder lifted in a slight shrug as Angel moved the package to the credenza behind her desk, the grin still plastered on her face. Damned if she could stop smiling.

"Aren't you gonna open it?" The woman demanded with a grin.

"Later."

"Why?"

"I need to prepare the questions for tomorrow. The giver of this gift is *far* too distracting."

Angel flushed guiltily at the memory of waking up in the tent with Alex after what felt like a minute and a half of sleep. Oh well, the punishment fit the crime.

"Wait. I thought all of the tests were standardized?"

"Um… sure. They are, but I've got a few extras on the Swanson case."

"That's not protocol, Angel. What's going on?"

"Nothing for you to concern yourself with; this guy is a slimy bastard and warrants more, uh… *extraction*. It's a gut feeling and I'm just being thorough."

Thankfully, the phone rang before more inquisition, and the young woman reached out and picked up the receiver on Angel's desk. Angel sighed in relief at the interruption. She had no intention of dragging someone else into this by saying more than she should.

"Dr. Angeline Hemming's office. How may I help you?"

Angel sank down in her chair and opened her Outlook email account, scanning for a certain address. She cursed her trembling fingers as they stumbled around on the keyboard, scrambling to open the one from Alex, the subject line causing her heart to beat faster.

From: A. Avery, CFO, Avery Enterprises International, Inc.
To: Angeline Hemming, Ph. D.
Subject: Us

I hated leaving. Waking up with you was magical. Thank you for an amazing couple of days... Now, go charge your fucking phone!
-A

Angel laughed out loud and quickly hit reply.

Liz's quizzical look said she wondered if the giggle was in any way connected to the beautifully wrapped gift on the desk. "Angel, there's a woman on the line regarding some sort of benefit for the Leukemia Foundation. Wanna take it?"

Angel glanced up, her brow creasing. She nodded, though she couldn't remember anything she'd committed to for that particular charity. Liz closed the door behind her as Angel picked up the phone.

"This is Dr. Hemming."

"Thank you for taking my call. My name is Ally Franklin, chairman of this year's fundraiser for the Chicagoland Chapter of the Leukemia and Lymphoma Foundation."

"Yes, what can I do for you?"

"Well, the event is in a month, a concert to be held at the Aragon Ballroom. It's usually a huge bash."

"Yes, I'm familiar with it. I attended two years ago, I believe. It was a very elegant affair."

"This year we were going for a more rock-like theme. We're recruiting a younger demographic of donors." Her voice was pleasant and her diction perfect.

"Sounds marvelous. Are you requesting PSAs on my radio program?"

"Well, yes, that would be lovely, of course, but not the reason for my call. The band we reserved canceled and I'm scrambling to find a replacement. There is one that I want badly, but they have refused me on two attempts."

"I'm sorry to hear that, Ms. Franklin, but surely, in a city this size, you should be able to find any number of bands that would want to help out."

"Oh, call me Ally, please. The band in question is Archangel."

Angel sat back in her chair in surprise. "Oh, I see. Have you been talking to Kyle, then?"

"Yes. Mr. Keith has been less than agreeable."

Angel smiled. *Mr. Keith. Hardly that.* Kyle was moody and difficult. He liked things his way or the highway, which was part of the problem where Angel was concerned, and the one thing he shared in common with Alex. She shook herself… *Can you get through one conversation without thinking about him?*

"Ah, yes, Kyle. There's a possibility the band is already booked for that date."

"No, I checked. I've been trying to book them for *weeks*."

"There must be a reason, then. He'd never turn down a gig that offered that much exposure."

"I think his words were: *it's not our scene*, something about blue hairs not liking rock-n-roll."

Angel chuckled quietly, wishing the call would end, anxious to reply to Alex's email, though part of her knew she should make him cool his heels. Girl games were so fun sometimes. "Yes, it sounds like him. He's very, um… direct."

"Yes. He told me to take my skinny ass and get lost." Amusement laced her tone and Angel burst out laughing, instantly taking a liking to this young woman. "If he wasn't so hot, I would have been really put upon."

"Oh, so then you spoke to him in person?" Angel smiled, thinking of this very refined-sounding woman in the presence of her ex, in all his tough and tattooed glory.

"Yes! I saw them at Excalibur two months ago. I was surprised how good they are. Some of their covers are better than the originals."

"Yes, I know. I'm surprised they haven't gotten a recording contract by now."

"I *really* want this band. They'd be a fabulous draw for the crowd I'm trying to attract. Can you talk to him?"

"Why me, Ms. Franklin?" Angel probed; the answer already niggling at her brain.

"I Googled the band and your name came up. So, you were lead singer for a few years?"

"Well, Kyle fronts the band. He and I… It was both of us."

"You must have a ton of influence. Will you help us? I understand you are huge into the charity circuit, so I'm hoping you'll take pity on my situation."

"My influence has been limited with him for the last couple of years, but I'll see what I can do. I can't make any promises. He's still mad at me for quitting."

"The band?"

"No, him. The band was just collateral damage."

"Oh, I see. Well, if it's too uncomfortable, I understand. You were my last resort."

"No, it's fine, Ms. Franklin. I'm going to give you back to my secretary, now. She'll take your contact information and I'll get back to you in a day or two. Will that be acceptable?"

"Yes! I really appreciate your help, and please call me Ally!"

"I'll talk to you soon, Ally. Have a nice afternoon."

Angel hung up the phone and resumed the email to Alex, a small smile playing on her red lips as her fingers flew over the keys.

From: Angeline Hemming, Ph. D.
To: A. Avery, CFO, Avery Enterprises, Inc.
Subject: Bossy, much?

Mr. Avery,
I don't take orders well, as you know. However, it suits me to charge the phone; so on this, I will acquiesce. I find the direct line extremely... er... stimulating. And yes, this morning was nice. Some of us aren't multi-millionaires and have to work. Please stop distracting me.
-A

She chuckled happily as she sent her message. The morning had been glorious. She awoke to warm lips on her shoulder, her naked body wrapped up tightly in his, still on the living room floor under the canopy of blankets. Her heart tightened inside her chest as she thought about it. It was exhilarating and unbelievable all rolled up together. It felt comfortable and right. She kept telling herself that it was too good to be true. However, his words and actions completely contradicted her original expectations and

Whitney's heated accusations. She had to admit that she was falling—and falling hard. Logic said she should get out now, but it just felt too damn good. And, not just physically.

Her heart constricted again, the pain a mixture of heady bliss and real fear. She closed her eyes, remembering the soft grazes of Alex's mouth on her shoulder as her eyes fought to open.

"You feel so good," Alex murmured as he dragged kisses over her collarbone and up the cord in her neck until his mouth seared hers. She was breathless and helpless under his merciless assault as he rolled her beneath him and pressed hard flesh into soft warmth. The events of the evening prior had proven he owned her, so she wanted nothing more than to experience every possible moment in this man's arms. Her hands roamed his naked back, reveling in the play of solid muscles as he moved.

When Jillian stirred in the other room, Alex had reluctantly pulled his mouth away. "Uhhh…" he sighed in frustration.

"Do you know what is most amazing about us?" Angel had whispered against his jaw, sighing in acknowledgment that she had to get up.

Alex huffed and smiled against the skin of her temple. "Is that a trick question?" He chuckled softly, his green eyes sparkling mischievously into hers.

"Not, that. I mean—" She shrugged and rolled her eyes with a grin. "Sure that, but the kisses…. are so silent. All breathing and brushing… sucking yes, but none of the sloppy, gross, smacking noises."

Alex burst out laughing, his eyes dancing at her. "I think there was a compliment in there somewhere."

"Yes…" she said breathlessly. "The kisses are more than amazing."

His answer was to take her mouth again hungrily, his tongue probing between her lips and finding hers in a frantic attempt to get enough to get through the day. Jillian's increased howl forced him to break the kiss and press his forehead to hers. "The most incredible I've ever had the pleasure of experiencing. I don't think I'll ever get enough."

"Never?" she asked hopefully.

"Never."

*****

Alex's morning was spent in meetings with Mrs. Dane rearranging his schedule and going over the expenditures that he would be granting Cole regarding the take-over of Swanson's business. He met Mrs. Dane's raised eyebrow with professional indifference, his demeanor clearly communicating that she was to ask no questions, just do as he asked.

Cole wouldn't be able to move into Angel's building until the end of the week, which made Alex uneasy. He was desperate to figure out a way to get her to stay with him until then, and he sure as hell wasn't going out of the country until he knew his brother would be within a few yards of her.

He ran a hand through his lush mop of hair and then over the stubble on his chin, sighing deeply. He left Angel's later than planned and rushed to the office after stopping briefly at his apartment for a quick change of clothes.

As much as he wanted to put Bancroft on her tail to make sure she was safe, Alex hesitated, unwilling to risk her anger if she found out. No, that wouldn't happen unless he felt he had absolutely no choice in the matter. It would be better to stay as close as he could, which had distinct advantages. Even hours later, after focusing on work and the laundry list of things he had on his plate, his body swelled to a painful throb at the memory. His mind could still conjure how she felt, her scent, the amazing way her body responded to his. The soft moans she made as he touched her most intimate places drove him wild with desire. As Alex pulled uncomfortably at the crotch of his dress slacks, he had to admit to himself that she excited him more than any woman he'd ever known, and the panic he felt over her current situation only reinforced more tender feelings he wasn't quite ready to face.

His phone buzzed and ended his musings.

"Your father is on line one," Mrs. Dane clipped, her even tone sounding over the intercom. "Are you available?"

"Yes, thank you, Mrs. Dane." Alex reached for the phone and leaned back in the dark brown leather chair behind the huge mahogany desk. "Hi, Dad."

"I thought you were going to Athens this morning? Has something happened?"

"Not at all. I just didn't feel like traveling this week. I had Blaine Foster handle it. He's been doing extremely well and deserves a shot." Alex tried to hide the agitation he felt at having to explain himself.

"You love Athens. You use any excuse to go."

"Sure, but I have a personal matter that needs my immediate attention."

"Are you ill?"

"Nothing like that," Alex dismissed shortly. "I'm fine."

"Okay, I'll leave you to it, then. How's Cole doing?"

"He's doing much better than I'd hoped. I put him on security and he enjoys it. Cole's not a suit and it was a matter of finding something he liked. He's really surprising me."

"What do you have him doing? Security is tight already, Alex."

"In house, yes, but he's investigating some businesses that I'm looking at acquiring."

"Oh. Well, wonderful. Your mother was upset that we didn't see you yesterday, so make sure you're there next week."

"Dad, you put billions of dollars in my hands; I'm an adult. I don't need to have brunch with Mommy and Daddy every Sunday," he said absently, not really concentrating on the conversation as he fiddled with a pen, twirling it on the smooth surface of his desk. "Cole hasn't been there in a month and a half, and you're fine with that."

"Maybe that will change. Your sister misses you. If you aren't going to come to family dinners, then at least give her a call."

"Yeah, okay."

Alex's door burst open and Cole stormed in with a flustered Mrs. Dane following. "Mr. Avery, you have to wait! Your brother is on the phone!"

"Alex, hang up the phone." Cole's tone was urgent as he stood waiting with his hands on his hips.

"Dad, I have to go."

"Is that Cole?"

"Yes. I'll call you later. Have a good morning."

When Alex hung up the phone, Mrs. Dane moved forward. "Mr. Avery, I'm so—"

"It's fine, Mrs. Dane. Will you excuse us?"

When the woman had exited the office, Alex took in Cole's agitated appearance. "What is it? What's happening?"

"Were you aware that Swanson was meeting with Angel this morning?"

Alex's brow dropped. "She didn't mention it specifically, but she hasn't named him to me. How did you know?"

"Well…. um, since you want me to move in next door, I figured you wanted a tail on her and Bancroft is watching Mark Swanson."

"As long as it's at her office, it's legitimate business. I don't want to scare her, so keep your distance." Alex motioned for his brother to take one of the expensive chairs that matched the leather sofa against one wall opposite the windows. "Thanks for doing that, Cole."

Cole smiled. "Sure, dude. I like this shit. It's fun!"

The corner of Alex's mouth lifted sardonically and he pushed his fingers through his hair, sighing. "Unfortunately, it is freaking me the fuck out. Angel won't tell me anything so I can't share what I know with her, or that I'm watching that bastard. I sense she's scared of him, but she won't admit it."

Cole took a notepad out of his jacket pocket and began flipping through it. "Well, I have everything you asked. I know which locations he owns and the property value, which properties he rents, who owns Angel's building.... all of it."

"Okay, so start buying the locations he rents as quickly as we can. We have an attorney on retainer, so use him. Offer the going rate. If that doesn't work, increase by twenty percent. Then begin issuing eviction notices."

"A couple of Swanson's stores are in strip malls in the 'burbs. So, eviction notices to only his business?"

Alex's expression hardened, his lips forming a firm line. "Only him."

"And the other locations?"

"It depends on how long this trial takes. We might be able to hurt his cash flow enough by closing down the rentals, but start looking for locations close to the ones he owns that we can convert. We'll start by hiring his employees away from him. He'll be scrambling at the very least."

"What will you do with them?"

"Put them on the payroll, find them jobs here; I don't care. Mrs. Dane will work with HR to do it. I've looked at his financial statements and he doesn't have enough liquidity to pay what Avery can. If he wants to make better offers, he'll have to try getting loans, and that would take collateral that he doesn't have." The smile on his handsome face spoke volumes.

"Alex, why don't you just tell the prick you're going to ruin him if he threatens Angel?"

Alex shook his head. "Because it would tip my hand, and it wouldn't be nearly as much fun. It also might make it more dangerous for her. The guy is bad news. Just consider what we're doing a community service."

"Okay, I'm gonna go over there and hang around, just in case."

"I appreciate your diligence, Cole. Really. But don't get creepy around her; she'll probably kick you in the balls." Alex was kidding, but only slightly; the amusement that danced over his features told Cole more than his words.

"Well, she must have a way with yours."

Green eyes sparkled with laughter. "If you only knew."

"So, I'll go, then."

Alex stopped him. "No, I think I'll go." He leaned forward and pressed the button on his phone that connected him to the outer office. "Mrs. Dane, please reschedule the rest of my day."

*****

"Angel, Mark Swanson is here." Liz's voice was soft on the other end of the line. She didn't use the intercom, knowing Angel wouldn't want the man privy to her response.

"Fine. Take him into the conference room. You remember what I told you?"

"Yeah. I got it. But he asked to speak to you first."

Despite her bravado, she was frightened. The man made her skin crawl; the way he looked at her was filled with hatred and lust. She'd use it to her advantage, but she'd have to keep her focus. She stood, smoothing down the wool crepe of her skirt before reaching into her desk drawer for lip gloss. "Fucker is going down," she murmured to herself as she applied it, and then threw it back into the drawer.

"Send him in, Liz."

He was dressed impeccably, his dark hair slicked back with some sort of gel that made him look more menacing. As always, he wore that same self-satisfied expression that Angel wanted to slap right off his face. She struggled to control her face; to keep her loathing for the man to herself.

"Good afternoon, Mr. Swanson." Angel extended her hand and he took it between both of his, pulling her toward him just slightly.

"So, we meet again. I take pleasure in it, even though I know what you're up to, Angel."

She itched to pull her hand away as he began to stroke her fingers with his. "Dr. Hemming, if you don't mind," she insisted.

"Ah, come now, Angel. You know you want to know me better. Why don't we just stop this nastiness, hmmm?"

She tugged her hand free and moved behind her desk, indicating that he should take one of the chairs in front of it. "Mr. Swanson, the nastiness is not my doing. I'm only here to see justice done."

His eyes narrowed, anger sparking in them. Angel flushed. The man was a hideous monster behind the polished and refined exterior. If she didn't know what lay behind his eyes, she would have bet money he wouldn't hurt a fly.

"My secretary is going to administer the tests this time. I appreciate that you came in. It was unfortunate that I lost the flash drive containing the first set."

"Cut the crap. We both know you didn't lose those results. They just weren't the results you wanted."

Angel's back straightened and she pursed her lips. "Okay, if we're being frank, I know you're guilty as hell. I think you are the lowest form of slime and I'm going to do whatever I can to nail your ass to the wall. Happy now?"

Mr. Swanson laughed, tenting his fingers in front of him as he studied the way Angel's chest rose and fell, his eyes drifting down over the full swells beneath her pale mauve blouse. "Your fiery disposition only makes you even more alluring, Angel. If that's possible. You are stunning, and I bet you're a real tiger in the sack."

"Ugh!" Angel was disgusted and scowled at him, her mouth thinning into a firm line as she tapped the end of her pen on her chin. "Now it's your turn to cut the crap, Mr. Swanson. I find you nothing less than repugnant, as I'm sure most women do. I wish I could say that's why you force yourself on innocents, but we both know you do it because you're a sick coward and can only feel like a man when you are controlling someone weaker. Coupled with a complete lack of conscience and your narcissistic tendencies... it adds up to a morally retarded sociopath. Textbook."

"You're crossing a fine line, Dr. Hemming," he said coldly, seething as the steel of his gaze bored into her as he moved forward in his chair.

"The truth hurts, I guess," she said with bravado she didn't feel. She squared her shoulders for the attack that would surely come next.

"You'd do well to remember who you're dealing with. It isn't just you who will suffer, little lady."

"No, you crossed the line when you hurt that young woman. I want to remind you that if you lay one finger on me, or anyone I care about, you'll be making the biggest mistake of your life. I have no time for your over-inflated, over-compensating ego, and absolutely zero interest in your teeny little weenie, other than to make sure it's behind bars!" She smiled brightly at her nemesis. "Did you know that inmates are notoriously hostile to sex offenders?"

Mark Swanson's face turned a mottled red. "I can do more than hurt you or teach you a lesson, you stupid little bitch! It won't be here or when you're expecting it, but don't underestimate me."

"Aspirations are always good, but I'm certain you don't have the balls to come after me yourself."

"Don't. Fuck. With. Me."

Angel forced a sly smile as hate welled up inside her. "Words to live by. You should practice what you preach."

"I'm warning you to back off." His tone was deadly quiet.

"Warn away." Angel sighed lightly. "Are we through? I really do have a busy day," she quipped, nonchalantly dismissing him with a wave of her hand and slight smile.

As if on cue, the intercom sounded. "Dr. Hemming?"

Angel watched Mr. Swanson as he worked to regain control of his temper. His face was red and contorted and his eyes blazed a trail of hatred. Angel inwardly blanched. She'd done what she needed to do. "Yes, Elizabeth?"

"Mr. Avery is here, and I'm ready for Mr. Swanson to join me in the conference room."

Shit! What is Alex doing here? It was a classic case of bad-timing. The last thing she needed was Mark Swanson knowing more about her personal life than he already did, but there was little she could do about it now, other than try to remain professional.

"Mr. Swanson and I are finished. Send Mr. Avery in, and let me know when you're finished with the testing. I'll be in my office."

Mark Swanson stood and buttoned the blazer of his grey suit. "Remember what I said, little miss," he said, pointing a finger at her warningly.

"No, you remember what I said, asshole. You have no idea what the first set of tests showed, the second could only be to reinforce what we found."

The door opened and Liz popped her head in. "Mr. Swanson? Please follow me."

"We expect full disclosure," the man said as he moved toward the office door.

"That's between you and the District Attorney's office. Now, if you'll excuse me?"

She watched him exit the office as Liz held the door. Alex passed the other man on the way into her office and, instantly, Angel's mood changed. He was impeccably dressed in a dark, expertly tailored navy suit, crisp white shirt, and a silk tie in shades of silvery grey and navy. She raised her eyebrow and grinned.

"To what do I owe this honor?"

Alex glanced around her office, registering the same elegant style that graced her condo: dark woods, sleek but plush upholstery, fine art, and a Persian rug that covered the majority of the floor in dark teals, ivory, and light mauves. He walked around her desk and took her hand, pulling her up and into his arms.

He'd recognized the bastard he'd just passed in the reception area. After seeing his face, he did recall the billboards and commercials for his dry cleaning business. Alex sighed. His determination to ruin Swanson's life renewed as he pulled Angel closer. He hated her job, hated the risks that came with it, hated the way it made him feel, and really hated the fucker that just left. If he had his way, he'd never let her out of his sight. But, he couldn't tell Angel any of that.

"It's simple. I wanted to look at you. You're beautiful."

Angel calmed as his arms wrapped around her and hers slid around his neck of their own volition. His green eyes burned over her face, the intensity out of place for a casual visit. "Well, you're seeing me," she said softly. The fingers of her right hand ghosted over his jaw as she met his gaze before her lids dropped and her chin tilted, silently asking for his mouth to find hers.

His lips hovered above hers as he breathed in her sweet scent; he moved the tip of his nose slowly around hers. "Are you okay? Who was that?" Alex wanted to see if she'd tell him the truth.

"Just a subject. Are you gonna kiss me or what?"

He laughed quietly as he teased her mouth with light licks and gentle brushes. "Depends on the *or what*."

Angel giggled. "Oh, baby, don't tease me."

"Oh, I will. You can count on it."

"Promises, promises."

Alex's hand moved up her back to thread through her silken hair that was falling in soft waves down her back. His pulse quickened as his mouth finally found hers in a hungry kiss, his tongue invading her mouth until she had no doubt how she affected him. Angel's heart thrummed in her chest and heat pooled in her core; she could almost feel her blood rushing in her veins.

"What are you doing to me?" he asked as his mouth dragged across her cheekbone. "I think of nothing but touching you, my mouth on yours, being inside you... just being able to look at you."

She clutched at his shoulders, his words and his kisses leaving her breathless. "It's no different for me," she admitted softly. Her statement was so true; it physically hurt. "But, I'll deny it if you ever repeat it."

2

In the Dark

ALEX'S HEART WAS pounding rapidly, his breathing shallow and fast. Words were impossible. The pleasure Angel was giving him was more than he'd ever experienced. That mouth on his body, her kisses, her voice, and her words were beginning to rule his world. It didn't matter that he'd known her less than a month, the emotions she generated were foreign but more amazing than he'd ever thought possible.

The fingers he'd wound in her hair tightened as his climax approached. The pleasure was unbearable, but he never wanted her to stop pushing him toward the explosion he knew was coming. Her beautiful mouth wrapped around his cock, sucking and licking in obvious mission to make him cum hard, was what his dreams were made of. His muscles coiled and stiffened, his balls tightened until his head fell back against the pillows and he finally couldn't fight it any longer.

"Ahhhh!" His cry of release echoed into the room, his body jerking with the intensity of his orgasm. Angel lightened her pressure as she swallowed, but kept the suction constant, her lips and tongue caressing gently until Alex relaxed. "Oh, baby…" He glanced down. The sheet was draped over her lower back, her hair wild and full around her satisfied expression. Alex sat up slightly and slid his hands over Angel's shoulders and down her arms to pull her up and across his body until she was lying with her head still resting on his stomach. "Oh, Angel… Oh, my God, that was so hot."

Angel tightened her arms around him, and he stroked over her hair and back over and over as his breathing slowed. Emotion overwhelmed her and she closed her eyes. She wished time would stop and the world would go away. In this man's arms, she found solace and ecstasy like she'd never known. In this man's arms, she wanted to give like she never had before. Giving pleasure was a way to be in control, to bring him to his knees, but it wasn't playing out as she planned. This was different. She cared about him against her will and pleasing him was a manifestation of her feelings. Her heart ached with it.

"You're so perfect," he whispered in the darkness, his fingers searching for her skin, never seeming to get enough. "Every god-damned thing about you is so fucking amazing."

"I'm not perfect, Alex." Her voice sounded like music, the syllables skittering over his skin like electric rain.

"Yes, you are. I never want to stop touching you, tasting you. I can't stand to be away from you." He inhaled deeply, surprised at his own admission.

"Is that why you didn't go to Greece today?"

"Yes," he admitted without hesitation, his chest still heaving.

"Who would have thought you'd be such a romantic?" she asked softly.

"Believe me, I'm as shocked as you are. Maybe you bring it out of me."

Angel's face was turned as she rested her cheek on his chest, but her breath fanned out over his skin and her fingers played gently, roving over his chest and down over the muscles on his lower abdomen.

"Hmmm," she sighed. Her throat tightened and her eyes welled. If only this could be *real.* If only it could last. She blinked away the tears, unwilling to let them fall, trying to concentrate on the warmth of his hands—in her hair, on her back—both caressing gently.

"Angel?" he asked after a few minutes.

Her arms tightened around his body again and she nodded. She wasn't sure she could trust her voice yet.

"That was him," Alex stated.

Angel's stomach fell, certain she couldn't lie convincingly enough.

"That was him, the guy… the case," he said again.

"Who?"

"That smarmy bastard in your office today."

"He's part of one of the cases I'm working on right now, yes."

"*The* case. The guy who raped his stepdaughter."

Angel lifted her head to look into his face. Despite the shadowy blanket of night, he could still see her brow furrow. "Yes. But why are we talking about this now?"

Alex ignored her question, determined to get some information out of her. The more he could get her to tell him, the more open he could be about protecting her. "I recognized him. He owns that dry cleaners, doesn't he?"

Angel moved off of Alex's body to lie next to him, propping her head on her hand.

"Yeah, but it doesn't matter what his business is. He's a creeper." The urge to tell him everything about the case consumed her. If only she could. She wanted to allow the protectiveness she heard in his voice to take root and make her feel safe.

"Has he threatened you?" The ominous tone in Alex's voice commanded a response.

"Please stop this, Alex. Don't ruin tonight." She reached out a hand and ran it down his chest, her eyes imploring.

He sighed again; this time, his impatience growing, exasperation lacing his low tone. "You might as well tell me. I have the resources to find out anything I want to know, babe."

She stiffened and, as she pulled away and sat up, looked into his face. "It's late. I should go."

He leaned up against the headboard, knowing it was an inane attempt to move the conversation in another direction.

"Why are you hiding this from me? I mean, what the hell is going on between us?"

She shifted, pulling the sheet closer beneath her breasts. "We agreed to live our own lives, and these questions, all the time we're spending together—" she motioned between them, "—this… it's getting out of hand. I want to keep it casual."

Under any other circumstances, with any other woman, Alex would have rejoiced at those words. "What are you afraid of, Angel?" His green eyes blazed in the darkness, sparkling pools trained on her face.

"Nothing. Why do you always assume I'm afraid of something?" Her voice took on an angry tone and he sighed, more heavily this time.

"I thought we worked through this last night."

The silence hung between them like the calm before a storm as she picked at the sheets, not looking Alex in the face. Her heart hurt and her throat ached. The emotions he caused were glorious, amazing, and so fucking painful. She swallowed hard, trying to get words beyond the lump in her throat. "I surrendered; you won. Do you have to rub it in?"

"There was no surrender. There is no *escape* in this," he said with quiet urgency and reached for her hand. His fingers were warm, his thumb rubbing over the smooth skin on the top of her hand. "For either one of us."

Her eyes lifted to his face… so incredibly handsome, his hair pushed back over his forehead by numerous trips of his hand, the strong jaw, straight nose, the slight cleft in his chin, and his soft expression, all added up to leave her breathless. She had to admit it to herself: she was in love. So in love she could barely function without him consuming her every thought. But she was a realist and loving him would leave her empty-handed.

"For now. Until you get bored."

Alex's mouth tightened into a thin line, anger and frustration filling him. "That's nonsense. I've never been more motivated, both in bed and out of it."

Angel shrugged slightly. *Did I expect him to say this was for forever? That he loves me?* "It's only been a few weeks. I'm not holding my breath."

"Can't you just have a little faith? I don't know what I can do to show you that I'm invested in this, Angel. We're spending every minute together when we're not at work and that is not what I do! Jesus! With Whitney, I couldn't wait to get away from her."

"I know."

"Do you?" Exasperation filled his voice, but his hand continued its gentle massaging of hers. "Will you trust me?" he asked, quietly, and she nodded without thinking. She wanted to build her world around this man, wanting him in ways she never imagined. "Then tell me if that bastard threatened you today."

"So much for the throes of passion." She tried to smile at him, thankful for the darkness of the room.

Alex's face tightened even more. "Angel… this isn't a fucking joke. None of it."

"No. It's not. It's my *job*, Alex. I don't need your permission. This doesn't concern you."

"The hell it doesn't! Everything about you concerns me now!" He flung himself back against the headboard away from her and it slammed loudly into the wall. "I want to make sure you're safe, goddamn it!"

Startled, Angel scrambled from the bed and began to gather her clothes from where they were scattered across his bedroom floor. He watched in silence as she began to dress without turning on a light before springing from the bed and gathering her to him.

"Stop." His fingers lightly traced her cheekbone, his forehead leaning down to hers as he inhaled her scent. "I know its nuts, but humor me. I won't let anything happen to you. Not when I can prevent it."

Her fingers closed around both of his forearms, flexing around the obvious strength she found there. "You can't get involved." Her eyes beseeched his as the silvery shadows from the moonlight filtering through the blinds cast her face in darkness. "Please? I'm a big girl. I can take care of myself," she whispered, already succumbing to his nearness. Her body reacting to his against her will. His lips blazed a hot path from her temple and down her cheekbone until they opened hotly on the skin on the arch of her neck. Shivers raced through her as his arms tightened, pulling her hard against his body, his arousal beginning to clamor against the softness of her belly.

"Not as well as I can," he said softly, an instant before his mouth claimed hers in a hungry kiss. Angel was helpless to deny him as his tongue invaded her mouth, and she whimpered in surrender, her mouth opening and kissing him back with equal fervor. Alex groaned into her mouth, his hands fisting in the back of her unbuttoned blouse. She was naked, save her shirt and a lace thong, and he wanted nothing more than to shed her of both articles and stake his claim on her body once again. Her skin on his was like a drug, so soft, alluring; the full mounds of her breasts pressed to his chest made him harder and hotter. "Damn, I can't stop wanting you," he growled, lifting her bridal-style and depositing her on the bed, only to follow her down.

Angel bucked beneath him, wanting to feel his hardness pressed between her legs, both of them frantic in their need to get closer. She clutched at the hair at his nape, their kisses hungry as Alex moved against her, his fingers hooking into the lace at her hip and starting to pull as his lips closed around a pebble-hard nipple and began to tease with the tip of his tongue.

Angel's soft moans were interrupted by the ringing of Alex's phone—the sound piercing the intimacy of the moment. "Hell," Alex complained, releasing her breast, but keeping her beneath him as he reached for his phone. "Sorry, baby, but it's the middle of the night and that's my father's ringtone. Something could be wrong."

Angel pressed her forehead to his shoulder as he answered.

"Yeah, Dad?" His breathing was heavy and he struggled to get it under control. "No, not a great time. What is it?"

Angel's fingers smoothed over the velvet skin that covered the hard muscles of his back, arms, and shoulders, her open mouth finding the pulse at his neck and sucking on it gently, her other hand closing around his full erection. She delighted in teasing him, knowing how difficult it was for him to keep his voice controlled as she stroked him in a steady rhythm until he was shaking with the effort of restraint. Her hips moved in unison with her hand, legs around his waist, as she showed him what she really wanted.

"Shit! When did you find out? Williams was supposed to keep me posted." Alex stroked Angel's cheek with the knuckles of his free hand, his eyes trained on her face. He wanted to throw the phone against the wall and bury himself in her warmth, but the urgency of the situation stalled him. He reached for her hand to still it around him.

"Apparently, he tried. We're going to lose that deal if you don't go. Benson is countering and we've already sunk a million dollars into the planning." His father was clearly frustrated.

"Jesus, Dad, I know. Okay. I'll catch a flight first thing in the morning."

"I already have that handled. Mrs. Dane booked you on the red eye. With the time difference, you'll get there at the start of business."

Alex's face tightened, and he moved away from Angel. The chill at his loss urged her to pull the covers around her as she rolled onto her side. She curved around him as he sat up on the edge of the bed, pushing his hand through his hair in agitation. "Okay, I'm on it. I'll call you later... when it's done."

He threw the phone on the mattress and grabbed Angel's hand. "I'm sorry, baby. I have to go to Hawaii. There's a property we're trying to purchase in Maui which will allow us to own a big part of the market there. Another company is countering, so I have to go convince the owner why Avery is his best option."

"Oh.... okay." Her disappointment was plain.

"Hey." He brought her hand up and placed his mouth on the inside of her wrist. "I'll make it up to you."

"How long will you be gone?" She hated her weakness, hated that she'd miss him, and more, that she wasn't able to hide it from him.

"I don't know. Depends on how much the other party is willing to deal. I can't spend more than I think it's worth, so I may have to figure out a merger or offer another property as an exchange. I won't know until I talk to them." He smiled softly. She was gorgeous, rumpled from their sex play, her lips swollen and bruised from his kisses, and her hair a wild mess. "It's damn hard to leave, but my flight is in two hours."

"Yeah, I felt how hard it was," she teased and he laughed softly. He rose and began to gather clean boxer briefs, a T-shirt and socks before flipping on the light in the bathroom and starting the shower.

"Yes," he called, "I'll have blue balls by the time I get back to you."

"Make sure that you do!" She wrapped the sheet around her body and followed him. He was just getting under the spray of the walk-in shower, his body blurred by the glass blocks making up one wall. The bathroom was elegant. Black marble topped the teak vanity and limestone lined the floors. The large whirlpool tub, black as night, reflected the gleaming silver fixtures and the light was on a dimmer switch, and Alex had it on low.

Another set for seduction, she thought wryly. "Humph!" Angel huffed as she sat on the edge of the tub.

Steam filled the air, making it comfortably warm.

"I want you to stay at my house while I'm gone."

"Well, I want world peace," Angel deadpanned. "But, I doubt either is likely."

She couldn't see his face, but the amusement in his voice was enough. "Can't you do this one thing without an argument? You'll be safer there and you can take care of Max for me. He adores you, and on such short notice, I doubt my housekeeper can do it."

"That's brilliant. What a way to suck me in." Her eyes raked over his perfect form, blurred through the wall.

"I'll suck you… in whatever way you want," he laughed happily, "for as long as you want, when I get back. In the meantime, you can use the pool, the Jacuzzi, and the personal chef. Ask Becca and Jillian to join you. Anything you want."

Cole wasn't moving in for several days and having Angel at his estate was the surest way he could ensure her safety without putting her under surveillance. His heart surged uncomfortably in his chest.

"Put your mouth where your money is," Angel quipped with a soft laugh.

"Oh, I will!" he chuckled.

"Again with the promises." Her soft laugh echoed through the space.

"I know. I'm even starting to freak *myself* out. Are you bringing your sweet little ass in here, or do I have to come out there and
get you?"

"I thought you only wanted me for my voice."

"I do. The rest of you is a bonus. Get in here."

"If I come in there, you'll be late."

"I'll make *sure* you come in here," he teased and looked
around the door before returning into the shower stream. "Well?"

"You'll be late," she stated again, grinning.

"If I'm late, I'll take the company jet."

Angel gasped. "I should have known. The great Alex Avery
will waste all that fuel, pollute the environment more than necessary, just for a little pus—aaaaah!" she squealed as he grabbed her
and pulled her, sheet and all under the spray, both of them laughing until his mouth swooped to take hers.

Soon words, pollution, the flight, and the soggy sheet were
long forgotten.

*****

It had been three days since Alex had gone. Angel padded through
the house to let Max outside. His house was massive and luxurious;
way too much for one person, she mused as the dog went out. It should
be filled with children and family and love. Her heart dropped at
the thought. What the fuck was she doing, thinking about such
things after knowing him for such a short time? Especially, about
this man in particular.

The air outside was hot, a stark contrast to the cool air-
conditioning inside. "There you go, baby," she murmured, caressing Max's golden coat as he passed her on his way out the door.
They had become inseparable. He even slept beside her in Alex's
room. She grinned at the thought. Alex would have an issue with
bed linens full of fur, no doubt.

The second set of test results had been no better than the first, leaving Angel, Kenneth, and the staff at the D.A.'s office floundering for ways to put Mark Swanson behind bars. For the first time in her career, Angel considered lying to get the conviction. She picked up her glass of chardonnay and settled on Alex's leather couch, recalling the conversation she and Kenneth had earlier.

"Angel, sometimes, you just have to let it go. Be thankful that the mother believes the girl and got her out of that house."

"But, she'll have to live with the fact that he got away with it, Kenneth! Do you know how horrible that will be for her? There should be some law in place to castrate fuckers like him."

Kenneth had grimaced. "Even if there was, he'd have to be convicted first. And it looks like all we have is the girl's testimony. I hope it will be enough."

"He'll probably threaten her within an inch of her life. I wouldn't be surprised if she refuses to testify."

"Stacey will call her as a hostile witness, if necessary. It's messy, but the charges were filed based on her statements and her physical condition. It's not up to the girl whether this goes to court. Even if he threatens her, the trial will commence, and I'll have her on the stand."

"But she won't say anything! She'll probably recant everything she said in her statement. He'll get acquitted, if the judge doesn't throw it out of court first. The only thing we have going for us is that Swanson and his slimy band don't know the results yet."

"But they will soon. Stacey will disclose as soon as my office has your reports, Angel. She has no choice. It's just one case. You can't win 'em all. Get over it."

She sighed into the big room. It wouldn't be enough, and she felt defeated by Kenneth's laissez-faire attitude and how the law seemed to protect the fucking criminal's civil rights more than the victim's. The entire thing wore on her, and coupled with the tossing and turning she'd been doing, she was completely exhausted.

The rock anthem that was Alex's self-imposed ringtone inter-rupted her thoughts.

Alex. Her heart lurched, excitement surging through her as she jumped up and ran into the hall to retrieve her purse from where it lay in a heap with her Gucci heels. She was still dressed in her chocolate brown suit and silk blouse in a soft, yellow pastel floral print. She shook her head and smiled at how her mood sud-denly elevated by a friggin' ringtone.

"Hello?"

"Hey, you. Are you home?"

"Oh, I just got in."

"Is the security on?"

"Well, I miss you, too! Alex, we go through this every night."

"Don't begrudge me knowing that you're safe."

She huffed and rolled her eyes.

"I do miss you. I miss your voice," he stated simply, his tone somewhat of a groan. Her heart began to race as she made her way back into the living room. "I wanted to call later, when you were naked in my bed, but I couldn't wait that long."

"Mmm…. How do you know I'll be naked?"

Alex chuckled. "Lucky guess?"

"It might be a sheer black chiffon baby doll. You never know."

"Angel… you're killing me, you naughty, naughty girl."

"You can call me again later," she suggested hopefully. "I'll plan on being naked if it seals the deal."

"I wish I could," he groaned. "I have a dinner meeting with the decision maker on this deal. You'll be sleeping long before I'm able to call you."

"I haven't been sleeping very well."

"Why? What's the matter? Is everything okay?" Concern laced his voice.

"Of course. But the results to my tests are back for Swanson's case and they're not what I'd hoped. The bastard could walk. I feel like I'm failing that poor girl."

"There are other ways to get at that prick. We'll talk about it when I get home."

Fear ran over her skin, leaving a trail of goose bumps in its wake. "I told you, Alex, I don't want you involved. It will work out."

"You're involved, so I'm involved." The tightness in his voice betrayed his irritation at her dismissal of his concern, but he did his best to mask it. "Has Max been good?"

"He's amazing. So sweet. I may have to steal him."

"Maybe we can share him."

"I'm trying not to get too attached." Her words carried a double entendre that she hoped he wouldn't catch. "Being gone this much, I'm surprised you have him. I think that's my argument for custody."

"I find traveling agrees with me less and less lately. What'd you do today?"

"Just patients and lunch with Kenneth." Angel relayed the information with a grimace, remembering Alex's behavior at the bar.

"Really," he said tightly. "About the case?"

"Don't get your panties in a bunch. It was strictly business."

"Yes, well, I'll venture business isn't all he has on his mind."

"Like you, he wants me to step back from this case. He doesn't feel we can win."

"Maybe he deserves more credit than I've given him, but when did it become *we*? You're just an expert witness, not part of his staff."

"So…" She was becoming irritated with the tack the conversation was taking. "When will you be ho… um, back in Chicago?"

"Not soon enough. Maybe late Friday."

"Crap. I have the show."

Obviously, she wanted to see him as soon as he got back and the thought elated him. Immediately, Alex took charge. "I can call Darian—"

"No. You can't just rearrange my life like that!"

"You call him, then," he said shortly. "The result will be the same."

"That's not the point, and you know it."

"I want to see you, so fucking sue me. The show won't go off-air if you miss one airing. I'd like to take you away for the weekend, somewhere with a crystal blue ocean and an enormous bed."

"You forgot teeny bikinis and Speedos."

"Yes on the bikinis, but there will be no Speedo."

"You have the ass for it."

"It's not my ass I'm concerned about, and you know it." Amusement laced his voice.

"Okay, you'll fill out the rest nicely as well. Is that what I'm supposed to say?"

"No. On that I am non-negotiable. Why don't you meet me here and we can fly back together? I'll get my sister to watch Max."

Tropical paradise and Alex? What could be better? Angel bit her lip. "It's tempting, but I can't."

"Think about it, at least. I'll call you tomorrow."

"Nothing will change."

"We'll see. I'll call you tomorrow."

"Okay. Goodnight, Alex. Good luck with your meeting."

"Thanks. Sleep tight, baby. Dream of me."

The house was dark except for one lamp in the living room and the light filtering through the blinds in the kitchen from the deck lights outside, and the giddiness created from Alex's words still enveloped her. The sliding door opened smoothly, but Max wasn't waiting as she'd expected. "Max!" Angel called. "Maxy Max! Here, boy!"

She stepped out onto the smooth cedar boards of the large, multi-level deck and moved to the edge of the highest one, peering out over the massive backyard. It was well-landscaped with large trees, bushes, and a limestone patio, which held expensive furniture, an outdoor kitchen and, at the center, a large in-ground pool. "Maaaaaaax!"

Angel strained to hear the dog's movements through the night and the jingle of his collar as he came closer but was met with only the sound of the warm breeze through the trees. "Here, Max!"

Unsure of what was beyond some of the trees, she scurried down the stairs to the lower levels, her eyes straining into the darkness. The estate was large, and the evening prior, he'd been out for a while, so after a few minutes of whistling and calling for the dog, Angel climbed the stairs and returned to the air-conditioned comfort of the house. The massive windows that soared in panels to the peak of the vaulted ceilings echoed the points of the roof.

When she flopped back down on the couch, she flipped on the big-screen TV and lowered the volume. She had yet to place the call to Kyle and decided this was as good a time as any to get it over with. She went to get her phone and refill her wine glass from the bottle in the refrigerator.

They hadn't talked in months, not since the last time he'd had an argument with Crystal and drunk-dialed her. Her disdain for the woman had not lessened as the years had passed. She was an airhead with a capital A, and Angel had little tolerance for her.

He answered on the first ring. "Hello?"

"Hey, Kyle. It's Angel."

She was met with silence for a few seconds. "Did you get a new number?" She could hear the band warming up in the background, a managed chaos of drums, bass, and guitar riffs.

"Oh. I have a new phone."

"Hey! Guys, can you wait a minute? It's Angel," he called loudly. "Sorry. What's up? Are you okay?"

"Yeah. I'm good. How have you been?"

"Good. The band is booked almost a year in advance, and we may be getting a manager soon."

"That's great. I hear nothing but good things about you guys. Do you have a contract yet? How is that going?"

"It's going. We'd be better off if you were still with us. What about you? Are you still with that douche?"

"Kenneth's not a douche. He's just…"

"A douche," he dismissed, and Angel had to smile.

"You'll never like any guy I'm with, but no, we stopped seeing each other."

"Good."

"Are you still with that *ditz*?" Angel countered dryly.

"Ha, ha," Kyle returned.

"I'll take that as a yes. How are the guys? Is Dennis doing better?"

"They're cool. He completed rehab and is getting married in November."

"Really? Wow! Good for him." Dennis was a good guy that fell into the trappings of the rocker lifestyle. Too much booze, too many women; he was a mess for a long time, despite the other band members' attempts to help him. Angel was happy he was finally getting his life on track. "Listen, Kyle, I'm calling because there's a benefit for leukemia coming up and they really want Archangel to play."

"Yeah, some high-society chick came to a gig and chased me around all night about it. It's not something I'm interested in. I can't believe she tracked you down, too. Damn!"

"It's a great cause, and it's on a Sunday night, so you should be open."

"We're open, yeah, but it's the wrong venue for us."

"They're targeting a younger demographic, so you could play your normal set list. Please consider it. For me." Angel knew it was low to use his feelings for her against him, but it was a good cause and she only had a second of regret.

"I'll do it if you come back to the band."

"Wha—What?" Shock resonated in her voice.

"Did I stutter? I want you back with the band. It's never been the same without you."

Angel hesitated for a stunned moment. "That's… impossible, even if I wanted to. What about Crystal?"

"She's not you. I'll deal with her."

"Kyle—"

"Do you want us to play this gig or not? Take it or leave it, Angel."

"You know I can't. I've got work and the radio show."

"Yeah, I heard it a couple of times. Just come to a practice and we can discuss this in person. The boys would love to see you."

"Umm…"

"Take it or leave it," he said again and gave her the address of a warehouse in South Chicago they used for practice; she ended up agreeing to come by on Sunday afternoon.

She showered and got ready for bed, deciding on some of Alex's boxers and a T-shirt before she put both of the phones on the chargers and then went in search of Max again.

The light above the stove was on but the rest of the house was dark. Angel hesitated. She didn't remember leaving it on. "Hello?" she called hesitantly as her steps slowed. Maybe the housekeeper had come back. "Hello? Please answer me!"

She stopped and looked around in the dim light, her ears straining for any sound, but she was met with only the sound of her own heart thudding wildly, the hair on her arms standing on end. She was shaking, fear making her sick to her stomach, yet she was frozen in place. Her fingers reached behind her in blind search for some weapon as she fumbled with the drawers until they closed around the handle of a large chef's knife, which she brought in front of her.

She searched the darkness, trembling as she slowly inched her way toward the light switch on the far wall, finally flooding the kitchen with fluorescent light. Her breathing was heavy and shallow, coming in frantic bursts. She turned in a circle, the knife pointing out from her body until she saw the note stuck to the stainless steel refrigerator with a large piece of duct tape. The message was simple and clear.

Next time it won't be the dog.

3

Heartbreak & Resolve

ALEX MADE HIMSELF focus on his dinner companions' conversation. He wanted the deal done. He wanted to get on the plane and head back to the mainland. He wanted to get back to Angel. His thoughts were consumed with her, the picture he'd taken of her last week at dinner smiled back at him from his phone. He loved the sparkle in her eyes, the curve of her face, and the luxurious mane of mahogany hair that danced with auburn light. He missed her voice. He was amazed it was the other stuff, as much as the incredible sex with Angel that filled his thoughts.

He glanced at his Rolex and it mocked at him. It was 4 AM in Chicago and he wouldn't be able to call before he turned in for the night. When she agreed to stay at his estate, he'd felt a little better about traveling, but worry still nagged at him.

"Hmmph," he sighed heavily. He'd never given a thought to any other woman during his business trips before: his head had been fully in the game. Although Angel's situation was more pre-carious than his other lovers' had been, he was certain he'd be thinking of her even if she were a barista at Starbucks.

Fuck! He rubbed a hand down his face and over his jaw as his mouth quirked in amusement at the thought. He was exhausted, and he was pushing himself to get a week's worth of business wrapped up in two or three days. Saving the deal was easy compared to fighting the urge to call the woman who was the focus of his thoughts, despite the lateness of the hour. He was itching to leave as he shook hands with the five other men in his party and made his way up to his room. The entire evening was spent in the hotel that was the subject of the offer. It was convenient, but it was below the standards of the Avery properties. There was much that needed to be changed. It was the details as much as the money, which tipped the scales in his favor.

Alex's phone vibrated in his pocket and he quickly grabbed it as he made his way down the long hallway to his suite, hoping it would be Angel. He didn't recognize the number.

"Alex Avery."

"Mr. Avery, this is Steven Frost. I'm with Werner Security Group. Is everything okay at your home?"

Alex pulled in a panicked breath. "I'm traveling. I'm not there. What's happening?"

"It seems that you lost power for a few moments and we were unable to monitor your property for about 30 minutes."

"What about the houses around mine? Were they affected?"

"No, sir."

"Damn it!" Alex yelled into the phone. The neighbors not losing power at the same time was bad. It meant his property was singled out. "Were the police called?"

"Yes, sir. They drove around the entire perimeter and nothing seemed to be out of the ordinary. The system is fully operational now and the cameras are showing no activity."

Alex's heart was racing so hard he felt it would fly from his chest; panic was freaking him the fuck out.

"I'm sure everything is fine. We'll pay special attention and let you know if anything happens," the man continued.

"I pay you to take extra care *all* the fucking time. See that you do," he growled into the phone.

"I'm sorry, but the problem wasn't with our equipment. Maybe a fuse blew on the property."

"Do you think it magically repaired itself?" Alex asked in disgust, opening the door to his room so hard that it slammed into the wall in the entryway. "Send a guard over there! *Now!* My girlfriend is there and I don't want her frightened. Just have the property patrolled quietly. Call me as soon as someone is on site. Jesus Christ! I knew I shouldn't have left!"

"Sir, things like this happen all the time."

"Not to me. Is there some sort of system that won't rely on electricity? Something wireless that can be installed?"

"Yes, sir."

"Then do it. Now!"

He hung up the phone without waiting for a reply and immediately dialed Angel's phone. When she didn't pick up, he impatiently rang her other one, ripping the tie from around his neck and unbuttoning the top two buttons of his dress shirt as it went to voicemail.

"Fucking hell!" he muttered as her message played; the feeling of helplessness overwhelming as he raked his hand through his hair.

"Angel. I know it's late, but call me as soon as you get this. I..." he hesitated. Should he tell her about his concerns? It could be nothing and he didn't want to upset her needlessly. "I miss hearing your voice." He struggled to control his tone. "Please give me a call when you wake up."

He kicked off his shoes and dialed Cole's number.

"Yeah?" Cole's voice was full of sleep.

"Hey, Cole. I need you go over to my house right away."

"Why? What's going on?" Cole was instantly alert and sounds of him opening drawers and slamming them closed followed his voice through the phone.

"The security system failed for a few hours. Angel's there and she isn't answering her phone."

"I followed when she left her office and waited until I knew she was inside the gates. That place is like Fort Knox. What happened?"

"As I understand it, the outage was just on my property."

There was a rustling on the other end of the line as Cole threw on his clothes and moved around his apartment. "Shit! Do you think someone broke in?" A jingling of car keys mingled with a loud bang as a door closed roughly behind Cole.

"Christ, I hope not."

"I'm on my way." Sounds of Cole leaving his building and getting into his car filled the background. "What do you want me to do? Should I go in? Make sure she's okay?"

"I don't want her to see you, but I need to know she's safe."

"Yeah, my cover as her new neighbor will be blown if I show up at your house. Unless…"

"What?"

"Maybe it would be better to just tell her, Alex. How will you explain who I am later? You like this woman; she'll meet the family eventually."

"I'll cross that bridge when I get there. She doesn't believe she needs to be taken care of, and it would upset her to know I'm having her watched. I'll fly back as soon as I can, but let me know what you find when you get over there. Security will be patrolling, so I'll let them know you'll be there as well."

"It's probably nothing, bro."

"I hope you're right, but my gut tells me otherwise. I'm going out of my fucking mind."

*****

Shaking, Angel fell to the floor of the kitchen, violent sobs shaking her small frame. "Max, noooo!" she cried, and she screamed at the top of her lungs. Frustration and fear for the animal she now loved like her own tightened her chest.

"You bastard! I hope you burn in hell!" She drew her knees up and buried her face in her folded arms. "You fucking deviant! I'll kill you! I'll fucking kill you; I swear to God!" She cried hard for five minutes then wiped the back of her hand across her nose and stood up, realizing her own situation was still precarious.

As she glanced around the kitchen, her eyes searched for signs of violence but there were none. *Was the house broken into? Did they take him while I was in the shower? What will I tell Alex?* Angel closed her eyes as more tears fell. *What did they do to sweet, innocent, gentle, Max?*

She ran back to the bedroom and scrambled into her clothes, her heart sick and her thoughts racing. If she had been in the shower, she wouldn't have heard them, and the possibilities of what could have happened to her flooded her thoughts.

There was a loud thudding in her ears as the blood pumped around her body so hard it almost hurt. She felt as if she would vomit, her heart in her throat, as she gathered all her belongings and threw them into her duffle bag. She didn't care that her expensive suits were smashed and hanging halfway out. She stopped, immediately still.

"What am I doing?" Her hand paused on its way to her temple, the fingers curling in mid-air. She went to the keypad on the alarm system and double-checked to make sure it was engaged. Her heart knocked painfully in her chest. Anger swelled, heat infusing every inch of her skin until she felt like screaming again. Now she was insane with panic over Max and what Swanson and his band of goons would do to him. Could she reason with him? Convince him she'd back off and get the dog back and once she did, call the police? She had to do whatever she could to save the dog and keep Alex out of the entire mess. But would it be too late? Alex's estate was too isolated, the neighbors not close enough, to feel safe calling Mark Swanson until she got back into the city. She'd be too vulnerable.

Angel swallowed and quickly pushed the angry tears off her cheeks. More than ever, she wanted to put Mark Swanson behind bars. She'd never hated anyone so much in her life. She left her cases in the hall and quickly rummaged around in Alex's kitchen for a plastic bag. Careful to only touch the edge of the duct tape, she pulled the note from the fridge and tucked it inside the bag, zipping it closed.

She gathered her things and ran from the house as if her life depended on it, frantically resetting the alarm. She struggled to the car, laden with her things.

Alex.

How would she explain this if she couldn't get Max back? She was still trembling, and silent tears still fell from her eyes. She was as terrified as she was angry. She wanted to talk to Alex but had no idea what she would say.

"Oh, God," she groaned as her car raced back into the city. Dawn was barely breaking, and soon she found herself in the garage of her own building, unsure of how she'd gotten there or why. Her hands gripped the steering wheel and her head fell onto them as sobs overtook her. She needed to call Kenneth and get his advice. Should she call the police right away? As far as she could tell, there were no signs of forced entry. What would she say? *I think this lunatic stole my friend's dog? And all I have is this stupid note? Would it be enough?* "Tell me what to do," she prayed aloud. *Is it better to let Alex think Max ran away and keep him out of this? I couldn't handle it if anything happened to him.*

She longed for Alex's presence. For the first time in years, she wanted someone else to wrap their arms around her and make everything go away.

"What is happening to me?" she said aloud. She grabbed her phone from her purse as she climbed out of the car and ran to the elevator. Alex had called twice on each phone. She struggled between her desire to call him and tell him everything and her need not to worry him. In the end, the latter won out and she dialed Kenneth's number, instead. She needed someone by her side when she called Swanson.

"Angel? It's so early. Are you okay?"

"Not really," her voice cracked. "Can you come over? Now?"

Thankfully, he didn't ask any questions. "Yes, I'll be there in twenty minutes."

"Thanks."

The elevator doors opened and she stepped into the hallway leading to her apartment. It was quiet, completely deserted, but there was the faintest sound of whining from around the corner. Her heart dropped and she broke into a run, stopping when she saw Max on a very short lead chained to her door. It was tight and he could barely move, his mouth muzzled with silver duct tape, his golden brown eyes pleading.

"Oh, Max! Thank God!" She quickly closed the distance between them and fell to her knees, frantically working the leash free of the door. She threw her arms around his neck and kissed his head before burying her face in his fur. It soaked up her tears as she clutched at him, and he whimpered again. "Max, my sweet boy. What did that bastard do to you?"

As if he understood, the dog put both of his front paws on her arms, resting his head against hers. Angel hugged him tighter and ruffled his fur gently. "I'm so happy to see you, boy," she said gently as she led him into her apartment and locked the door behind them. She threw her purse down and went to the kitchen, returning in seconds with paper towels and olive oil. "Come here, Maxy. Let's get this crap off your face. Poor baby; come."

After several minutes of trying, Angel only had the edge of the tape loosened, her heart hammered painfully. She was so thankful Max was okay and she wouldn't have to tell Alex any of it. The dog was incredibly patient, sitting and letting her work, his eyes full of trust as she massaged the oil into his fur and tried to pull the tape free without hurting him. "How can anyone be this mean?" she muttered. "That sick bastard is evil."

When Kenneth arrived, she met him at the door and Max followed, never leaving Angel's side. Ken looked rumpled, his clothes wrinkled and his hair uncombed. "What's wrong?" he asked urgently as he folded her in his arms. She couldn't help it; tears burned her eyes again and a small sob broke from her chest. He'd never seen her so shaken.

"It was Mark Swanson! I was house sitting and he took Max!"

Kenneth's eyes dropped to the animal with the silver tape still half wrapped, half dangling from his muzzle and he frowned over Angel's shoulder. "It was Swanson? Are you sure?"

"It had to be him or his goons. He warned me something would happen when he was in my office earlier this week."

"What the hell? I've never seen you this upset. And why didn't you tell me about his threats at your office?"

Angel pulled from him and put her hand on Max's head and stepped aside so Kenneth could enter her apartment, ignoring his last question. "This is Alex's dog, Max. Alex is out of town and I was taking care of him at his house. I let him outside, but he never came back, and then I found this note in the kitchen." She pulled the bag she'd put it in out of the pocket of her jean shorts and handed it to Kenneth. "When I got here, he was tied to my door with the duct tape all over his face."

"You're off the case," Kenneth said abruptly. His expression hardened as he read the note and her eyes widened at his response.

"No! I can't let that fucker win." She walked back into the living room and resumed her place on the floor, continuing to work on Max.

"Angel! It could have been you! He's just proven he can breach security here and at Avery's estate. Think about it!"

"I can't let him get away with the horrible things he does, Kenneth. *Please*. I mean, just look at this! Children and helpless animals? I hate that sick bastard!"

"You're too close to this now."

She ignored him and continued to work oil into the golden fur on Max's face, carefully prying the tape away a millimeter at a time. "Who knows what he's capable of? We have to stop him."

Kenneth sat on one of the stools by her counter bar watching her, his leg dangling half off the chair. He sighed. Angel was determined. His eyes roved over her swollen eyes and messy hair, down her bare arms and legs, open to his view in the tank top and shorts she wore.

The phone Alex had given her rang in the other room, the rock music echoing off of the walls. "Shit." She scrambled to get it from her purse and answer, but then stopped. What would she tell him? Her brow furrowed and her throat thickened. She knew what she had to do and it would hurt like hell. She stared at the phone until the music stopped playing, wondering what he would say, flinching when the phone beeped as the message came in.

"Angel, what is it? Why didn't you answer? Do you think it was Swanson?" Kenneth asked.

Angel flushed as she resumed her work. Her eyes glanced up and then back down and shook her head. Max whimpered as the tape was pulled free another inch. "No, not on that phone. He doesn't have that number. That prick wouldn't call on either of them because there would be a record, right? I'm surprised there was even a note."

"Yes, it's doubtful we'll find any prints, and even if we did, it's not likely he constructed it himself. Still, we need to get it to the police."

"No. What's the point when we can't prove anything?"

"The point is building a record of violence against you! You know that!"

"But I didn't see any signs of forced entry at the house. The place is like a fortress: stone walls, locked metal gates, and security cameras."

"You have to ask your boyfriend if there's any damage." His face was sober and Angel could see the hurt in his expression.

"Alex isn't exactly my boyfriend."

"Spare me the details."

"In any case, I don't want him involved."

"His home was breached, so, he's involved."

"I haven't spoken to him since last evening. I told you, he's out of town."

"A guy like Avery knows every detail at all times, trust me. If the security was down, even for a short period of time, I'm sure he was notified."

Max cried again as the last piece of tape was pulled free of his face. Angel rubbed through his fur and kissed him after she'd rubbed most of the oil away with the towels. "I'm sorry, baby. It's all better now." She got up and went to the refrigerator to pull out three bottles of water, handing one to Kenneth and pouring another in a bowl for Max. "I'm not even sure what happened. These guys are pros. Who knows what Alex is aware of? He's working on this billion dollar deal in Hawaii; his focus is elsewhere."

"Was that him on the phone?" he asked, before taking a long pull of his water.

Angel didn't answer but unscrewed the cap on her own and then jumped as his ringtone flooded the silence again.

"That's him?"

Angel nodded and picked up the phone. Her heart dropped and her pulse thundered in her veins. "Hello?"

"Angel! Where the hell have you been?" Alex demanded harshly.

"Nowhere. I'm home, at my place."

"Why didn't you answer your phone all night? There was some sort of problem with the security last night. I was out of my fucking mind when I couldn't reach you!"

"Calm down. I'm okay. I came home just this morning and Max is with me."

Kenneth shook his head. "Tell him the truth, Angel," he mouthed.

She scowled at him and turned her back.

"Why didn't you answer the phone?" he asked again. "I've called several times on both phones. Didn't you get any of my messages?"

"I didn't hear the phone, I guess."

"For four hours?"

"Alex, stop with the Spanish Inquisition. I was sleeping, in the shower, whatever."

"No, not whatever! Jesus Christ, Angel!"

"Alex, I said I'm fine. Max is fine. As far as I know, the house is fine."

"The security company called me and the system was down for a while. It's functioning fine now, but they're on site. I didn't want you to be frightened by them."

She heard the stress behind the words and her heart swelled. "I'm fine. I think I should stay at my apartment tonight, though. I'll keep Max here."

"They're installing a new system. It's top-of-the-line and not as vulnerable, so I'd feel better with you there."

"But…"

"Just—*don't* argue with me!"

She sucked in her breath. Her instinct was to tell him to go to hell—that she'd do what she damn well pleased—but the panic in his voice stopped her. Despite the decision she'd made, she needed to see him and feel his arms around her with his body claiming hers one more time.

"Okay, okay. When will you be finished there?"

"I'd hoped today, but no later than tomorrow evening, Chicago time. Should I send Mrs. Dane to collect Max? Are you going into your office?"

"Yes, thank you. I'll pick him up on my way home."

"Sounds good." He sighed, the sound whooshing through the phone. "Please keep your phone near you. I want to be able to reach you at all times. I'll have someone meet you there to tell you the new combination around six."

"A little bossy, aren't you?" She tried to tease him, even though her heart ached.

"I'm a lot bossy, so do as you're told." He was indignant and pissed.

"Alex, I'm fine," Angel reassured him.

"All right, but do as you're told." He chuckled softly, relief flooding his voice, and she smiled slightly.

"I only do as I'm told when it suits my own agenda. That's part of my appeal."

"Behave or I'll have to spank you."

I miss you so much, her heart cried. Tears stung at the back of her eyes and she tried to swallow the lump in her throat. "Um…" she cleared her throat. "Listen, I gotta get ready for work."

"Angel, tell me what's wrong."

"Nothing. I'm just running late."

Alex hesitated only briefly. "Okay, I'll let you get to it. Be careful, and I'll see you soon."

"Yes. Have a safe trip back. Goodbye."

When she turned back to Kenneth, she faced his disapproval. "Angel, why didn't you just tell him?"

"Because, I can't involve him in the case… professional ethics bullshit! Why worry him for nothing, anyway? This happened because of me. Alex was not Swanson's motivation."

Kenneth's eyes narrowed. He understood. Alex Avery meant more to her than she was letting on. "No, but he's yours," he said knowingly.

"Look, what I choose to tell him is my business. I'm not discussing the case with him, counselor, don't worry."

"I'm dropping you from the case. I'll have Stacey assign someone else."

"You forget I'm getting paid for this. So, essentially, you're firing me?"

"It's just a case. It seems like you've got more important irons in the fire, anyway."

"I need a little more time. I have to reconcile the two sets of tests and write up the reports, do depositions. I need to wheedle him a little more."

"Until he kills you?"

"He wants me to feel helpless and in his control. He wants to teach me a lesson, and if I were dead, I wouldn't learn a damn thing. He doesn't want to kill me." *He's more likely to hurt someone I care about.* Angel tried to hide the tremor that ran through her at the thought.

"You're so goddamned blasé about it. This isn't something to mess around with. At the very least, he'll hurt you. Just walk away, Angel. I'm telling you to walk away."

"Not yet."

"Are you in love with him?"

"Where the hell did that come from? In love with whom?"

"You and I both know you can't play dumb and succeed. Why Avery?"

"I don't know."

"Be honest. I can take it."

"I honestly don't know!" She paced back and forth, talking with her hands. "I feel all tied up in knots, and I need to keep my head on straight right now. I didn't want this. Needing Alex makes me weak. I don't want to care about him."

"But, you do."

"Yes, I do. That's why I don't want him involved. Swanson would kill him because he knows it would punish me. He wanted to get my attention by taking Max, by showing me he could infiltrate the life of someone I care about, and it worked. His point is made, so Alex and I are over."

"Angel, do you think he will go down without a fight?"

"Not at all, but I'll find a way to make charges stick. I'm not an adolescent girl who will crumble under cross-examination."

"I wasn't talking about Swanson."

*****

It was late and the house was dark. The new security system was in place, and Max was on the bed next to Angel as she rolled onto her back under the thick comforter and stared at the ceiling. The soft candle glowing on the bedside table cast eerie shadows all around the room. She tried to figure out how to goad Mark Swanson into a coming after her himself. It was a risk, but her abhorrence for that fucker gave her bravado that she might otherwise lack. Her mind turned to the man who had altered her view of so many things.

Her slender fingers traced over the iPhone that Alex had given her, willing it to ring. He was working like mad to finish in Hawaii, and though she yearned to see him, she also dreaded it.

"Max, I'm going to miss you both so much," she whispered brokenly.

She willed herself not to cry as sadness overwhelmed her. It didn't matter that she reminded herself a million times why she was doing it; it didn't matter that she'd been telling herself from the beginning that she'd bleed over Alex Avery. All that mattered was that she wouldn't be with him. And worse, by the time the case was wrapped, she was sure he would move on, because that's what men do—especially the sexy, intelligent, strong, and wealthy type. He'd never take her back, even if she begged, which Angel would never do.

"How stupid am I, Max? I lie here dying just to hear his voice. I'm not sure I'm strong enough to walk away." *Fuck my life,* she thought when the tears finally won out.

The phone never rang and as the hours wore on, Angel finally fell into a fitful sleep, her dreams a collage of wondrous touches and magnificent kisses intermingled with fear, worry, and sadness.

A sound in the other room had her heart beating faster when she was startled from her dream. Her hands clenched at the sheets as she sat bolt upright, her eyes wide and her ears straining. The sound of the door to the bedroom opening made her jump, her chest constricting. "Alex?"

Instantly, she recognized his tall form, his white dress shirt outlined his strong shoulders in the dark. She let out her breath, unaware that she'd been holding it, and fell back onto the pillows.

"Expecting someone else?" His voice was husky and she could tell how tired he was.

"No. You scared me."

"I'm sorry. I didn't mean to wake you, baby," he said softly as he unbuttoned his shirt, pulling it free from his pants. "Angel?"

She watched him, her eyes adjusting to the darkness so she could see his movements. "It's okay. I wasn't sleeping well, anyway."

"Miss me bad, huh?"

Her throat constricted as he leaned across the bed and touched her chin. She couldn't speak, so she only nodded and wrapped her fingers around the ones cupping her face. She pressed into his hand and nodded again, trying to memorize his touch. His hands were warm and strong, capable of bringing such immense comfort or pleasure. He touched her chin with his thumb again.

"Pffttt!" he whistled. "Down, Max." The dog scrambled off of the bed but went to lie beside it on Angel's side. Alex began to move away to discard his clothes. Unable to help herself, Angel held onto the hem of his shirt and pulled him back. This time it was her hand that reached out, moving along his jaw and pushing his hair back.

"Angel," he said throatily as he leaned down and took her mouth hungrily with his, arms pulling her easily up off the bed and fully into his embrace. He tasted good and she clung to him, her mouth open and responsive under his, her fingers sliding up his hard stomach and chest until they reached up his neck and into his hair. He groaned and kissed her harder, his mouth sucking on and then ghosting over hers.

"I missed you," she breathed against his lips, her chin rising, silently asking his to return.

"I was so worried when I couldn't reach you." His forehead rested on hers before he placed one more open-mouthed kiss on her temple and Angel's heart exploded.

Alex moved away to shed the rest of his clothes, discarding the expensive garments carelessly on the floor before he slid in beside her, gathering her close and tangling his limbs with hers. "God, you feel good." His hands roamed over her back and down the curve of her hip and his mouth found her shoulder in a series of kisses.

"I didn't expect you back tonight."

"I fully expected you to defy me and not be here."

"I should have. Then I'd have gotten my spanking."

Alex laughed and his chest rumbled beneath her check as he swatted her rump once. She smiled, her breath rushing warmly over his skin.

"You sound so tired."

"Not too tired to touch you."

Angel curled closer into him, Alex's arms tightened around her and his lips found her forehead. Her fingers played over the smooth skin on his chest. She felt safe in his arms despite the precarious position they were both in. Angel concentrated on the glorious feeling of his fingers threading in her hair and smoothing it down her back, in the rise and fall of his chest beneath her cheek, and the warmth of his body entwined with hers.

"Angel, what's wrong?" His deep voice broke into her thoughts.

Her arm wound around his waist and she placed an open-mouthed kiss on his neck and then another.

"Tell me," he commanded. His voice was quiet but the tone demanded no less compliance.

"Nothing." The lie forced itself from her lips. "I know you're tired, so I was trying to let you fall asleep."

"Has something happened?"

"No."

"Angel." He wasn't asking, he was demanding an answer she didn't want to give.

"Can't I just lie here and enjoy being with you?" She ran her tongue along his jaw, the stubble sharper than she expected, and her hand slid up his face and into the hair beside his ear.

Without releasing her, Alex moved her up until her head was beside his on the pillow and he could look into her eyes. Despite the darkness, the glistening pools drew him in. His fingers traced over her skin, gently kneading.

His expression was serious as he regarded her. "Yes, all I've thought about was having my hands on you, smelling your skin, tasting your mouth… making sure you're safe."

Love flooded her heart and she closed her eyes, resting her forehead against his as her fingers clutched in the hair at the back of his head. Alex pulled her leg over his hip, his strong fingers reaching almost around her thigh.

"I want you, Angel." His mouth reached for hers. The kiss began tentatively but quickly became intense and passionate. Both of them were lost in the other: lips moving in perfect unison, breathing increasing, and bodies tightening. "Tell me you want me, too."

"You know I do," she breathed against his mouth.

"Say the words." Her body's response should have been enough for him; he'd never questioned his ability to make a woman pant and moan, but with Angel, he needed her words as much as he needed her body. He needed to know she was as addicted to him as he was to her.

Alex pushed her shirt up until his hand closed around the firm mound of her breast, his thumb circling her nipple until they were both moaning between kisses. Heat pooled between her legs and she arched forward, longing to feel his hardness grinding against her.

"I'm aching, Alex, please."

"Please, Angel. Say, you want me. Only me."

His fingers pushed the shirt up and over her head, his mouth closing around her breast while his right arm pulled her closer, finally letting her feel his arousal.

"Mmmmm…. Uh…" she moaned.

"Fuuuuck! The sounds you make go straight to my cock." He resumed his exploration of her body with his mouth, moving slowly lower until she was writhing beneath him. He ran his nose along the lace at the top of her panties, inhaling her scent. "Mmmm…" he murmured as she arched up toward his mouth, urging him to end her suffering.

His fingers hooked around the lace at her hip and began to drag it down, his hot mouth wild against every inch of skin that was revealed. "Say it, Angel. Just fucking admit it."

"Yes! Yes, I want you. Just you. Oh, God." Her heart screamed. How was she going to leave him after she'd just admitted what she had?

Her legs fought to be free of her panties as he flung them aside and settled between them, finally spreading them wide. Right or wrong, he wanted to own her and he proceeded to prove to her that she wanted it, too; his tongue and mouth laving and sucking in relentless pursuit of her pleasure. Soon Angel was clutching the sheet, as he pushed her body over the edge.

"Uh... uhhhh.... Aleeeexxxx," she moaned. "Uhhhh.... Mmmm..."

His hand flattened on her abdomen as his mouth eased off slowly, gently teasing every last pulse from her orgasm.

Angel's heart ached even as her body shuddered in explosive ecstasy. She reached for him, pulling him up and wrapping her legs around him, urging him frantically inside her body. "I want you; I want to make you come hard."

"Wait, baby," he said quietly as he found a condom and rolled it down his considerable length.

"No. No waiting," she almost cried. She loved this man, she knew it, and she was in agony knowing she had to end their relationship. She wanted this one last night in his arms, to memorize his voice, his breathing, his body as he claimed his ownership, and she wasn't going to waste one second of it.

They both groaned as he found her entrance and filled her. Holding her knee up, he moved inside her, each thrust longer and deeper, taking her slowly, savoring every inch of her as she clenched around him. "This is mine," he said just before his mouth claimed hers and he lost himself in her body. "No one fucking touches you but me. Ever again."

4

Sacrifice

ALEX ROLLED OVER in the bed, the cool sheets alerting him to Angel's absence. His arm reached out, fingers fanning over the soft surface of the sheet, only to find it empty. He sat up with an unfamiliar feeling of panic. "Angel?"

His eyes strained in the darkness, quickly glancing around the perimeter of the room. "Angel?" he called again, louder this time. Silence answered; it's voice a black hole of nothingness. Alex quickly pushed back the covers and rose from the bed. The carpet beneath his feet was plush, but the air was a stark contrast to the warmth of the bed and goose bumps covered his skin. Despite the chill, he walked down the hall, oblivious to his nakedness, his only thought to find her.

He glanced through the doorway of the smaller bedroom next to his and then walked quickly down the hall and descended the long staircase. The light of the moon filtered softly through the skylights in the kitchen and a few of the windows, casting an eerie blue glow that left twisted and over-sized shadows falling from the furniture. They stretched out on the floor as if in search of something just their beyond reach.

The jingle of Max's collar drew Alex's attention and he turned toward the great room. The dog was on the couch with Angel kneeling in front of him, her arms wrapped around his furry body and her words soft and soothing. Alex felt the coil of his muscles unwind as relief flooded through him.

"Such a good boy. I'm so sorry." Her low murmur throbbed with barely veiled emotion. "I'll miss you, Max. So much. I love you."

Never had three words caused more longing in his heart as Alex slowed his pace and observed Angel comforting the dog. She'd thrown on his dress shirt with the sleeves rolled up above her elbows, and her firm legs were curled beneath her. Alex wanted to make his presence known, yet was content just to gaze at her. Something in her tone gave him pause, and he frowned as questions rolled through his mind.

"You won't need to miss him, baby. You'll see him often," he said softly, moving to her side.

The hand cupping her head felt like heaven, any excuse to have him touch her was welcome. Her soft eyes looked up and glistened in the low light, beseeching Alex with some unspoken need. His breath caught at the picture she made: a mixture of sensual allure and sadness—her complexity mirroring his own.

"We've become sort of close." Her voice was thick and strained. "I mean…" she searched for words and laid her head against Max's. The dog responded by throwing a paw over one of her arms. "He's my buddy now. We're sort of used to each other."

Alex settled on the floor next to her and reached a hand out, his knuckles brushing the petal softness of her cheek. "Lucky dog," he murmured—his eyes more serious than his words and the slight smile that played on his lips. He studied her, searching for an understanding of her sadness.

"He is. He has you." Angel's eyes were intense, never leaving the green depths of his.

"You have me, too."

Angel's heart seized. Those words should have been nirvana, but instead, they ripped through her like a knife. Her chin trembled slightly as her throat swelled and tears burned her eyes. *God, help me keep it together,* she prayed. It was going to hurt like hell, but she would do what she needed to do, no matter the consequences to herself, no matter if he never forgave her for her deception. Keeping him out of harm's way was the most important thing.

Angel was unsure if she just wanted more precious time with him or if she was unwilling or unable to win the fight should he choose to resist her decision. Alex would resist; she was sure. His relationships ended when he said they ended and not before. Who in their right mind could fucking leave him anyway? No matter the circumstances, the boundaries he put in place, or how small the scraps he threw, who was strong enough to walk away from Alexander Avery?

Suddenly, she felt very sorry for the woman she spoke with on her program, empathy painting an all too vivid reality of what the prospect of losing this man felt like. Angel swallowed hard, trying to clear the pain from her throat.

"No one has you, Alex," she said simply, her hand coming up to wrap around his wrist while he continued to stroke her cheekbone, his touch feather-light and gentle. His tenderness tore at her heart. "Not completely."

Alex seemed oblivious to his nakedness, sitting with his legs stretched out in front of him and crossed at the ankles, leaning one elbow on the cushion of the sofa, facing her. His eyes bore into hers. "You have me more than anyone ever has," he admitted. His hair was wild from sleep, and she yearned to wrap her fingers in the silky strands. There was no end to his sexual magnetism. Her heart was aching, and yet, she wanted him. Always wanting him.

Alex reached up and ruffled Max's furry mane. "Are you taking good care of Angel, boy?"

Angel's eyes were still trained on Alex's face and following every movement. "Are you cold?"

Alex smirked. "If you're insinuating that my dick's shriveled, save it. It is cold in here."

Angel couldn't help the grin. "No. Sorry to disappoint you, but um... I wasn't referring to your *man banana*," she said cheekily. "Just because it's all you think about, don't assume everyone else is also preoccupied with it."

Alex burst out laughing, his brilliant green eyes crinkling at the corners. "Oh, really?"

"Yeah. I mean, no!"

"Man banana?"

"Perhaps you prefer tube steak, pork sword, or my personal favorite; stinky pickle?" She bit her lip and tried not to giggle but gave up when Alex threw his head back and laughed uproariously.

"Oh, my God! Angel!"

"What?" she asked innocently with wide eyes and raised eyebrows. "I had a patient with a penis obsession last year! I've heard 'em all!" She fell over into Alex's arms, giggling uncontrollably. A miracle considering the overwhelming sadness she'd felt only moments before.

"I doubt I'll ever be able to get it up again after that! I think I prefer man banana!" He chuckled, enjoying the way she felt in his arms—her warm breath on his neck, the soft curves beneath the expensive linen. She always smelled so good.

"I have faith in your ability," she murmured, sobering. Her hand traced his jaw softly.

"You do, huh?" His lips found hers, softly, and he closed his eyes, inhaling her scent.

Angel nodded and yawned, drawing her hand to cover her mouth. "Yes."

Even with Angel in his arms, Alex got easily to his feet. "Come on. Back to bed with you, young lady."

Angel laid her head on his shoulder and snuggled in, memorizing the feel of his arms around her and his firm chest, warm next to hers. The clink of Max's collar followed them down the hall and the dog found a warm spot on the floor next to Alex's bed.

When Angel was tucked back in, Alex slid in behind her and gathered her back against his body. The heat radiating between them quickly warmed the covers and created a cozy cocoon around them both. The duvet was plush and fluffy, and Angel mused how everything that surrounded her was soft as silk, even Alex's skin. His body was solid muscle, but she fit so perfectly to him: it was heaven. Angel's fingers ran over the soft hair on his forearm that was wrapped around her and let her feet rest between his calves.

Alex hugged her closer still. "Mmmm... this feels nice." His lips found her shoulder in a gentle caress that ended in the soft bite of his teeth. "Go to sleep, baby."

They lay in the darkness, but Angel continued to stroke Alex's arm, her fingers entwining with his when she reached them. "How am I different?" she wondered aloud, needing an answer that she might never have the chance to hear again.

Alex's eyes snapped open and he frowned. The hand holding hers tightened, and he kissed her shoulder again. "How aren't you different, Angel?" he responded.

"But... *how?*"

He considered how to make his meaning clear; how best to communicate her significance. "Well, you're amazingly gorgeous, and your body anticipates and reciprocates every move I make. I let you tongue-lash me and, the strange thing is, I like it. You give as good as you get."

"You don't *let* me do anything. I do what I want."

"Exactly." He laughed softly, his chest shaking gently against her back. "Soooo fucking sexy."

"So it's about the sex?"

"No." He shook his head. "I mean, sure, it's incredible, no question. My dick has never been happier, but it's your wit and your intelligence that I adore, the many ways you affect me."

He ran a hand over the soft swell of her hip and down her thigh, only to retrace the movement. "Your body is irresistible and fits mine perfectly. It's like you were made just for me."

She listened, her heart aching yet anxious for the comfort of his voice.

"I miss you," he said quietly after a moment's pause, the realization a surprise, even to himself. "That's the biggest thing."

"What?" she asked so softly he barely heard her.

"*I miss you.*" He shrugged slightly, the admission leaving him vulnerable—which was new and uncomfortable. A position he avoided at all costs most of the time, but with Angel, he was driven to spill his guts. "I never missed anyone before. In fact, I couldn't wait to leave. But when we're not together, I can't wait to be with you, and when we are, I never want to leave." He huffed in realization. "It's ridiculous. You're always on my mind, Angel. When I woke up earlier and you weren't in bed, I panicked. It's just stupid."

Tears filled her eyes as they slammed shut, then seeped from the corners to fall softly on her pillow as he echoed her feelings with his words. She brought his hand to her mouth and placed a series of butterfly kisses on his knuckles. She drew in a steadying breath. "No, it's not stupid."

"I've been summoned for brunch with my family this Sunday. My mother won't take no for an answer, and I'd like you to come with me. I think even Allison and Josh will be there."

Iron bands of emotion wound tightly around her chest making it difficult to breath, and she struggled to could keep the tears out of her voice. "What about your brother?"

He knew that couldn't happen right now, not if Cole was to be successful watching over her. The repercussion would bite him in the ass, he knew, but it was a price he was willing to pay to make sure she was safe. "No. No, he won't be able to make it."

*****

"Angel?" Elizabeth's voice interrupted her attempt to concentrate on the report she was working on. Her heart was heavy and her mind wasn't focused on work. "Mark Swanson is on line one. Do you want to take it?"

Angel pushed the pause button on her handheld tape recorder and threw it carelessly on her desk. It landed with a dull thump.

Shit, she thought. Her heart skipped a beat. Just the mention of that fucker's name made her skin crawl. "What does he want?"

"He didn't say. Should I ask?"

"No. I'll talk to him." She hesitated only briefly, her hand pushing the soft tendrils of hair behind her ear, before she picked up the phone. "Good morning, Mr. Swanson. What can I do for you?"

A harsh laugh fell into her ear. "I've got a surprise for you, sexy doctor."

"A repeat performance?" she asked stiffly.

"Ah. Well, whatever. Did you enjoy that as much as I did?" His voice slithered through the phone and wrapped around her.

Her back stiffened and her hand clenched around the phone until her fingers hurt. "Yeah. It was a barrel of laughs. Sick motherfuckers like you fascinate me. If I were a man, my dick would be hard."

She was chilled by the low chuckle that followed. "Come now, Angel, play nice. I know where it hurts, so remember that."

"You're not taking into account that I'm a cold bitch and I have a purpose here. It doesn't matter what you do, my agenda will not change."

"I love your defiance, but we both know the tests show nothing."

"Your crystal ball needs adjusting." Anger flooded her until she thought she'd burst, and she knew this was the time to push his buttons. When he called her office, he gave her the opportunity to engage his rage without initiating contact. "I'll do what needs to be done."

"As will I. Accidents befall important men all the time."

A chill ran over her skin like lightning. "Well, you might have a point, but you'll come up empty."

"I know you're involved with Alex Avery."

"Not involved, exactly. I *was* fucking him. We had an arrangement, but it's over. I got bored."

"I'm not convinced, but maybe you need a real man."

She rolled her eyes in disgust. "Well, let me know if you run into one. Until then, I'll just concentrate on putting your sorry ass behind bars. Have a nice day."

Somehow, Angel had ended up on the far side of her office to stare out of the window and didn't notice that she'd inadvertently knocked her latte over with the cord from the phone. The tan liquid was dripping down the side of her desk, and the reports she was working on were ruined.

"Oh, crap!" she moaned, returning the phone to its cradle and pulling tissues from the dispenser near the corner of her desk; she began to frantically mop up the mess.

"Mr. Gant is here."

"Thank you, Liz. Send him in." She glanced up as she threw the tissues away. He looked anxious as he entered her office. "Hi, Kenneth."

Kenneth deposited himself in one of the sleek black leather chairs opposite hers. "Angel, I wanted to let you know that I got word the victim is refusing to testify. Apparently, Swanson offered his wife a huge settlement and a quickie divorce to keep it all hush-hush."

"But—it's a criminal matter. It still goes to trial, right? Regardless of what she wants, it isn't up to her."

"Well, yeah, technically, I could push it. But if the victim is called as a hostile witness and then refuses to talk, she'll be charged with perjury and contempt of court. Frankly, Angel, it's a huge waste of taxpayer money to take something to trial that we'll probably lose. And, don't you think that poor kid's been through enough?"

Angel tugged at a tendril that had fallen free from her chignon to softly frame her face. She sighed heavily. "It's better than knowing that fucker got away with what he did to her! He'll just do it to someone else! Creeps like Mark Swanson don't stop because they *almost* got caught. He'll just feel empowered, like he can get away with anything!"

"Angel, there's not a whole hell of a lot I can do. It's my job to take cases to court that I can win, and I don't think I'll win this."

"That bastard!" she breathed. "I've never hated anyone so much in my life. Maybe, if I talk to the girl again?" Her face felt like it was on fire even as the color drained from away and desperation clung to her soul. After all of the torment that he'd caused, he would get off scot-free? Her heart fell and she felt like she would vomit, her hands shaking to the point where she had to steady them by smoothing out her navy skirt.

"It's doubtful it will help. You can't win 'em all, Angel. I know how much this means to you, but you have to let it go."

"Can't you stall for a little while? Give me some time to crack this asshole on my own?"

"It's too dangerous, Angel." Kenneth shook his head. "And I've already stalled so you could repeat the tests."

"He's threatened me and had his thugs break into Alex's house. I have to get him on something, for God's sake!"

"*You* don't have to do anything! Stay out of it! He'll screw up on his own; trust me. We just have to wait him out."

Her upper teeth gnawed on her lower lip, and Kenneth knew that look well.

"Angel! It's not worth it."

"Ken, there's nothing you can say to change my mind. It's personal now. He's invaded my life and threatened people I care about."

"What will your boyfriend think of you chasing rapists around? You're too smart to put yourself in such a dangerous position!" Kenneth argued.

"Alex is no one's boyfriend!" Angel admonished. "Even if he were, I wouldn't ask his permission. You know me better than that. But, it's moot." She paused, unsure how much she should say. "I'm not seeing him anymore." She concentrated on keeping her voice steady despite the ache the words caused. The burning behind her eyes resulted in tears welling up. She blinked rapidly and turned away so Kenneth wouldn't see, absently digging around in her desk drawer.

Kenneth's tone softened. "Avery's reputation is what it is, but I never expected him to be through with you so soon."

Her cheeks burned at the implication, but she had no desire to give the wrong impression either. "Naturally, you assume it's up to him." She scowled, anger a welcome distraction from the ache in her throat. "That just pisses me off! This is my decision and it has nothing to do with Alex. He's been... really wonderful."

There was a long pause as Kenneth digested the information. "I'm not sure if I'm relieved you're not with the guy or frustrated because I'm not the reason why. I hoped after this affair burned out, you'd want to try again."

Angel's face crumpled. "Kenneth, I can't." Her voice broke slightly. "I'm not leaving Alex because I don't want to be with him. Swanson has threatened to hurt him and I can't risk that."

"Oh, I see." He sighed. "If you feel this strongly, just tell him what's going on and agree not to see each other until this is over."

She shook her head adamantly. "I wish it were that easy. My conscience won't let me abandon what's right, and Alex isn't the type to wait in the wings. God knows what he'd do. He's not as invincible as he thinks he is, and I don't want him hurt."

"Don't you think ending the relationship will hurt him?"

"His ego may be bruised, and I expect he'll be madder than hell, but better that than the alternative. If anything happened to him, I'd never forgive myself." She closed her eyes against the sting.

"Did you ever consider that even if you stop seeing Avery, Swanson might not believe you're done with him?"

"I'm not a moron," Angel almost spat out.

Kenneth sat still as stone and studied her absolute resolve until she shifted in her seat.

"Look, I have a full load of patients today, and I need to get my shit together."

He stood reluctantly and came around the desk, pulling her up by her hand and hugging her gently. "I'm here if you need me. Don't do anything stupid. I'll stall this thing as long as I can."

"Thank you."

After Kenneth left, Angel sank back into her chair and let her head fall onto her arms on the top of her desk. Her shoulders shook in an effort to hold it together. The loss and regret overwhelmed her. She knew that she'd have to be stronger than ever when she faced Alex. He was a predator who was used to winning, and he wouldn't play fair. He'd pull out every weapon in his arsenal to prove just how much power he held over her. Power her heart already acknowledged without hesitation.

She felt physically ill when she considered the scene she'd have to get through, what she would need to do to convince Alex she wanted him out of her life. She grabbed the black wastebasket

from under her desk and vomited up the latte and what little break-
fast she'd had earlier. The convulsions continued until dry heaves
racked her slight form. When they finally subsided, she sat back
and grabbed a tissue from her sideboard next to her desk, wiping at
her mouth and then at the tears clinging to her lashes. Angel picked
up the phone and buzzed Liz.

"Yes?"

"I can't see patients today. I'm ill. Please call and reschedule
my appointments."

"Are you okay? Do you need anything?"

"No, thank you. I just need to go home."

"Okay, Angel. I'll take care of everything."

"Thank you."

Angel stood on shaky legs and pulled both of her phones
from her purse. Of course, there was a message from Alex.

*Hey, babe, it's me. I thought I'd take you out to dinner. I'll have Mrs.
Dane make reservations wherever you'd like. Meetings this morning but I'll
touch base over lunch. Talk to you soon.*

How easy it would be to allow things to continue as they had
been. Every second with him had been magical. She loved the thrill
of thinking about him and knowing that every night she could be
wrapped in his arms if that was what she wanted. Except, she
wouldn't be.

Suddenly, she was desperate to put it off for one more day.
She pushed his phone aside and picked up the other phone, quickly
dialing her best friend.

"Hey, stranger!"

"Hi, Becca. Can you meet me tonight? Just you?"

Becca heard the weariness in Angel's voice; the stuffiness of
her nose was a clear sign she'd been crying.

"I think so. I'll ask Mom to watch Jilly. Are you okay?"

"Oh, sure." Angel forced an enthusiastic tone she didn't feel.
"I just miss you."

"Okay! Where and what time?"

"My place? It doesn't matter when. I'm going home early."

"Sure. Should I bring anything?"

"No, I'll stop and pick some stuff up on my way home."

"Is Alex out of town? I didn't think you'd ever come up for air!" Becca laughed happily.

Angel was not willing to disclose anything until she saw Becca in person; she needed time to get her game face on. "So, around six?"

"What's wrong, Angel?" Becca asked, the somber tone of her friend giving her mood away.

"I'll tell you tonight. I promise." She brushed the remnant tears from under her eyes and gathered her purse.

"Okay. See you then."

"Thanks."

Angel leaned back in her high-backed leather chair and closed her eyes. She cleared her throat. It was now or never. "Fuck my life."

*****

"Is she home?" Alex asked as the door shut heavily behind him.

Cole's eyes roamed over his brother's unusual appearance. He was without a jacket or tie, shirt untucked, sleeves rolled halfway up his forearms, and the dark shadow of a day and a half's worth of beard covering his jaw.

"Yes. Since early afternoon." Cole was in the process of moving into Angel's building and overseeing the installation of the new security system after Avery's purchase was final. "She passed me in the hall but seemed distracted. I don't think she even noticed."

Angel hadn't answered his request for dinner, and he'd been unable to reach her all day. So he ended up in the room that was supposed to be Cole's living room but now looked more like a security office with several monitors that wired into cameras placed around the entire building.

Alex, hands on hips, looked closely at the screens. "Where the fuck is Bancroft? He was supposed to be watching her, wasn't he?" Tension filled him, tightening the muscles of his arms and shoulders with a painful burn.

"Downtown, digging around to find out how much weight Swanson's mob connections afford him. It doesn't look like the organization gives a fuck about the guy. He's basically a joke. It doesn't help him that the girl is Marvin Standish's niece." Anyone connected in Chicago, knew that the Standish family was heavy into the mob, even though they had legitimate business fronts as well. The man attended some of the same events as Alex did and his wife ran in some of the same circles as the wives of other Chicago businessmen. His kids played in the same sports leagues. Most people knew but it wasn't exactly a topic of conversation. "I'm surprised he's still breathing, to be honest, but then his sister Carol is married to one of them. I doubt his sister's husband is significant, so I doubt they will protect him or retaliate, but we should still be careful, Alex."

"I'm paying him to watch her!"

Cole frowned as he glanced toward his brother. "Alex, are you listening? This is great news! No one is going to save this dude's ass by pouring money into his business. Three of his locations are already closed. It's happening just the way you planned."

Two hands ran through his thick mop of dark hair as he inhaled deeply. "Bancroft should've been doing his fucking job!" The tenor of his words bounced off the walls and echoed around the empty apartment.

"Alex!" Cole said sharply. "She's safe, for Christ's sake!"

"Until that fucker is locked up or so broke he can't afford to take a cab across the street, I want someone watching her around the clock! Is that clear, Cole?" He leaned down, looking closely at the monitor that was trained on the hallway in front of Angel's apartment. Cole turned and stared at his profile, watching the muscle twitch in Alex's jaw. "I *said*, is that clear?" His voice was menacingly low.

"Alex, I know I'm just a hired hand, but I'm still your older brother. Remember that." Cole got up and went into the kitchen, pulling two beers from the refrigerator.

Alex waved the proffered can away and Cole's brows rose.

"You need a drink. Take it." He offered it again and Alex reluctantly took it.

"Only one, Cole. You can't protect her if you're drunk." His voice was softer now.

"Aren't you on your way over there? I figure I can get some sleep as long as she's with you."

"I don't know." Alex opened the can and downed half of the contents in one long pull.

"Since when? You always architect every move you make."

"I've uh…" he paused. "It's the Angel affect, I guess." The corner of his mouth quirked slightly. "Sorry about before. The guy's slime, and he openly threatened her."

"He threatened you both. Don't forget that."

Alex shrugged and sank to the floor, leaning his back against a wall, his legs out in front of him as he finished the beer. "He's not interested in me, but I need to take care of Angel… she doesn't make it easy. But you're right. I shouldn't take it out on you. Bancroft, on the other hand, will hear about it."

Cole sat back down in front of the monitors and adjusted something in front of him. "She had a visitor earlier, a woman. Pretty, with long blonde hair."

"That would be her best friend, Becca. Is she still there?" Alex pulled out his phone, longing to see that Angel had returned his message. He frowned at the blank screen. "What the hell is going on?" he murmured under his breath.

"No, she left around 10:30. She's gorgeous, too, Alex."

"Don't get any ideas." The last thing Alex needed was Cole to become distracted; plus, he wasn't convinced his brother was up to a woman with a kid and he didn't want either Becca or Jillian to become fallout. He might be changing his ways, but Alex wasn't confident it would stick just yet.

Cole smiled. "Are you going to call her?"

Alex shook his head and rose to his feet. "I'm going over. I'll check in with you in the morning."

When he found himself in front of Angel's door, his ears strained to hear something from inside. Was she asleep already? His mind cranked through the possibilities about her lack of contact. His hand connected with the wood in four loud raps. "Angel?" he called.

The door opened and Angel appeared in a pair of navy blue sweatshorts and a white tank top. Her eyes were red and swollen, her hair falling down around her face in a rumpled mess from the topknot.

His eyes swept over her face and then the soft curves of her body, as relief washed over him. "Why didn't you answer my calls? Are you okay? I was worried." He walked toward her, taking for granted that she'd allow him in, sliding his arms around her waist and kissing her on the temple.

Angel closed her eyes briefly, letting herself inhale his scent before she forced herself to stiffen in his arms. "I'm fine."

"Then why didn't you answer my calls?" he questioned again.

"You're not my father or my boss, so it's really none of your concern," she said softly, forced sarcasm lacing her tone. Her heart was screaming. She hated herself for what she was about to do, when all she wanted was to melt into his arms and never leave.

Alex moved back to look into her face, a frown settling on his handsome face. "What's your problem? Don't I deserve a little respect?" He walked past her and into the apartment without waiting for an invitation.

"By all means, do come in."

He turned toward her, though still hovering in the entryway. His head cocked to the side, his expression perplexed. "What the hell is going on?"

"Nothing!" she said harshly. "I'm a grown woman. I don't need to report in to you or anyone else!"

"Stop acting like a spoiled child, Angel. It doesn't suit you," Alex said blandly, the anger he'd managed to quash earlier rising anew. "This has turned out to be one, great fucking day."

"So sorry if I've inconvenienced you, but since you're not my husband, or even my boyfriend, stop with the inquisition." She went into the kitchen and picked up a half-full bottle of white wine, refilling her glass without offering one to him. She turned her back to him looking out of the window, the burn in her throat threatening to choke her. Her heart thudded abnormally, her pulse pounding abnormally hard in her neck as her eyes blurred. "We fucked, that's all. There really is no point in continuing something that was doomed from the start."

Alex heard the words but didn't believe them. "I know why you're doing this, and it isn't going to work. Come over here." His voice was soft as silk, and she swallowed, trying to ease the lump in her throat.

"It has to be over, Alex."

"Angel, come on. I know it's only been a few weeks, but I know you better than that. Everything will be okay. You'll see." He had moved to her side and reached out, his hand ghosting over the outline of her head and then slid down the contour of her neck.

She jerked away from his touch as if he had burned her. "Don't touch me!" she hissed. "Is it so impossible to comprehend that a mere woman would leave the great Alex Avery? Is it so hard to believe that your dick doesn't mesmerize me? You're a great fuck, I'll admit, but there's no substance. You said it going in. It is what it is, so let's cut our losses."

His hand hovered in the air and then fell to his side before he walked quickly into the other room, found the Chivas in her bar, and poured three fingers into a crystal tumbler before bolting it. The liquid burned on the way down and he set the glass down hard. "Stop it, Angel. You're not a common whore, and I won't have you talking like you are!" he said angrily.

She turned to look at him. His shoulders were solid, his back straight, and her eyes drank him in. He was pissed. She could see it in the way he moved, the way he poured another shot and swallowed it. It almost radiated off of him like heat waves off pavement in the desert.

Pain wrapped itself around her chest, and she wondered if she could keep from screaming out loud. She blinked at the tears forming, quickly wiping at one that managed to escape. Angel was trembling—breaking from the inside out—but gathered the resolve she needed to harden her voice and her expression. "I need you to leave. *Now.*" *Please, God. Make him go. Let him go before I fall apart,* she prayed.

"The fuck I will," he rasped out.

"Get out!" she screamed at him, hurling her glass across the room toward him. It whizzed past his head and slammed into the mirror over the bar, splattering him with droplets of wine on the way and leaving the mirror shattered. "Leave!"

Before she knew what had hit her, he was across the room, and she was hauled backward and pinned by his body pressing her into the wall. His arms caged her in and he was breathing hard. She turned her head away, unwilling to see the questions or the pain in his eyes. "The fuck I will," he repeated again, but softer and deeper this time. His breath fanned out over her face in series of hot, liquor-scented blasts, and she wondered if she'd ever feel him this close again.

Angel could feel the fury churning within him but she couldn't bring herself to be afraid. This was Alex. Alex, who touched her with tenderness and passion. Alex, who would never hurt her, but wanted to protect her. She knew it like she knew her own name.

He moved on her, his hands and mouth seeking and finding tender flesh, his body arousing hers even as her heart broke within her chest. His hand moved frantically up under her shirt and closed roughly over her breast, his thumb working the nipple into a hard pebble. He pushed against her, rubbing his groin against hers and hoisting her in a thud against the wall with each thrust of his hips.

"Tell me you don't want this. Say it and I'll stop. Say it, damn you!" His voice was raw with passion and something else she couldn't fathom.

Angel clutched and clawed at his shoulders and the back of his head, lost to the love she felt. Tears rained from her eyes to soak into the white linen on his shoulder, her body throbbing in surrender. She turned her face into his neck as the clink of his belt somehow found purchase through their heavy breathing. "Tell me you're immune to this thing between us! Tell me to stop, goddam-mit!" he ground out. He pulled the crotch of her shorts and panties aside, his fingers finding the dampness that belied her desire. "Fucking hell, tell me to stop!" Alex was as close to begging as he'd ever come in his life.

His eyes locked with hers, taking in the shimmer of tears still clinging to her lashes. She shook her head and closed her eyes, forcing more tears down her face.

"No," she whispered brokenly. Her fingers found the side of his jaw just before his mouth took hers in an angry kiss. His teeth pulled on her lower lip until she cried out, and when their tongues met, he slammed into her with one quick thrust, burying himself in her moist heat.

They fought each other with their bodies, trying to be the first to wring pleasure out of the other in ruthless pursuit, their mouths at war. Her fingers threaded in his hair as his mouth dragged from hers and down her chin and neck.

Angel's head banged against the wall as he fucked her, but it was only the sound that registered. She only felt his body claiming hers; his mouth, hot and needy, taking from hers. "Not in anger, Alex. Please," she begged.

He groaned against her shoulder in regret. "Oh, God, Angel. I'm sorry. I'm sorry, baby, but I can't stop. You make me insane. I don't even know who I am right now."

Her thighs tightened around him and her hips moved with his as they both raced with frantic abandon toward release. When he felt her shudder around him and stiffen in his arms, he came hard, emptying himself deep inside her body.

He held her against the wall, their bodies trembling and jerking with the aftershock, until their breathing evened out. Angel's crying intensified when he tenderly pushed her hair, now damp with tears, off her face. His lips traced the outline of her face at the same time his arms tightened around her. Her heart exploded, ripping her apart as the shards fell. Angel's hand stroked his head and her other arm wrapped tightly around his shoulders. Sobs threatened to break as she turned and kissed the side of his face, damp with perspiration. "Alex," she choked out.

"Oh, Angel," he sighed. "Are you okay?"

They clung together for long moments, but when she didn't answer, he stood away from the wall and pulled out of her body, letting her feet find the floor. Angel moved away from him, bringing the back of her trembling hand to her mouth. Alex watched her and began to unbutton his shirt, taking it for granted that he'd stay with her now, moving to her and leaning in to kiss her mouth.

"Physically, I'm fine, but I still need you to go," she said stoically before their lips met.

"What?" he asked in disbelief, pulling back from the almost-kiss.

"Nothing changes because of... this. It seems fitting we say goodbye this way. You can let yourself out."

Angel walked numbly to her bedroom and locked the door, leaving a stunned Alex standing alone in her living room. She grabbed a pillow to muffle the sobs she knew would erupt in the following seconds and prayed he would leave before the proof of her grief would be undeniable.

5

Light and Dark

ALEX STOOD, STUNNED, in the middle of the silent living room, unsure of what to do. Angel was as stubborn as he was, and when someone pushed him, it only made him more determined. So, he stood for several minutes until he finally poured himself another drink and lay down on Angel's couch. He was shaken, no question. Her demand that things were over was unexpected after the evening and night they'd spent together the day before. In fact, every moment between them had been spectacular. Everything inside him denied that she would walk away from him and something that felt so amazing.

He ran a hand over his face as his mind fought with his heart. His chest resisted the deep breath he tried to draw in, his lungs aching. The scotch that burned all the way down did nothing to dispel the feeling, but maybe he'd get inebriated enough to shut off his mind. He couldn't reconcile what had just occurred. She'd goaded and prodded until he'd lost control; in fact, she'd begun the process earlier in the day when she wouldn't return his calls. She'd orchestrated his reaction perfectly.

"Humph!" he mused. His anger had gotten the better of him with Cole as well. He didn't like how he felt. He was never out of fucking control like this! Instinct told him to fight for what he wanted, to get her to surrender—except he admired her strength and didn't want to see her broken. He sighed deeply. For the first time, what someone else felt and what someone else wanted was more important than his own needs.

Alex turned his head in the direction of Angel's room, straining to hear something, but there was only silence. It screamed back, mocking him like the class bully in sixth grade after he'd pushed you down in the dirt and kicked you in the stomach.

The silence confused him. Maybe she was unmoved; though her tears, while they battled it out with their mouths and bodies, told a different tale. His mouth thinned in anger. Something must have happened while he was in Hawaii. Yet, last night… He had to admit to preoccupation: the security breach at his estate, getting that damn deal finalized so he could get back to her, and methodically taking down that twisted bastard she was trying to put away. Had he missed something?

If that prick was leaving threats similar to the one he found on his car, her nerves must be shot. She put on a good show, but under the bravado, he sensed her fear. Alex's blood boiled at the thought as he launched off the couch and down the hall.

His steps slowed as he approached her room, and his hand reached out to rest on the frame around the closed door. "Angel?" His tone was tempered with concern.

On the other side of the wood, Angel flinched at the sound of his voice. She was on the floor of her walk-in closet, clutching the pillow to her chest in the dark, tears still leaked in a steady stream down her face. Her eyes closed as she drew a gasping breath.

"Don't let that prick separate us. Can you trust me? I won't ever let anything hurt you."

How does he know? She scrambled into a sitting position against the wall.

"Baby, you have to talk to me." Alex paused. "Let me in."

"It's not about that," she murmured softly. Her resolve to keep him safe laced her lie with conviction. Alex didn't know how deviant that asshole was, or how far he would go, but she did. "It's just not working out. I know myself, and I know you. It's better to end it now. Quit while we're ahead."

Alex felt heat creeping up under the skin of his neck and rush toward his face. His heart fell, leaving an uncomfortable hollowness in his chest. He was filled with a mixture of disbelief and anger, not comprehending that this was what she really wanted.

"Was I the only one there? You still think I'm *that* guy? After how we've been together? You think it's all been a fucking *act?*" His voice was deep and menacing.

No, I think you're amazing, loving, witty, smart as hell, and so completely wonderful. "I can't talk about it anymore. Can you please just go? If it's like this now, imagine what it will be like if we keep going." Her voice was weak, but he didn't hear any waiver, no emotion to indicate she was lying.

"That's all I fucking do is imagine it! I don't believe this!" His fist connected with the door so hard it shook the walls. "I don't fucking believe this! Angel!" He hit the door again, making her jump.

With her elbows on bent knees, she dropped her head into her hands and closed her eyes. "You don't want a relationship with me. I'm too complicated. I don't follow rules set for me by men who want to control me. In the end, you'll thank me."

"Don't tell me what I want! Apparently, you don't know me at all. Maybe I don't know you, either." Alex cleared his throat and dropped his hand from the door. He wasn't used to being dumped, but by God, he wouldn't grovel. He reminded himself who he was, and he would never beg. For anyone. "But, if you've decided this is the end, I will thank you *now* and leave it at that. Goodbye, Angel."

She bit her lip to hold back the sobs, shaking until she heard the door slam in a cryptic bang behind him. Angel fell over and wrapped her arms around herself, gasping for breath she couldn't find. Pain wrapped around her like a vice, her eyes hurt, and her throat ached, but still, she held it in, her body jerking in defiance. If Alex heard her cry, all of it would have been for nothing. After a few minutes, when she was sure he had gone, she finally allowed the hiccupping sobs to fill the silence.

*****

"Alex!" Charles Avery startled his son out of his reverie. His eyebrow rose at Alex's apparent preoccupation. It was bad enough that he'd shown up looking disheveled and unshaven, clearly preoccupied and unprepared for the meeting. "Son, are you with me?"

"What?" Alex was staring out the window at the haze that covered the city and blurred the blue of Lake Michigan into a sort of dark, murky grey. He turned abruptly at the harsh tone of his father's voice and leaned forward on the table, glancing into his stern expression. "Sorry, what were you saying?"

"I was asking what all of these local expenditures are about. You never mentioned to me that you had taken an interest in a local business. It's so small, hardly the scope of our usual dealings."

It was a week since the night at Angel's, and though Alex tried to keep things business as usual, he was distracted. He spent most of his time hammering Cole and Bancroft about where Angel was or what she was doing and what remained to cement Swanson's financial ruin. He was on a mission and worked tirelessly, driven until he exhausted himself. He ignored Darian and Cole's invitations to go out, telling his friend he was too busy and demanding his brother forget socializing and get back to work. He wasn't eating like he should, drinking way too much, and working out until his muscles shook.

"It's a new idea. Give me some latitude, will you?" he retorted sharply.

"I never interfere," Charles began.

"*And*, we've made billions, so relax."

"Can you assure me that we'll make money on this? The investment is almost as much as the last acquisition, but you aren't buying anything. If it's a takeover, their assets don't seem worth the trouble or the money."

"They aren't publicly traded, so I couldn't take that route." Alex picked at his eyebrow absentmindedly.

"So, what is this about, then?"

"Dad, I don't ask for much, but this is personal. I'm asking for a little latitude without a barrage of inane questions."

"The one question I must ask you is what you yourself are always so good at asking, Alex. How will Avery and our shareholders benefit?"

"Let's just say I'm doing a public service, creating jobs and making someone a whole hell of a lot happier. I always find a way to make money for the company and its benefactors, Dad. For Christ's sake!" His tolerance with the conversation came to a head.

The diners at the few nearby tables sent them awkward glances, so Alex lowered his voice. "This is personal," he insisted again.

"What's it about?"

"Something I wanted done, and it evolved into a way to include Cole. It's something that he can really sink his teeth into. He's doing well; extremely well. And, my requirements are being met. Not as fast as I'd like, but that's not his job. If I didn't care about the company making money, I'd forget negotiating contracts and just pay out the ass to get what I want accomplished."

"Does this have anything to do with why you look like hell?"

Alex's lips quirked in the start of a grin. "Awww, thanks for noticing," he said with mock sarcasm. "I didn't think you cared."

Charles scowled. "Don't be petulant. Your mother noticed last Sunday that you weren't yourself."

"Well, Allison bothered me!" Alex complained. "She's always yapping at me about one charity or another. I already wrote her a check for twenty thousand toward whatever she's working on this month, but all she does is go on about the tax write-offs and how I should give more. Who in the hell does she think she's talking to? Is she the one with the MBA?"

"Alex, Allison may get a bit overzealous, but her heart's in the right place."

"Her incessant nagging wears on my nerves," Alex huffed. "It's not her place to question my decisions with the company or my personal life."

When his father continued to glare at him, Alex shifted uncomfortably in his chair and ran a careless hand through his already unruly hair.

"Whitney is her friend, Alex. It's only natural for Allison to ask about her."

During the family get-together, Allison took him aside to admonish him for not telling her that his relationship with Whitney had ended. Alex had been hungover from a night of feeling sorry for himself, liquor giving him the strength to resist calling or going to Angel, and he didn't take it well.

"Whitney is a money-grubbing little bitch, Allison."

"She said you dumped her without an explanation!"

"That's not true. I told her that she's a money-grubbing little bitch," he said with a distracted smirk, humor replacing his irritation. *"I'm sure she failed to mention that she called in to a live radio show about how horrible I was to her? If I wasn't already out, that would have sealed the deal."*

"Shut up! She did what?"

"Oh, yes, she did, Allison. I'm not surprised she didn't mention it. She never was any good at accepting responsibility for things."

"You mean that new show that's getting so much buzz? Which was it? At Darian's station. Umm," she pondered.

"Angel After Dark," he grumbled, pouring himself another drink and holding the glass out to her. "Want one?"

Allison shook her head. "No, thanks. I know her. I mean, I spoke with her."

Alex's curiosity was piqued and he turned, leaning back against the bar while Allison sat opposite him in one of the wingback chairs. Tension tightened the muscles in his neck and increased the throbbing in his head, but the ache eased by just being able to talk about it. "About what?"

"She has connections to a band I wanted to hire for the benefit."

Alex relaxed slightly. "Oh. When was this? Have you met her?"

"Two or three weeks ago, I think. No, I haven't seen her, except for the shots promoting the show, but you know how those things are. It probably isn't her anyway."

"Mmm hmm."

"Why?" They were close and Allison's eyes narrowed. Alex was out of sorts, quiet, introspective, and not himself. He looked tired, like he'd rolled out of bed and threw on the first thing he found, and more telling, he didn't argue when their mother asked personal questions. He simply left the room. "Do you know her? Do you know what she told Whitney?"

He contemplated how much to say. He hadn't confided in anyone, not even D. "She told her to get her shit together and walk away," he answered quietly. He took a long pull on his drink and the ice clinked on the side of the fine crystal glass. "Whitney didn't have the balls to follow through, and I called the show the next week and told my side of the story. Whitney, no doubt, painted a biased picture. Angel, however, had her own ideas on men like me. User, womanizer; you know the classic stereotype. She had no problem showing her distaste."

"Oh, my God. I can only imagine. I'm sure you were ruthless in defense of your position." Allison's eyes sparkled as she teased him. "And it's Angel, is it?"

"Yes. Angel. Don't worry, Allison, she gives as good as she gets."

Understanding dawned on his sister's face. "Oh, I see."

"Do you?"

"I know you, Alex. Nothing gets your juices flowing like a good challenge."

He nodded and moved into the room. "It may have started out that way."

"Tell me, Alex."

"She's... not like anyone I've ever met. She's very provocative. I wanted her like I've never wanted anyone. Like—I couldn't help myself."

"Apparently, she couldn't either."

Alex stared into his glass, examining the ice as if it were a precious diamond. He shrugged.

"So Whitney should hang up any hope for reconciliation, I see."

"Please, Allison." His reluctant eyes met hers. "You've spoken to Angel, then?"

"Yes, but it was all business. I thought I'd hear back from her by now."

"Do you think you will?"

"Most likely. The band isn't booked and she'll be instrumental in securing them."

"Do you know what her connection is?"

"Yes. She fronted the band a few years ago."

"I believe she was involved with one of her bandmates for a time."

"It seems you have a lot of information, Alex."

"Does she know you're my sister?"

"No. I mean I don't know how she would. I had no reason to mention you and our last names are different."

"Can you keep it that way?"

"Why?"

"We're taking a break. I'm trying to give her just enough space to miss me."

"Was this your decision or hers?"

"It took me completely by surprise. I thought things were going well. Better than well."

"Wow." Allison's eyebrow lifted. *"You've always been the one to walk. How are you handling it?"*

He shrugged, ignoring the gravity of her statement. *"I'm a little off-balance, Allison, but I'm still me."*

"Is there anything else?" Alex asked, shaking himself out of his thoughts.

Charles set his napkin on the table with purpose. "It strikes me as strange that you are keeping this deal a secret."

Alex smoothed down his tie. "Do you know who Mark Swanson is?"

"I've heard the name, but no."

"He's a small-time hood who runs a chain of dry cleaners in the Greater Chicago Area. He's been charged with raping his step-daughter. However, it looks unlikely he'll be convicted."

"It's news, so what? It seems an unlikely business opportunity. Maybe, if the man was getting convicted and the business was being sold off cheap. But, this?" Charles frowned.

Alex sighed heavily. "He's guilty, but he's able to pass the psychological tests, even the polygraph."

"That doesn't explain your involvement," his father insisted.

"The psychologist profiling the case is a friend. The bastard is threatening her."

"Just a friend?"

"No."

"I see. So you think that justifies using company resources?"

Alex shook his head. "Not exactly, but it's something I need to do, Dad."

Charles's eyes studied his son. He was dressed impeccably, as always, but he looked exhausted, his face drawn, his eyes bloodshot. He had new hope his son would find new faith in love. It was perplexing to Charles that Alex would be so cynical when his parents shared such a close relationship. He nodded. "Okay, son."

Alex was thankful his father let the subject drop and the conversation continued on to less personal matters. The situation he shared with Angel felt too intimate to share, like he'd be betraying some sacred bond. Cole knew by necessity, and Darian knew they were seeing each other, but nothing more. Other than that, and the short mention to Allison, he kept it close to the cuff.

"Alex, you haven't mentioned it in a few weeks, but we're still on track with that London acquisition, aren't we?"

Alex flushed. "It's sort of taken a back burner, but I'll work on it this week."

"Did you forget we're supposed to close the deal in two weeks? You told me a month ago it had to be done by the middle of this month."

"No, I didn't forget," he lied. "I'll take care of it."

"I expect you to be there to finalize everything."

He didn't feel like arguing, but going to England was the last thing Alex wanted to do. If the issues with Angel weren't resolved before then, he knew it would make him nuts. He didn't relish being so far away when everything was a clusterfuck with an uncertain outcome. Even with Bancroft and Cole watching her around the clock, his gut told him to stay close.

As father and son left the upscale restaurant, Alex reached for his phone. Cole was supposed to check in every couple of hours, and he'd been tied up with his father for more than three. Although he hated to admit it to himself, he was also hoping to see a message from Angel. He chastised himself for being such a pussy and quickly connected to his voicemail.

Hi, Alex. She's at her office, and it's been quiet. Nothing to report. The message was short and cryptic.

"Excuse me. Alexander Avery, isn't it?"

The two men paused, and Alex's eyes narrowed on the man attached to the voice. His back stiffened and something close to hatred slithered over his skin with agonizing slowness, making the hair on his arms and the back of his neck stand up.

"It is." As if it needed confirmation. Alex turned to his father and extended his hand. "Dad, thanks for lunch. I'll call you later."

Charles glanced between the other two men, the tension between them more than obvious, and it was unlike Alex not to introduce him. He nodded and shook his son's hand. "Sure."

Alex buttoned the jacket of the black Gucci suit, a stark contrast to the white shirt and blood red of the silk tie he wore. "What can I do for you, Mr. Swanson?"

"Oh, so you know who I am?"

Alex's lips thinned and he huffed. "Your reputation precedes you," he replied.

"As does yours."

"No doubt. This chitchat is nice, but I have obligations to attend to, so if you'll excuse me?" Alex dismissed the other man but he put up a hand to stop him.

"Mr. Avery, we have things to discuss."

Alex contemplated his next words carefully. "Really. Like what?" he asked dryly, wondering if the prick had the balls to mention Angel. The notion made his blood boil, and he'd be hard pressed to keep the control necessary not to rip the other man to shreds.

"I'm not stupid. I know what you're doing."

Alex felt his lip twitch, although he felt less than amused. "Then I guess that makes us even." He turned and began walking out of the restaurant.

"Mr. Avery! We're both good at negotiation. I'm sure we can come to a mutually agreeable solution."

Alex turned and looked steadily at the man he'd come to hate. "I don't negotiate with fuckers like you, and I doubt you could keep up, in any case. You may have missed it, but I'm not doing this because of your stellar business practices."

"You don't know who you're dealing with. You'd be better served—"

Alex laughed harshly, interrupting abruptly. "I know exactly who I'm dealing with. *Exactly.*" His tone was harder than iron.

"You understand what I mean. Back off of my business! You don't need more money."

Did this asshole really think it was about money?

"If you knew *who you were dealing with*, you'd know I always finish what I start, and I make it a point to know my adversaries inside and out before taking them on. You're a little greasier than most I deal with, I admit, but I have more resources and more connections than you dream about. Plus, I always win. If you were an honorable man, you could go about your meaningless life of dirty laundry, and I wouldn't give a shit." Alex's chest tightened despite his outwardly calm demeanor. "But, since you're slime, you'll be lucky if you have enough left for a garage sale when I'm finished."

"You're not as infallible as you think you are, Avery; a fact which was illuminated while you were in Hawaii, I believe." The older man watched the younger one's muscles coil under the expensive suit, and satisfaction at Alex's discomfort caused a wicked smile pulling his lips away from his teeth. "Dr. Hemming is less, shall we say, evasive than you... much more easily *penetrated*." His emphasis on the word had Alex's blood boiling. "So alluring and full of fire, hmm? It makes her vulnerable and even more attractive."

Alex's hands curled into tight fists. It was all he could do not to beat the smug look off Mark Swanson's oily face. In three quick strides, he was a foot away from the other man. The scent of smoke that clung heavily on the other man's breath and clothes assaulted him.

"Your so-called *connections* don't give a fuck about you. You're a bug, an annoyance that needs to be squashed. Nothing more. As for Angeline, touch her and I won't be responsible for my actions. If you hurt her, I swear to God, you will beg for death."

Alex turned, inhaling deeply at the same time, and stalked away from his enemy. His chest hurt, he was hotter than hell, and his skin was burning. He'd never experienced hate to the degree he felt it now. Right there in the middle of the restaurant, Alex wanted to kill Mark Swanson with his bare hands and damn the consequences.

*****

"Huh! Huh!" Angel punched, and then attacked the bag with a round kick, followed by more punches. "Huh! Arrrrggggghhhhh!" She was out of breath; sweat plastered the tendrils that had worked their way out of her ponytail to the sides of her head. She could feel the moisture soaking through her sports bra and around the top of the yoga pants she was wearing. "Huh!" She kicked the bag again.

"Angel, I think that's enough!" Becca let go of the bag and moved away. "You almost knocked me down. I think you've still got your groove on."

Angel picked up a towel off the mat next to her and slung it around her neck, using the ends to wipe the perspiration off of her face. Her chest was still heaving as she shot Becca a disgusted look, took a long pull on her water bottle, and began walking off toward the locker room. "I sucked, Becca!" she said indignantly. "It's been too long since I practiced. Don't fucking placate me."

Her friend sighed. Angel had been quiet all night, and when she did open her mouth, she complained about everything. "Look, Angel, you're not as good as you were. Okay? But you're already being a bitch tonight, so why would I want to make it worse, huh?" she asked loudly, her words bouncing off the tile walls of the locker room.

Angel kicked off her shoes and threw them in her locker and they landed with a loud thud. "I don't have time for this shit. I have to take a shower and go to the station."

"What the hell's your problem? If I didn't know better, I'd say you're upset because Alex let you dump him. You didn't bargain for that, did you?" She sat down on the wooden bench and watched Angel angrily strip her clothes off and wrap a towel around her. "You have no one to blame but yourself."

"Shut up, Becca. See what I get for telling you about it. You know why I did it."

"Yes, but it's the dumbest thing you've done since I've known you. Why didn't you just tell him the truth?"

"Because." Angel felt her throat thicken, making it difficult to get the words out. All she wanted to do was disappear inside the shower where her tears would be invisible. "He wouldn't have stayed away. He'd only get more involved. I told you because I needed someone to talk to. I shouldn't have, and if I'd known how you'd bitch at me about it, I wouldn't have! I don't want to go over it again. I don't want to think about Alex."

"But he's... *him*, Angel! A guy like that doesn't roll over with his legs in the air."

"That's the problem. I have to put this bastard away, and Alex would stand in my way. I don't want to argue with him about it, and he might get hurt in the process. I couldn't take that chance."

"I think you should just leave this alone, Angel. It's too dangerous. From what you've told me, this prick will stop at nothing."

"Exactly the reason he has to be put away. For God's sake! Not you, too! I shouldn't have told you any of it! I needed someone to support me, Becca."

"I will. I am! But, you're in love with this guy. Why risk losing him?"

"I didn't want to care about him," Angel said weakly, picking up her shampoo and trying not to let Becca see her face. Her heart hurt and she wasn't sure she could keep it off of her expression. "Long-term relationships are not Alex's forte, and you can't lose something you never had. This is for the best."

"Who are you trying to convince?"

Angel ignored the other girl and left her on the bench. She yanked the shower curtain closed, letting the hot water rush over her hair and body, wishing it could wash all of her problems down the drain with it. She missed Alex more than she wanted to admit and ached for him to call. He didn't. It had been almost two weeks and she hadn't heard from him. Not once.

Her reports would go to the D.A.'s office next week, and there wasn't a damn thing she could do about the charges being dropped. Kenneth wouldn't take a lost cause to court, and if the girl refused to face her attacker, that's exactly what it was. What a fucking waste!

Angel leaned on folded arms against the tile wall, resting her head against them. She was exhausted, and not just because of the brutal workout she'd just subjected herself to. She wasn't sleeping well at all; each night, her comforter and sheets wound up in a wad on the floor or tangled up at the foot of her bed. Even though her building was secure, it wasn't more secure than Alex's estate, so it was only a matter of time before Swanson and his band of thugs tried something. She was sure of it, but she didn't know when or where. At the office, her apartment, the station, or the gym? It could be anywhere and she was always on edge. She'd even considered getting a gun, but her father had always said if you have a gun for protection, you better be prepared to use it or else it could be used against you.

The threats had been intermittent. One call on her cell phone threatening to kill her if she didn't get Swanson off, but the voice was raspy and unrecognizable. She'd been ready to record any others, but all that followed were voicemail after voicemail of heavy breathing and creepy laughter. Always the number was restricted and couldn't be traced. It was frustrating as hell. She stopped answering her phone when she didn't recognize the number, but calls kept coming. If she didn't know better, the situation would almost be comical. She got hate mail at her condo, and after the first one, she made sure to open them with latex gloves on and save them in a Ziploc bag. The fear was worst when she was alone at night. Despite the fact she wanted the prick to attack, she was scared to death and longed for the safety of Alex's arms. He was always on her mind and that wasn't good. She struggled to keep her wits about her and not let the overwhelming sadness distract her.

Being at the station late on Friday nights was a risk, not just for her, but for Christine, too. On her way through midtown, she called Darian.

"Can you be there for the show tonight?"

"No problem. I'll meet you there."

Angel's brow furrowed. No questions? No complaints about missing boy's night out? Again, Alex surfaced in her mind. "Thanks," she replied into her phone. "No boy's night tonight?" she asked; the lights of the Chicago night were a blur against her windows.

"Nope. Are you okay?"

"Erm… yeah? Why?" She wondered what Alex had told his best friend. Was he struggling as she was, or was he full of arrogant bravado, making it seem like she was just another casualty in the Alex Avery relationship train.

"Nothing. You sound different, and you're asking me to be at the station. It's weird. Are you feeling all right?"

"Not really. That's why I thought you could be there for moral support. Plus, I haven't seen you in weeks."

Darian laughed. "Well, I'm flattered; although, since I haven't seen much of Alex either, I figured the reason was obvious."

Angel doubted that Darian was as ignorant as he was playing, but she didn't want to discuss the subject. "Yeah. See you in a bit."

*****

"This is Angel After Dark on KKIS FM. Thanks for all of your calls and dedications. Love and peace until next week."

Alex lay on his bed in the dark as he listened to her voice. The last words he'd hear from her mouth until her next broadcast. He'd itched to call her voicemail, just to hear her, but he resisted it at every turn.

He'd been staying at his apartment because it was closer to Angel, and Max was with his parents. Cole was firmly ensconced in her building now, and Bancroft had hired a few others to follow her around the clock. He let out a deep sigh. She'd probably scratch his eyes out if she knew, but at this point, he'd take any contact with her he could get.

After the confrontation with Swanson over lunch last week, he'd ramped everything up, even hiring security for himself and to watch Allison, Josh, and his parents. It was getting damn expensive, but it wouldn't be much longer. Maybe a month before the business was bankrupt. The cocksucker had too many outstanding loans to avoid it with two more of the dry cleaners closed. That made five, in all. Alex bought the leases out on three more with eviction notices going out the same day he closed escrow. Step by step, he was getting it done, but he was impatient for it to be over.

It was all he could do not to hang out at Cole's stakeout digs, but when he did, he only got a glimpse of Angel coming and going. There were privacy issues and legalities involved that prevented them from setting up cameras on the inside of anyone's living space. And, he drove his brother crazy. It was agony being so close and not being able to talk to her or touch her. She was beautiful still, but she looked tired and skittish.

"Fuck!" he shouted into the lifeless room.

The satisfaction he got taking Swanson down was worthless with the way he felt. Did she really believe that things weren't different with her? Hadn't he held her in his arms when he told her? Hadn't he made a big enough ass of himself over it?

Alex pushed off the bed and went to his liquor cabinet in the other room. Bancroft had assured him that two armed men would be near her at all times. Alex insisted on meeting them one by one and poured over each of their dossiers personally. Two of them were retired DEA agents, used to dealing with hardcore criminals, and another had been head of security at Bank of America. They didn't come cheap, but you got what you paid for. At least he'd get some sleep.

He swallowed three fingers of scotch in one gulp and poured another as he made his way back to his bedroom. The apartment was dark, and he was so tired. Downing the amber liquid, he peeled off his boxers and T-shirt and climbed between the sheets, willing himself to relax.

The cell phone on the bedside table beeped and lit up. Alex picked it up to retrieve the message.

Dr. Hemming has left the radio station and we have her. We are relieving Mr. Avery until 8 a.m. and will let you know when she arrives home. Have a good night.

A good night. He hadn't had one of those in two fucking weeks. He threw the phone down on the bed and closed his eyes.

6

Dreams and Nightmares

ANGEL SWORE AS she pulled off the road; the thud, thud, thud of the flat grated on her nerves as the car ground to a halt. Her breath rushed out as she considered her options and turned on her emergency flashers. A flat tire was the last thing she needed in the middle of the night. The streets in the small mid-town neighborhood were all but deserted.

The evening was cooler, and the September breezes coming in from Lake Michigan rustled the leaves that clung to the trees. She angrily alighted from the car with a slam of the door and stomped around to stare at the deflated tire. She frowned at the damn thing. The car was fine, working perfectly, and she'd had the tires rotated with her service less than a week before.

"Ugh!" She kicked the tire in disgust. "Really? Are you kidding me with this shit?" Angel crouched down to get a closer look but couldn't really tell the cause of the damage. There weren't any big obstacles or potholes that she'd run over.

She stood up and walked back around, pulling the driver's door open on her Lexus and sliding back inside. Could she change a tire? Yes. Her father wouldn't let her drive until she could change

a tire and the oil all by herself, but at this time of night, she was too
tired and too aware of being alone in the darkness. A shiver ran
through her as it registered this could be one of Mark Swanson's
warnings, or worse, a setup to leave her stranded and vulnerable.
She hated it that a creep like him could frighten her so badly, but
she wasn't stupid, and fear only strengthened her determination to
see him put away.

She quickly reached over to the passenger seat and dug
through her purse in search of her phone. Her hand closed around
the phone that Alex had given her, and despite her circumstances,
she couldn't help but check the screen. Angel was rewarded with
more of the same nothingness before she threw it down on the
leather seat next to her. She didn't even know why she bothered
keeping the damn thing charged since he hadn't called or texted in
weeks. Becca was right, though, what did she expect?

She scrolled through her contacts on her other phone and dialed the roadside assistance number she'd gotten from her auto
insurance agent. She sat there, frustrated, as she listened to the
automated message and hammered out the various policy numbers
it asked for. It seemed like hours before an actual voice came on
the line and took her location.

She sighed and settled in to wait the thirty to forty minutes she
was told it would take for the technician to arrive. Her eyes felt as if
they were full of sand; the burning only intensified as the streetlight
she was focusing on blurred. She shook her head and glanced around
through the tinted windows.

She picked up the iPhone again, her thumb rubbing over the
screen once again. Somehow, holding it in her hand calmed her
nerves but made her heart ache. She closed her eyes briefly, and her
mind willed Alex to call. She missed him like it had been years
rather than weeks.

Angel glanced at the clock in her dash. Barely five minutes
had passed since she'd gotten off the phone. She closed her eyes

and leaned back against the headrest, attempting to calm her panic. She tried to concentrate on the soft notes drifting from the speakers, the songs on her iPod her only company.

The shrill electronic ringing made her jump in her seat. Who could be calling at such a time? Her heart thudded heavily in her chest as she glanced toward the offending object. She knew. It had to be Mark Swanson.

A restricted number registered on the screen, and she picked it up with shaking hands.

"What do you want, you fucked-up bastard?" she spat into the phone. She'd be damned if she'd let him see how terrified she was. Despite her self-defense training, she knew how vulnerable she was.

Mark Swanson's low chuckle resonated through the earpiece. He sounded maniacal, like some character out of a horror movie. "Are you enjoying your little situation, Angel?"

She steadied herself. "I'm just fine, but your concern is so touching," she replied as calmly as possible.

He laughed again. "Oh, Angel." He tsked his tongue against his teeth a few times. "Always so defiant. That's what I love about you. It will make your surrender that much sweeter. I'm going to fuck you senseless."

"You'll have to kill me first."

"Be careful what you wish for."

"We both know you don't have the balls for that. Gonna call in your cronies for the big boy stuff?"

The loud crash of glass breaking had Angel scrambling away from the sound. The tire iron hit the car again and again, making her cower across both seats with her arms curled around her head and her knees pulled up. "Ahhhhhhhhhh!" she screamed, frantically glancing around at the two shadowy figures moving around her car. They were dressed in all black with creepy Halloween masks covering their facial features and all but blended into the night. The tire iron hit the roof of her car, making her scream again as a gloved hand reached in the broken passenger window and unlocked the door.

"Get her out." A deep voice said from somewhere near the rear of the car. The adrenaline pumping through her veins got her heart beating so fast she felt it would fly from her chest. Her purse still clutched in her hand, she twisted so that when the man reached for her, she could use her feet to defend herself. She watched his arms grasping at her ankle as her other foot delivered a sound kick to his shoulder.

"Guh! You little bitch!" he groaned as he began to yank her out.

"Huh!" She kicked at him again, this time hitting the man soundly in the forehead and snapping his neck back. His hands left her as he fell backward briefly before lunging forward and grabbing her again by both feet. He dragged her out of the car while she struggled for dear life. Her lower back hit the door frame and pain shot through her pelvis as she landed on the pavement with a thud.

"Let go of me! Let go!"

The bigger man came forward and wrapped his arms around Angel's body, the two of them lifting her and hurrying toward a black van. Angel heaved in their arms, pulling at one of the masks and kicking at the other man's head. She screamed again, the sound shrill in the dead air. "Ahhhhhh! Somebody, help me!" Steel arms clamped around hers and imprisoned them close to her body so she couldn't move; both her assailant's meaty hands imprisoned her wrists tightly.

"Just get her in the goddamn van, Nick!" The other one mumbled, followed by a grunt as one of Angel's feet broke free of his hold and found purchase on his jaw. "Motherfucker!"

"Get off of me!" she shouted, her voice showing none of the terror she felt.

The door to the van protested in a loud grating of metal as it opened, and they were about to throw her inside when another voice rang out. "Leave the young woman alone!" His tone was hard and authoritative, but Angel didn't recognize his voice.

Angel landed with a heavy bang inside the back of the unfinished conversion van, moaning as pain shot through her hip and arm. The two men were besieged by two others, and Angel's eyes squinted to get a better look. She could only see a dark blur of bodies among a series of grunts and punching noises.

Angel crawled to the front of the van and over the seat to scramble out the driver's side door amid the sound of a body being slammed against the side of the vehicle with a sick thud and a bang. The echo of one gunshot filled the night air. She fell onto the pavement, slamming her knee. Pebbles jabbed into the heels of her hands, leaving a deep sting when she pushed herself to her feet in the start of a run.

She ran as fast as her feet would carry her despite the burning pain in her hips, knee, and back. Angel wanted to put as much distance as possible between herself and the scene. She didn't think twice about leaving her car behind; the blood pounding in her ears and the throp, throp, throp of her feet on the pavement grew louder as the sounds of the fight diminished behind her.

"Dr. Hemming!" Angel heard the faint sound of her name in the distance as she turned down a dark residential street and glanced over her shoulder to see if she was being followed.

She ran until her sides hurt, zigzagging through the backyards of the houses and dark side streets. She finally slowed her pace and leaned against a tree, placing her hands on her knees as she struggled to regain her breath. Her hair had worked its way out of the ponytail and hung in damp tendrils around her face, and her lungs ached in angry protest as she pulled in oxygen with heavy pants.

Her mind reeled. She knew the first two men were Swanson's hired henchmen but wasn't sure about the other two. Maybe they were just passersby and had come to her aid when they heard her screams, but Angel didn't consider that in her haste. She was too uncertain to stay and watch the scene play out, instinct telling her to get the hell out of there as quickly as possible. She straightened up, thankful she was in casual attire and Adidas. By some miracle, her purse was still looped over her arm.

She opened it to inspect the contents. Her original cell phone was gone, and she'd left her keys in the ignition. She still had the phone Alex gave her and her wallet. Angel's eyes closed in relief. *Thank God.*

Angel didn't feel safe going back to her condo; someone would probably be waiting. It was too obvious that was where she would go, and Swanson would be furious that his plan was foiled.

"Stupid bastard! I fucking hate you," she murmured softly, thinking how little effect she had on the outcome of the case; it wasn't even going to make it to court. She knew Swanson's grudge was personal now. He wanted to prove a point.

Angel held her hand out in front of her and felt her whole body begin to shake as the adrenaline wore off. Her hip ached and she was sure in a few hours she'd find bruises on her body from landing in the van and the fingers biting into her tender flesh.

It was pitch black, the trees blocking any moonlight, as she continued to rummage through the contents of her purse. She walked beneath a streetlight, just as her hands closed around a different set of keys.

*****

Angel peeled her clothes off in the guest bathroom, the only light coming from a candle on the granite vanity. The décor was simple, but the colors were obscured by the golden light and flickering shadows. She was exhausted and frightened, the soreness she knew she'd feel in a few hours had yet to take hold.

Her jacket was left in the backseat of her mangled Lexus, and the shower's steaming surge lessened the chill on her skin. It was hard to know what damage had been done to the car after she ran away, but the light of day would tell. There wasn't anything she could do about it now other than what she'd done. She called the police, and they told her she'd have to file a report the following day, but that a patrolman would go to the scene, and her car would be towed to the impound lot until she could pick it up.

She drew in a shaky breath, doubting her recent decisions as she pulled her hair down and found a brush in the drawer. As she pulled it through the long, silky strands, her heart was heavy, yet it beat in frantic anticipation. Angel was drawn to Alex like the moon pulled the tide; it was the most natural thing in the world to end up here. Like she had no conscious choice; she didn't even remember telling the cab driver the address a half an hour earlier.

She'd been unsure if Alex would even be there, and she still didn't know. Part of her hoped he wouldn't be, and the other part needed to feel his arms wrapped around her because it was the only way she'd be sure either of them was safe. Water Tower had armed security and would be harder to penetrate. It had been pure luck that the security codes were the same as his estate. But what if he wasn't alone?

Her heart fell as the realization hit her; she wasn't prepared for that possibility. He might be angry, and he'd probably tell her to get the hell out. She was feeling fragile, and her eyes flooded with tears as her throat began to throb.

Somehow, she'd managed to enter and shower without detection. The evening had been surreal, like some scene from a low-budget horror flick, and she was shaken. If it weren't for her aches and pains and the rips in her shirt, she could've sworn it was a nightmare.

Her hands paused midway on their way to pick up her discarded clothing, and soon, her towel joined them on the Italian marble floor.

She leaned on her hands and bowed her head in defeat. She should leave. If she wanted to keep the carefully constructed, yet delicate, walls in place, she needed to leave now. But she needed the comfort of his touch, to smell his skin, to hear him breathe. Even if, to her horror, he was in bed with someone else, at least she'd know he was okay.

Angel swallowed and pushed open the door, and the contrast between the steam-filled bathroom and the cool air of the rest of the apartment caused her nipples to pucker as the chill skittered over her skin. Her feet were almost silent as they sank into the plush carpet of the hallway. As she drew closer to his bedroom door, she heard a low moan and she froze, her hands clenching in protest.

Please, God, no, she prayed in her thoughts. Her conscious mind knew she had no claim on him, but her heart screamed in protest. She padded closer, her feet carrying her forward of their own volition, and her heart tightened painfully.

"Mmmmm..." Alex murmured. The sound of his voice begged her to push the door open further. The smooth mahogany gave way beneath her trembling fingertips to reveal a lone figure sprawled face down on the bed.

Angel's breath left her lungs in a grateful rush as she leaned on the door frame, hands reaching out to take her weight. Relief washed through her. He was here and he was alone. God help her, that fact was just as important.

The sheet was falling low on his waist, clinging precariously to the curve of his butt, the strong expanse of his shoulders presented to her below the dark hair. It looked longer than she remembered, and she stood there, willing him to turn so she could see the lines of his face. Her lips parted to call his name, but he stopped her by calling hers first.

"Angel, don't do this."

She gasped softly and moved to the side of the bed, crawling gently onto it to kneel beside him, her rear resting on her feet. His scent surrounded her, a mixture of musky cologne and Alex. The skin, molded over the strong contours of his back, fascinated her. She wanted to touch, to feel the silken texture beneath her fingers, to run her nose down his spine, to taste the salty tang on her tongue.

Angel was falling apart, her weakness overwhelming her. Earlier, she'd fought ruthlessly, but now, she had no fight left. With Alex, she wanted to surrender. The truth of it was undeniable.

"What am I doing?" she asked softly, reaching out to smooth her hand over the back of his head and down the strong muscles of his back. He was warm, a sharp contrast to her own skin, and the familiar electricity ran between his flesh and hers—tangible and alive.

Alex shifted, turning his head toward her. He was still sleeping, his features soft in the dark blue glow of night. "You deny us. You left me."

"Oh, Alex." Angel's heart swelled to the point of bursting. "That seems impossible," she whispered, continuing to rub his back and then gently kneading his shoulder and the back of his neck.

"That feels so good. Your hands on me."

"I miss touching you." The words ripped from her, her voice trembling.

Suddenly, Alex turned, his hand closing around her forearm and pulling her forward and closer until her face was inches from his.

"Am I dreaming?" His green eyes looked black, but glittered in the darkness. "Angel?"

Angel nodded, unsure what else to do. Maybe she could get away with being here if he believed she wasn't real. "Do you dream of me often?"

"Every time I close my eyes." He cupped her face, his big hand easily reaching around the back of her head to tangle in her long hair, his thumb brushing her chin. "But this time, you feel so real. I want you to be real."

She leaned into his touch, rubbing her face into his hand, and the harshness of the day melted into nothingness. Her eyes burned as emotions threatened to overflow. This man was the only thing that mattered, and she would allow herself to get lost in him, even if only for an hour or two. "Then don't wake up."

"Your voice is different."

She flushed. The screaming and the running had left its effect. Her throat felt sore, but in the spontaneity of the moment, she hadn't even noticed. "Shhhh…" Angel murmured. Her hand smoothed along the strong line of his jaw; it was lined with stubble that poked gently at her fingertips. "Just, shhh…"

Alex pulled her forward, his lips finding hers. The kiss was gentle, yet hungry and urgent, his other hand running down her body, over her hip and to her thigh, finding her naked. He wasn't surprised. She was always like this in his dreams.

Angel did her best not to wince when his hands came across some of the tender flesh now marred by bruises. She couldn't let him know she was hurting or he'd wake up for sure.

He pulled her down beside him, shifted until she was half beneath him, when his mouth reluctantly pulled from hers, but still hovering, to glide like hot silk over her cheek and down the side of her neck. He inhaled the scent of his own shampoo, his nose finding the subtle dampness at her hairline as his hands continued to explore her willing body. "Your skin is like velvet."

"Touch me," she begged in a whisper. "Kiss me, Alex."

Alex loomed over her, his eyes searching her face. She seemed vulnerable, aching, needy, and demanding all at once. "These last two weeks have been torture. I've been so worried."

The frown on his face and the look in his eyes made her heart ache. "So have I."

"I want to look at you." He had a hard time articulating exactly what he wanted, but he knew that he wanted something from this woman, dream or no, that he'd never wanted. "I want..."

Her forehead leaned into his jaw and her hands slid up his chest over his shoulders to thread through his hair. He groaned when her fingers tugged gently, urging his head down to hers. Angel's chin lifted and she licked at his top lip, then pulled his bottom one between both of hers and let her teeth tug on it gently. The heat pooling in her body wouldn't be denied; the familiar ache that settled in the pit of her stomach and around her heart whenever she was with him grew more intense. She didn't care if she had to beg. "What? This is your dream. Anything you want, it's yours."

His heart beat furiously under the fingers of her hand, and his full erection throbbed and pulsed against her thigh, yet he was hesitant, studying the apparition before him.

"I don't want anything between us, dream or not, Angel." His hand flattened out on the smooth plane of her belly and moved lower, his fingers parting her flesh, seeking the warmth between her legs as his mouth traced the swell of her breast. She arched her back as her breath left her. God, she loved his mouth on her, his fingers as they pushed inside her, seeking the place he knew would drive her wild. She understood what he was asking. But the last time, they hadn't used protection in the heat of that moment either. Angel hadn't been concerned because she was on the pill. But apparently, Alex was.

"I'm safe, Alex. We're safe."

"Then you trust me?" he asked softly, his lips finally closing around her nipple and sucking gently as his fingers worked in and out of her body, his thumb pressing against her most sensitive flesh with a purposeful rhythm. He enjoyed the panting breaths and soft mewling moans, her hips gyrating as her body begged for his.

"With everything I have," she breathed.

"Then I want to make love to you. Slow, languid love. I never want this to end."

Angel's heart felt as if it would fly from her chest; her hands roamed lovingly over the smooth skin, hard with the strength lying beneath it. Her eyes squeezed shut, forcing the moisture to leak from the corners as her mouth found purchase against his bicep. "Oh, God, Alex," she cried even as her body came around his fingers. "Uhhh, Uhhh!"

Alex's mouth skimmed her skin, tasting the soft, salty sheen on her shoulder as he rolled her beneath him. The aftershocks of her orgasm were still rocking through her when she felt his hardness push against her, his pelvis rocking into hers, seeking entrance. Both of his large hands closed around the sides of her face. He was moving gently, his arms holding his weight, his mouth taking hers in a hungry kiss.

"You have to know what you mean to me," he whispered urgently, softly licking and then roughly forcing his tongue inside to war with hers. She lifted her knees to curl around the side of his torso, and he slipped inside her tight, moist heat. "Beautiful, Angel. Ahhhhhggggh," he groaned, pulling out almost completely to fill her again in a deep thrust.

Over and over, he repeated the action, pulling out slowly and thrusting in with a deeper force, letting her feel every inch of his length, the fullness of the head opening her up, and each ounce of his possession of her. She clenched around him, unsure if she wanted to prove to him he belonged to her just as much as she did him or whether it just felt too fucking good to stop the reaction of her body or her heart.

They kissed hungrily, their bodies moving in sync and with slow purpose, clinging to each other, pulling and grasping to get closer, even if it wasn't possible. Alex stopped suddenly, fully embedded in her flesh, as he fought for control of his own release. Angel didn't need words to know why he stopped or that he would begin the delicious dance again in a few seconds time.

Even if it was a dream, Alex made love to Angel until his body was pushed to its limits.

When she cried out his name and heaved against him as he made her come for the third time, her fingers raked painfully down his back. Alex let himself give in to his own release, his muscles tensed as he finally burst inside her and her name was forced from his lips like a prayer. The magnitude of it rushed over him in waves as Angel's body closed around him, milking the fluid from his body and pulling it into her own.

Alex couldn't stop kissing her, even as his body calmed and their breathing evened out. His fingers stroked her hair back from her temples, and his mouth worshiped hers—his lips slanting and sucking, giving and taking what he needed in return. Angel was just as unwilling to end the connection; her arms and legs still caged him in, her hips still heaving against his.

His heart exploded like a firework of light. His chest ached, his eyes burned, and his throat refused to allow him to swallow the tightness. The pain was enough that he thought it would kill him. The mixture of pleasure and pain was the most amazing, confusing, incredible feeling of his life.

He rolled over and gently pulled her with him, and she curled easily into his arms. His hand moved up to stroke down from the back of her head to smooth her hair down over her spine. Over and over, Alex soothed her, wondering if she were real, and if she was, would she be as fucked up by this as he was? Her little arms tightened around him, and her lips pressed into the pulse at the side of his neck.

Angel's face turned into his neck as her shoulders started to shake, and he felt the hot sear of her tears run over his skin as she nodded against him. Her fingers curled around his neck as she gasped.

He sucked in a painful breath. "Oh, Angel. Jesus Christ, it hurts so fucking bad! It hurts… so fucking bad."

7

Upon the Rising Sun

ALEX STARTED VIOLENTLY and sucked in a deep breath. He was lying sprawled diagonally across his king-sized bed, one leg hitched and both arms wrapped around two of the six pillows. "Angel?"

His eyes adjusted to the sunlight streaming through the cracks in the vertical blinds as he rolled over and scrubbed his face with both hands. "Angel?" He called again and sat up, the sheet all but falling away from his naked body while he looked around the room.

She wasn't there.

He closed his eyes again as disappointment crashed into his conscious mind. It was all a dream. He told himself he should be thankful that he remembered every second of it: unlike most dreams when he was left with hazy remnants, unable to piece them together in the morning.

"Goddamn it!" He threw a pillow across the room, and it knocked his reading lamp off the small side table by a big leather chair. It landed in a loud crash of glass breaking against the wall.

His chest ached. He fell back and rolled over, burying his face
in the pillows again, inhaling, in search of her scent. His fist pounded
the headboard causing it to bounce back against the wall in another
loud thud. "Angel!" he shouted into the empty room as his body
uncoiled in defeat and sagged against the mattress; his blood was
thick as molasses and heart working overtime as it struggled to pump
it around his body with sickening, hollow thrums.

He felt unhinged by her absence, emptiness eating a tangible
hole in him from the inside out. Alex hated feeling helpless, but
there was absolutely nothing he could do to ease it. His chest
burned with something horrible and completely and utterly
breathtaking at the same time, and it filled him up to the point of
bursting yet left him empty and consumed. She was present in
every waking moment, haunted his dreams, and drove him to lose
his preciously guarded control. The feeling was unbelievable and
amazing, incredibly wonderful and agonizing as hell.

Bzzzzzz! Bzzzzzz! Bzzzzzz!

The sound had Alex bolting off the bed and rummaging
through a drawer for something to wear. Banging began after a
series of impatient buzzes, followed by his brother's bellowing
voice.

"Alex!"

Alex scrambled to don the black silk pajama pants before
running down the hall into the great room and finally the entryway.
"Alex! Are you here?"

"Yeah! Hold on!" he shouted back as he deactivated the security system and locks fell away. He finally pulled the door open.
Cole stormed past his half-naked brother and into the apartment.

Alex's heart tightened as fear flooded through him. "What is
it, Cole? Is Angel okay?" he asked anxiously.

"Why in the hell haven't you been answering your phone? The
security desk can't even let you know I'm here when I've been trying to call you for several hours!"

"Forget the phone," Alex dismissed with an impatient wave of his hand. "Just tell me what the hell is going on!"

Cole paused, unsure how he would break the news without Alex going ballistic. He decided there wasn't one and blurted it out. "On the way from the station last night, something happened."

"Cole! What?" Alex's lungs constricted painfully.

"Angel had a flat tire, and Sid and Wayne were watching her from about 200 yards back. While she waited for a tow truck, two men in a black van took a crowbar to her car and tried to take her away." Cole registered the panic on Alex's face and put up a hand to stop him from speaking. "She's okay, she got away."

"I'm going to kill that motherfucking bastard! Where is she now? Was she hurt?"

"Angel is at her place, and Bancroft is monitoring, along with one of the others. She was moving a little slow when I saw her, but from what Sid said, she ran from the scene like hell was on her heels. They threw her in the van, so yeah, she's probably beat up a little. There's no way of knowing for sure."

"How in the hell did you let this happen?" Alex's expression twisted with fury. "The two guards were with her, weren't they?"

"They maintained their distance as instructed. When they radioed in, Bancroft decided that stepping in might compromise our cover. If she saw their faces, they couldn't trail her anymore."

Alex's whole body tensed up. He'd never been so incensed and scared at the same time. "Her safety is first and foremost! I don't give a fuck about anything else! If you need to hire different men, do it!"

"Alex, be reasonable! If you want her protected, we don't have time to do that!" Alex began to pace in front of him like a caged animal. "Bancroft... Well, we both thought we might be able to catch the asshole in action. Both of the new guys are PIs and can make arrests. It was the right way to handle it. She's okay! She got away on her own."

"How?"

"When they intervened, she ran off. Sid tried to stop her, but then one of them pulled a gun."

"If she's hurt in any way, I will fucking kill Bancroft! I'll kill him!" He took off down the hall, rushing into his room to search for his phone. "I ask for one thing. One fucking thing, Cole!" Alex shouted angrily over his shoulder.

"Are you gonna kill me, too?" Cole's voice followed but Alex ignored it as he pulled the sheet from the bed. The last time he remembered having his phone was right before he fell asleep. He'd thrown it on the bed beside him.

"I might," he muttered as he finally found it lying on the floor on the far side of the bed, the battery lying next to it. Alex shoved the battery back in place and swore at the length of time it took to power up. "Why in the name of God didn't you come and get me before this?"

"I thought you'd prefer if I found your girl, and what would you have done?"

Alex walked back into the other room, stopping dead. "You better not be telling me that you lost her." His skin was on fire, and he was dangerously close to losing it, but his voice was cold as death. "Answer me, Cole!"

"Yes, okay! The men fought off the bad guys, Alex, but Wayne got shot in the process. Sid was able to call the ambulance and capture one of them, but he couldn't keep Angel there. The guy with the gun fled the scene. I was worried he followed her, so I tried to find her. I called, but you didn't answer. We knew locating Angel was the most important thing and what you'd want."

Alex's legs were shaking, refusing to take his weight, and he sank down onto the couch. "Angel's okay? You're sure?" His voice was quieter now.

"Sid said she kicked one of Swanson's men in the head during the struggle. The guy they arrested has a black eye and a broken clavicle!" He chuckled, but Alex found nothing funny in the situation. Cole couldn't help himself. It seemed absurd that such a small woman would kick the shit out of a man twice her size. Alex scowled and Cole continued, his hand moving up to try to disguise the smile still playing on his mouth. "That girl has balls of steel."

The thought of Angel being alone and vulnerable, probably scared to death in the middle of the Chicago night, made Alex's chest constrict. No matter if she appeared tough, he knew the vulnerability that lay beneath. "How do you know she's safe?"

"I waited for her, and she returned home a couple of hours ago. Her Lexus was towed to the impound lot; it's in pretty bad shape. I'm not sure if it's worth saving." He thought better of telling his brother that it took them three hours to find her. "What are you doing?"

Alex rested his elbows on his knees and dialed Angel's number. "What does it look like I'm doing? I want to make sure she's okay."

"Don't let her know you know what happened, Alex. Our cover will be blown."

Alex pressed send on the phone and lifted it to his ear. "Right now, I don't give a flying fuck about your cover. I'll protect her even if she hates me for it."

"You do care, Alex." Cole reached out and wrenched the phone from Alex's hand and turned it off. "Think about it! Why are you keeping it a secret if she'd agree? I'll just go knock on her door. *Hi, I'm Alex's brother, Cole. I'm here to follow you around!*"

"Don't be a smartass!" Alex yelled, jumping up to rush toward Cole. "Give. Me. The. Fucking. Phone!"

"Having her hate you is the last thing you want. You're totally screwed over this, and I'm not sure how you're gonna fix it but don't fuck it up even more."

"I need to see she's okay with my own eyes!" Alex reached for the phone again, and Cole's hand came down on his shoulder and squeezed.

"Man, you need to calm down. Bancroft and Sid are watching her, and she'll probably be filing a police report today. Sid already did, as will Wayne when he is well enough, but they're just gonna say they were passersby who stopped to help. We still don't have proof Swanson is behind it, and we won't unless the guy in custody cracks. We need to catch him red-handed. Give us more time to get this prick, Alex. His business is almost flushed."

"It's not enough anymore. I've never wanted anyone dead so much in my entire life, Cole. I can't sit by and wait until Angel gets hurt or worse!"

Cole pushed Alex back down on the couch with both hands on his shoulders. "Alex! Who are you right now? Where is the cold, level-headed bastard I know and love?"

Alex shook his head. "Shut up! I can't risk her safety."

Cole sat down next to Alex. "Angel's doing a damn good job of risking it on her own. For once, it's not up to you."

"Arrrghhhh!" Alex let out a frustrated yell. "She's too reckless. Swanson all but admitted he was behind the security breach at the estate and that he was after her. He knows Avery Enterprises is taking his business down, too. He's like a rabid dog now, fighting for his life."

"He has nothing to gain, anyway," Cole said, scratching his head. His dark hair was mussed and the plaid flannel shirt he wore over his jeans was wrinkled. "Unless... you're willing to negotiate."

Alex looked at Cole in disgust. Nothing would be gained by showing weakness. "Not a snowball's chance in hell."

"There are a couple more things you still need to know, Alex. Yesterday, Gant's office dropped the case... but I guess that wasn't enough for Swanson to lay off Angel."

"Watch her twenty-four seven, Cole. Tell Bancroft I want a meeting, and I want more guards on Mom, Dad, Allison, and Josh. Oh, and Angel's friend, Becca and her daughter, and Angel's dad in Joplin, Missouri. No loopholes. Nothing left to chance. Understand?"

"Completely."

"What else?" Alex asked.

"The guy who got arrested is Swanson's nephew, the one who lives in Angel's building, remember? He'll probably get out on bail in a couple of hours."

"Instruct the lobby security that he's not allowed back in, and let the building management know that we are not accepting new tenants, even if there are some in process. Everything gets put on hold, immediately."

"It's illegal to prevent a tenant from entering an apartment he has a lease on, isn't it?"

"Not when his victim lives in the building! Even if it becomes a legal quagmire, I'll deal with it."

"Dad said you're supposed to go to London in a couple of weeks. Are you still going?"

"I don't want to, but it's my bargaining chip for Dad's acceptance of all... this." He ran both hands through his hair and sighed. "It's unlikely this will all be resolved before that trip. Mark Swanson wants revenge. I could see it in his eyes. With the case out of court, it would be logical that he'd leave her alone, but in light of last night, that clearly isn't his intention."

"Right." Cole agreed and nodded toward the door. "I'm gonna head back."

Alex was already dialing Angel's number when his brother left, but it went straight to voicemail.

This is Dr. Angeline Hemming. I'm not available...

With a deep breath he ended the call without leaving a message, unsure what his next step should be. Half of him wanted to confront that cocksucker, but the more dominant, logical half argued that doing so would only give the bastard a sick sense of satisfaction. He wouldn't affirm the chink in his armor or that Swanson had succeeded in scaring the shit out of Angel. Alex ran a hand through his slightly overlong hair and walked back into his room. That was unacceptable.

Alex allowed himself a small smile; an image of Angel kicking the ass of one of the thugs almost medicated his anxiousness and discomposure over the whole event, but not quite.

His mind reeled, and his emotions only made matters worse. He needed to get his head in the game so he could get the business end in the can. When Swanson was no longer able to pay his lawyers, he'd be at the mercy of his mob connections or the public defender.

Alex huffed. Neither one would be much help to that sick motherfucker. Hardened criminals had more pressing concerns than to clean up what, in the grand scheme of their operations, was nothing more than a bothersome ripple. Alex felt certain of it, even if Cole and Bancroft hadn't confirmed it yet.

He'd have to come clean with Angel after Swanson was bankrupt. She'd have no choice but to understand that everything he kept from her and everything he'd done was for her own damn good. He breathed in deeply and looked up at the ceiling. He hoped.

He tried Angel's cell again, but it went to voicemail once more, and even though Cole assured him that Bancroft was watching her and she was safe in her apartment, he was filled with trepidation. "Damn it!"

His second call was answered by a soft, sweet voice. "Hello?"`

"Allison, I need you to do me a favor."

*****

Monday morning, Angel walked out of the police station with Kenneth at her side, glad the last few grueling hours were finally over. Hearing that one of the men who stopped to help had been critically injured had left her shaken and overwhelmed. Should she have stayed?

"I think I should go by the hospital, say thank you." Her body ached with every movement; the night before had been the most terrifying and beautiful one of her life. If it weren't for the pain, for the police report, and the absence of her Lexus from the garage this morning, she wouldn't have known if it was real or imagined.

"He's in pretty bad shape from what Dave said; you should wait awhile," Kenneth replied, referring to the police sergeant that had taken Angel's statement. "At least there's a tangible connection to Swanson now. His nephew lives in your building, for God's sake!" He stopped her and took hold of her shoulders. "I'll get the restraining order in place within the hour, honey. Don't worry. He won't be able to touch you."

Angel swallowed and raised her eyes to his face. The day was bright and clear, but brisk; the sunlight behind him throwing Kenneth's features into shadow. "Do you think a stupid restraining order will stop them? He'll just send someone else. It won't end until I get that prick to come after me himself. He's such a coward!"

Kenneth took in Angel's appearance. She was put together, but her demeanor was off—subdued, introspective, and distracted. It was so unlike her.

"Angel," Kenneth said. His finger prodded her chin up. "It's not worth it."

"Then tell me that this so-called connection is enough to lock him up?" Her eyes threw fire, and her expression was determined. "You can't, can you?"

Kenneth sighed, searching her worried expression. He couldn't and she knew it. "What are you doing today?"

"I don't know. I have to deal with the car, call the insurance agent." She shrugged. "Why?"

"Just be careful." He held up his arm to hail her a cab. "Take some time off to regroup."

Kenneth's arms slid around her, but she didn't fall into them as he'd hoped. She was stiff, her arms crossing her chest between them, and she visibly winced. He was hurt, but it was only to be expected. She'd just been assaulted and, surely, the touch of any man would repulse her in her current state. Not to mention all of her bruises had to be painful. He reluctantly let her go.

"Yeah, I will."

"If you need me—anything…" His eyes searched hers for some sign that she missed him. "Just call. I can come over tonight. You shouldn't be alone."

Angel flushed and touched the front of his cream-colored dress shirt, hating the hurt she saw in his eyes. "I'm okay, but thank you."

She slid gratefully into the cab and gave the address of her office to the driver just before her phone rang. *Alex.* She closed her eyes and leaned her head back on the seat, gathering the strength to let it go unanswered. It was the fifth time he'd called in the past two days.

Would he leave a message this time?

She needed his voice, his arms, and his mere essence to make some sense out of the chaos. She was angry and frustrated. Angel was angry that she allowed her fear to put him at risk and at her own weakness. Swanson had to believe Alex was out of her life or he'd use him, hurt him in order to hurt her. She had to keep him safe at all costs. If anything happened to Alex, well, she'd never forgive herself.

It would've been easy to give the driver his office address and tell him everything. It didn't feel right keeping things from him, but no good would come from telling Alex now. She opened her eyes and squared her shoulders, her focus renewed as the cab came to a stop in front of her office. She made her way inside, her bruised muscles protesting with each movement.

Liz was busy working on the monthly billing statements and barely looked up from her computer screen or Angel's slowness would have been cause for concern. Angel's hip burned at the place she had landed on when she was thrown into the van, and the rest of her body ached. The angry, purple bruise that she noticed while looking in the bathroom mirror earlier that morning, was shocking.

"Morning, Liz," Angel murmured as she walked past her into her own office. "Would you mind getting me some coffee and then coming in?"

"Sure, boss." She glanced up, smiled brightly, and pushed back from her desk to do Angel's bidding. She showed up with a cup of black coffee, quickly placing it on the desk.

"The schedule is all regular patients except there was a call earlier today from Ally Franklin. She mentioned she'd spoken to you about the leukemia benefit that she's chairing and asked for a meeting. You have time before your first appointment, so I scheduled her in. I hope that's okay?"

She'd forgotten all about that. Angel reached for the coffee, taking a quick sip. The liquid was hot and burned her tongue. "Ouch!" She almost spilled the steaming coffee on her lap. "Oh, um, sure."

Kyle was expecting her to attend band practice yesterday, but it had completely slipped her mind with everything else going on. Maybe it would be the distraction she needed, and it could also take Swanson's focus away from Alex. Maybe if he saw her around her ex, he'd believe she wasn't involved with Alex.

Angel was in a sort of haze, hearing but not registering much of what her assistant said as she went over her patient load and arranged the files on her desk.

"Do you have enough blank tapes and notepads?" Liz asked, rising to leave. "Angel?" she asked thoughtfully. "You're not yourself. Are you still feeling ill?"

"No, um, I'm fine. Just tired, I guess."

"Party too hard this weekend?" Liz asked with a laugh. Her eyes twinkled. "I listened to the show Friday night! You were brilliant. I can't believe that one woman believed that guy! Just because he said the other girl was just a friend with benefits."

"I know, right?" Angel said with a roll of her eyes. "She's infatuated, but it will wear off when she sees he's playing them both."

"Silly girl!"

Angel sat back in her chair and blew on her coffee before raising the rim to her lips for another sip. "She's in love." She shrugged. "Love is blind, and when you've got someone in front of you that is larger than life, it's hard to know what the truth is."

Liz's eyes narrowed. "What?" She shook her head with a smirk. "I expected you to say something like 'she's getting what she deserves for hiding her head in the sand!' Followed up by a resounding, 'Stupid cow!'"

Angel laughed lightly, pulling the files close to her, and setting her cup on her desk. "Yes, normally, but lately, my black and white world is muddying up in certain places."

Liz stopped in the doorway, her eyebrow shooting up quizzically. "What? Something's up."

Angel flushed guiltily. Liz didn't know about Alex; she didn't know about her feelings, but Angel felt as if her deepest secret was about to be laid bare. She bit her lip and flipped on her computer. "In talking with all of these women, who are so fucked up by relationships, I just… I've started to empathize a little."

"Empathize, huh? Angel, you don't empathize; you tell people to get their heads out of their asses."

Angel's face burned, and she scrubbed at one of her cheeks with the heel of her hand. "Not everyone can be a cold-hearted bitch like me, you know." Her teasing brought a smile to the older woman's lips.

"You never fooled me. You have a big heart."

The outer door to the office opened and someone walked inside. "That must be Mrs. Franklin," Liz murmured and turned to go.

"Send her right in."

Angel stood, her hand smoothing down her black pencil skirt, as a willowy young woman, impeccably dressed in a dark green silk blouse and subtle green and brown tweed suit, entered her office. The scarf she wore was the perfect frame for her heart-shaped face and brunette hair that bounced around at the top of her shoulders. She was polished and fine, her expression pleasant as she extended her hand. "Angel, right? Or should I call you Dr. Hemming?"

"Angel, please. It's my pleasure to meet you, Ally." Something about the calm green eyes put her at ease as she accepted the outstretched hand with a smile. "I'm sorry; I was supposed to go to the band's practice yesterday, but I forgot. Can we get you anything to drink? I think I have Pellegrino or tea if you don't like coffee."

Ally's eyes looked over the other woman who walked across the room to the sideboard along one wall and pulled open the small refrigerator door hidden there. Angel was beautiful, and Ally could see Alex's fascination, though she was different from a lot of his previous girlfriends. Being a fiery brunette was the obvious difference, but it was the way she held herself, the confidence with which she moved, and the intelligence behind her dark eyes which would trigger his fascination. Yes, she could certainly understand Alex's infatuation.

"Pellegrino is perfect; thank you. I tried to call your friend again, but he's not taking my calls, I'm afraid. The date is getting so close, and I have no back-up plan. I really don't know what I'm going to do."

Ally's voice was light and flitted around the room like a butterfly in a meadow of buttercups despite her dilemma. Angel's mood lifted as a result, and she thought Ally's blood red nail polish against her pale skin was a pretty contrast as the long fingers wrapped around the crystal tumbler full of the sparkling water.

"Thank you," Ally murmured as she accepted the glass.

Angel settled back in her chair across from the other woman. "I can't promise anything. Kyle put a condition on the benefit when I spoke to him, and I'm not sure it will work out."

"What sort of condition? Is it about money?" Ally's brow creased. "I told him the most the foundation could afford was $10,000."

"Ugh. If only that was it," Angel answered. The confused look on the other woman's face propelled her forward. "He requires that I resume my position with the band for this gig or he won't agree."

"Oh, my gosh! Angel!" Her face lit up. "That would be fabulous and would certainly add to the draw of the event! Will you?"

"Hmmm. It's not exactly one of my top priorities right now. It's been a few years since I've performed with them and some of the players have changed." She grimaced as the image of the airhead blonde that took her place crossed her mind. Surely, Crystal would protest at her guest appearance and Kyle's insistence. It wasn't like they parted on the best of terms. "It could be a disaster, and I wouldn't want that for you, Ally."

Allison leaned forward in her seat anxiously. "What could happen? You sang with them for years, you said. It's only a few hours, and it's such a worthy cause."

"Oh, I'm not disputing the worthiness of the cause, but—"

"Then what?"

"Kyle and I were together, and we split because he was screwing this bimbo groupie that used to haunt every gig we did. Her stupidity used to annoy the shit out of me, even before that happened." Angel glanced up and caught herself, but Ally was grinning, two dimples prominent in her cheeks. She looked familiar in a way Angel couldn't place. "Er, excuse my choice of words. Anyway, I caught them backstage after a particularly important show. We were on the verge of getting a record deal with Sony, but then I walked out on Kyle and the band. Everyone was pretty mad at me."

"Pfft!" Allison's hand dismissed the notion with a wave. "They should have been pissed at Kyle, not you. Er, excuse my choice of words." Ally grinned. "It was his fault for not keeping his prick in his pants."

Angel's face split into a brilliant smile. "I think this could be the start of a beautiful friendship."

"So, you'll do it?"

"Only if Kyle agrees to keep Crystal Light away from me."

"Oh," Ally responded with another chuckle. "The airhead?"

Angel nodded, her face contorting with a mixture of amusement and disgust. Allison laughed louder this time. "More like brain-dead. I was being kind. Why'd you think I call her Crystal *Light*?"

The other woman laughed again. "She can't be that bad."

"It's painful. You'll see."

"I will?"

"Yes. You're coming with me when I show up at practice. I'll call Kyle and let him know."

Allison's face lit up. "I can watch? I always wanted to be in a band, but my training was classical strings. I think my mother had a wet dream about Mozart. Or it may have been Vivaldi."

Angel's head fell back as laughter shook her shoulders, both of them giggling until they were gasping. Ally Franklin was a breath of fresh air and just what the doctor ordered.

"I studied classical piano, but rock-n-roll is where it's at, you know? I think I'll put a couple of conditions out there of my own." The devilish gleam in Angel's dark eyes didn't go unnoticed. "How extensive is this fundraiser, Ally? Is everything being donated?"

Allison nodded. "We're catering the event with a full bar, and the venue has agreed to only take the cost of food and beverages out of the gross. The net proceeds go to the foundation."

"What if the band were gratis, too?"

"I already have a commitment from my father and brother to front the cost of the band and the staff, so that's unnecessary."

"Well, if Kyle wants me, he has to pay. And, he has to let you sit in, too. That's if you want to."

"What? Are you kidding?" Ally's face flushed with excitement and her green eyes danced.

"Nope." Angel was reaching for the phone when Liz walked in with a bouquet of Canna lilies in a huge crystal vase. Angel's heart fell like lead to her stomach. "Oh, my God," she gasped.

"Sorry to interrupt, but you girls sounded like you're having so much fun, and these just arrived. The purple color is gorgeous! I've never seen anything like them! Have you?"

The thudding of her pulse pushed so hard she could feel it in her wrists and neck. "Uhhhh…" She breathed. "Uhm, yeah."

"Wow. They're beautiful, Angel. From anyone special?" Ally asked with a raised eyebrow and a smirk.

Angel could do little more than nod as she sat there without moving. Liz placed the large arrangement on the edge of her desk and her shaking hand reached for the card.

Angel-
Please meet me at the Navy Pier at 10 tonight. I
miss you.
   -Alex

8

The Tangled Web We Weave

TIME TICKED AWAY. She didn't own a watch, and the digital numbers on her phone were silent, but still, each second that passed screamed as loudly as a banshee. Angel's hand moved up to rub her temple as if it would erase the fight from her mind. The struggle tightened her lungs as anxiety wrapped around her chest and squeezed.

"What the fuck am I doing?" Angel muttered to herself as she glanced at her phone again. Alex's phone. He'd called twice during the day, and she'd ignored him both times. He didn't leave messages, and both calls came in before the flowers arrived at her office. How in the hell should she know what he was thinking?

She inhaled again and her lungs protested painfully. It was only 7:00 pm and she still had a little more than two hours to decide what she was going to do. The flowers on her table seemed like some beautiful prop in a horror flick, the way they loomed there, mocking her, laying in wait to pounce. Either way, it sucked. The flowers symbolized something wonderful, and now? It could turn into something ugly.

Angel wasn't kidding herself. As much as she wanted the flowers to be from Alex, it was more likely Swanson sent them, and she wasn't ignorant enough to blindly walk into an ambush at the pier. She'd come home, changed out of her suit into old sweatpants, a Northwestern sweatshirt, and big fuzzy socks in an attempt to keep herself at home. The slightest chance that Alex did send them was enough to torment her to know for sure. To hope. Admittedly, he was a chink in her armor. She pulled her knees up and rested her arms on them, as a rerun episode of *House* droned on one of the cable stations.

Her hand hovered and picked up the phone only to throw it down on the sofa next to her ten seconds later. She laughed harshly, wondering if she was more scared of what might happen at the pier or finding out for sure that Alex did not send the flowers. She pulled the elastic from her wrist and worked her hair up, twisting it around three or four times until it flopped in a lopsided knot on the very top of her head.

"Ugggghhhh!" Hating her weakness, Angel picked up the phone, quickly pressing the speed dial that would give her the answer she sought. Her heart was beating as fast as a hummingbird's as she fought between fear and anxiousness when it began to ring on the other end. It didn't take him long to answer.

"Hello? Angel? Is that you?" Alex's voice was strained, and Angel couldn't tell if he was angry with her or merely inconvenienced.

"Yes. I'm sorry, I uh…"

"No," he interrupted abruptly. "I'm glad you called."

"Um, I saw you called earlier but my day was so busy." She was hedging because he seemed pensive and impatient.

"Have you been busy for two weeks? I was worried about you. You couldn't spare a moment to respond even with a text?" The anger that laced his tone was expected and she flushed.

"We decided we needed a break," she said simply, hoping her flustered explanation would halt the inevitable confrontation.

"*We* did nothing of the sort."

"Look," she began, "I just wanted to say thank you for the lilies." There, it was out, and in a matter of seconds, she'd have confirmation of the answer she dreaded.

The silence that loomed made her sick to her stomach, even though it was only a couple of beats. Angel was certain she heard his quick intake of breath.

"They aren't from me." His voice was deep and stoic.

"Oh." She rubbed the back of her neck as embarrassment burned in her cheeks, falling back against the sofa and sinking into the plush cushions. "Well, I guess I have a secret admirer," she said, attempting a light tone designed to keep him from asking questions.

"It's not a secret admirer and you fucking know it. Was there a card?" he asked tightly.

Angel didn't want to answer, and Alex lost his temper at her hesitation.

"Look, stop the bullshit! I know who sent them, so just tell me what was on the goddamned card!"

"Wha-at?"

"Angel, please. Just tell me what was on the card." Alex struggled to regain control, but his words held a sharp edge that belied her disobeying his request.

"That you missed me, and you wanted to meet at the Navy Pier tonight at ten."

"You're not to go!" he commanded.

"Stop yelling at me! I wasn't planning on it! Didn't you hear what I said?"

"Yes, but that was when you thought you were meeting me."

She shook her head as pain filled her, hating the abyss she had created between them. "That was an asshole thing to say."

"You're so careless! You know that bastard is stalking you, and yet you lie to me and flit around as if you don't have a care in the world!"

"Fuck you! I don't flit around anything!"

"The hell you don't! What have you gained by keeping it from me? It's making me nuts!"

"What I gain is professional integrity! What do you know about it, Alex? How do you know anything at all?"

"That's irrelevant. I know about Friday night and more. If you'd have told me, as you should have, this all could have been avoided. You could have been kidnapped, raped, or killed! Damn professional integrity! It's moot now anyway since the case has been dismissed."

Heat was readily creeping up beneath the skin of her neck and face and her free hand balled into a fist. "You arrogant bastard! It's none of your business! Do you think you can just nose around in my life like it's front page news? Do you think you can control me, or what happens to me? Tell me how you know! Have you been in touch with Kenneth Gant? Are the two of you in cahoots?"

Alex laughed harshly. "Hardly! Give me some credit. If I need answers, I get them! Do you really think I'd need to ask that piss-ant anything?" he asked in disgust.

"You're not my husband or my father, so stop acting like it! When I want your help, I'll ask for it!"

"You don't think you need help, Angel! That's the problem. Even if you don't want to admit it, you need me. Mark Swanson's prick is in a vice, which makes him dangerous. He knows things about you. About us. Think about it, for Christ's sake!"

"Well, maybe when he needs answers, he gets them," Angel spat viciously.

"Don't push me on this! I don't give a damn if I've pissed you off as long as you're safe. We'll discuss it after this behind us."

"There is no us. Haven't you been listening?"

"The hell there isn't!"

"Hmmph!" Angel huffed angrily. "I'm not like your other bimbos that fawn all over you and take your orders, Alex! I'm not sticking around until… I'm not leaving it up to you."

Alex snorted bitterly. "That's insulting. Is that what you seriously think of me?"

She felt defeated; positive Alex was entitled to his anger. He was clearly concerned, and yet she felt compelled to push him away. "I don't need to remind you of our first conversation."

He sighed heavily. "You're right. I have no one to blame but myself. If you want it ended between us, it's done. I'm tired of this merry-go-round. But, I won't let him hurt you."

Angel started to tremble as tears welled, surprised Alex would acquiesce so easily. "Have you been watching me just like he is?"

"What do you think?" Exasperation and disgust laced his tone. "When something needs to be done, I damn well do it."

"How can there be anything between us when you keep this from me?"

"Do you hear yourself? You're as guilty as I am. How could I tell you when you denied you were in any danger? Did you really think I'd just sit around until something happened to you? Give me a God damned break!"

"All of this mistrust isn't much of a foundation to build on, is it?" Angel gathered her strength, preparing herself as much for the words she was about to say as for his reaction. "Even if I wanted to."

"You're upset and angry right now. You're not rational. I'll come over and we'll talk. When you think about it, you'll—"

"I'll *nothing*, Alex! I don't want to talk to you. Please, for both our sakes, just respect that." She felt her throat tighten up and she swallowed hard, her eyes burning. She knew she had to get off the phone before she started to cry. She felt so fucking weak when she cried. "I gotta go."

"Angel, wait."

The seconds ticked by, both of them struggling for words.

"What is it?" she finally asked tightly.

Alex cleared his throat. "The watchers will remain in place until this is over, but I'll stay away from you if that's what you really want."

Angel closed her eyes. It was the last thing she wanted. She wanted his mouth on hers, his hands on her flesh, strong arms wrapped around her, his body deep inside hers, and his beautiful face turned into her neck as he came. She wanted the sound of his voice groaning her name as he made love to her. At least... it always felt like making love.

"Who are they? How many of them are there?"

"It's best if you don't know. Your actions could be suspicious if you're constantly looking for them, and we don't want to tip Swanson off. He may leave you alone now that the case is over, but I doubt it."

"Okay." Angel gave in, silently thankful for the protection.

"I'd prefer if someone other than you were his target. Just... don't go to the pier. Angel, promise me you'll be careful, and you'll call me if something happens. No matter what he's done, that bastard isn't worth you getting hurt." Alex's voice was tight and his anxiousness made her heart speed up.

She was so full of him it hurt but yet his absence caused a deep seated, hollow ache.

"I promise," she said softly and then ended the call without giving him the chance to say anything more.

*****

Angel's week passed with the days dragging in an uneventful routine, always trying not to search for the men she knew were watching her every move, not knowing if it was Swanson's goons or Alex's protection detail. Either way, it rattled her nerves.

The phone he had given her remained obnoxiously silent, which bothered her more than she wanted to admit. Twice, she had nightmares that left her sweating, panting, and screaming into her dark apartment; each time she'd woken shaken and reaching out to the emptiness beside her. Several of Swanson's business locations were closing, and Angel hoped it was enough to keep his revenge plans at bay, but logic told her it was only a matter of time until he came after her again. If Alex had engineered his business problems as she suspected, he'd be even more dangerous than before.

On Friday afternoon, she fought the temptation to bail on that evening's radio show. The events of the prior week were enough to make her think twice, in addition to the fact she didn't feel up to listening to other people whining when her own heart was so sore. In the end, Angel was relieved when Darian showed up at the station and stayed for the entire run. It wasn't necessary to ask if Alex had filled him in since his presence alone spoke volumes.

As Darian walked with her to her rental car, she felt safer, and she was silently thankful for his company. She glanced up at him and pulled her wool suit blazer closer around her body to ward off the damp evening air. Angel fought down the words that seemed to rise of their own volition. Her throat caught painfully when she tried to swallow, the way a knuckle sometimes does when it needs to be cracked. The distance to the car was waning, and the only sound was the scuffling of gravel and loose rocks beneath their feet.

"So…, um, have you heard from Alex?" She fumbled for the keys in her purse, even though the over-large key chain with the rental company's logo and the car's identification number should have made them easy to find. "Er… I mean, how is he?"

Darian stopped and looked into Angel's face as the moon bathed it in soft blue light. He could see the struggle on her features. "He's okay." His cryptic response did little to dispel her anxiety.

"Is that all?" She shook her head, her brow wrinkling as the words tumbled out, not knowing exactly how to ask what she wanted to know. "Did he tell you not to say anything to me?"

Darian could see the conflict dance on her features. "No, but he's preoccupied. Not himself. He's really been an asshole, if you want the truth. Even fifteen-year-old scotch doesn't soften his mood."

Angel nodded and unlocked the economy car that her insurance company had rented for her, using the remote on the key chain. "He's angry with me. I apologize if he's taking it out on you."

Darian's hand reached out and grasped Angel's upper arm to stop her. "He's worried sick about you. Alex is a good man, Angel. The best. Sometimes he screws up like the rest of us, but his intentions are always good."

She nodded and looked at the ground, her teeth coming out to bite her lip. "I know, Darian."

"You're so alike in so many ways. I knew you'd shake him up, but it didn't occur to me that he'd have you so off-balance." She shifted uncomfortably in front of him, and Darian continued. "Alex has been different since he met you, Angel. You've changed him."

"He's changed me, too. He makes me weak."

Darian's face split in a knowing smile. "Needing someone doesn't make you weak, doll. It makes you human."

*****

The warehouse hadn't changed much. It was still run-down, and the land around it still barren. There were a lot of good memories between these walls that Angel acknowledged as the familiar sounds of the band warming-up echoed around her. She and Ally walked through the heavy door, and it slammed behind them with a loud bang. She grinned when confronted with the same old sofa cushions nailed to the walls to absorb the sounds and create better acoustics than the old metal building allowed. Kyle and David had stolen them from three couches as they waited on curbs for the Salvation Army truck to come and cart them away. Kyle knew she was coming, but she wondered if the others did.

"So how is this going to go?" Ally asked.

Angel glanced over at her new friend and grimaced. The warehouse was an abandoned auto shop that belonged to Kyle's grandfather. It still smelled of grease and cigarette smoke, and Ally looked completely out of place in her Dior get-up. Angel was in jeans and an old royal blue hoodie with the words *Northwestern* in white print, faded from years of wear and washing. "You should have worn sneakers and jeans," she pointed out with a smirk.

Ally laughed. "I don't think I've worn jeans more than three times in my life, and then only because my brothers forced me to build a fort or play football in our backyard when I was younger."

"Ugh," Angel groaned. "You're kidding me, right?"

Ally's nose wrinkled slightly as she shook her head. "No. My mother is very, um—" she stopped as she searched for the words. "Well, let's just say proper young ladies wear frilly frocks and Mary Jane's."

Angel felt a small pang rush through her at her own lack of female intervention. "My dad didn't know much about that stuff."

Ally's arm went around her. "From what I've seen, you have an amazing sense of style."

"Angel! Is that you?" A freakishly large Hispanic man jumped up from behind the black pearl drum set with a huge grin plastered across his plump face. Angel scurried into his waiting arms, only to be hoisted up and then twirled around, and at the same time, bounced up and down. "My little Angel!" His accent was not as thick as she remembered, but the voice still bellowed.

Angel giggled despite the iron vice of his arms crushing her small frame. "Sa-Bad Ass-tian!" she squealed as her little arms wrapped halfway around his massive shoulders while her feet dangled almost two feet off the ground. "I've missed you!"

"Where you been?" he asked as he finally set her down. "I told Kyle to get you back countless times. Stupid ass!"

Angel's eyes scanned the space and found five other sets of eyes on them. Kyle's gaze burned into her as he examined everything about her. He looked good; his body was still fit but with more tattoos than she remembered, and his head was shaved. He looked tougher.

Crystal, in her cheap punk-rock style and spiky blonde hair laced with pink, stood with her hand possessively on his arm. *Don't worry, bitch. Been there, done that*, Angel thought with barely hidden disdain. David, Owen, and Jay—the other members of the band— all came forward to hug her one by one, their smiles clearly communicating they were as happy to see her as Sebastian had been.

"Hi, Angel," Owen said quietly. He was the bass player, and his mop of reddish hair still hung in boyish disarray above his bright blue eyes. David and Jay had a rougher look than she remembered, both of them with longer hair and more expensive holes in their jeans.

"Hey, guys." Angel smiled brightly, trying to ignore the daggers that Crystal was shooting with her eyes. "This is my friend, Ally Franklin. She plays strings with the Chicago Symphony and wanted to check out practice. Kyle, you remember Ally?"

"Yes, hello," he said softly and extended his hand in greeting to Ally. "It's good to see you, Angel." His eyes seemed sad, and his mouth twitched slightly at one corner. Angel took the three steps needed to slide her arms around his neck in a short embrace. Kyle left his arm around her waist a moment too long as she turned back to the others.

"Ally, this is Owen on bass, David plays keyboards, Jay is on rhythm guitar, and you've already met Sebastian, the drummer." Her jaw shot out as she tried to stop herself from laughing, not really sure how she'd introduce the woman, but afraid of what word vomit would spill out. "And this... is... er, Crystal."

Allison shook hands with them all one by one. "How do you do?"

"How do I do?" Crystal spat out, hatred dripping from her words. "I was better before she got here!" She turned on Angel. "Let's get one thing straight! The band doesn't need you to come back."

Angel rolled her eyes as she peeled off her coat and flung it on one of the chairs that surrounded the open area where the instruments were arranged. "Kyle, can you do something with that?" she asked dryly. "All that screeching gives me a headache."

Most of the guys did their best to hide their amusement, but even Kyle couldn't keep the slow smile from creeping across his features, and Sebastian burst out laughing. Sebastian blamed Crystal for Angel's speedy exit and so never even gave the other girl a chance. The band had suffered as a result. Angel's fiery presence had been missed dearly.

Crystal took two steps toward Angel, her expression furious, when Kyle's fingers clamped firmly around her arm. "I asked her to be here."

"What about what I want?" she sneered.

"Look, I'm not all that thrilled about seeing you either, but this is for a good cause. So grow up already."

Ally's eyes widened, and she bit her lip trying to suppress a giggle. Sebastian and the boys didn't feel the need and laughed out loud. Vivid color flooded the other woman's face, and Kyle visibly stiffened.

"Look, Crystal! Your face matches your hair!" Owen said, as he strapped on his guitar. He smiled and winked at Angel. "Awesome!"

"Don't worry; I'm not here to steal your boyfriend."

"As if you could…" Crystal began.

"Oh, sure I could," Angel stated matter-of-factly, still laughing as she took a seat on the bench next to one of the keyboards and ran her hands over the keys. Her eyes shot up to lock with Crystal's.

"He left you for me!"

"Hmmm. That's not the way I remember it. Kyle, is that the way you remember it?" Her words were soft and distracted, clearly communicating that she didn't give a shit one way or the other. Of their own accord, Angel's fingers began playing one of the songs she loved from the Adele's latest album.

"Just because you can't face it, doesn't make it the truth. Right, baby?" she cooed and wrapped her scantily clad self around Kyle. His focus was on the woman at the piano, her thick auburn hair tied up in a knot and her face devoid of make-up. She could still make his heart speed up.

"Isn't this fun?" Angel asked Ally with a wry huff, wrinkling her nose playfully. "I bet you're so glad you decided to join." The electric piano filled the empty space with the melodic strains. "Crystal, as enjoyable as it may be for you, this childish bullshit is not on my agenda. I'm here to work up a set list for the benefit, so can we get started?" Angel stopped playing and looked at Kyle. "Are you still doing any of our old stuff?"

"Quite a bit, but we should add in some new songs," Kyle said.

"I want to do something from Britney Spears," Crystal interjected.

"Ugh," Angel rolled her eyes again. "Really?"

"Why? She's a huge superstar!" Crystal protested.

"So is Barney the dinosaur, but you won't see us doing his top ten songs for tots," Angel said, unable to stop the start of giggle. This was too much fun. "We need songs with meat in them."

"Lady Gaga!" Crystal was obviously unaffected by Angel's snarky response.

Angel pounded out the first five bars of *Poker Face* and Crystal perked up. Sebastian added a light dusting on a cymbal and started singing "Ma, Ma, Ma, Ma," clearly buying into Angel's humor.

Crystal's expression changed to a frown when Angel banged her hands against the keys in a loud clang, startling the other woman.

"Not that kind of *meat*," Angel said sweetly, twisting her mouth into a sly smile.

"What's that supposed to mean?"

Sure, this airhead is so mentally challenged, she doesn't get it.

"It means, if you want me to sing about dick, okay, but I won't call it a disco stick or vertical stick or any other fucking kind of *stick*," Angel deadpanned with a bored look on her beautiful face. "Understand?" Her left eyebrow shot up. "Now, can we move on?"

The boys burst out laughing, even Kyle couldn't keep the deep rumbles from bursting free. Allison put a hand over her mouth and tried her best to hide her amusement, but the shaking of her shoulders and sparkle in her eyes gave her away.

"Classic Angel!" Jay laughed. "I'd shut the hell up if I were you, Crystal. You can't keep up; trust me."

"Fuck you, Jay," Crystal huffed.

"No, thanks," he retorted.

Angel couldn't keep the laugh from erupting. "Well, this is entertaining anyway."

Crystal stomped to the opposite end of the warehouse and perched on one of the speakers as the others discussed the music.

"Kyle, I thought it would be fun if we let Ally sit in. She plays cello, and with that thingy you have for your guitar, we can do some cool stuff. I was thinking an Evanescence cover or two. It could be cool."

"It's called an E-bow," Ally put in. "That thing for the guitar that makes it sound like a violin. Right?" Her eyes shot to Kyle.

"Yeah." He nodded with a smile. "It could be cool."

Ally's face lit up with excitement. "Really?" Maybe this guy wasn't so bad after all. He certainly looked tough enough. She took note of the tattoos that covered his arms, especially the one on his left shoulder.

"Sure."

"Now there are two of them?" Crystal whined. "What about me?"

"What about you?" Kyle asked. "You're still part of the band, babe."

"Yes," Angel agreed. "I'm only here for one gig, and I don't want to upset the entire balance of the band." No matter how much she disliked the blonde woman, she didn't intend to misrepresent her intentions.

"I was hoping we'd get Angel behind the mic. Isn't that the point?" Sebastian asked. His deep baritone voice matched his huge form.

Kyle nodded. "Fans ask about you all the time. It would be nice to have the old version of Archangel, at least for this one gig. Maybe more."

Angel could see the jealousy burning in Crystal's expression and couldn't help a small bit of smugness at her discomfort but chose to ignore the last part of Kyle's comment.

"I think we should do a mix: songs you're doing currently, some of our old stuff, and brand new material. Don't you think that would be best, Kyle?"

"I agree. We're gonna promote the fact you'll be with us that evening, so hopefully we can boost the numbers of attendees."

"This is going to be so exciting!" Ally exclaimed.

"Joy." Crystal's face contorted in barely concealed disgust.

*****

Angel was satisfied with the result of the session. They'd spent three hours arranging the harmonies and practicing, and she and Kyle got right back into their groove on their old numbers. Crystal came around about halfway through, though she was still pouty, she did participate, and overall, the sound was solid. It was three weeks until the benefit, and there would be only four more practices. Ally was excited about playing with them, and they'd come up with several songs that could incorporate her cello or violin.

The evening air was getting colder and the breezes coming off Lake Michigan were chilly. Angel shivered and turned on the heater in her rental, and when she did, a stale, unused smell flooded the passenger compartment.

"I hate this stupid car," Angel grumbled.

"Why don't you get a new one?" Ally asked as she studied Angel with knowing eyes.

"This is a rental. My Lexus is in the shop."

"What's wrong with it?" Allison wondered if Angel would tell her the same story that Alex had.

"Oh, some vandals took a crow bar to it." Angel didn't elaborate, and Ally didn't need to ask.

"That's strange. My brother had his car beat up a few weeks ago, too."

"Yeah, that is weird." Angel shrugged.

"I had a great time. Thanks for inviting me!"

Angel smiled as she merged onto the interstate that would take them back downtown. "Oh, my pleasure. I wasn't sure what we were going to walk into. Kyle was nicer than I expected him to be."

"Really? I mean he was a jerk when we first met, but with your history, I expected today to go well. That Crystal is a bitch, though."

"She's always rubbed me the wrong way. Especially after she rubbed Kyle the right way, if you know what I mean."

"She's a little trashy-looking, and the rest of the guys don't seem to have much time for her," Ally said offhandedly. "Oh! I guess I shouldn't have said that out loud."

"No, it's okay. They blame her for me leaving. Kyle's affair with her was a big part of it, but honestly, it was time I moved on. I wanted to go to grad school, and I knew a full-time job and the band would be too much for me to handle in addition to a full-course load. I had to prioritize. Kyle was angry and unable to accept my decision, so I suppose he tried to get back at me."

"I saw his tattoo. He must have loved you very much."

Angel shrugged again, feeling like it was a lifetime ago. "It's all history now."

"Are you dating anyone?" Ally probed. "You're quite a stunning woman, Angel. I can't imagine you being single."

Angel's eyes stayed on the interstate and the red lights of the cars driving in front of her. "Not at the moment."

"There isn't anyone?"

Angel bristled. "Mmm… I was seeing someone for a while but not anymore."

"Oh, I'm sorry. Am I being too nosey if I ask what happened?"

"Nothing really. I work with women everyday who piss and moan about how one man or another used them, broke their heart, and left them with a mess to clean up. I see it all the time, and it just opens my eyes a little wider than most. I don't want to end up like them. I worried it wasn't going anywhere beyond the bedroom, so I ended it."

"My husband is a saint. He puts up with all my chattering and shopping sprees without one complaint! And I'm always doing some charity thing, so I'm gone all the time."

"You're one of the lucky ones, Ally. Hold on to him."

"Tell me about the man you were seeing. What was wrong with him?"

Angel drew in a deep breath, her mind flooding with images and memories. "Not much, other than he's a little obstinate, sometimes. He thinks he can do whatever he damn well pleases and have whatever he wants when he wants it. He's too beautiful."

"Is he a womanizer?"

"At first glance, you'd think he would be, but…" Angel shook her head. "No, he's not. He's really quite wonderful."

"Then what?" Ally asked hesitantly. "I don't get it."

"He's a heartbreaker. Alex isn't the type of man for happily ever after. When we met, he was quite upfront about his requirements in a relationship—which was sex without strings. I'd just taken a call from his current girlfriend, who was miserable. And I can't believe that his ideals will change overnight."

"Yes, I can see why you'd think that way."

"What?"

"Oh, nothing. Is there any way you'd get back together? Has he tried?"

Angel nodded after a short hesitation. Talking about Alex made her heart hurt and her need for him intensify. That, and always wondering if or when Mark Swanson would strike again, wore on her. She was tired. "I think his reluctance to accept it was due to the fact it wasn't his decision, and he never loses. He's very powerful in business and has been in his relationships. It's very difficult for him to let go of control in anything."

Angel pulled into her office parking lot to drop Ally off, her eyes scanning the parking lot for other cars, and was relieved to find it vacant.

"I'm sure it will work out, honey."

Angel felt the need to change the subject. "I can't wait to hear how we sound when you play with us."

"My brothers will be so jealous! We used to play *Rock Band* when we were small. My mother thought rock music screwed up our minds, so we had to sneak away to the fort my brothers built in the woods behind our house. The neighborhood kids would all gather to watch us. It was a blast!"

"It sounds like it!" A small nudge of envy rose inside Angel as she compared the situation to her own childhood sans siblings. "Do you have the schedule for the practices?"

Allison leaned over and gave Angel a hug before she exited the car. "Yes! I'll be there with bells on!"

Angel was glad when Ally was safely in her car and on her way, and she had a moment of relief as she made her way back to her apartment and pulled into the underground garage. The worst part of her day was the time it took to get from her car to her apartment, which was when she felt most vulnerable.

The garage was dark and quiet, but a car had pulled in just seconds behind her. She didn't recognize the large, black SUV, and after the experience with the van, she wasn't willing to take the chance. A large man dressed all in black jumped out of the passenger door and purposely made his way toward her.

Her earlier calm left in a mad rush, and her heart started to pound. She had a better chance fighting if she started out on her feet, so she reached into her purse for the mace she kept there and jumped out of the car. Her eyes were blazing as the man approached.

"Dr. Hemming? I'm Cole Avery. Alex's brother. My associate and I are here to protect you."

"Anyone could say that." She took a fighting stance, the mace still firmly ensconced in her right hand. "Prove it."

"How? Alex is public property. Everyone in Chicago's heard of him." He folded his arms across his chest. "I assure you, I'm his brother."

Angel's eyes roamed over the tall, dark-haired man. The shadows in the garage prevented her from seeing his face clearly, but there was something familiar about the angle of his jaw.

"Why didn't he let me know in advance?"

"He doesn't know I'm talking to you because he's in England on business. We're trying to catch that bastard in the act, and I told Alex it would be better if you knew what we were doing. He's brilliant, but in this, his judgment is clouded."

"How'd he take that?"

"Not well. He's pissed, but what can he do from across the pond? Take away my birthday?" Cole asked with a smirk.

"I'd hate to be you when he gets back. Can I see your ID?"

Cole reached into his back pocket for his wallet. "Of course."

"How long have you been following me?"

"A few weeks. The two guys that saved you from the abduction attempt work for Avery Corp."

Angel relaxed slightly when she'd seen his driver's license, but anger boiled beneath the surface. "Alex should have mentioned it."

"Alex doesn't discuss things: he gives orders. Besides, he knew you'd be angry, and I'm not sure he'd know how to deal with that." The phone began ringing from his pocket. "That's him now. I'm going to take it, okay?"

He waited for her nod and then reached for the phone, turning it so Angel could see Alex's name flashing on the screen. "Hey. Yeah, I got her. She's at her apartment. Okay. Bancroft and I are on it. Get some sleep. It has to be four in the morning over there, dickhead."

Angel smiled as Cole hung up the phone and used his right arm to usher Angel to walk in front of him toward the elevator. "Would you feel more comfortable if I accompanied you to your door?" Cole took out his own keycard and swiped the access on the elevator. Angel's brow creased.

"I still don't know if I can trust you."

"Fair enough." He handed her a piece of paper with his phone number on it. "If you see me or a shorter dude that looks like one of the *Men in Black*, don't panic. We'll keep a low profile, so try not to watch for us. Alex's main concern was that our cover would be blown. I'd appreciate it if you didn't mention this conversation to him, Dr. Hemming. I like this job."

Angel's mind was reeling with questions, but she did feel relief that she now knew at least part of the puzzle. As she stepped into the elevator, Cole's phone began to ring again.

"I guess he doesn't like being called a dickhead." Cole laughed as the elevator doors closed.

9

Impasse'

ALEX PACED BACK and forth in his office on the 23rd
floor that housed the elegant European headquarters of Avery
Corporation. He was impatient and hadn't slept more than two
hours the night before. The goddamned contracts weren't signed as
he'd hoped, and the general manager of the branch was at the mahogany conference table reprimanding her assistant in a stern
voice. Her attempt to transfer the blame only pissed him off.

His mouth thinned into a firm line. "Miss Morrison, would
you excuse us, please?" His voice was cold and calm, but the un-
derlying tone brokered no defiance. Alex didn't look at the
chubby young woman as she left, his gaze never leaving the
horizon of the London skyline over Canary Wharf, the lights of
the buildings a stark contrast to the dark night. The blurry re-
flections in the Thames were pretty but vaguely registered in his
consciousness.

Normally, Alex loved the history and beauty of London, but
his focus wasn't where it needed to be. Preoccupation with the
events in Chicago made him impatient for his work here to be
completed.

The sleek woman in the Stella McCartney suit and black patent leather pumps eyed Alex warily. Her blue eyes narrowed and the red-tipped fingers moved up to smooth back the sides of the fiery hair that was neatly pulled back in a tight chignon. Her pursed lips were coated in a glossy shade that matched her nails.

"Alex, relax. The deal will go through. It's just delayed a little. What's another day or two?"

He ignored her obvious skirting of the issue as his hand ran through his thick shock of hair. "Not only does it cost us money, it's a waste of time that I can't spare right now, Helen."

The woman sighed and turned, crossing her legs. The casual way she leaned back in her chair, as he continued to pace, caused his temper to flare. He stopped and waited for her response, the stern expression on his handsome face clearly communicating his annoyance.

"Well, the lawyers didn't get the contracts finished in time, and when they finally did, I rejected the counter-offer and sent it back for revisions." She took in the broad shoulders beneath the tailored fine white linen of his shirt, the way his body tapered in at his waist, and then the grey wool that was tailored over that sumptuous ass. Alex had always been coldly professional, but that didn't stop Helen from wishing for the day when he'd show some interest in her womanly charms.

Alex shoved his hands into his pockets and stared out the window. He turned as a scowl settled on his handsome features. "I'm not interested in excuses. You knew when I'd be here and what I expected to accomplish within that timeframe!" he said sternly. "The offer was enough to get the deal done. The money we piss away on minuscule bullshit does little to help the bottom line," Alex said with barely concealed disgust. He quickly shoved a copy of the other company's dossier into his expensive Italian leather briefcase before closing it with two loud snaps. He was impeccable as always, despite his sour mood, but he was exhausted.

"Yes, but you are two weeks early," Helen pointed out.

Alex couldn't argue, which only increased his agitation. He loosened the knot in his black and grey silk tie. "I have more pressing issues that demand my attention back in the States." He huffed, unsure why he was giving explanations to an employee. She'd made it obvious on numerous occasions that she'd be responsive if he had the slightest inclination, but his commitment to monogamy had always kept a more intimate relationship at bay. He could hardly remember a time in his adult life that he wasn't involved with someone. His eyes drifted over her with obvious disinterest. She was beautiful, with a feisty personality to match her red hair, but there was little more to separate her from any of the women he used to be attracted to.

He snorted, pissed that he'd thought about it in the past tense. Even if he weren't going crazy over Angel, he'd always kept business and more pleasurable endeavors apart and he sensed Helen would be more demanding than a brief sexcapade was worth. No, even if he weren't her boss, she meant nothing more than a passing stroke to his ego.

Helen stared at him, her expression a mixture of incredulity and mocking. "How can you be so blasé, Alex? The money on the table is—"

"I'm not sure why you feel the need to lecture me," Alex interrupted coldly. "I penned the goddamned offer, for Christ's sake! Get them on the phone and tell them to take it or leave it. No more revisions. Do I make myself perfectly clear?"

Helen's shoulders stiffened as she sat up straighter in her chair, her eyes widening in surprise. "But, Alex, we can express them to Chicago for your sig—"

"Just do it!" he commanded. "If it isn't closed by 10 a.m., it's off the table."

She opened her mouth and then closed it again as Alex walked out of the room without waiting for a response. Experience told her that he was not in the mood to listen to anything she had to say.

Alex was already pulling his phone out of his inside breast pocket as the expensive wooden door closed with a bang behind him. He called for his car to take him back to the hotel. It was 10 p.m. on Thursday night, and he was determined to get back to Chicago before Angel went on air the following night. The time difference meant he had to be on a plane in less than fifteen hours. Helen and this deal could go straight to hell as far as he was concerned.

The building was deserted except for the security station, and he wearily said goodnight as he passed and exited through the glass door being held open for him. A black limousine waited by the curb across the concrete plaza to take him back to his equally luxurious hotel suite; the thirty yards Alex had to cross to reach it seemed endless. Exhaustion waged a war with his mind, and he hoped he'd finally find the blissful relief of sleep, knowing that soon, he wouldn't be halfway around the world from where he wanted to be.

The aroma of new leather wafted around him as he leaned back in the plush seats of the car. He didn't speak to the driver as the car started to move, dialing Bancroft's number instead.

"Hello, sir."

"Anything new?"

"Nothing. Dr. Hemming didn't go into her office at all today."

Alex's chest tightened slightly. "Did something happen to her?" Panic edged his voice.

"There hasn't been any activity out of the perpetrator, and we've got cameras on all of the entrances, as you know. Nothing seems out of the ordinary. No new people that we've seen."

"Is she ill?"

"We don't think so."

"Find out and call me back," he said shortly and abruptly ended the call. He had four missed calls and not one of them from the one person he wanted to hear from. He debated whether to return any of them before finally throwing the phone down on the seat beside him. His hand rubbed over the day's growth of stubble on his chin. "I am so fucked."

*****

Angel lay stretched out on the couch, her hand resting on her stomach. The muscles were sore from the night spent heaving her guts out, and the only sleep she'd managed was leaning up against the wall in the bathroom, sitting within close proximity of the toilet. Her head hurt in the way that makes nausea worse, and the clamminess of her skin spoke of a fever. She didn't do sick well. It was just a different type of weakness.

"Ugh," she moaned as her stomach turned again. "How many times can I puke?" She reached down for the large metal bowl strategically positioned on the floor next to the couch and lurched into it violently. The contents of her stomach were emptied some five hours earlier and she was left with dry heaves, which seemed even worse. She'd tried some ginger ale but even that wasn't staying down.

She rolled onto her side, set the bowl back down, and pulled her blanket closer around her body as a new set of chills made her teeth chatter. Becca wanted to bring over some soup or Pepto Bismol, but Angel had adamantly refused the offer. It seemed selfish to risk Becca or Jillian getting the horrid virus, so the knock at the door came as a surprise.

She wearily got up, her blanket still wrapped firmly around her, the fuzzy socks on her feet making her steps silent. "Bec, I told you not to come," she muttered as each step she took pounded in her skull.

"Dr. Hemming, it's Cole Avery. Are you all right? Can I please speak with you?"

"I'm sicker than a dog, Cole. It's not something you want to catch, so another time?"

"Just for a minute."

Angel hesitated, leaning her forehead on the door, the coolness a stark contrast to her burning skin. "It's your funeral," she said as she undid the deadbolt.

"Dr. Hemming, you shouldn't open your door without verifying who it is," Cole warned as he entered toting a brown shopping bag.

Angel rolled her eyes. "I recognized your voice. Did Alex send you to check up on me? And you can call me Angel." She gestured him in with a wave of her hand, forgetting the bowl by the couch. "Oh, God." She put a hand to her head as he noticed it.

"You really are sick."

"Really? I thought I was on vacation."

Cole's mouth lifted in a sly smile, and Angel couldn't help but see the resemblance to Alex. She picked up the bowl to take it down the hall and into the bathroom.

"You never answered me. Did Alex send you?" she called.

"We've all wondered why you didn't go into your office today, so yes."

Angel walked back in and crawled back onto the sofa, curling in on herself. "Well, you can tell him that you've personally seen me and I look like hell."

"No, because he doesn't know we've spoken." He grimaced as he noticed her shivering. "Can I get you anything?"

She shook her head. "Nothing, thanks. I think it's a twenty-four hour bug. But it's miserable."

Cole sat down in a chair across from her and pulled something from the bag. "The surveillance equipment is three flights down, and as a precaution, I'd like to set this up."

"You have an apartment in this building?" she asked incredulously. "Are you fucking kidding me?" She was starting to get pissed. It was too much, even if it was for her own good. Alex was an arrogant bastard!

"Um, yeah. Actually, we've got the whole building wired in the common areas. It's illegal to set up cameras in here…"

"The whole building? Did he bribe the landlord or what?"

"Alex will be pissed that I'm telling you, but, uh, he is the landlord." He shifted uncomfortably under Angel's surprised glare. "Sort of. Sorry."

"He's gone too far with this. If I wasn't so freaking sick, I'd be yelling my head off."

"Angel, he's Alex. He doesn't follow the same rules as normal people. I'm not saying it's right, but he means well."

She sighed but didn't answer.

"In order to protect you, I came up with this. It's a baby monitor modified to handle the extra distance. I can't watch you, but I can listen. If you'll agree."

"It's a little late to be asking my permission, don't you think?"

"It's for—"

Her hand shot up to stop him, even from her prone position. "Don't say it's for my own good. Will you run to Alex with reports and audio tapes?"

Cole flashed a smile and shook his head. "No tapes. I only tell Alex things regarding your safety. But these—" he held up a handful of gadgets, "—will make sure we have the opportunity to get to you if needed. I also need a key. If you don't mind."

"Oh, sure. Next you'll want to know what kind of tampons I use." Angel's stomach protested again, and she grimaced as she went to the drawer in the kitchen where she kept a spare key. "How do you think your brother will react when he hears you have a key and he doesn't?"

Cole placed a monitor on one of the end tables and plugged it in. "I don't really care. He asked me to do a job, and I'm doing it. Alex can bite me."

Angel paused as a small laugh broke from her chest. "I think... I really like you, Cole. *Alex can bite me*," she mused. "I love it."

*****

"This is Angeline. It's just about midnight, so what's your confession?"

"Which one do you want?" The unexpected familiarity of the voice made Angel stiffen in her chair and her heart sink. Angel glanced quickly up at the window toward Christina, but the other girl had ducked around the corner and out of her eye line.

It was three weeks since that beautiful, horrible night. Two since the stilted phone conversation when he said he'd let their relationship go. Angel thought, surely, if he were going to call and confront her, he would have done so before this. She'd been nervous about it, never expecting Alex to slink away into nothingness, and spent the past Friday evening sitting on the edge of her seat waiting for a moment just like this.

Her stomach did somersaults, and her heart beat wildly in her chest.

"Whichever you'd like my opinion on," she said cautiously.

Christina was looking through the window, totally aware of who was on the phone. What the fuck was she thinking putting Alex's call through? Angel shot her a hateful glance.

"Huh, you'll regret saying that," he said caustically. His tone was hard and cold, miles away from the hot, husky voice she'd heard the last time they'd made love or fucked or whatever the hell it was. At this point, she wasn't sure. Her emotions were all over the place when it came to Alex. She was scared for him, but worse, scared of him, and she was smart enough to recognize it. Running away was uncharacteristic; she didn't run from Mark Swanson as much as she ran from Alex Avery.

Silence boomed like a bass drum.

Angel was sure she could hear him breathing—in and out, in and out. Her chest hurt in sympathetic unison, and she glanced down at her shaking hands, clasping them together to try to still them. She could almost hear the wheels cranking inside his brain, searching for the words that would ruin her resolve.

"Aren't you going to ask me my name, Angeline?" He was mocking her in the silken voice. So smooth, but harder than she'd ever heard it, and it hurt like hell.

"Names don't seem important tonight. Uhhmmm…" she cleared her throat. "What did you want to discuss?"

"I thought discussion wasn't something to be valued, relationships… dispensable."

"You sound angry and unlike yourself."

"Careful. Your listeners might think we know each other; unless you're a mind reader, Angeline. Are you?" His voice was a soft seduction, his words measured for ultimate impact. He knew how it affected her, and he was using it like a weapon.

"Not at all. Who has affected you this way?" Angel's own voice took on a harder tone as she dared him to expose her own relationship on air. She knew he was angry, but she was growing more impatient as the seconds ticked by. Although he deserved more, and part of her ached for him, she couldn't tell him that she was too afraid of heartbreak to be with him. Especially when he'd professed that love wasn't even real.

"I don't even know what the hell to call her. My lover or my obsession… Whatever she is or was… She disappeared from my life without much of an explanation. Something was going on and she wouldn't tell me the truth, so I was left wondering what the hell happened. She kept me in the dark and then got angry when I took it upon myself to find out what was going on."

"Maybe she had a good reason to leave you." Angel closed her eyes, her heart thudding sickeningly in her chest as she struggled to keep her voice even. Her hands were shaking, so she once again clasped them together on the desk in front of her.

He laughed out loud. "That's funny. I mean, freaking hilarious," he said bitterly.

"Is that such an impossibility?"

"What do you mean?" he questioned but then he continued. He knew. "Oh, yeah. Yeah, right. She thinks I've always been the one to walk away in relationships. I guess it was true. But this was different, and she didn't even give me a chance. Not really."

"Maybe she was afraid she'd become another notch on your bedpost."

"Maybe she should have *talked to me*," he spat bitterly. "We agreed to be honest. I meant it, but apparently, she didn't."

"What was your relationship based on? Possession of the unattainable? What was the attraction, really?"

He huffed loudly into the phone. "It was... everything about her. She was definitely high maintenance. But she was beautiful. Soooo, so beautiful."

"Maybe she wanted to be more to you than beautiful. Sometimes being a pretty possession isn't enough."

"How could she be a possession when we were both possessed? Every time I tried to get closer to her, I felt her pull further away. She seemed so strong. I never expected her to turn tail and run away."

"Did you ask her? If she was afraid, I mean."

"Not like I should have. That was my mistake. How do you think she was afraid of me?"

Tears pricked at the back of Angel's eyes and her throat tightened. She tried to breathe and then to speak. "Uh... most women

are afraid of beautiful men with the world at their fingertips, who
think they can have anything just by reaching out and taking it,
usually with no regard for the havoc they cause."

"Who said I was beautiful?" he goaded, and Angel had the
grace to flush.

"Maybe she is stronger than most; strong enough to think and
protect her heart; to put more worth on herself. Maybe she needed
to be more than a conquest."

He could hear the tightness in her voice, and his heart ached,
but he laughed bitterly. "She made me the conquest! In ways I
never expected or knew how to deal with—I've been hungrier than
I've ever been."

Angel laughed, but it was forced. So forced. "You poor thing.
Did you have a hard-on and nowhere to put it? I'm sure there are
hundreds of orifices at your disposal."

"What the hell are you talking about, Angel? I've had enough
of this ridiculous game! You know how fu—"

Angel quickly hit the hold button and ran a hand through her
hair. "Um… we need to take a quick break. I'll be right back."

She was trembling as she stood, leaning over the desk, bracing
herself on her arms, and wondering how in the hell she was going
to get through the next two hours. She wanted to leave and lock
herself away somewhere. Not in her apartment because now his
presence lingered. *How could I be so fucking stupid?* She sank into
her chair and buried her face in her hands.

Shaking, she pushed the button to connect the call off-air.
"Alex… just let it go. You agreed the last time we talked. It's
done."

She ended the call without letting him answer. What a coward,
but she couldn't listen to that voice without giving into the weakness he created.

It wasn't Alex that she hated. In fact, the opposite was true,
but love made her weak. Want made her weak, and she knew what

it meant to be hungry. It was the weakness she despised. She was unable to stop herself from feeling and falling... terrified of losing herself and all of the things that made her, *her*. She couldn't let it get to a place where she was absolutely unable to save herself. But maybe it was already too late.

*****

Alex stared down in disbelief at the now dark screen of his cell phone, her words echoing around him. Damn it to hell! It was bad enough that he hadn't been able to talk to her when he was worried sick, but to have her hang up on him?

"Alex, just let it go. You agreed the last time we talked. It's done." Angel's voice had been contrite and she'd hung up before he could answer. Alex was boiling.

He had said it, but it wasn't even fucking started as far as he was concerned! There was an ache in her voice and it called to an answering pang deep inside himself that he didn't even know existed before her. He'd never been this ready to take hold of someone in his whole goddamn life! Angel could *fuck* letting go!

"Ahhhhhhhh!" he yelled into the darkness of his apartment.

He stopped, torn between smashing the phone against the wall and rushing across town to confront her. The hand that wasn't holding his phone clenched, opened, and then clenched tight again. He walked back and forth in front of the windows in his great room, the lights of the Chicago night blinked for as far as the eye could see and the black inkiness of Lake Michigan along the East Side was the only interruption. It was raining hard, the droplets running down the windows in sheets. He wasn't sure if it was rage or the water that made the lights blur before his eyes. Alex's skin felt uncomfortably hot—burning—and his throat ached.

How does one woman turn your world completely upside down and leave you completely fucking reeling? He was still off-balance as much as he'd been the day after they'd made love. It took that beautiful, surreal night when they both surrendered to each other to show him the truth of what he wanted. Unlike anything he'd ever experienced, it left him stunned and elated, completely unprepared for how it ripped at his guts and filled his heart. For the first time, he felt vulnerable and completely helpless to change it. She owned him, but surprisingly, his eyes were finally wide open to possibilities he'd never believed existed.

When he called her later the same day and then the days after and she wouldn't take his calls, he was left wondering if it really had been a dream that was driving him insane. He'd barely been able to keep his head in work, thinking he imagined her scent on the sheets the next morning. Angel completely closing off after they had been so incredibly close left him bereft. So close; barely any words had been spoken, yet he remembered every breath she'd taken that night, every touch of her fingertips, her body's immediate response to his, and each searing kiss. And how he'd lost himself in the dream of her. She was a beautiful, real dream… and nightmare at the same time.

Alex looked down at his phone again in disbelief. His heart was racing as if it would fly from his chest and the skin of his face and neck burned like fire. As he stood motionless in the middle of the room, he couldn't breathe.

"What the hell is happening to me?" Alex ran a hand over his jaw and swept it across the back of his neck. His breathing labored in frustration; anger and something he couldn't define seething through his body. "That's it. I'm done with this bullshit!"

*****

Alex wasn't sure how, but minutes later he was driving through midtown toward KKIS. He didn't know whether or not he'd be able to get in, but then he hadn't stopped to think. Period. Alex shook his head as he realized where he was headed and why.

It had been three weeks since he'd laid eyes on her. Three weeks since he'd kissed her mouth. Three weeks since that night when everything he believed, all his carefully built delusions, had come tumbling down around him in a thunderous heap. He closed his eyes briefly and was brought out of it as the shrill cry of a horn blew in front of him. His eyes flew open in response, and he swerved sharply to avoid the other car. He sucked in his breath.

Holy shit!

He was at the complete mercy of his wants, his needs… his goddamned emotions. Steeling his resolve, Alex pressed his foot down on the accelerator, despite the weather, as thoughts of Angel raced through his brain. The first time he'd seen her at Home Depot and then, fatefully, at the karaoke bar in that amazing dress she wore their first night together. The way her mouth felt under his, the incredible passion they shared that last night, and his incredible need to protect her. All of it was stunning and unfamiliar. As foreign as everything else he'd been feeling.

Blinking his eyes twice and shaking his head to try to clear it, he muttered under his breath. "I am completely losing it."

It wasn't long before he was pulling up outside the radio station. Angel's newly repaired Lexus was still there, and his eyes flickered over the parking lot. It was well-lit, the new security cameras in several places, but it was still the middle of the night and it left Alex uneasy about her walking to her car alone.

The doors were locked and the lobby dark. Alex dialed Darian's number and waited for him to answer.

"Alex, are you back in Chicago?"

"Hey, D. Yes. I'm at the station. Can you come down and let me in?"

"Whoa. Think about what you're doing, man." Darian paused. His friend was acting completely out of character. It wasn't like Alex to run across town for a woman, especially one that wasn't giving him the time of day. "How long has it been since you've seen her?"

"Darian, don't fucking lecture me. Just... I only want to talk to her."

"Call her then. Don't ambush her. It might do more harm than good."

Alex sighed heavily as he leaned up against the white brick beside the glass doors on the front of the building.

"I have. I did. A few weeks back, she came to me in the middle of the night. I thought I was dreaming, but I wasn't. Angel came to me, and now she won't answer my calls? And, all of the other bullshit with that psycho-bastard? It's driving me fucking crazy." His hand raked through his damp hair. "Chris put me through to her tonight. It turned into a confrontation."

"Didn't it start that way, too?" his friend asked knowingly.

Alex ignored the question. "Blow me, Darian. I have to talk to her."

"Jesus, Alex. I've never seen you act like this."

"Yeah, I know. I'm sorry. I... care about this girl. Shit, it actually matters to me if she's hurt or if she has the wrong idea of what I'm thinking. It's complicated and I don't have time to go into it, but I'm completely out of my element," he ground out. "Truthfully, I don't know what the fuck I'm doing here other than I have to see her."

Darian sighed into the phone, feeling sorry for his best friend's struggle. "Is Chris still there?"

"I think so. There are two cars."

"I'll call her and have her let you in, but please wait until Angel is off-air. Let her finish the show before you go into the studio."

"Have you talked to her? While I was in London? Has she said anything about me?"

"Not much, Alex; only once. She wanted to know how you were. I'm sorry, man. Besides that one minute of concern, she's been all business and sort of closed off. She's working on some sort of charity thing, so I haven't really seen much of her other than the one night I sat in on the show."

"I see." His heart fell.

"I'll call Christine now. Alex, just—take it easy on her. For both your sakes."

Alex breathed in deeply, filling his lungs to their max capacity. "I don't feel easy, D. It's like I'm ready to explode."

10
Fine Line

THERE WAS MUSIC playing over the station intercom as
Alex walked down the hall following Christine after she'd let him
in. Wide-eyed and staring at finally seeing him in 'real life', the
young woman pointed out the direction of the studio where
Angel's show was being broadcast. Alex felt at a loss for what to
say to the girl. He was more concerned with seeing Angel.

"Thank you, Christine. It's nice to finally meet you." Alex extended his hand, and she shook it limply.

"Oh, yeah. Angel's mad at me for taking your call earlier. She
hasn't talked to me all night, and I'll probably get fired."

"Isn't Darian your boss?" He tried to concentrate on her
words but all he really wanted was to bolt through the door that led
to Angel. It was unsettling to be so uptight and worried. He was
Alex 'fucking' Avery, and he tried to remind himself of that fact
and also that Angel was a woman. And women had never been his
weakness. He was controlled, confident, and in charge of his environment. Usually.

Christine shrugged. "It's Angel's show. I don't know."

"Is she off the air yet?" He glanced at his Rolex and then looked anxiously down the hall again.

"She was on her last call when she basically kicked me out." Christine looked at the floor, clearly uncomfortable with the situation. "So, I guess I'll go. Can you tell Angel that Darian let you in? Please?"

Alex's brows dropped over his green eyes in sympathy. He was grateful for her help and certainly didn't want her to get in trouble. He pulled a business card from his wallet and handed it to her.

"If she fires you, give me a call. But, I'm sure she'll be too angry with me to wonder how I got in." His disarming smile had the desired effect, and the girl smiled back as she waved and walked toward the door.

"Lock this behind me. I hope you have your armor, Prince Charming. That princess has claws."

Alex's face twisted sardonically and he nodded. He doubted Angel would agree. "Yes. I have the marks up my back to prove it." He flushed as he realized how true that statement really was.

The hallway was long and the walls were lined with old records and CD's, autographed photos of musicians, and windows into the various sound booths. It was dark; only low lights in the corridor with the remainder of the studios deserted.

He walked toward the one Christine indicated and glanced through the window that made up the upper half of the wall. The door was on one side of the window, and Angel's back was to him. She was still seated at the desk as he looked upon her. There were some headphones thrown down on the desk in front of her, and she was digging in her purse for something.

Alex's pulse quickened, and he paused to watch her unobserved. She was so beautiful, her long hair like silk waves down her back over the dark burgundy top. There was a sad expression on her face when she looked down at the phone she'd just retrieved; her chest lifted as she sucked in a deep breath and bit her lip. The three weeks since he'd seen her felt like years. He drank in the sight of her like he'd never get enough, almost content to do nothing else.

Setting the phone down on the desk, Angel clasped her hands in front of her and rested her forehead on them. Alex hesitated only briefly as he struggled with how to approach her. He decided to give her what she'd expect from him: sarcasm and pith. It put him in control, and he didn't want to reveal how much the outcome of this confrontation mattered. He yearned to gather her close and kiss her until she was breathless, but he couldn't. Not until he was sure how she'd take seeing him. He didn't expect it to go well.

When Alex pushed the door open, she was startled and glanced up quickly.

"Looking for another call from me? You'll be disappointed," he pointed out dryly and regretted his words when anger replaced the surprise on her face. "I'm not a masochist."

Her eyes shot in his direction, taking in his casual elegance; offensively expensive designer jeans just tight enough to accentuate his delicious body, under a dark grey, long-sleeved V-neck that hinted at the smooth muscles of his chest, signature messy bed-head, and scruff on that incredible jaw. So fucking sexy it was criminal. Testosterone practically dripped off him in puddles. Her eyes dropped to the hem of the soft cotton shirt, her carnal knowledge of the happy trail just beneath it was enough to make her mouth go dry.

Angel forced herself to look away when her pulse quickened. She wasn't sure if it was the surprise of him being there or the memory of his chest brushing against her nipples that fucked her up so badly, but the reason was irrelevant. She was embarrassed by her body's violent reaction to the mere sight of him.

"Then what the hell are you doing here?" She grabbed her purse and shoved the iPhone into it, pointing at the door. "Leave!

Didn't the dial tone in your ear communicate well enough? I don't want to talk to you!"

Alex glared at her for a split second before he exploded.

"Too. Fucking. Bad, Angel! I want some goddamned answers! The last time we were together, it was incredible. So what the hell is going on?"

She hesitated briefly, unsure when he meant. Every time with him had been incredible, but the last time had been indescribable. Did he know it was real?

"Everything isn't always about what you want."

He almost laughed at that, thinking how he'd been willing to give her everything she'd asked for and more. He'd been fucking dying to do it.

"I've been worried sick about you! I told you I know what's been going on with Mark Swanson, and yet you leave me out here floundering!"

Angel said nothing, her eyes shooting fire at him.

"I want an explanation why you won't talk to me or keep me informed of what the fuck is happening! And more importantly, why you're running away?"

She turned from him and looked down at the purse in her hands, leaving Alex to bristle.

"It isn't fucking brain surgery. You're a smart guy—smarter than most, so figure this shit out already!"

They stood frozen in place, both of them heaving with the effort of their yelling, their eyes locked.

Alex softened his voice. "I thought we… were so connected. Why are you doing this? There's something tangible here," he said as he used his hand to indicate them both. "Is it only because of that prick? I took him down. He's ruined. He can't afford a pot to piss in, let alone a legal team. If he tries anything else, he won't find it easy to get out of it."

"Why? Why did you get involved? I didn't want you to!"

"Are you really asking me that?"

"This isn't about Swanson. It's about us. It isn't a game!" she shot back, her brown eyes flashing fire. "I just… It's not going to work."

"So you just slink away and cut me off? I never thought the great Dr. Hemming would ever run away from the damn truth! Please explain that to me. What exactly isn't going to work? I know you enjoy being with me." His tone was softer now, and when she answered, so was hers. "The fucking earth moves when we're together!"

"Yeah, well, there's more to life than getting off, Alex."

He shook his head and laughed bitterly. "This isn't about sex, Angel."

"Isn't it? I thought that was all you wanted in your *relationships*, and I use the term loosely," she murmured in defeat, using both hands to place invisible quotes around the word.

"You know damn well it was different with you!" He ran both hands through his hair as he moved toward her, his voice growing softer. "I'm not sure what I want right now, but it's not this abyss looming between us." He reached out a hand to run a single finger down her back. "Yes… with you it's more than amazing, but sex is only a vehicle. I can't lie, Angeline," he almost whispered. There was something in the way he said her name that pulled at her. "When I touch you, I'm… out of control." It was an admission he wasn't ready to make. "Once I start, I can't stop. It's never enough."

"Alex. Please. Then don't. Don't touch me."

He ignored her plea and both of his hands closed over her shoulders and ran down her arms.

He let out his breath as his forehead came to rest on the crown of her head. "Hmmph. That's like asking me not to breathe." His voice was back to the velvet tone, the one that coaxed and excited; the one that he used in their most intimate moments.

Why did his words melt her so easily? Why wasn't she stronger? Why *him*? Why was she helpless toward a man who could break her so easily? Angel closed her eyes as the shockwaves caused by his light touch ran along every nerve in her body.

"Do you think I'm such an idiot that I don't realize how many women you've said those same words to? I'm not good at this shit. I don't fuck around, and you make me..." She stepped forward until she was almost free of his hands.

"I make you what?" He didn't hesitate to take the opening she left hanging there.

She turned on him, twisting out of his hold and backing away slightly, her eyes accusing and the index finger of her right hand pointing in his direction. "You make me feel out of control, okay? I don't like not knowing what comes next or feeling like I have no choice. I don't like worrying about you when I can't do anything about it. I don't want to give a shit if you're fucking half the women in Chicago!" Her voice was frantic and louder as the words ripped from her. "I don't want to give a shit, Alex!" She stopped and centered herself. Alex could visibly see her regaining her control, and it was evident in the calm tenor of her words when she continued. "I can't keep this up and not care. I know this about myself, and that isn't what either of us wants. Is that what you want me to say? Let's just cut our losses while we still can."

Alex's jaw shot forward in protest as he pulled back. "It's too late! I am right there with you, and I'm not happy about it at all!" He was yelling at her. Alex didn't even realize it until Angel flinched in front of him, yet it didn't make him back down. "But it is what it is, Angel! I asked to spend time with you, so it is unfair to say I just want sex! And I'm not fucking half of Chicago and you know it. How have I made you feel like this? I've worshiped you!"

"Stop talking! Just shut up! This is pointless!" She put both hands up to the sides of her head and closed her eyes, unable to hear anymore or she'd give in. "You'll never convince me I'm any different than any of your other fuck buddies of convenience and that's fine! You never lied about how you are. I get it; it just isn't for me. I should never have gotten involved with you." She looked straight into his face and dropped her hands to her sides.

"Oh, right. You'd rather have a lesser man following you around like a puppy on a leash. Does Kenny get a hard-on on demand?" he spat in disgust. "I bet he never opens his fucking mouth without asking permission first. I'm sure that's immensely stimulating for you. Forgive me if I don't fit your mold."

"That's the point, isn't it? Swanson was just my excuse to end things! Neither one of us fits the other's mold, so where can this go? If amazing orgasms were all I wanted, you'd definitely be my go-to guy."

A few months ago, that comment from a woman would have pumped up his ego, but coming from this woman, one he wanted beyond all others, it left him as cold as ice.

"That's enough! Stop belittling the time we've spent together! What do you want from me? If it's for me to disappear, forget it!" Alex was more pissed than he'd been in a long time, and he couldn't believe his ears. Nothing had been defined between them other than the insatiable need they had for one another. "Weren't you listening when I told you that I don't fuck around? I'll be damned if I'll sit still for you doing that just to prove you're not in this!"

Angel was visibly shaking with the strength of emotions rushing through her. If he only knew she had no interest in anyone else and there was no way she was able to let anyone else near her now. Not while he was in her head… the memory of him inside her body, his kisses and his scent, his sounds, how much he made her laugh. She shook her head in disbelief. Alex wasn't the type to allow anything beyond lust, and she'd already lost her heart. She'd known this would happen the first time she heard his damn voice.

"Hmmph!" she huffed. "Doesn't Cole give you a play-by-play?"

Alex paused as the implication of her words sank in. She knew.

"Don't you know where I am and who I'm with every second? You know I'm not seeing anyone, but if I were—it's none of your business!"

"Like hell, it isn't!" he said. The words tore from him without his consent.

It wasn't possible to face him and still walk away. She should have known he wouldn't accept defeat with grace. Not without a fight and here it fucking was.

"It's just the chase you love, Alex. What would happen if I stopped running? Would you still want me?" Her eyes challenged him.

Alex didn't speak for a few seconds and just stood there staring into her face. "That's just it," he said softly. "You weren't running. We were together. I want to be again."

The blood drained from her face.

"No. Just… No. This will never work."

"Why do you fight something that feels so fucking good? God, I'm so pissed at you I can't stand it, but my cock is hard enough to pound nails! Do you think I'll let you twist me all up in knots and then just walk away? I can't. You. Want. Me, Angel." He punctuated every word and each one was like a knife piercing her heart.

She met his gaze without flinching, but her hand landed over her heart. "Yes… I do want. I want badly. Too much. And it does feel good. But, eventually, it will hurt like hell. I'm not willing to hurt like that. Happily ever after doesn't start off this way, no matter how earth-shattering the physical connection is between us."

Alex had moved and was leaning up against the desk, half sitting on its edge with his arms crossed over his chest.

"How do you know what will happen? You won't give us a chance." He looked at the ceiling and rubbed the back of his neck with one hand. "It already hurts like hell, doesn't it?" It wasn't a question she wanted to answer, but the pain in his voice was as vivid as the anger. "I can't even fucking believe I said that out loud," he said in disgust.

The words he said the night they made love in his apartment resonated in her head. *"Oh, Angel. Jesus Christ, it hurts so fucking bad! It hurts... so fucking bad."*

She could feel him behind her, even if he wasn't touching her. "You told me the first time we spoke that sex was what mattered in relationships. Remember?"

"I'm so sick of you reminding me of those words. I know what I said. Things change," he said softly with a shrug of his shoulders. "We have to take a chance or we'll never know, Angel. It's like anything else. The risk is directly proportional to the pay-off."

Her shoulders slumped, and her voice trembled. "This isn't a damn boardroom, Alex. One of us will bleed out." She knew who it would be because her heart was already aching over him. "You have to see it coming."

"At least I have the balls to try. I want you and no one else. I'm admitting it, Angel."

She sighed as her eyes closed tightly, feeling the fight drain from her body. *If only that were true.*

When she didn't answer, he rushed toward her and pushed her up against the glass window. Angel gasped in surprise as one of his large hands came to rest beside her head and his face stopped just inches from hers.

"Tell me what is going to happen now. If you can read the future, then just tell me what you're thinking." His hand came up to cup her face, the thumb of his right hand pulling on her lower lip and his pelvis pressing into hers.

"Alex, stop. You don't fight fair." She didn't push him away because she didn't have the strength. She inhaled his scent, his breath, and she craved his mouth on hers even though her mind screamed that they shouldn't be in this place.

"You don't expect me to, do you?" Alex repeated the words she said to him that first night they went to dinner. "I always fight to win. But, I don't want to fight right now."

"Then what do you want?"

His nose brushed hers and he loomed over her, his green eyes burning into hers. "You already know. I want you to trust me and to let me take care of you, to make sure you're safe. I want you to take my calls and let me take you out. I want to spend time with you. Just let it happen. That's all."

"Spend time—fucking?" She knew it would piss him off and shatter the intimacy of the moment. She needed to do it or she would only get weaker.

His handsome features hardened. "Stop saying that shit!" he said angrily, his grasp becoming more urgent. "Stop taunting me! You know what you're doing when you're doing it! You tease me until I can't stand it, Angel. If sex was all I wanted, do you think I'd put myself through this?"

"But…"

In frustration, Alex interrupted her and he shoved her up against the glass yet again, this time with more force, making it impossible for her to move even if she wanted to.

"Okay, yes! Do you want me to spill my goddamned guts? Is that what it will take? Then, yes!" he hissed, but never let her go, his lower body now pressing into hers and leaving her in no doubt he was as aroused as she was. "It's indescribable! I've never been so consumed with desire. Is that what you want to hear? Then fucking *hear it!*"

He pushed his hard length into the softness of her stomach, and Angel's fingers fisted around the material on the front of his shirt, her resolve quickly melting into nothing. She closed her eyes and turned her face away.

"Feel it. Yes! I want you, but you drive me crazy in a million other ways. I want to know you not just your body. I want to hear about your work, your family and friends, to sleep in your bed, and share meals with you. I want your voice calling my name in the dark. I want you to let me into your world, and for the first time in my life, I want to let someone into mine. And I don't want secrets between us. Christ!" he ground out.

The indescribable burn between them scorched them both. They were both furious as his body held hers in place, and they raged at each other with their words. Angel's chest was heaving at the magnitude of what he was saying. Alex's gaze dropped to her mouth and his thumb brushed against her cheek as she softened against his will. He ground his pelvis into the softness of her stomach again, and she gasped at the implication, her brown eyes challenging him fiercely, yet she was unable to speak.

"I'm not going to be a hypocrite and lie about the want, Angel. Even if every cell in my body weren't aching with it, you wouldn't believe me even if I said it weren't true."

"I know it is," she breathed, and suddenly, the energy changed as his mouth bent toward hers and he took it gently, licking her top lip and urging a response by nudging it with his full lower one. Her breath was hot and rushed from her chest in anticipation, her scent intoxicating and exciting Alex further.

He could feel her body relaxing as she gave into her own desire. Desire for him. The knowledge of it filled him with elation and something that went deeper. Control over her wasn't what he required, but he needed to know that she was as helpless to this thing between them as he was.

His hot breath rushed over her cheek as he bent to nuzzle against her skin, one hand starting to roam down her shoulder and collarbone and then ghosting over her breast, sliding down the side of her body, over her hip, and lifting one leg up. The fingers of her left hand curled into the front of his shirt and under it until they flattened on the hard muscles, curling in the stream of hair there, while her right slid over his shoulder to clutch into the hair at the back of his head.

"Clearly," he moaned as her hips surged into his, pressing his aching erection more firmly into the heat between her legs. He needed her to know how deeply he was affected because he wanted her to feel safe, to know he needed her, too, and that they were in this together. It was the only way she was going to open up, and he knew it. She whimpered softly into his mouth, and he loved it.

"Uhh… Alex."

The sound of his name falling from her lips in passionate surrender urged him on. "Do you feel how on fire I am for you?"

Her arms slid up over the solid muscles of his chest, around his neck, and into his hair. When she did that, he lifted her like she weighed nothing, to press her higher up on the wall creating more of the friction they both needed. "I need to hear you say it." His mouth hovered over her open one, refusing to kiss her until she admitted to the same need he had. "Tell me you want me, too."

"We can't be in the same room without wanting to rip each other's clothes off. It's not healthy." Her voice was breathless and her words broken. "God—you know I do."

"Mmmm…" His mouth took her lips roughly, passion and need filling them both. Angel opened her mouth to his invading tongue and clung to him as he pulled her closer because there was no thought of denying the raging need. They were both starving, the impact of the words they'd just exchanged feeding their desperation even more.

She broke the kiss and twisted her head away leaving him to bury his mouth in the side of her neck.

"It's been too long."

"It's like an obsession, Alex. It's not real."

"I don't care. Whatever it is… I want it."

His arms tightened and he lifted her up off of the floor, turning around toward the center of the room where the desk was situated. The computer and the soundboard prevented him from laying her down, so he perched her on the edge of the desk. Her legs came up of their own volation, wrapping around his, one heel digging into his muscled thigh. Alex's hands closed around her lower back to pull her hips flush against his groin and it was heaven.

Her head fell back and her mouth dropped open before it closed and her teeth emerged to bite her lower lip. She leaned back on one elbow and the other hand frantically pushed up the hem of his shirt, the hard muscles tightening as he sucked in his breath. She looked into his glowing eyes as he pulled her still tighter to his body, a low growl escaping his chest as another wave of lust flowed through him.

"I can feel your heat coming through all of these layers," he groaned, resting his forehead against her cheek before his mouth found hers in another hungry kiss. Their hips rocked into each other as they worked frantically at each other's clothing, hands clawing, mouths seeking the delicious skin that was bared. The position on the edge of the desk was awkward, and Alex longed for a way to get her skin on his and fast.

Panting, he pulled away from her and looked around for his discarded shirt on the floor. There was carpeting in the studio but it was low pile and rough. Angel watched in silent awe as his perfect body moved in front of her, laying the shirt out on the floor. The muscles on his back were so well-defined, his shoulders strong, and the biceps flexing in the shadowed light made her tremble.

Why is he so beautiful? Why does he take my resolve? She lifted a shaking hand and pressed the back of her hand to her mouth.

Angel made short work of her shirt as Alex undid the button and zipper on his jeans, exposing the grey boxer briefs he wore beneath, the strong column of his erection drawing her eyes, and she thrilled to see how affected he was. He fell to his knees in front of her where she was still sitting on the edge of the desk.

"Alex, we should stop." The words weren't easy for her to say; stopping was the last thing she wanted. Her voice was soft, barely audible.

He didn't say anything, just reached out a hand and pulled her forward roughly by fisting his hand in the front waistband of her jeans. His eyes were wild as he made easy work of the closing, and Angel said nothing nor did she make a move to stop him.

He pulled the material down her legs and let it drop the few inches from her feet to the floor. His hands closed around her thighs, kneading the silken flesh as he ran his mouth from the line of her neck up over her cheek, his tongue leaving a trail of fire behind it. His mouth opened over the skin of her shoulder and sucked hard, causing Angel to gasp, his teeth grazing her skin as his hands raked down her back.

"I thought I could get you out of my system, but every time we're finished, the ache comes back worse than before. You're all I think about," he whispered as his mouth moved to hover over hers, and Angel pushed off with her arm to sit up straighter, causing him to move back at the same time. The movement brought her torso in closer contact with his face, and she wound her arms around his head, her fingers tugging through his hair.

"Oh, God."

Alex's description had slammed through every synapse in her brain, and his whispered words were her very own thoughts. It was insane. It was indescribable and impossible. This insatiable longing was growing as if it had a life of its own, and she hated herself for not being able to resist. She hated that this one man's touch could reduce her to such clinging desperation.

Alex bent to kiss the luscious swell of her breast, visible over the sheer black lace of her bra, his fingers brushed across the crotch of her matching thong, and he moaned at the moistness he found there.

"Your body tells me you want this as much as I do. This is going to happen and *keep* happening. Stop fighting it."

Angel writhed against him as Alex's fingers closed around the lace and practically ripped it from her body as his lips crushed down on hers roughly. His hands moved up over her hips then her ribcage and around her back as he kissed her over and over. She clung to him, her mouth wild beneath his, as he quickly rid her of her bra. He was delirious as every inch of her skin was available for his eager hands.

Angel whimpered when Alex pulled his mouth from hers to let it travel down her body. "Uhhh…" She sucked in her breath when he pulled her leg up until her foot rested on his shoulder and she felt his scruffy chin rubbing on the sensitive skin of her inner thigh. His breath was hot as he blew out his breath and then, deeply sucking in the scent of her arousal.

She might have been embarrassed with Kenneth because sex with him had been awkward, but with Alex, it was a raw, animal need and neither of them could hide one damn thing from the other. He was intoxicated further. "Jesus… Angel, you don't know what you do to me."

After that, there were no more words. His mouth drove her insane as he licked and suckled her heated flesh. Angel couldn't stop the soft moans of pleasure bursting from her, and it drove

Alex on even more. His hands pulled her hips forward to give him better access so he could thrust his tongue inside her. He loved the way she sounded, the way she tasted, his cock aching like it would burst, so jealous of his mouth.

Looking down and seeing this beautiful man between her legs and getting into it so much had to be the sexiest thing she'd ever seen. He moaned deeply against her and sucked her flesh between his lips and flicked at it with the tip of his tongue. Her body tightened and clenched in response.

"Uhhh... Alex..." His name fell from her lips in a rush of breath. "Aaaleeeeexxx!"

A rush of satisfaction filled him. Wrapping his arms around her hips, he kissed her stomach and the underside of her breasts as she lay heaving in his arms.

"Yes, Angel. God, you're so beautiful when you come for me."

Her arms automatically wrapped around his broad shoulders, and he started to pull her from the desk, supporting her so she wouldn't crash onto the floor, and moving her as if she weighed nothing. He laid her down on the shirt he'd put down earlier and kissed her mouth softly.

"Mmmm... See how good you taste? I could do that every day and still want more, baby." He sat up on his knees between her bent ones and pushed the top of his jeans and boxers down. She couldn't help but reach for his cock as it sprang free, the silken steel hot as he twitched in her hand.

"Your cock is so beautiful." Her eyes ran up his body. It was perfection. "How many women have told you how beautiful you are?"

"Only one that matters right now." His hands ran over her knees and up her thighs as he bent to take a hard, pink nipple into his mouth. "Tell me what you want."

As he kissed her breasts, Angel heard the crinkling noise of the foil wrapper on a condom as he pulled it out of his pocket.

"I want you inside me." Alex kissed up her chest to her neck, over her chin and cheeks until he was looking into her eyes. "Without that."

"What?" He smiled softly and nuzzled her cheek again, throwing the packet aside. "I didn't hear you."

He was going to make her beg.

"You know you want to fuck me, Alex. Why must you make me beg?"

"Because I'm so turned on I'm going to explode, and I need to know you're just as fucked up by this as I am."

"Then do it," she breathed. "Now! I want you, too."

"Ungggg…" Alex groaned as he rubbed the head of his cock along her wetness. Just a little push and he'd slip inside. Angel arched her back, raising her hips in invitation to show him what she wanted. "Nnn… baby. I want you sore tomorrow. Every delicious ache will be because of me and you'll know it. You'll think of me every time you move."

Angel gasped and bit her lower lip as he pushed in hard and started moving in long, hard thrusts. She closed her eyes and pulled him closer, wanting his mouth on hers, but Alex wanted to watch his body slide in and out of hers. It was the most erotic thing he ever experienced as he looked down on her and plunged inside over and over again. He held her right leg for leverage as his thumb moved to rub her sensitive, still-swollen nub. Her mouth fell open in audible pants, and she closed her eyes. Her hair was strewn out around her head like a dark halo, and her pale skin glowed in the half-light.

He was lost. He knew it. For the first time in his life it was more than fucking, and if it ended, it would matter. He'd gotten a taste of her absence these past weeks, and he was determined to give her so much pleasure she'd be unable to deny what was between them. "Angel. Look at me."

Her eyes opened languidly and burned into his. "You feel so amazing. God, I'm... Uh, I'm going to come again."

"I'll make you come a hundred times if you'll let me."

He pounded into her harder, feeling his own orgasm build to the point of no return. When her back arched and her legs started to shake as she lost it, he fell on her body and kissed her deeply, his tongue thrusting into her mouth with the same intensity and rhythm as their mating bodies. Angel held onto him for dear life, taking him deeper and deeper, and needing to bring him more pleasure than anyone before her, she rocked her body into his and clenched around him. Even if this was all there was, if it was the last time, she needed to brand him like he was branding her.

"Uhh....Jesus, Angel!" Alex cried out as he finally spilled deep inside her. In an instant, he'd brought his mouth back to hers. Their mouths moved in perfection together, sucking, clinging, giving, and taking. She clenched around him, her own orgasm and the determination she felt to milk every last shudder from him, making her the aggressor. Angel moved on him until the very last jerk was pulled from him.

He kissed her again, not wanting to let her go, and he realized his back was on fire from the nails she'd raked over his back.

"Good God, that was incredible." He turned his face toward hers and rested his forehead above her ear. Angel nodded in agreement.

They were both panting and utterly exhausted as they came down, still wound up together.

Angel's hands ran over his back and up into his hair again, partly because she couldn't help herself and partly because she didn't want to let go of him. The knowledge unsettled her as she traced over the skin of his shoulders, now ripe with welts. She touched him again and he winced slightly. Did I do that? Regret surged through her that she could have hurt him.

"Why did you have to come here tonight?"

The silence was broken only by the soft strains of the syndicated music now playing over the airwaves, her softly spoken words hung like screams between them. Her voice was low and trembling, and Alex wondered if it was pain he heard there.

Alex's face was buried in the curve of her neck, a thin sheen of sweat covering both of their bodies. He rose up on his elbows and looked into her eyes. Angel's heels still pressed into his calves, and his cock, still embedded within her softness, had not yet lost its erection. He pushed his hips into hers, and her body answered automatically. They were calm and languid, studying each other with lust-clouded eyes. Seconds ticked by until Alex bent to take her mouth again, licking and teasing until she sighed and kissed him back. When he did pull back to answer, she caught his lower lip between her teeth and pulled gently.

Christ, she's the sexiest, most beautiful creature I have ever seen. The world could end around us and I wouldn't even know it was happening, he thought in wonder.

His right thumb ran down her cheek as he looked into her dark brown eyes and decided to answer honestly, no matter the cost.

"Because, I can't stay away. I don't know if I'd be strong enough to fight it even if I wanted to."

"You're the strongest man I know."

"Not when it comes to you."

Angel stared up at him, afraid to speak lest she say something that would expose too much. She was filled with strong emotions and struggled to reconcile what was happening.

She wanted him; there was no denying it. He created a need in her like she had never known, but he was still Alexander Avery. He could have any woman he wanted, and he could walk away at any time. She fought against letting his words woo her into believing there would ever be more between them... Wooed into wanting or hoping for more.

He nuzzled into her and made no move to pull out or move away and, instead, ran a series of soft open-mouthed kisses along the side of her face and then back to her mouth, to tease and coax. Angel's arms tightened around Alex which he took as acquiescence to the inevitability of their situation. He moaned softly and slid his tongue deeply into the warm recesses of her mouth. She opened and returned his ardor, kiss for sucking kiss. Alex loved how she felt beneath him, and her response to every touch was nothing short of miraculous. "It's always so magnificent. Each time, I'm left amazed at the perfection of every touch."

There was no denying the incredible pull between them. It was hard enough when he was miles away, but here, while they were in each other's arms, she'd never be strong enough to deny him.

Angel knew he desired her intensely. So there were two questions that needed answers and they threatened to explode over her like a bomb.

Where in the hell do we go from here? And will I be able to handle it when he walks away?

11

Co-habits

ANGEL WATCHED ALEX hand Cole her keys as she sat in the front seat of his expensive car and rolled her eyes in exasperation. She should have known the well-oiled machine would be running in spite of Alex's presence; or maybe, because of it. She was still stunned by his appearance and what had occurred after he got to the radio station, despite the closeness and familiarity she felt with him.

Unable to tear her eyes away, she searched for the brotherly similarity beyond the brief familiarity in the eyes, coloring, and line of the jaw. Cole was broader, but Alex was slightly taller, more commanding and polished. His confidence and sexuality oozed beyond his perfect features and lithe body. It was in the graceful, unconscious way he moved, the tone of his voice, how his eyes caressed her, and the strength in everything he did.

She inhaled deeply and leaned back against the headrest. After their session in the studio, he'd dressed and silently pushed her hands out of the way as she buttoned the front of her blouse, his eyes never leaving hers and silently daring her to protest when he took over the task. She didn't. She wasn't embarrassed or ashamed that she'd lost control or that her body quickened again when his fingers accidentally brushed the top swell of her breasts when he buttoned the top button. For once, she let someone else dictate her destiny, at least for the moment, and it felt damn good.

Angel wanted to acquiesce to Alex's wishes and let it all happen, to believe that this intense love affair could turn into something real. She wanted to forget her trepidation, melt into him, and just *feel*. She wanted... Alex. Always. Not just his body and the powerful, shuddering release he gave her, but the touch of his hand, his tender words, and, more than any of it, his love. Her eyes closed as her heart contracted at the realization.

The door opened and he slid inside, starting the car before glancing in her direction. They hadn't spoken a word after they'd made love, and his green eyes took in her mussed hair and swollen lips. One side of his mouth lifted in the crooked smile she loved. His hand reached out to hold the side of her face, his thumb brushing back and forth against her cheek.

"I asked Cole to take your car back to your place, but I'm taking you home with me. Okay?" His voice was like a silk cocoon that slid around her and squeezed, making it impossible to refuse. Even if he worded it like a question, Angel knew he wasn't asking permission.

Angel shifted in her seat as her hand came up to cover his. "Yes."

"Now, that didn't hurt so much, did it?" he teased, a sparkle coming into his eyes as they crinkled at the corners.

"Yes." She smiled back weakly. "You have no idea how excruciating."

His soft laugh vibrated around her as Alex put the car in gear before reaching down and lacing his fingers through hers. "I wouldn't bet on it."

They drove in silence, hands entwined, both lost in their own thoughts, afraid of ruining the moment with the wrong words.

Angel studied his profile, drinking in every line of his face as the
lights of the passing streetlights threw them both into shadow and
then light again. He looked tired, jet lag from the six-hour time difference and the lateness of the hour clearly taking their toll on him.
Angel's fingers tightened around his, and he lifted her hand and
pressed his lips in a slow sensual caress across the back of it. Her
body, even so recently sated, opened and throbbed as he recreated
the need once again. She said nothing as Alex deftly maneuvered
the car onto I-90, the soft music from the satellite radio coming
through in surround sound. Contentment took hold like a vice. She
longed to be closer and wondered if, when they reached his apartment and despite his exhaustion, his arms would come around her
and his mouth would find hers again.

Finally, she spoke, her tone soft. "Are they following us?"

Alex glanced at her quickly before turning his attention back
to the interstate. "Security will follow until we're safely in the garage of my building and the gate is secure behind us, yes. Then tomorrow, they'll have you, as usual."

Angel inhaled deeply. "I wish this were over. I'd like to live
my life without observation."

She watched his muscles visibly tense. "I don't feel comfortable discontinuing the surveillance yet. I'm sorry."

"But… you said Swanson wouldn't be able to—"

"I said he wouldn't be able to afford a decent attorney, but
he's probably enraged right now and that makes him extremely
dangerous. Most of his locations are closed, and he has no way to
cover the operational expenses of those that remain; his outstanding loan payments are more than his cash flow can handle, and he's
in default. Stupidly, he didn't protect his personal assets with an
LLC incorporation. Plus, his wife is divorcing him. Logically, he
has more pressing things to contend with besides hurting you, but I
can't take that chance."

Angel's brow crinkled. "That's why I didn't want you involved, Alex. Now, he'll just come after you. Do you have bodyguards?"

Alex's mouth quirked in the start of a smirk.

"What's so damned funny? You're just as much of a target as I am." She huffed, but inside she was heartsick at the thought of the break-in at his estate and what they did to Max.

"I can take care of myself."

"Well, I'm not some helpless damsel in distress, either. I can probably fight better than you."

A deep laugh burst from him, and Angel couldn't help but smile. "Humor me," Alex said.

Angel's smile faded. "Seriously, he might come after you."

"He knows my Achilles heel. If he wants to get at me, you'll be the target. So Cole and his team stay in place."

"Until when? The end of time?" She pouted, and he rolled his eyes.

"Until I say so. End of discussion."

"Well, if you would've stayed out of it then you'd be left untouch—"

Alex's irritation got the better of him, and he interrupted her impatiently. "Angel! If I'd stayed out of it, they would have succeeded the night they tried to kidnap you! The sooner you accept how serious this is, the better off we'll be!" he practically shouted.

She jumped in her seat, her eyes wide. "Not true! I kicked the shit out of that asshole!"

"If my guys weren't there, those scumbags would have chased you down. I don't care how well you fight, they would have succeeded!"

"It's just as dangerous for you!"

Alex sighed, his fingers tightening around hers, refusing to let her go as she tried to pull her hand away. "Maybe, in certain ways, but I'm more concerned about you."

Angel stared at Alex's profile, the muscle in his jaw working overtime, his expression stern. "Then let's make a plan to put him away," she said matter-of-factly.

Alex inhaled a deep breath. "Hasn't your lawyer-boyfriend explained the perils of entrapment to you? We have to wait until the bastard fucks up."

"But, if the offense isn't serious enough, he'll just be back at it after he gets out! Surely, some well-placed goading or loosening of the security won't qualify as entrapment."

Alex shook his head. "Forget it. It's too dangerous."

"I can't stand waiting day after day, always looking over my shoulder and worrying all the time! I can't sleep."

He sighed wearily. "I know. I have the same problem. Except tonight, with you beside me, I'll sleep like the dead. It's unlikely Swanson will try anything at Watertower. The security is too tight."

Angel's features softened as she looked at him, the love in her heart filling her up.

Alex glanced at her face briefly. "You're not arguing. Are you ill?"

A gentle laugh escaped her. "It's only because I see how tired you are. It wouldn't be fair to take advantage of your incapacitated state."

He chuckled again. "Keep telling yourself that, baby."

Alex pulled into the garage and parked, using his phone via Bluetooth to communicate with Bancroft and Cole. When he was satisfied that Angel's car was secure and they were safely ensconced behind the security gates, he walked around and opened her door. Proffering his hand before their arms slid around the other's waist, he placed a soft kiss on her temple as they walked.

"I don't have my pajamas," she said with a devilish grin.

Alex played along. "I guess I'll have to suffer through." He breathed in the scent of her perfume and shampoo, grateful she was safely wrapped in his arms.

The ride up the private elevator was spent in gentle nuzzling and soft kisses, his lips teasing and lightly sucking on hers, neither of them able to keep their hands off the other. Angel's fingers stroked the side of his face as his lips lifted and then returned to hers over and over. She wanted to melt into Alex's arms for tonight and forever, even if she was still apprehensive of the pain to follow.

His tongue snaked out to nudge her top lip before his teeth pulled gently on her lower one. "God, you taste good."

"I've missed you," she admitted unwillingly as the elevator dinged and the doors opened.

"It's been so unnecessary."

He reluctantly pulled away from her, and her hands slid from over his strong shoulders and down his arms, her fingers taking in the contours of the muscles that lay beneath the material of his shirt. His hand closed around hers as he led her into his apartment. There were low lights on in the entryway, further into the great room, and from the direction of the kitchen.

Angel's mind flashed to the last time she was here, when he made love to her unknowingly in a dream-like state. Her heart hammered as she followed him in, her fingers still threaded through his. It was as if Alex didn't want to lose contact with her, and she didn't protest. The prospect warmed her heart and a thrill coursed through her.

The stainless steel appliances reflected the light from the single light over the sink. The kitchen was spotless, even though he'd been gone, and a full bowl of fresh fruit was on the table. It occurred to Angel that Alex would most likely be hungry. It would be nine or ten a.m. in London. "Would you like something to eat? I can make an omelet or something."

He shook his head and pulled her into his embrace, holding her tightly against him. Angel let her head rest on his chest as her arms slid around his waist. His chest rose and fell beneath her cheek when he inhaled and expelled a deep breath. "No food. Water and then bed."

"You must be exhausted."

"Yeah. It's been 24 hours since I've slept."

Alex carried a glass of water as he led her up the stairs and into his bedroom with one hand entwined with hers. Setting it on the nightstand, he pulled off his shirt in one smooth motion and tossed it on the chair on the far side of the room near the window. This room, like the others, was dimly lit from a small light in the bathroom, and Angel's eyes followed his movements as he kicked off his shoes and opened his jeans.

"Do you want something to sleep in? One of my T-shirts?"

"Sure."

He smiled and tossed her one and then watched her as she undressed and turned her back to take off her lacy bra. Probably best, he thought. *Sleep. I need sleep.*

The shirt came to the middle of her thighs and she pulled the bedcovers down and crawled beneath them. Alex peeled his jeans and boxer briefs off and left them where they landed on the floor. Walking naked to his dresser, he pulled out some black silk pajama pants and quickly put them on before joining Angel in the over-sized bed.

"Fuck, I'm tired," he murmured as he sank into the several pillows at the head of the bed. She could feel the heat seeping from their bodies into the comforter. The Egyptian cotton sheets were so fine; they slid against her bare legs like silk. She itched to reach out and run her hand over the smooth skin and firm muscles of the man before her, even as her own eyes got heavy. As if reading her thoughts, strong fingers reached around her arm, gently pulling her closer and across his body. "Get over here," Alex commanded softly.

"Bossy, much?" She smiled into the dark, her breath bathing his chest in a warm rush as she settled her cheek against over his heart; both of them now in a tangled embrace of arms and legs.

"Ah! At last, she understands!" he teased. She heard the smile in his voice and smiled.

"Like I said, you're incapacitated. I'm taking pity on you for the moment, but don't expect it to last." His strong arms around her and the firmness of his chest beneath her head were what dreams were made of. Even as she goaded him, she was thankful they were both safe and together. Her heart filled to capacity and contentment settled around her more closely than the blankets, now warmly infused with the heat from their bodies.

His lips pressed to the top of her head and smiled sleepily. "Incapacitated, my ass."

Angel couldn't help a short laugh. Why did she have so much fun with this man? It boggled her mind how he could be so many things to her. "Nice ass."

"I think yours is nicer."

"Nah." She giggled openly now as she poked Alex in the ribs. "Yours is."

"Hey!" he protested. Before she knew it, he rolled over and her body was pinned securely beneath his, her thighs snugly cradling his hips. "Angel," he mused before his lips traced up from her shoulder to the gentle slope of her neck and along her jaw. "Must you argue with me about everything?"

"Not everything," she said softly, unable to stop herself from rocking her pelvis into his now apparent arousal. Her hands ran up his back, kneading the muscles.

"Wanna argue about how incapacitated I am?" he asked seriously, pulling his head up and searching her face. He knew he'd get no argument. The backs of his fingers brushed her cheek while his other hand traced her temple on the opposite side of her face. His hips moved against hers then, mirroring her movements. She gasped and closed her eyes, shaking her head. "No?" he whispered, his voice was thick with desire by now. "Good, then kiss me," he commanded as his mouth hungrily latched onto hers.

*****

Alex's heart raced. It was pouring rain and very dark. He couldn't see much, save for brief seconds when lightning lit up the night sky, followed by the loud crack of thunder.

"Angel!" he called. "Angel!"

She screamed in the distance, and his heart constricted with panic as he broke into a run toward the sound of her voice. His ears strained to hear her, but all he could hear was the rain, thunder, and the slap of his feet on the wet pavement. Alex stopped, panting; his head snapped around and he turned, searching for some clue to which direction he'd find her when her scream split the air.

"Ahhhgggggg! Stop! Please, stop!" she begged. She was sobbing and her voice broke. "No! Please let me go!"

"Shut up, you little bitch! I will kill you and then fuck you, but either way, I'm going to fuck you!"

The expletive was followed by another scream, scuffling and the sound of someone falling against the pavement.

Alex started running, taking a right down an alley between two old brick buildings. As he came closer, he could hear a man grunting and Angel choking. He felt like he was drowning; unable to catch his breath, his lungs were ready to explode.

The alley seemed to stretch on forever, then finally, he saw them. Angel's arms were clawing at her assailant but she could only reach his chest, her hips bucking underneath his heavy weight as she tried to fight the man off. One arm was straight, his hand wrapped around her throat, while he sat on her hips to hold her down. His free hand ripped at her blouse.

Alex was paralyzed, his lungs unable to function as he begged his legs to move.

"Angel!" he croaked. He wanted to save her, he wanted to kill that piece of shit bastard, and he wanted to die himself. "No! Get away from her!" Her arms dropped to her sides, and she stopped struggling as she lost consciousness, but the man continued ripping open her blouse and pushing up her skirt. "Aaannnggeeellll!" Alex screamed in agony.

Alex's hands flailed in front of him, searching in the dark; they pushed across the sheets. The bed was empty, and he rolled over onto his back and sat up. "Stop!" He was panting heavily, his heart hammering, as if he'd run five miles in a full sprint. "Angel?" he gasped.

Angel suddenly appeared as a shadowy figure in the bathroom doorway, quickly walking to the edge of the bed. "What is it? Are you okay?"

Alex's hand wiped at the perspiration on his forehead as his chest rose and fell. He pulled up his knees beneath the covers and leaned both arms on them before dropping his head between them. He felt sick with panic at what he'd dreamed. It could happen; it almost did. "I can't fucking breathe."

Confusion wrinkled Angel's brow, and her hand reached for his shoulder, worried at his words and the anxiety in his voice. "Alex, what is it?"

"Where were you?" he asked.

"Just in the bathroom." Her hand moved in the direction she'd just come from. "I was only gone for a minute."

He sighed again and nodded, still seeming a little disoriented.

"What's the matter?" she asked again, her voice wary. She began to knead the muscles beneath her fingers. "You're scaring me."

Alex moved to the edge of the bed, reaching for her arm and pulling her close. He buried his face in the side of her neck and the curtain of her silky hair fell around his face, her scent assaulting his nostrils. His arms wound tightly around her body to reassure himself that she was safe.

Angel wound her arms around his shoulders and head as she kissed the side of his face in a series of light kisses, and she could feel his heart beating frantically, pounding against her ribcage. "What is it, sweetie?" Her heart filling with a mixture of love and pain, she ached for him.

"Four hours ago you hated me; now you're calling me sweetie?"

"Well, four hours ago you were yelling at me, but, you know I don't hate you," she said against his temple. Her fingers threaded through his hair and curled, moving over his scalp in a calming motion.

"I was yelling out of frustration. I'm sick of you denying what's between us. I just wanted you to admit it." He lied, unwilling to scare her with the implications of his dream.

Angel closed her eyes as tears pricked at the backs of her eyes. "I didn't want to accept it."

"Why?"

"I told you earlier. Let's not rehash it, or you'll only yell again." She tried to tease him, but it didn't quite make it into her tone.

"Hmmph." Alex made his best attempt at a laugh he didn't feel.

"Stop trying to change the subject. Was it a bad dream?"

"It doesn't matter." He pulled back and searched her face, using both hands to brush her hair back, his green eyes glistening black.

"Tell me."

Alex shook his head. "We both don't need nightmares. Come back to bed."

They stared at each other, both of them unable to stop touching the other. Finally, she nodded and he scooted back, holding open the covers. They were both naked; even though they'd intended to sleep, somehow their clothes ended up lost somewhere between their passion, the tangled sheets, and the floor.

Angel slid in next to Alex, and he pulled her back against him, one arm sliding under her head and the other wrapped firmly around her as their bodies spooned together. He drew in a deep breath and pressed his lips to her shoulder, finally relaxing when she threaded her hand through his.

"Jesus, it feels so good to be with you like this."

"Mmmm... I was thinking the same thing."

"I think you should move in." The unexpected words left Alex as stunned as they did Angel.

"Wh... What?" Incredulity laced her voice. She laughed nervously before finally finding her words. "Are you insane? What'd you do with Alex?"

"This isn't a joke, Angel. I want you with me."

"How'd we go from 'I don't want to see you at all to living together?" She let him hold her, enjoying the contentment that washed over her at being so openly possessed by him. It was an amazing feeling. Too amazing.

"The same way I went from dickhead to sweetie, I suppose."

Angel smiled and shook her head.

"You don't have to do that. I'll let Cole and his band of merry men tail me without protest."

"You're right; you will. But I still want you to move in. It's not just about keeping you safe."

"It's most of it."

"I'm not saying that I don't want to protect you; I do." *Mostly, so I don't lose my fucking mind*, he thought. "But, there's more to it, and you know it."

Angel's heart constricted, knowing it would only add to the pain if he decided he didn't want her. "Can't we leave things as they are? I'll let you take me out, blah, blah, blah, but only after Swanson is out of the picture. Before that, I want to keep it behind closed doors."

"What? Am I mentally challenged now?" he murmured in disgust. "I know you want to keep me at arm's length, so stop trying to pass it off as something else."

"Apparently, I suck at it." Her arm pressed down on his.

"Babe, I don't want to keep it quiet. I want a normal relationship."

Angel froze. "Normal for me or normal for you?"

"For you." Her eyes shot to his, and he frowned at the doubt he found there. "Are you ever going to believe me? Give me a chance to prove it to you."

Angel nodded, seeing his sincerity and allowing herself to give in to the hope in her heart. "You don't have to club me over the head and drag me off to your cave to have a relationship with me."

"Whatever."

"Where I come from, 'whatever' translates to *fuck off.*"

He laughed. "Every instinct tells me to do whatever I have to do to protect you, and it would be easier if you'd cooperate. Mark Swanson would know you're not as vulnerable if you're with me." He spoke against her shoulder, his warm breath rushing over her skin. Alex enjoyed the closeness and the feeling of release from the worry. She was here, and he knew she was safe. "But, more than that, I just want us together."

Angel's heart thrummed and swelled. "Alex, I need to make him do something criminal. It's the only way I'll have any peace. Making myself unavailable won't accomplish it."

He sighed again, but said nothing as her fingers traced the soft hair on his arm. He enjoyed her touch too much, and though the thought crossed his mind the morning after she'd come to his apartment, now he knew it. He was in love. There was no other explanation for the desperateness, the elation, the worry, or the insatiable desire he felt for her. He couldn't wait to see her, to get his arms around her, to talk to her, to please her.

"I want to see you. I really do." Alex's arms tightened, and he kissed her shoulder and then the side of her neck, sending shivers through her whole body. "But, I have to put this guy away. Please help me."

"I will if you move in."

"I'll move in after it's done. Doesn't that make more sense? It will drag on too long if I make it too difficult for him. I just want it over."

"Angel, you're asking me to risk your safety. That's impossible."

"I'll be careful. I'll have Cole's team... and you."

The seconds felt like hours as she waited for his answer. Alex waged an internal struggle, the protectiveness he felt battled with his need to have the threats behind them so they could concentrate on each other.

"Okay, we'll make a plan. But what I say goes. No arguments."

*****

"Mr. Avery?" Mrs. Dane's voice broke into Alex's thoughts as he worked to reconcile the coming year's budget of one of the Avery properties. He had ten more to get through. Even having the CFOs submitting them in rounds, this time of year was always hectic. It didn't help that his head wasn't in the game. "The travel arrangements have been made."

"What about the meeting?" His hand ran over his face and then began tugging his tie loose. It was close to six and Mrs. Dane would be leaving soon.

"Yes, sir."

"Good. Have a good night. I'll see you in a few days."

"You, too."

The week had dragged. After last weekend when he and Angel had been locked away in his apartment, spending most of the time making love, watching movies, and cooking late at night by candlelight, he hadn't been alone with her at all since. Every second of it had been glorious and flew away at the speed of light. He especially loved playing Rachmaninoff on his Fazioli piano at her prodding, enjoying that she'd wanted to hear him play, since it was something he loved so much. The piano was one of his most prized possessions, and he found it even more beautiful with Angel draped across the mahogany, her dark eyes shimmering with the candle's reflection as he played for her. His grandfather had it handmade in Italy as a reward after he'd been accepted to Julliard. It was during that time, as he played on autopilot, that they had conceived their plan. He still wasn't certain it would work and part of him prayed it wouldn't.

Alex's heart fell as he threw the report on his desk and pushed away from it. They'd agreed to compromise. Angel wouldn't move in until after Swanson was caged, but they were spending a lot of time together. The best part of his day came when they were together. Every minute he spent with her, he fell more deeply in love. It was a course he never expected his life to take, but he found himself seriously thinking about the future, introducing her to his family and meeting her father. He huffed. His mother would do fucking cartwheels.

Their plan meant they would be seen out together often, making it obvious they were a couple. That was the easy part. Surely, that bastard would know that if he went after one or the other, he'd injure them both, and that was tantamount to making it work.

Alex made his way out of his office, carrying his suit jacket over his arm and his briefcase in the other hand. The pounding in his head echoed his footsteps as he made his way into the elevator and then into the dark garage. Angel wouldn't tell him what her plans were for the early part of her evening, only admitting that it was a surprise. Not knowing where she was worried him more than it pissed him off, but she assured him that she'd keep Cole in the loop. He sighed as he got in his car and drove into busy, Friday evening traffic.

"Fucking traitor," Alex muttered. How Angel had converted Cole from loyal employee, never mind brother, to keeping her secrets, he'd never know.

So, absent Angel meant he could go see Max at his parent's estate, call Darian, or maybe Allison and Josh would meet him for dinner downtown. He pulled out his phone and dialed his sister's number.

"Hey, Alex." Allison answered.

"What are you and Josh doing tonight? I thought we might get a bite to eat."

"I can't tonight, but Josh is at loose ends. I'm sure he'd love to."

"What are you doing?"

"Nothing special. Girl time. How are things going with Angel?"

"We're… really good." The grin that settled on his face wasn't surprising.

"Hmmm," Allison mused. "Methinks the boy has finally met his match."

"I agree."

"Really?"

Her incredulous tone made Alex grimace. "Don't sound so surprised. I'm not made of stone."

"I was beginning to wonder if anyone would ever get through to you. I'm glad to see things have changed."

"Have you talked to her about me?"

"Not about you. She helped me secure the talent for the benefit, so of course, we've had contact."

"But, recently? Have you told her you're my sister?"

"Not yet, but I think one of us should."

"I know. I don't want her to think the benefit was all a setup, but I'm not sure how to bring it up."

"It was just a coincidence. I'd talked to her before I knew you were seeing her."

"Yes, well…" Alex didn't feel up to explaining the entire situation, but he was concerned Angel would automatically assume the worst, given the secrets they'd already kept from each other.

"It's the truth, so she'll believe it," Allison said simply.

"We'll see."

"What has Angel told you about the benefit?"

"Not a lot, but I had Mrs. Dane acquire tickets for us, so I hope she'll attend with me. I have to support my little sister's causes, you know."

"Uh huh," a wariness crept into Allison's voice. "What's Angel doing tonight? You didn't mention her joining you for dinner."

"She has the radio show later but something to do first. She said it was a surprise."

A small giggle escaped Allison.

"Why is that funny?" Alex asked, but Allison ignored him.

"Call Josh if you're lonely. And, what about Cole? It could be fun for all of you to get together."

"Cole's working, but, sure, I'll call Josh. Maybe Darian."

"Alex, I'm late, so I gotta go. See ya later. Love you."

"You, too."

*****

It was dark in her apartment and Alex lay on Angel's bed, enjoying the fact that her scent permeated the air around him as her voice filled the room as she counseled her callers. He was showered and was lying back against her pillows, a fluffy white towel wrapped around the defined muscles of his waist.

"My husband said he doesn't love me anymore," the woman whined.

"Why would you want to be with someone who says he doesn't love you? You need to take more pride in yourself."

"But, I love him!"

"Ugh! Sally, you need to love yourself. How can you expect to command respect when you don't have any for yourself?" Alex could hear the undertones of Angel's chagrin at the woman's lack of balls. His lips curved up in a smile, anxious for when she'd finally be home and in his arms.

Cole had the night off and Bancroft would be following her home. Despite Angel's pleas to leave her vulnerable, Alex refused to do so unless it was contrived, designed to support the illusion, but never for real. His chest tightened. This next week would be the test and he was worried sick.

12
Cat and Mouse

ALEX GAZED DOWN at the woman lounging on the bed. She was so fucking sexy; it was all he could do to finish dressing. Her bare legs were tangled in the sheet, the top of it leaving the swell of her breasts open to his view, but it was her face that drew him in the most. Her hair was tousled, her lips parted and swollen, her dark eyes soft and beseeching. His lovemaking had certainly left a stamp on her, just as he'd wanted it to do.

"Angel, don't look at me like that," he murmured. "I'll never leave."

Angel bit her lip as she watched him button his cuffs, turn the collar of his deep merlot-colored shirt up, and slide the striped tie around his neck.

"I don't want you to go," she said with a small shrug and soft smile. It was a simple statement but loaded with meaning.

His hands stopped what they were doing as he studied her face. "You want to catch this bastard, don't you?"

She sat up, letting the sheet completely fall to her waist. "Right now, it doesn't seem as important." Her heart tightened. Alex was meeting with Mark Swanson to put their plan into play.

He sat down on the edge of the bed next to her, his warm hand cupping her satin-soft cheek, as he tried to ignore all of the creamy skin and luscious curves open to his view. "It will be important to you tomorrow. You talked me into this, so let's just get it over with, shall we?"

Angel wasn't meeting his eyes in her effort not to show too much emotion, but she swallowed hard as she nodded in his palm. Shimmering brown eyes finally lifted to meet intense green ones.

"Hey," Alex murmured. "I won't let anything happen to you."

"I'm protected. I have Cole and his monitors, Bancroft and his guys. It's you—"

"I'll be fine," Alex interrupted. "He won't do anything in public, babe." One hand brushed the top of her breast as the other pushed her hair back. "Stop trying to distract me."

"Could I?" Her chin lifted as she sought Alex's mouth with her own. He kissed her back softly but pulled away when the kiss became more heated. Angel was less willing to break contact, her mouth clinging to his.

"Not today, honey. This thing is burning in my gut, and I need to have it done so we can move on." He had plans, plans for their future, to take her to Missouri so he could meet her dad, to introduce her to his family, to lay it all on the line and admit his feelings. He couldn't do that when they were both worried and preoccupied. "I don't like seeing you so worked up."

Angel blinked at the burning behind her eyes and tried to lighten the conversation. "That's not how it seemed last night." She tried to smile and tease, but her lips trembled as her brow knitted. Alex saw her struggle and rested his forehead on hers, his hand moved back to cradle her head, his thumb stroking the side of her neck, his fingers twined in the soft strands of her hair. She was pensive, and he saw right through her ploy.

"Angel," he breathed. "I won't be far away. You know that, don't you?"

She tried to push down the sob that threatened to erupt from her chest and kept her from speaking. Her forehead fell to his strong shoulder, and she inhaled the spicy scent of expensive cologne, fine soap, and Alex. She wrapped her arms around his neck and slid her fingers into the hair at the back of his head as he gathered her close. Alex loved the possessive feeling of her embrace, and his heart ached with hope that maybe she did love him in return. He held her tightly against him and waited for her response, content to have her nestled in his arms with her heart beating against his.

"It's not fair. You'll get to see me, but I can't see you." She winced at the whining undertone to her voice.

"The monitors are hardly as satisfying as holding you like this. Is that what you mean?"

"It's better than nothing."

"When you're home, I'll only hear you." He turned his face and kissed the side of her neck beneath her ear, his breath washing her skin as he spoke. "Please don't take chances. Go about your normal routine, but don't take unnecessary risks. Promise me."

He felt her body expand with a deeply inhaled breath. He knew her well enough to know her determination would give her undue bravado and make her do things she shouldn't. "Angel? Promise me."

"Ugh." She pulled out of his arms and shook her head. "You just said you want it over with!"

"I do." Alex got up and finished tying his tie and then shrugged on the jacket to his dark grey Armani suit. "But not if it means taking stupid chances," he said sternly. "I mean it. It's bad enough that I'm deliberately going to piss him off. If, or rather when," he amended, "Swanson comes after you, I want it to be in an environment and situation we are in control of."

Angel scowled at him. "No shit. We already discussed this."

"Right, so why do I have the feeling you're going to try to egg him on without telling me, at a time or place that I'm not prepared for?"

"That's what you're doing! So, why can't I? The longer it takes…" *the longer we have to be apart.*

"Angel, just stick to the goddamned plan! If you deviate, we won't be in place to protect you. I'm already against this. I'm not taking my life in my hands, I'm just pushing him a little to get him moving."

"You don't know him. He's a deviant, capable of anything. Just… Please be careful." Her voice shook with emotion.

The sorrowful look on her face softened Alex's temper and the corner of his mouth lifted in a half smile. "Piece of cake."

She watched him put on the gleaming Rolex watch that was his only piece of jewelry, pick up his wallet and car keys and shove them in the pocket of his pants. He already had his shoes on, and it would be only moments before he walked out the door. "Are you at least taking Cole or the others with you?"

"If I take any of them in with me, it blows their cover and leaves you vulnerable. Bancroft will be nearby, okay? I won't take undue chances, trust me." He sat down on the bed again, unable to resist touching her one last time before he left. Alex sighed, his fingers tracing the side of her face and pushing a soft, curling tendril behind her ear. He couldn't seem to keep his hands off of her.

"The worst part of this whole thing is I won't be able to touch you. You're so damn beautiful." His index finger curled and nudged her chin up as he leaned in and kissed her softly on her mouth. His lips lifted and then brushed over hers again, his tongue coming out to nudge her mouth into play. The soft sigh that was elicited in response as her fingers curled around his forearm and into the hair at his nape made it difficult for him not to deepen the kiss, especially when it was evident that was what Angel wanted.

Alex's hands held her head, both thumbs brushing her cheek-bones as he gave in and kissed her deeply, his tongue finally parting her lips and laving against hers. Angel's response was explosive, and his body instantly reacted. Alex softened the kiss again, know-ing he didn't have time to make love to her like he wanted. When she pulled his lower lip into her mouth with her teeth, he pulled away with a reluctant groan. "You don't make leaving easy."

"Get used to it," she whispered against his lips as they left hers for the last time. Alex smiled brilliantly at her as her hand dragged down his arm to capture his hand as he rose from the bed.

Alex looked down at her and briefly touched her chin with his fingertips. "This thing between us... It's real, okay?"

"Okay." Angel's hand tightened around Alex's fingers.

"Mmmm. Honey, I really need to go. Mrs. Dane has it all set up, and Bancroft is waiting for me downstairs."

"Okay." Angel flopped back against the pillows and rolled onto her side.

"Make sure to call Cole and give him your itinerary for the day."

"Already done. I spoke with him last night on my way to the station."

Alex's eyebrow raised and he smiled. He'd expected more re-sistance from her. "Are you going to tell me what you were doing before that?"

"Nope." Angel smiled slyly and shook her head.

"I'll just ask Cole."

"He won't tell you. He promised."

"We'll see." Alex was pleased that Angel and Cole had be-come friends though he did worry that Cole might fall in love with her as easily as he did. She was irresistible and brotherly love only went so far.

"Yes, we will," she retorted smartly, her lips lifting in a grin.

"Okay." Alex hovered in the doorway of his bedroom, not wanting to leave her. His heart tightened inside his chest as he looked at her. Their eyes met and held.

"I'll miss you." *I love you*, her mind screamed.

"Me, too. I'll call you tonight, baby." And with that, he was gone.

*****

As Alex walked into the swanky gentleman's club, the fine hair on the back of his arms and neck stood on end. His jaw set and determination settled on his features as he made his way toward the table in the back where the other man and his entourage were waiting. It was an expensive, members-only establishment, and the atmosphere reeked of money and unspoken possibilities. Anything could be had between these walls: drugs, kinky sex, and assorted fetishes, all for a price. The air smelled of cigar smoke and the haze it created blurred the low lights that glowed red. The bass from the music boomed, and as almost-nude women danced, others waited tables in various states of undress.

Alex never considered himself an actor, but he was adept at adopting a façade when needed. Bluffing was the name of the game and it was a skill he'd honed to a fine edge during the past few years while at the helm of Avery Enterprises. He usually loved the cat and mouse games in business as much as he had enjoyed them with the opposite sex, but this was different. The stakes were higher.

He cleared his throat as he approached the table. "When my personal secretary told me this was the venue you chose, I thought she was joking. I should have known better." His lips thinned and his brow rose. A sleazy setting for a sleazy bastard, he thought with disdain. "It is rather fitting, I suppose."

Mark Swanson rose and offered Alex his hand, the four men gathered on either side of him rising. Alex inwardly balked but shook it firmly and then sat down. "How do you mean? I like to surround myself with beautiful women."

"It's low rent and distasteful," Alex said without qualms and with barely hidden amusement as he took a seat opposite.

A scowl replaced the swarthy smile on Swanson's face at the smooth delivery of the slam, but it left Alex nonplussed.

"Do you have an aversion to beautiful women, Mr. Avery? Surely, you are a member here as well?"

Alex laughed shortly. "I admire beautiful women as much as the next man, but I never have to pay for sex, and this is no place for business." He held up his hand dismissing the waitress without a glance before she barely reached the table. "I had to acquire a membership just for this meeting."

"You've effectively ruined my business, so I assume you have another reason for this meeting. Are you afraid Dr. Hemming wouldn't approve?" Mark Swanson smoothed his shiny hair back, and Alex's mouth tightened: the two men on either side of him shifted and one of them crossed his meaty arms across his chest.

"Hardly. In any case, Angel is not up for discussion. I'm well aware of your intentions with respect to her. I thought I'd made that painfully obvious."

Swanson's face hardened. "So, it wasn't just good business," he stated. "You ruining me, I mean."

Alex's expression twisted, his brows drawing together sardonically and he scoffed at the other man. "Dirty laundry is way out of our scope, and we never bother with companies of such small... consequence. No, I think we both know that my interest here had little to do with business." He ran a hand down the front of his tie, closed his mouth, and watched, his hard gaze never flinching from his adversary's. "You threatened my girl, invaded my home, and destroyed my property. You needed a lesson in limits."

Mark Swanson was impeccably dressed, as were the men surrounding him, but he still had that greasy air about him that made Alex's skin crawl. Knowing what that bastard was capable of, it was all he could do not to fly across the table and rip his head off. His fists clenched at his sides as he struggled to maintain the control he needed to keep focused on the outcome he wanted.

"I could kill you for what you've done to me."

"Likewise," Alex answered. The cold steel in his voice married with the one word response stunned the other man, his surprise showing clearly on his face.

"I hardly think some cross words at your girlfriend equate to the way you've ruined my entire life."

"You did it to yourself; I just aided and abetted. Let's not insult each other by pretending we don't know exactly what the other has done."

A slow, smug smile spread across Alex's handsome face as he regarded his enemy with disgust. "I'm a man of honor, and I thought you should know that every move I made was calculated and very deliberate. I take full responsibility for my actions while you hide behind the skirts of your mafia connections. Although now, after what you've done to your wife's daughter, I'm honestly surprised you're still breathing."

The other man's face swelled and flushed as the blood rushed to his head, his features contorting in rage, and the men at his sides shifted uncomfortably. It was apparent that Alex's words struck a nerve. Satisfaction, mixed with trepidation at what Mark Swanson would do to retaliate, rushed through him. He took a calming breath and reminded himself that this was all a well-staged part of the plan.

"I took you down with no regard to financial loss or gain and, make no mistake, I'd do it again without flinching. There is nothing more important to me than Angel. Touch her again and I may have to sink to your level. There will be no place you can hide from me. Is that clear?" He coolly glanced at his watch and rose from his seat, effectively dismissing the other man without so much as a glance in his direction. "I have a plane to catch, so if you'll excuse me?"

With a flick of his finger, Swanson motioned for his men to move on Alex.

"Are you really that stupid? As sleazy as this joint is, it's still a public place." With that he turned and walked from the club, pulling his sunglasses from his breast pocket in preparation for the bright Chicago day and its stark contrast with the dark confines of the club. The scent of sex, sweat, smoke, and alcohol permeated the air and Alex wrinkled his nose in distaste.

"Hey, baby, wanna private dance? I could make you feel real good." A buxom blonde leaned down, smiling, from the stage, her overly long, red-nailed hand raking down the sleeve of his fine wool suit as he passed. Alex continued out of the club without a pause or a word to the woman.

Bancroft was waiting in the back of the limousine when he slid inside. "How'd it go?" the he asked.

Alex sighed and shrugged slightly. "We'll see. I hope it registered that I'm going out of town. That slimy cocksucker! It was all I could do not to rip him apart."

Bancroft instructed the driver to pull out and then radioed the other car waiting in the parking lot. Alex glanced out the window, his elbow resting on the door while his hand plucked at his lower lip. "Well?"

"We're definitely being followed."

"Let's hope they take the bait. I want this bullshit over with."

"It looks like they have, sir." He watched his boss stare out the window, his face somber, a frown knitting his brow. "The boys are with her. They're taking shifts."

Alex nodded but didn't speak.

"I have a driver ready to meet you in Milwaukee."

He hated that he had to go to this extreme ruse to make sure Swanson believed he left town. Alex's voice was low. "This is going to be a fucking long three hours."

"It's necessary, sir." Bancroft studied his boss as he looked out the window, noting his jaw muscles flexing.

"I know, but it would be easier to just run through O'Hare— in one terminal and out another."

"They'll be watching. We have to solidify the illusion."

"But flying to Milwaukee and driving back... I don't want to be out of town that long."

"Sorry to remind you, sir, but this was your plan."

"I realize that, but I don't have to like it." Alex scowled at having the obvious pointed out, and Bancroft thought better of expounding on the matter. "It might not even work. It's probable Swanson would realize that I'd never leave Angel vulnerable, no matter what my obligations might be."

"Forgive me, Mr. Avery, but Dr. Hemming... has become much more than a... pleasant distraction, am I right?"

Alex's brow raised in introspection. "She's always been more than that."

"Cole just texted that she is with your sister at Paddy O's for lunch."

"Great. That's just what I need, two of them to worry about. Christ!"

Alex's mind raced. What was she doing with Allison? The benefit was in a few weeks, but he thought the details were ironed out. Angel didn't mention anything, nor, for that matter, had Allison. Alex pulled out his phone and banged out a text message.

Bancroft lifted an eyebrow. "We did tell Dr. Hemming to go about business as usual."

Alex's hand raked through his hair. "Yes, I know. Even if I told her to lay low, she wouldn't respect my wishes."

Bancroft smiled. "She seems very strong-willed."

"That's one way to put it. You're insanely diplomatic, Bancroft." Alex chuckled and shook his head.

*****

So Alex was Ally Franklin's brother. *Allison* Franklin.

Angel turned on the television and fell onto her sofa with her laptop and an armful of files. She needed to work, but confusion clouded her mind and her heart was heavy. Should she believe that the world really was as fucking small as Ally had insisted, or had Alex deliberately deceived her?

Ally was adamant that neither she nor Alex was even aware that the other knew her. So, why hadn't he mentioned it when he figured it out? Angel sighed, wondering if either he or his sister would have spilled the beans if Angel hadn't shared her own desire to surprise Alex with her performance with Archangel at the benefit. In the face of Angel's giddiness at finally admitting that they were indeed a couple, Ally had sobered and grabbed her hand.

"Angel, I need to tell you something…"

Ugh! she thought as she replayed that part of the conversation in her mind. "He should have told me, Ally. Or is it Allison?" she'd asked angrily.

"Allison is my given name. My husband and some of my friends call me Ally, but to my family, I've always been Allison." She flushed as Angel pulled her hand away. "Please, Angel. Don't let something so silly come between you. Alex… cares about you very much."

Angel looked at Allison with wide eyes, over their half-eaten lunch, as her heart began to beat a little too quickly when the hot rush of embarrassment flooded her skin. She was unable to let her heart miss those last words. "Then, he should have told me. He knew I was helping with the benefit."

"Did he mention his philanthropic sister?"

"Yes, but he didn't say anything specific."

Ally threw her hands in the air. "Because he doesn't care what it is specifically; he just throws money at me whenever I ask for it! Please don't overreact. Alex and I haven't talked that much lately. He's so busy; he rarely shows up at family gatherings. I nagged him about the reason he's blowing us all off and he told me he was seeing someone. You."

It sounded reasonable, but it still bothered her that Alex hadn't mentioned it himself. They'd gotten so close, and doubt dug into her at the prospect of any lies or disillusionment between them. She was already teetering on the edge of insanity.

When Alex left her place in the morning, after he'd had a clean change of clothes sent over like it was an everyday occurrence, she'd missed him so much she ached. Not just because it was unclear when they'd be able to be together again but because love filled her up to bursting. Angel desperately wanted to believe his simple statement. *"This thing between us… it's real, okay?"*

His ringtone screamed on her phone, which was never far from her. As she put it to her ear, her chin jutted out involuntarily. "Hello?"

"Hey," Alex said and Angel closed her eyes. That damn voice! "Are you in for the night? I'd love to chat online later."

"I'm sort of busy."

"Angel, Allison said she told you she's my sister."

"Yes, I guess I'm the only one left in the dark."

"Is it really that big a deal? Despite the fact I feel like I've known you forever, there are still so many things to learn about each other. I wasn't thinking about Allison; I was concentrating on you."

"Stop trying to sweet-talk me. I'm upset with you."

"Yes, I hear it in your voice, but get over it. This exact conversation is why I didn't tell you. I knew you'd question my motives. You don't trust me enough, and it pisses me off!"

"I trusted you with everything!" she spat back.

"Not in the beginning. It didn't come up, and when I found out you were working with Allison, it was just when we were making progress. Call me crazy, but I didn't want to fuck it up."

"All you had to do was tell me."

"I know. I should have mentioned it. I don't want to fight, Angel. We can't have make-up sex since I'm *gone*."

Angel bit her lip as a smile worked its way, unwillingly, across her face. "Shut up."

"I will if you will."

She laughed despite herself. "It's not fair. I can't stay mad at you."

"Thank God," he said, his voice laced with amusement. "I miss you already."

"Me, too," she agreed.

"It sucks as bad as I knew it would."

Happiness washed over her and she giggled. "Are you... um, I mean, did you reach your destination safely?" They'd agreed not to say anything too telling on the phone since cell phones were easily monitored.

"Yes. I'm here." He was telling her that he was safely ensconced in the apartment Cole had in the building; the ruse of leaving town was fully played out by taking the private jet out and changing the flight plan mid-flight, land in Milwaukee, and then take a car back without being discovered. "It was a looonnnngg freaking day."

"Poor baby."

Alex laughed. "Sorry you have to work tonight, babe, but get to a place where you have some time and I'll be waiting to speak to you. Bye, sweetheart."

Angel's computer's instant message chimed a second after the phone call ended.

Moneytalks Hi, baby.

AngelWings Hey. Are you with Cole?

Moneytalks Unfortunately. He's in the other room shoving a whole pizza down his throat. Say something. I can hear you on these monitors Cole rigged up.

AngelWings Nope. I only give as good as I get.

Moneytalks LOL. Don't I know it! But I reeeaallly want to hear your voice.

AngelWings Well, I want world peace and zero unemployment. Did Cole cave on where I was last night?

Moneytalks No. You were right. He wouldn't budge.

AngelWings Told ya. How'd it today go? Did Swanson bite?

Moneytalks He was seething, but I'm not sure it was enough.

AngelWings I hope so.

Moneytalks I'd rather that bastard just slink off and disappear.

AngelWings I was worried about you.

Moneytalks Well, I was worried about YOU. And then Cole texted you were with Allison, which only compounded things. What did you tell her?

AngelWings Nothing! I was afraid someone would be listening, and she doesn't know about this, right?

Moneytalks I didn't tell her.

AngelWings I almost spilled after I found out who she was.

Moneytalks Angel, I would've told you she was my sister if I thought it was an issue, but I didn't think you and Allison were friends. All I knew was that she contacted you about booking your boyfriend for her benefit. Allison rambles on so much; I tune most of it out.

AngelWings Kyle is not my boyfriend.

Moneytalks Whatever.

AngelWings Whatever = f**k off, remember? ☺ And stop
rolling your eyes.

Moneytalks LOL! Are you naked? Thanks for the visual this
morning, btw.

AngelWings Not completely. Is that all you think about?

Moneytalks Guilty. How naked?

AngelWings LOL

Moneytalks What about you? Don't you think about us like
that?

AngelWings I'll never tell. ☺

Moneytalks You don't have to. Say something. I want to hear
your voice.

Angel contemplated torturing him some more, but decided
against it. "Cole, can you please excuse us?" she asked into the air.
"I mean, give Alex some privacy with these monitors?"

AngelWings Make sure he leaves the room and can't hear
me.

Moneytalks Okay. He's going.

AngelWings Is he gone?

Moneytalks Yes.

Angel took a deep breath and set her computer on the ottoman in front of her. The lights in her apartment were low, and she
curled into a ball with her arm under her head. She swallowed, her
throat suddenly tightening. Her computer chimed again. She didn't
need to read it to know Alex was impatient.

"Okay, here goes. I was so worried today. I hate that sick
bastard, and I know what he's capable of. I... uhm..." She cleared
her throat. "Oh, God. Imagine me at a loss for words?"

The computer remained conspicuously silent as Alex waited
to hear her words.

"You... *terrify me*, Alex. You're everything a woman could want, and I'm not blind or stupid. I've seen how hurt women get by trusting men with everything to offer, when they have absolutely no intention of offering it. I've been hurt before, dealt with an unfaithful man. You and Kyle are different in so many ways, but similar in that a lot of women want you. You—even more so than him. You have the power to hurt me, even more, if that makes sense?"

She waited, mostly to try to control the trembling in her voice. Her computer piped up.

Moneytalks I understand.

"Well, I didn't want to risk a broken heart, especially when you told me that you didn't believe in love. But, despite what I went through with Kyle, I do believe in it. I believe in the kind of love that leaves you breathless, aching, and feeling like you're flying and dying all at the same time. I knew if I let myself enjoy being with you, I'd probably get hurt. So I tried not to care, and um... I tried to be the man. You know what I mean—have sex without emotion. That's what I wanted."

By now her eyes were flooded, emotion ached in her voice, and her fingers tugged at the pillow near her head. She glanced at the screen as it blurred before her eyes, but no answer was forthcoming.

"Then all the shit with Mark Swanson happened. I've never been one to lean on anyone because there never has been anyone to lean on, except my dad. I never meant to turn into a hard bitch that wouldn't let anyone in, but it's just been a circumstance of my life. I don't know why it's so much easier to tell you this when you're not in the same room."

Moneytalks I'm having a hell of a time not coming up there right now.

"Yes, well, just let me get it out. Swanson threatened me, but also you. The break-in at your house while I was there with Max scared the hell out of me, and by then, I was already in too deep and didn't want you hurt. It just gave me another reason to push you away, and I needed one. I'm sorry." The computer chimed.

Moneytalks It's okay, baby.

Angel closed her eyes, pushing the tears that hovered to tumble silently down her cheeks. "No. You didn't deserve it. You've been nothing but wonderful to me. You didn't deserve my doubt or my stupid preconceived notions. You're so much more than I thought you'd be. You're a really good person, and you've been more than I deserved."

She drew in a shaky breath, begging her voice not to crack. "And, Alex, I really do care about you. I can't fight it anymore, even knowing you'll probably break my heart in the end. No matter what my head says, I can't stop it. Which is really what has had me scared."

Silence boomed around her as she waited for the computer to sing out Alex's answer, and her heart pounded, pushing the blood to visibly throb at her pulse points. She bit her lip, holding back the sob that threatened at his lack of response.

Finally, it came.

Moneytalks You overwhelm me, Angel. I wish you'd told me this in person so I could touch you and make love to you … to show you how much you've come to mean to me. I'm crazy about you. *Fucking insane.*

Angel smiled tremulously as she brushed a tear away. He didn't say he loved her, but it was close.

13

Pounce

ALEX PACED BACK and forth in the surveillance apartment. He felt like a caged tiger, starving and helpless: what he craved most was just out of his reach. His work was suffering despite the daily calls and meetings via Skype. And, he was driving Cole crazy. Bancroft and one of the others were following Angel, and the time it took for them to travel from her office until she was safely ensconced within the building felt like forever. Cole could come and go, but the illusion they'd built for Swanson's benefit demanded that Alex stay inside the stark space.

"I can't stand much more of this!" Alex picked up one of Cole's free weights and lifted it over and over. "I could throw this fucking thing through a wall!"

"Alex, man, you have to chill. This has to stop." Cole watched his brother rub the back of his neck, agitation painted across his features. "Why don't you go to Mom and Dad's? Spend some time with them and see Max."

"I didn't hole up in this goddamned place all week just to blow it now." Alex's brow furrowed in anger as he scowled. "What in the hell is he waiting for?"

"Maybe the lockdown is too tight. Swanson might know we're watching her and that we've got the place wired. I know you don't want to, but, Alex, we have to give him enough rope to hang himself." Cole reached for the peanut butter sandwich in front of him and took a big bite as Alex sat down on the couch only to get up seconds later and continue pacing. "You're irritating the shit out of me, bro. Go back to work. Obviously, you being *out of town* isn't helping," Cole said with his mouth full.

Alex stopped pacing and studied the screens from the cameras that monitored the hallways, entrances, and parking garage. Maybe Cole was right. He was so frustrated with the situation and with not seeing Angel, but yet he resisted. His chest tightened and he sighed heavily.

Cole shoved the last two bites of his sandwich into his mouth and raised his eyebrows, mid-chew. "What?" he asked.

"It's just very difficult to put Angel in a place or situation where I don't have absolute control."

"Do you want this over or not? I mean, I could do this forever if you'd just get the fuck out of here, but I doubt Angel would be as accepting." Cole grinned and then shrugged. "When this is done, I'm out of a job."

It was unnecessary for Alex to agree with Cole's assessment of Angel's attitude, and his lip twitched in the start of a smile. Cole's comments relaxed him slightly. "You've really surprised me with how you've embraced this assignment, Cole," Alex said seriously. "I'm impressed, and I've felt a lot better knowing you're with her when I can't be."

"I like her. She has spunk." Cole leaned forward to grab a bottle of water and shot a fleeting glance at Alex, whose eyes narrowed.

"Don't get any ideas."

Cole smiled, purposefully ignoring the warning and deliberately provoking instead of backing off. "And, she's really hot!" He loved getting a rise out of his little brother. He'd never seen Alex so worked up over a woman or anything else for that matter. He was usually so cool and collected; it was nice to see the façade melt away. It made him more human somehow and more relatable to someone less than perfect like himself.

"Stop," Alex warned as he finally sank down in one of the desk chairs in front of the surveillance monitors as Angel's car appeared on the one in the parking garage. The muscles in his body visibly uncoiled.

"What? She is. You never got pissed when I talked about Whitney's big tits or Ashley's fantasy blowjob mouth. They were all beautiful, but Angel is… real."

Alex studied his brother, his green eyes shooting fire. "Cole, stop thinking about her that way. To me she's real; to you, she's an assignment. Don't lose sight of that."

"What? Am I dead?"

"No, but you're skating on thin ice." His eyes were cold and his expression hard as stone when he turned back to the monitor. Cole could see the muscle working in Alex's jaw and decided to take pity on him. Alex leaned forward as Angel got out of her car and began walking toward the elevator.

"I understand your frustration. I mean… shit. Now that you've been with her, it must be killing you."

"The whole thing is frustrating. Being this close and not—" He shook his head and huffed, his hand pushing under the hem of his navy T-shirt to scratch along his stomach. "Worrying all the goddamned time is driving me mad."

Alex had always been the perfect one: never disappointing his parents, making the right decisions, having the best grades, being a member of the high school honor society, and having the most beautiful girlfriends. Shit, he accomplished everything he did with barely a finger lifted. When they were growing up, Cole had been so jealous, thinking that it all was some gift bestowed on Alex from

Heaven. But being this close to him for an extended period of time, and listening to him work, he had a new respect for how much effort Alex invested in everything. The most amazing thing about his brother was that, to the world, it seemed effortless, and he was un-touchable. In reality, he worked his ass off, took his responsibilities seriously, and he had a deep capacity for love. Deeper than even he knew himself.

"I never thought I'd see the day, Alex." The walkie-talkie on Cole's hip beeped and flashed red and he grabbed it. "It looks good on you," he said before he spoke into the device. "We see her. Did you see anything suspicious?"

Alex balked at his brother's comment. His lungs filled to ca-pacity in a frustrated sigh as he sat back in his chair again, waiting to hear the response. He groaned. He was more a prisoner than Angel despite the fact he had engineered the entire operation. He pulled his iPhone from the pocket of his expensive jeans and pressed the button that would speed dial the woman in his thoughts. Cole got up and walked into the kitchen with his plate, and Alex wondered if his motivation was his bottomless appetite or a subtle attempt to give him some privacy.

"Hey." Angel's breathy voice answered before the second ring.

"Is something wrong?"

"No, I'm changing clothes. I promised to meet Becca at the gym and I'm running late," she explained. The sound of her voice over the monitor speakers echoed around her voice over the phone. It was too loud and the feedback hurt his ears. He leaned forward and switched them off.

Alex relaxed slightly. "Oh. Did you tell her what's going on?"

"She's my best friend and I had to explain why I haven't been around. She's not mental, Alex."

"I get it."

"Are you okay?" Angel asked thoughtfully. He could hear the rustle of fabric and the change in her voice as she struggled to change clothes and hold the phone simultaneously.

"I feel like a caged animal."

"Alex, why don't we just—"

"Just what, baby?"

"Can you sneak up here after I get back from the gym? I'd like to see you."

He groaned. "Don't tempt me."

"Nothing's happened in a week. How long can you hole up and stay away from work? Maybe Mark Swanson has given up or moved beyond it."

"Honestly, I didn't think that prick would be able to resist this long."

"Just… please? Come up later?"

Alex's sour mood changed in an instant. "I want to, babe. You know that."

He could hear a smile in her voice that echoed the stupid grin on his face. "I want, too. As in, also."

"Mmm…" His tone lowered and smoothed out as his body reacted to her words.

"So do it." Angel's low murmur was laced with promise.

"What is it you want me to do? *It?*" Alex chuckled softly, and Angel burst out laughing.

"Yes, that. *It.* Do *it.* With me." She continued to giggle.

"Only with you. You've ruined me."

Cole came back in the room with two more sandwiches and some chips loaded on the plate. His eyebrow shot up at his brother's happy expression as he offered him a sandwich. Alex shook his head and turned away.

"I have to go. Consider coming up."

"Okay. Be careful."

Alex waved his brother toward the door. "She's on the move. Take Wayne with you."

Cole pushed his plate away and stood up. The keys he dug from his pocket jingled as he walked quickly toward the door. "Am I out of a job after this thing is done?"

Alex moved to take the seat in front of the monitors that Cole had just vacated and shook his head. "You're not out of a job. You've proven I can trust you, and you're good at this. It depends on what you want to take on, but I'm thinking of putting you in charge of security at Avery. Bancroft handles the local stuff well, but you can oversee all of the properties. If you want... but you'll probably have to wear a suit for part of it." Alex smirked. "Mom will be placated at least."

Cole was happily astonished, judging by the smile that flashed across his face. "Seriously?"

Alex nodded. "I've already told Dad."

"Cool."

*****

Angel walked into her apartment and found it dark. Her heart fell as she turned and bolted the door. Apparently, Alex had resisted her invitation. She sighed, her gym bag thumping as it hit the floor by the door, along with her purse. She pushed one of the tendrils back from her face but it resisted, the sweat, now dried from her workout, making it stick to the side of her face. The light from the refrigerator flooded the room as she pulled a bottle of water out before walking through her apartment on the way to her bedroom.

It had been a long, boring day. Aside from her brief conversation with Alex, and Becca's rant about the hot guy she met the previous weekend, Angel couldn't find much else enjoyable about it. She glanced at the bed longingly, passing the dark laptop sitting on the desk by the window and running her hand along the edge on the way to the bathroom. She smiled softly, chastising herself for not being able to pass the bed without thinking of Alex and wishing she'd managed to convince him to give in and spend the night with her. It amazed her how quickly she'd been able to reconcile being with him and come to depend on his presence. All of her convictions about giving over control and protecting her heart now lay in shambles. That was the nature of giving up control, though. It was unavoidable. He was a force to be reckoned with. Angel huffed as the stupid grin settled onto her face.

She kicked off her shoes and peeled off her shirt, tank, and sports bra before pulling the tie out of her hair to allow the thick locks loose while her hands scratched wildly against her scalp, shaking the chestnut curls into a flurry. She could almost feel the thin layer of residual salt hardening into a shell on her skin. The workout felt good, but Becca pushed her hard. and Angel's muscles protested. The past couple of weeks had been filled with so many other things that she hadn't spent enough time at the gym and she was paying the price. Her arms were quivering slightly and her legs shaky when she turned on the shower and then pushed her black yoga pants down her legs, leaving them in a pile on the floor with her thong.

Steam began to fill the bathroom, and she padded back into her bedroom to grab a soft silk chemise to sleep in. She stopped on her way back, lighting two candles at the bedside, before flipping open the laptop and quickly loading Skype. Standing naked in front of the screen was a risk considering Cole might be in the room with Alex when they connected, but she was feeling mischievous and decided it was the best way to get what she wanted: Alex, in her apartment and her bed.

She was certain Alex would be more upset if Cole saw her naked than he would be with her for being that way in front of her monitor. She smiled, waiting for Skype to load, and turning on her iPod so that music flooded the room. Her skin flushed warm in anticipation of his reaction. Her teeth pressed down on her lower lip: her plan was to give a little tease and then disappear into the bathroom.

Alex's image materialized on the screen. "Yeah, I'm here, honey." He was adjusting the monitor and hadn't looked at his screen. "How was the work—Holy shit!" he said as he sat down in his chair and finally saw her, standing naked to his gaze. His arms immediately covered the monitor and Angel giggled in delight. "Cole! Vamoose!"

"What?" Cole's voice was somewhat muted. "Why?"

"Just get the hell out of here!"

"This is stupid, Alex." Angel could hear Cole muttering as he left the room followed by a door slamming loudly.

Alex moved away from the monitor enough so Angel had a full view of his face. He smiled. "What are you doing to me?"

"Nothing."

Alex took a deep breath and leaned in toward the monitor. "It doesn't feel like nothing in my pants. Are you trying to kill me?"

"Is that what I'm doing?" Angel asked with fake innocence, moving back and turning around to give him a good look. She bit her lip to keep from grinning.

"Aren't you?"

She shook her head. "Nope. I'm all sticky, so I'm going to shower and then climb into this big, huge bed right over here." She pointed to it and smiled slyly. "See this big bed?" She used a breathy, bimbo voice and widened her eyes in over-exaggeration.

Alex laughed out loud. "I see it."

"Of course, I don't know why I bother showering since I was hoping to, you know… get sticky all over again… in it."

"Angel, stop it." His words belied what his eyes were saying as they roamed over her body. Alex brought one hand up to his mouth, his index finger and thumb messing with his lower lip.

"Oh, Alex, come on!" Angel shot back with a small stamp of her foot. "You can protect me better here. How will Swanson know, anyway?"

"It isn't a matter of him knowing, but he won't get the chance you seem to want to give him if I'm in your bed. All we'd have him on is breaking and entering."

"Have you been talking with Kenneth?"

"A bit."

"Is he your new best friend?"

"Don't be ridiculous. We have the common interest of keeping that pretty little head of yours on that delicious little body."

Angel scowled because he wasn't giving in, and she felt weird about Alex and Kenneth comparing notes.

"All talk and no play, Alex. Please?"

"No. Sorry, babe."

Angel got up and moved toward the bathroom. "Fine!" She all but screamed as she slammed the bathroom door behind her. "Ugh!"

The steam-filled air was heavy, and the mirrors were fogged over. Angel leaned her hands on the vanity and tried to push down her disappointment and blink away the burn of tears that pricked at the back of her eyes.

Her heart seized when a vice-like grip closed around her throat and she was lifted up and slammed back into the cold ceramic tile of the wall opposite the mirror. Her eyes widened and a scream rose in her chest but the hands tightened and made it all but impossible to breathe. Angel's hands clawed at the face of her attacker but encountered not flesh and bone but the fabric of a ski mask; her legs flailed, her feet kicked out and tried to find purchase on his chest, hips, or legs.

"You little bitch!" he snarled, and she recognized the raspy voice. "I decided I'd just kill you and get it over with, but since your boyfriend is such a motherfucker, maybe I should have a little fun first. Just for him."

Angel continued to struggle and was rewarded with a grunt when her knee pushed against his groin with all the force she could muster. Her heart pounded in her ears, her hands still clawing at him, finally pulling the mask from his face. She scratched her nails down both cheeks and felt the flesh give way beneath her hands. Mark Swanson hissed and dropped her to the ground followed by a loud clatter of metal hitting the ceramic. Pain shot through her hip and shoulder as she landed in a heap at his feet. She moaned at the sharp burn that spread like wildfire beneath the skin on her left hip.

Angel's heart beat as if it would fly from her chest. She was gasping to regain her breath as she used her hands to push up and scramble to her feet, racing past the man into the other room. Her frantic eyes went to her laptop in search of Alex's face but he wasn't at the desk. "Alex! Cole! He's here! Aaaallllleeeeexxxx!" she yelled as she ran through the bedroom door and down the hall.

"Ahhhh! Ummph!" The air rushed from her lungs as she found herself face down on the taupe carpet of her hallway; Mark Swanson was suddenly on top of her, one hand twisting in her hair and yanking so hard she was sure her neck would snap. Angel tried to roll over but his body was holding hers down, his legs pushing between hers. Suddenly, she was fully aware of her nakedness and the helpless position she was in; her struggles resulted in nothing more than rug burns on her body. Her skin ripped as she heaved and bucked, her position preventing her from using her hands to defend herself. His rancid breath rushed over her shoulder, into her ear, and over her cheek. He smelled of alcohol and smoke, and worse. Her stomach lurched.

Dear Jesus. "Alex!" she screamed as she heard the clank of Mark Swanson's buckle. Tears started to seep from her eyes. "Alex! Help me!" The high pitch of her cries made her throat ache. "He's in the building!"

"He'll be too late, anyway."

"He'll fucking kill you, you bastard!" she spat out, pulling her arms beneath her body and trying to use them to pull herself free from the dead weight over her. "You're such a coward! You can't even face me, and I'm half your size!"

The chuckle that followed was chilling. "He fucked my life beyond repair, so I'm going to fuck the only thing he cares about. I wish Avery could watch this happen. Maybe you'll like it. Play nice and I'll get you off."

Angel could feel her knees and elbows burn, the warm wetness of her own blood starting to ooze, her arms and legs shaking with the extent of her effort. "Fuck you."

"I have a knife, Angel. Play nice or I'll use it."

"Then use it! You'll have to kill me!"

A thunderous boom was followed by the sound of wood splitting and the door falling off its hinges and cracking against the hardwood floor in her entryway.

Angel's knees were quickly and forcefully pushed wide despite using every ounce of strength she possessed to counter his efforts. She felt the cold metal of the knife slide along her thigh and the burn as it finally sliced along the flesh. A piercing scream burst from her chest in the same instant she was suddenly freed of the weight. Mark Swanson was hurled away from her, landing with a loud crash on his back, the knife flung roughly with a clang into the wall and then a dull thud on the carpet. He grunted as Alex landed on top of him, effectively pinning him to the ground.

"Take care of Angel!" Alex's voice rang out as she pulled her knees up and crawled up against the wall. Her hands wrapped around her bleeding thigh and tears stained her cheeks. A sob rose in her throat, and her eyes followed Alex's voice. She barely noticed Cole's presence beside her or that he removed his shirt and draped his shirt around her.

Alex's knees were on top of Swanson's biceps and he was sitting on his chest, was using both fists to pound the other man repeatedly. Angel couldn't see his face but she could hear the frustration pouring from him as his fist slammed into Swanson's face repeatedly.

"Ugh! Ugh! Ugh!" Alex's grunts seemed to punctuate each and every blow. The other man tried to struggle, much in the same way Angel had, and was just as helpless as Alex pummeled him. The sound of fists hitting flesh with sickening thuds, Swanson's moans, and Angel's soft crying were like sonic booms against the music echoing down the hall from her room. "Die, you motherfucker! How dare you touch her? Fucking die!"

The other man's legs stopped moving and it was apparent that he was unconscious, and still, Alex beat him over and over, never lessening the force he used. His chest was on fire and his eyes burned.

"Alex! That's enough!" Cole shouted. "He's unconscious!"

"No! It will never be enough!" His voice was thick and broken as his fist landed again, harder, and he pulled his arm back to repeat the motion again.

"Alex," Angel called tearfully, her trembling hand reaching toward him but fell upon empty air. The space between them was too great for her to touch him, yet still, she reached out. "Baby, he's not worth it."

She watched him sit back on his haunches, his chest heaving as his arms dropped to his sides and his head dropped back. "Jesus Christ!"

Cole's arm was around her as she huddled underneath his blue-button down. Her shoulders began to shake in soft sobs which snapped Alex back to reality. Instantly, he was kneeling at her side and pulling her onto his lap as his arms enfolded her gently while she crumpled into him, her arms lifting around his neck. Alex pulled the hem of the shirt lower to cover her.

"Cole. Call the police if Bancroft hasn't already." His hands drifted gently over her, checking for broken bones but seeing the blood running down one leg in a series of streams. "And, an ambulance."

Shirtless, Cole got up and quickly walked down the hall and into the kitchen, already speaking into the phone.

"Oh, God, Angel… are you all right? He didn't…" The fingers of his right hand moved to her blood-stained thigh. "If he— Jesus, I will fucking gut him, right now!"

The tears still clung to her lashes, her dark brown eyes glassy as they gazed into his. Alex's face was full of sadness, the back of his knuckles bloody as he brushed them along her cheekbone. She shook her head as her hand threaded through his.

"I'm sorry I wasn't there, honey. I should have been at the monitor. When I heard you scream, we got here as fast as we could. Fuck! This is all my fault."

"No, it's not. It's okay. I'm okay." Her fingers reached out to trace the strong lines of his jaw, but his mournful eyes met hers. "I'm okay."

*****

Angel noted Alex's restlessness as he removed his wallet from his pocket and took off his Rolex to gently place them on the dresser in the low-lit room. He'd taken her to his apartment after the police had left hers, anxious to leave the scene behind. The doorjamb was shattered anyway. She'd been treated in emergency, her thigh stitched and her rug burns bandaged up, but she was thankful that she didn't have to stay overnight. After the ordeal, Alex needed her as much as she needed him.

He looked tired, even though he still moved with grace and elegance. She sensed his muscles were protesting as much as her own.

Love swelled within her as she remembered how he'd swooped in and pounded Mark Swanson to a pulp, his aggressiveness a stark contrast to his tenderness afterward. All through the police questioning, he never left her side. Her heart squeezed. He'd wanted to clean her up and make sure she was okay, but her experience with rape cases taught her that nothing could be touched. Not the scene, not the victim, not until all of the evidence was collected. The whole process was humiliating, and she understood why some women decided not to report assault.

He seemed too far away when she ached to touch him.

"Alex," she called softly. He turned toward her as he pulled the tails of his shirt from the waistband of his pants and undid the buckle of his belt.

"Yes?"

"Aren't you coming to bed?"

He sighed and finished unbuttoning his shirt and began to rummage in a drawer for something. "I'll lie down in the other room." He sat down on the edge of the bed with his back to her, and Angel rolled carefully onto her side. Her bandaged thigh still throbbed, and pain shot through her hip and limbs, and her knees still burned. She winced silently.

"This is a big bed." She reached out and ran a hand down his back and up again, softly kneading his firm muscles. He placed his pajama pants on the bed and rubbed the back of his neck wearily.

"I can't, Angel." Defeat laced his voice. "I can't be next to you and not touch you."

Tears stung at the back of her eyes as she rested her forehead on his back. "Then... touch me," she whispered in a tremulous voice.

"You don't need a man's hands on you tonight. Not after what that bastard did. When I thought that he—"

Angel reached out and grabbed one of Alex's hands. "These hands don't hurt me," she insisted softly and pressed her lips to his palm and then held it against her cheek, bringing her eyes up to meet his. His brow crinkled in confusion.

She moaned softly as she moved behind him to wrap her arms around his middle and plaster her body as close to his as possible. Her hands flattened on his bare chest and flat stomach through his open shirt. "I want to be with you. I always have."

"Then maybe you can explain why you've run away from me so much."

"I was scared."

"Not of me, surely?"

She nodded. "I told you. You're going to break my heart if I let you too close."

"Closer is where I want to be with you. More than I've ever wanted it with anyone."

"You say that now, until you get bored. Men always get bored after a while."

"You're saying this to me tonight?"

"I'd rather talk about this than dwell on what happened, okay?"

Alex knew what she was saying; she didn't want to relive it, so he was okay with letting her distract herself. "Did you ever consider that it could be the women who were fucked up?"

"Sure, sometimes, but you're the epitome of generalization!" Amusement laced her tone as she gently nudged his body with hers. "Cold, unavailable emotionally, yet the handsome, powerful, and unattainable man all women want. You draw us like moths to a flame, and we're held helpless by your superman skills."

Alex pulled one of her hands forward and held it between both of his as he huffed skeptically. "Superman skills, huh? Do all women want me?" She could almost hear the smirk on his face in the darkness. "Do you really believe that?"

"He asked with false modesty," she teased gently, her lips moving against the fine cotton covering his shoulder.

"You don't seem so helpless to my, uh, skills." He smiled gently; his fingers played with hers until they twined together, and he lifted her hand to his lips and brushed them across her knuckles. Desire tightened in the pit of her stomach.

"I'm completely helpless."

"Really?" he asked in disbelief. Tiredness was written all over him.

"Yes, but I think more than most women. My professional training and personal experience make it difficult to shut off the warning in my head. It's annoying as hell." Angel snuggled further into Alex's embrace, her head coming to rest beneath his chin, the rise and fall of his chest beneath her cheek comforting.

"I agree. You over-thinking everything annoys the shit out of me, too."

"Huh!" she huffed with a smile. "Like now. I'm thinking that you should be amazing in bed since that's how you define your relationships. I should expect you to be magnificent and you haven't disappointed me."

Alex scowled. "I'm not a robot. With you… it's different."

"Okay, *defined* relationships," Angel amended with a chuckle. "Define—d."

"With you, I'm highly motivated," he said seriously.

Angel sobered. "Why? I don't measure your worth by how many orgasms you give me."

"It's just—" He paused, searching for the right words. "I enjoy giving you pleasure. I love the way it sounds and looks on you. And, your responsiveness blows my mind; it makes me insane to have you. I can't stand the thought of anyone touching you with violence or in passion. Even in tenderness. Beyond that, it's like I've told you, I want to see where this goes. Can we stop with the doubt? I don't enjoy discussing it. I need you to trust me."

"Okay."

Alex pulled back and turned in her arms, seeking her eyes. "Just like that?" His hands moved gently up over her shoulders and down her arms until they wrapped around her forearms.

Angel winced slightly but nodded. "Yes."

Alex instantly gentled his grip, one hand moving to cup her face and the other down to hold her hand in his. "I'm sorry, baby. I didn't mean to hurt you."

Angel tightened her fingers around his. "I'm okay."

His green eyes narrowed and turned to glittering black. "It makes me sick to think what he did to you," he growled. "What he almost did."

"Shhh. It's over. Thanks to you, I'm fine."

"I barely got there in time. Seeing him over you—" he closed his eyes as the image of her struggling with the other man between her naked thighs flashed in his mind, "—the world exploded. Angel, I wanted to kill him with my bare hands."

"I'm glad Cole stopped you. Are they sore?"

"Not as much as my shoulder. I'll live." He grimaced. His hands ached and burned at the same time. "You stopped me, not Cole."

She nodded, eyes still locked with his. "Alex, I..." Angel paused, trying to get past the tightening in her throat. "Thank you." He brushed his thumb back and forth across her cheekbone, and the tenderness in his touch made her want to cry. "I don't know what I would have done without you tonight."

Alex leaned forward and kissed her temple. "You don't have to do without me." He breathed in the soft floral scent of her shampoo, the warmth of her skin beneath his caress somehow reassuring. He closed his eyes and slid his arms around her, the softness of the towel reminded him of her state of undress. The familiar ache that took root every time he was near her was accompanied by tenderness and a need to protect her. He wanted to wrap her up in his arms and never let her go. His heart ached with it. He was still reeling from the unfamiliar emotions that consumed him, but the feeling was as incredible as it was terrifying. "I'll get you something to put on and tuck you in."

Alex started to get up but she caught his hand. "Will you stay with me? Don't leave."

"Okay. You've convinced me."

14

Duplicity

ANGEL AND ALEX spent a week holed up in his apartment, taking time to heal physically and recover mentally from all that had happened with Mark Swanson. Alex insisted Angel take time off from work and the radio show to recover and offered to take her away for a while, to Joplin to see her dad or Hawaii like they'd planned, anywhere she wanted to go. But Angel just wanted to be with Alex, alone, without obligations to anyone else except Max.

When Angel told him what she wanted, Alex was more elated than he'd wanted to admit. Mrs. Dane shopped for everything they needed, and Alex whisked Angel away to his estate without argument, both of them returning to his downtown apartment only last night. It was time to get back to reality and work.

Alex had the door to Angel's condo repaired, and the only evidence that it had ever been damaged was the large yellowish bruise on his right shoulder. The bloodstained carpet had been replaced as well. That, and the skin they had recovered from beneath Angel's fingernails, would be enough DNA evidence to put Swanson away. The only thing hanging in the balance was how long he'd be locked up. He was released from the hospital three days after Alex's beating and arrested, albeit with a broken jaw and nose. The D.A's office threw a slew of charges at him, the worst of which included two accounts of assault with a deadly weapon and attempted rape. But still, the asshole was out on bail. Alex was doubly frustrated because he'd hoped he wouldn't have the money after his company was flushed. Some family member must have stepped up; he just hoped it wasn't of the organized crime variety. Surely, after raping the niece of one of the family members, it was highly unlikely. Still, it was a constant concern.

Since the incident, Alex spent more time speaking with Kenneth and, though a part of him was loathe to admit it, discovered he was a good guy and genuinely concerned about Angel's well-being.

Angel glanced at Alex as he read the morning edition of The Wall Street Journal, a cup of steaming black coffee and the waffle she'd made for him sitting on the marble surface of the table. His brow was knitted in concentration, and she smiled to herself. She kept waiting to wake up and have it all blow up in her face but had finally accepted their relationship and their time together. While expected now, it was still very fragile in her eyes and part of her was still worried she'd lose him eventually. Logic told her she couldn't worry about the future and just enjoy each moment they had together. Still, it nagged at the back of her mind.

Alex was still the strong, sexy, and super-confident man she'd met in the bar a few months back, but when she looked at him now, she also saw his soul and something deeper in his dark green eyes that made her pulse pound and body quicken. He was passion personified; the epitome of sex for sure, but he possessed an unexpected tenderness that made her heart swell, even as the urgency in his touch reduced her to shuddering ecstasy in his hands.

He glanced up as she pushed the syrup she'd warmed in the microwave toward him, the look in her eyes giving a hint of her thoughts.

"What?" he asked, the left side of his mouth curving into the start of a grin.

"Nothing. What are you reading?" She smiled softly back at him.

Alex threw the paper aside and shook his head. "I can't focus on anything."

"Then what are you thinking about?" She leaned her forearms on the back of the chair next to his and dug one foot into the floor.

"Ken called. Swanson is out on bail."

"I figured."

Alex glanced up and his eyes locked with hers. She knew what he was thinking but she wanted to distract him, not wanting to think about it herself.

"You haven't touched the waffle. Aren't you hungry?" Her eyes roamed over his shower-dampened hair that, while combed, was still falling in perfect disarray over his forehead. She bit her lip as he reached up to thread his fingers through it in a failed attempt to push it back. Alex looked handsome in his crisp cream-colored shirt and a patterned olive green and black tie. The jacket to his deep black Hugo Boss suit hung over the back of the chair opposite him, the olive silk pocket square already nestled in the breast pocket. She rolled her eyes at the easy elegance he exuded and huffed out loud.

His eyes narrowed in amusement and he shoved some of his waffle into his mouth after cutting a piece with his fork. "Yum!" He flashed a smile as he chewed and readied another bite.

"Don't rub it in. You know I don't like to cook."

"You made this…" he mumbled with his mouth full and wide eyes that mocked her.

"All I did was 'leggo your Eggo'. That doesn't count." She grinned.

Alex burst out laughing and leaned forward to take her hand in his. "I'll miss you today."

Her smile softened as his thumb traced over the top of her knuckles. "Me, too. This week was nice."

Angel got up and squeezed in between the table and Alex, settling onto his lap, facing him. Alex leaned back in surprise, his hands finding purchase on her bare thighs as she settled in. She was wearing a pair of cotton pajama shorts and a some-what-fitted white, V-neck T-shirt. Her hands flattened on his chest. He'd been trying to ignore the way she was flirting with him. The sexy way the shirt hugged the rounded swell of her breasts and outline of her nipples, and the bare expanse of her long legs weren't helping, and his dick twitched in response to her touch.

"Don't go to work," she whispered, leaning in and brushing her nose against his neck behind the strong line of his jaw. "Just one more day?"

She closed her eyes and inhaled his masculine scent then opened her mouth hotly over his skin. She sucked slightly and licked at his neck, her fingers sliding up to curl in the hair at his nape. "Mmmm... you smell so great."

Alex tensed and his fingers closed around her flesh tighter, hips moving of their own volition against her. "Angel, I have a meeting with the board at nine. Don't torture us both by starting something we can't finish."

"Boo," she said softly, even though she'd already known that he wouldn't blow off a board meeting. Oh, well. It didn't hurt to try. Her face took on a pretty pout, and Alex couldn't resist kissing her tenderly on the mouth. She tasted sweet, so soft, and he sighed at the perfect way their mouths played with each other's.

"I'll make it up to you tonight. It will be better when you get your stitches out, anyway." His thumb traced lightly over the rough 6-inch line down the inside of her left thigh. Something between rage and regret flashed over his features before he was able to mask it. Alex hated that her perfect skin had been forever marked by that heinous bastard, and the fire in his gut still burned as hot as it did the day he'd almost beat him to death. Part of him wished he could have. No one deserved death more.

Angel's own eyes softened as she took in his expression. She sat back and looked into his eyes, her arms still around his shoulders, and her fingers playing lazily in his hair. After a moment, she leaned down and kissed the corner of his mouth lightly. "I forgot about that."

Alex's hands slid up her back and over her shoulders, gently kneading as he went. Angel's head fell back, exposing the column of her neck for his lips to explore, and he couldn't resist the obvious temptation. "How could you forget? It looks so sore," he murmured against her skin.

Angel shivered in his arms. "Just a little. It's a badge of a battle well fought."

"I hate seeing your skin marked in any way. *Any* way."

"It'll fade." She nuzzled into him, and he continued to rub her back, his fingers drawing little circle patterns. "I could always get a tattoo to cover it up. Property of Alex Avery." Angel pulled away just enough to see his face.

Alex smiled and ran his index finger down the side of her cheek but shook his head. "No tattoos to interrupt the perfection of your skin." He went back to nuzzling the side of her neck. "Why don't you take it easy today? Shop. Buy something new to wear this evening, and I'll meet you at Tru at seven. We'll have an early dinner then I'll make slow love to you for hours and hours. How does that sound?" Hot breath washed her skin as he spoke.

She nodded and turned her head to kiss his cheekbone. "Nice."

He huffed softly with a smile. "Just nice?" The warmth in his languid eyes made her pause.

"Okay, orgasmic!" Angel said with a smirk. "Like heaven."

"That's better."

Her eyes turned serious as they searched his expression, seeking something, but she was unsure what she would find. Her brow furrowed, uncertainty flashing across her face. "You know, you don't have to change for me. I mean, this whole cohabitation-relationship thing is new for you."

Alex held her gaze, unflinching, but he paused a few seconds before answering.

"I didn't change *for* you, baby. I changed *because* of you."

"Is there a difference?"

"You know there is, Angel. Stop over-thinking. This is good. It's how I want it." His index finger ran down the outline of her face again then his hand wrapped around the back of her head so he could kiss her more deeply this time. Angel's mouth opened underneath his and she kissed him back with fervor, her heart hoping she could still convince him to stay, even though her mind protested. Her pulse raced at the point under his thumb, and his body swelled painfully in the confines of his slacks. His mouth dragged from hers reluctantly, yet still their lips clung together. "Ung… I gotta go. I don't want to, but I must."

Abruptly, Alex stood with Angel still folded in his arms, her legs wrapped around his waist. They hugged tightly, both of them reluctant to let the other go, before he finally set her down and reached for his jacket. She watched him shrug into it and shook her head.

Alex's eyebrow shot up. "What is that look for?"

"You. Are. One. Sexy. Bastard." Angel punctuated each word with a pause.

A brilliant smile split across his face as he came back and placed a hard, but brief, kiss on her willing mouth. "I thought I'd convinced you," he whispered. "I'm not really a bastard."

She smiled against his mouth, her eyes still closed as he kissed her again, more leisurely this time. "I know you're not," Angel agreed as he pulled away from her. "I hate being wrong, but in this case, I'll acquiesce."

Alex laughed softly. "See you tonight at the restaurant. Call me after your doctor's appointment, please," he said over his shoulder on the way out of the kitchen.

Angel followed him into the foyer, her bare feet registering the cooler temperature of the marble tiles. "Stop worrying."

"Not gonna happen," Alex retorted as he left.

After the door closed, Angel turned back to the empty apartment and sighed heavily at the sudden starkness. It was still the same elegant place it had been, full of luxurious furnishings and expensive art, but now it was without Alex. She sighed at how huge his presence really was. He was definitely a force to be reckoned with, admired, and completely enveloped by. She adored him.

Her fingers ran across the back of the soft, leather couch as she made her way back to his bedroom, acknowledging that she really didn't mind being consumed by him and, for the first time in her life, welcomed it, maybe even reveled in it. She was giddy with emotion. Alex never left her thoughts, and she wanted to be with him every second they were apart. This was the part of love that no one called into her radio show about, the part of love that lifted people to the highest highs and made the possible crash even more agonizing. Angel mentally chastised herself for the weakness that had her slipping into doubt.

Their time together this week proved they did a great job of taking care of each other, neither in the other's shadow. He hadn't said he loved her, but then, neither had she. It was in the little things; the way his green eyes burned into her, the reverence of his

touch, the passion-filled nights, and his fierce protectiveness. It felt
right. Angel was at ease and finally willing to risk combining her life
with his, he'd invaded her heart completely and, really, what was
the point in fighting the rest of it? It was nothing more than logis-
tics. Alex had initiated a conversation a few weeks back about living together, and Angel knew he'd be revisiting the subject that
night at dinner.

She dialed Becca's number and waited for her best friend to
pick up. Who better to confide in? A silly smile settled on Angel's
beautiful features, and she tugged on a lock of her long hair. She
couldn't wait to tell Becca about her plans.

"Hey!" Becca answered.

"Hi! I've missed you and my little Jillybean."

"Me, too. I have so much to tell you! Can you meet for
lunch?" Unmistakable excitement laced Becca's voice.

*****

By the end of the afternoon, Angel was a little tired and hoped a
long dip in Alex's over-sized Jacuzzi bathtub would help to revital-
ize her. The doctor's appointment, the shopping, and afterward,
going to her own apartment to get a few things, had taken longer
than she wanted, and she was anxious for her evening alone with
Alex.

Cole brought her packages in, carried them upstairs, and left
them on Alex's bed. She blushed when he'd followed her and
Becca into Enchanté despite Angel's urging that he could wait in
the car. It was by far the best lingerie retailer in Chicago, and she
was looking for something special to knock Alex's socks off. She
wanted this evening to be unforgettable for both of them.

Unpacking the sheer, black silk bra and matching Brazilian bi-
kini panties, Angel laid them out on the bed. She smoothed the
hand-crocheted lace that adorned the inside edge of the halter cups

and made up the delicate fringe around the bottom of the bra. Both pieces sparkled just slightly with well-placed Swarovski crystals, which would be perfect in candlelight. The humanitarian side of her cringed at the $350 she'd dropped on the two scant pieces, but the hungry look in Alex's eyes when he peeled off her new dress would be worth every cent. The thought alone had sensuality oozing out of every pore.

Angel placed the silk crepe dress next to the lingerie on the bed. The dress was a deep purple, reminiscent of the lilies he'd given her before their first date, the design fitted with small horizontal openings running below the neckline, just above the hemline which skimmed the middle of her thighs, and three places on the long sleeves. Each one lined with matching sheer silk chiffon. It was classy and drop-dead sexy at the same time. The barely-black and filmy thigh-highs she laid next to it would be another wow factor when Alex stripped off her clothes. The box containing the new Prada pumps were the final touch. They were simple elegance and relied on their cut and stiletto heel for the desired effect. She nodded, satisfied with the choices she'd made, confident of Alex's approval.

Tonight was the night. The night she'd say those three little words that would let Alex know she'd given up on her tightly held convictions to keep her heart completely out of this equation. Part of her still trembled at the power she was about to hand over because he was the one man who could now totally destroy her heart. She'd resolved to tell him, and she'd show him how she really felt, and hopefully, he would echo her feelings. The thought of it alone made her body hum.

"Angel?" Cole called from the other room. "I'm gonna go back to my place and take a shower, but I'll be back to take you to the restaurant, okay? Don't let anyone else in."

Her hand smoothed down the fine fabric of the dress once more. It was soft as satin but richer. "Okay, but wait a second."

Angel rushed down the hall and down the stairs into the foyer where Cole stood. "Thanks for putting up with me today. You're a great sport, letting me drag you all over Chicago." She smiled and hugged him hard.

Cole's big arms closed around her back and he lifted her small form into a bear hug. "Alex's one lucky mofo, that's all I have to say."

"Yes. He's got a great brother!"

"Naw. It was fun. Your friend is kind of a smartass, though, but she's cute."

He turned to leave, and Angel made her way back toward the stairs. "Oh, she's a smartass, all right."

"I'll be back in what? Two hours?"

Angel paused on the third stair and turned. "You don't need to—"

"Oh, yes, I do. Alex would blow a gasket if I let you go alone. That prick's out on bail."

"You're the second Avery brother that's warned me about that today. I get it, but with a broken jaw and shattered cheekbone, it's not likely he's feeling up to revenge."

"Alex—" Cole began, only to be cut off by Angel.

"I know! *Alex!*" She sighed and shook her head as happiness flooded through her.

"Alex doesn't take any chances," Cole concluded with a grin that echoed the one she loved in his brother. "Gant said he got wind that Swanson's mob connections deserted him so he shouldn't have his band of goons in tow either. Apparently, his brother-in-law feels that he's not worth engaging with a big conglomerate like Avery. We have more resources."

"Yeah, but they have bullets." Angel's brow furrowed, wondering why Alex hadn't shared this piece of information. Neither had Kenneth, for that matter.

Cole shook his head. "Swanson's not blood and only con-nected by marriage. They won't invest in someone as trivial as that asshole. Alex and you, well, you're both a little high profile to risk attracting attention, and Mark Swanson is inconsequential to their organization. The girl he assaulted being the big man's family, I'm really surprised they didn't put a hit out on him. But," his eyebrow shot up, "just to be safe, we're on it for a while longer. Boss' orders."

"Ugh! Alex needs a hobby." Angel chuckled and Cole burst out laughing.

"You're it. Didn't you know? See ya, later."

After Cole left, Angel took a long bath, letting the hot water soak into her skin. She lingered, paying careful attention to shav-ing her legs, and later, perfuming every inch of her skin with ex-pensive silk body lotion and meticulously coaxing her hair to fall in a mop of loose, sexy curls that cascaded in waves down to the middle of her back. Her make-up was meticulous, her eyes done in dark plum and shimmering silver. She was deep in thought when a text from Alex beeped on the phone he had given her.

I'm sending you something, so it's okay to open the door in three, two, one...

She rolled her eyes at the knock that accompanied the end of the text and threw on his burgundy robe and padded down the hall, tying the belt as she went.

She was met with another large bouquet of the Canna lilies; similar to the one that Alex had sent to her on their first date, and held by the same delivery boy. Pleasure rushed through her and a big smile spread across her face.

"Hello, again," she said happily.

"Dr. Hemming," the young man answered. His grey eyes wid-ened as they skated over her face and hair. He was dressed in baggy shorts that hung loosely to his knees, an over-sized red T-shirt and unlaced Nikes with no socks. A worn New York Giants cap was shoved on his unruly mop of dark hair. "Gosh! You look amazing! Er, I mean… not that you didn't look pretty last time. You did. But, uh…"

Her smile softened at his outburst, his face turning red at the speed of light.

"Thank you."

"I think I'll just shut up now," he murmured.

Angel laughed and took the bouquet into the apartment but the boy lingered in the doorway, her delight at Alex's thoughtfulness and the boy's compliment bursting forth. "Come in, please."

His eyes took in the size and elegance of Alex's foyer and he didn't move. "Uh, no, it's okay. Have a good evening, Dr. Hemming."

"Wait. I'll get you a tip." She set the crystal vase down on the mahogany entry table and reached for the card, unable to wait even a moment to read it. It was written in Alex's own bold handwriting, and his words filled her with pleasure and an incredible rush of love. She inhaled deeply as she read them again.

Remembering the night that changed my life.

Warmth spread through her at the implied meaning. Yes, tonight she would make sure he would know she loved him.

The boy called after her. "No need, remember? Have a nice evening."

Suddenly, the idea of a crowded restaurant wasn't as appealing. It was nearly six o'clock and she still had time to change their plans. Unsure if Tru offered take-out or delivery, she paused before closing the door. "Wait!"

"Yes, ma'am?" The boy loped back down the corridor away from the elevators to the door.

"Um… can you wait a second? I'm going to call the restaurant to see if they offer take-out, and if so, would you mind running to pick it up for me?"

"Oh, yes, ma'am! I'd be happy to!"

"Great. Will you hold on a second? I have to call to see if it's possible."

She left him in the foyer and proceeded down the hall into Alex's study. The room was much like the man, very masculine and strong. The furniture was solid but elegant and there were bookshelves lining one complete wall, some of the books clearly first editions, old and worth a great deal of money. The fireplace on the opposing wall was constructed of large Italian marble in dark browns and more of the large leather furniture that seemed to be his preference was sitting in the middle of the room.

His laptop was on the large desk and she fired it up, hoping she'd be able to find the menu online. Her eyes scanned the top of the desk. It was mostly unadorned, save for a leather desk protector, a few photos, and a makeshift award of one octave of piano keys mounted on a wooden and metal base. A metal plate on the front was engraved in cursive:

"Neither a lofty degree of intelligence, nor imagination, nor both together, go to the making of genius. Love, love, love… that is the soul of genius." – Wolfgang Amadeus Mozart

Angel's fingers traced over the words, perplexed at this obvious contradiction to Alex's self-confessed feelings on love, and her heart contracted in response. Maybe he'd been hurt. He'd never mentioned anyone breaking his heart, but it wouldn't be like him to admit to pain.

"Oh, Alex," she said softly, running her fingers over the words.

The shuffling in the other room, reminded her that the boy was waiting.

She wanted to write down the address of the restaurant, in case the young man didn't know where it was, but there was no paper on the desk. She pushed the massive chair back and turned toward the printer positioned behind her on the matching credenza situated beneath the only window in the room. She rolled her eyes when, pulling out the paper tray, found it empty. "Figures," she huffed in amusement.

She quickly began rummaging through the top drawer but found nothing but expensive pens, Alex's passport, a calculator, and nail clippers. She moved to the other drawers and quickly rifled through them, her fingers and eyes searching. When her fingers passed over something silken in the bottom drawer, Angel stopped dead.

A pair of blush and black silk panties stared her in the face. *Her panties.* She flushed, remembering how she left without them the first night she'd been with Alex, the same night he referred to in his note. Her fingers ghosted over the soft material as she pushed it to the side, chuckling; she decided to tease Alex about hoarding women's underwear later in the evening.

The only other occupant of the bottom drawer was a red file folder. Angel pulled it out, hoping to find the needed paper, but was instead confronted with a copy of her driver's license. Confused, her fingers sifted through the other contents, her movements slowing as what she was holding registered in her mind.

"Uhhh…" Angel's breath left her lungs in a whoosh. Heat burned in her cheeks and her heart thudded sickeningly in her chest as she saw her name repeated over and over again on the documents. Her eyes scanned the letter that was the second item in the folder. After registering the date, her vision blurred, anger and pain rising up inside. Her entire life was there; high school and college transcripts, her Ph.D. dissertation, a list of her old addresses and lists of friends, an article she'd written, her birth certificate, an old picture of her mother and father... and pictures of Kenneth along with his résumé.

When her eyes found mention of her mother's location in the letter, she couldn't read any more and slammed the folder shut. "What the fuck?" she breathed out.

Her lungs constricted, and she leaned back in the chair while it felt like a gaping hole was rapidly replacing the heart inside her chest. The blood pounding through her veins thudded loudly in her ears.

"Dr. Hemming?"

Her hands covered her face, and she inhaled until she thought her lungs would burst, the air rushing in and out of her lungs in shallow pants.

"Dr. Hemming? Did you still want me to run to the restaurant?"

Tears pricked at the back of her eyes, and her throat tightened painfully; the beautiful evening she'd planned seemed like a lie now. Her elbows rested on the desk, her head still in her hands as she willed herself not to lose it, not to cry or scream out loud. Shaking, it felt like the earth opened up and swallowed her whole.

How could Alex do this? Who in the hell was he? How can I love him when I don't even know him?

"Excuse me? Is everything all right?" he called.

She pushed back from the desk and walked on shaky legs back toward the boy who waited in the other room, blinking rapidly and swallowing down the emotion threatening to choke her as she tried to smile at the boy.

"Um, change of plans. I'm sorry I made you wait. You can go. Thank you."

He took in her flushed cheeks and the glisten in her eyes, uncertainty flitting across his features, but he slowly turned to leave. "Okay. Have a nice night."

"You, too."

When the door closed, Angel leaned against it. "Oh, my God. This isn't happening," she murmured softly, before yelling. "This isn't fucking happening!" Her fist slammed into the door beside her thigh.

Angel hurried back into the study once again and still glaring at her from the top of Alex's desk were all of the documents that summed up her life. It was like some stupid scene from "Who Framed Roger Rabbit" where the thing you despise most comes at you in an oversized, 3-D cartoon. She felt disgusted and betrayed. Amazing how one's entire existence could be reduced to nothing more than a meaningless paper trail. Her eyes darted from the desk to the fireplace. All of the hopes and dreams she had of a future with Alex had just gone up in smoke. Just like the contents of that file were about to do. Without trust, there was nothing. The first broken sob finally erupted and filled the room.

*****

Alex glanced at his watch. It was eight o'clock. An hour past the time Angel was supposed to meet him at Tru. After three glasses of Chivas on the rocks and a lot of inquiring glances from the staff, he'd gotten up and left the restaurant. Angel wasn't answering her phone; in fact, it wasn't even going to voicemail. He tried Cole and was unable to reach him either. His heart filled with sickening dread, and his stomach burned.

Alex tried her cell phone again, and, finally, he was able to leave a message. "Angel, where the hell are you? I'm on my way back to my apartment. For Christ's sake! I'm going crazy with worry. Call me the minute you get this."

When Alex's driver dropped him off, he paused briefly with the doorman. "Brody, did my brother and Dr. Hemming leave?"

"Mr. Avery left a few hours ago, sir. He was smiling big. Said he hadn't had a night off in three months and he'd be back to pick Dr. Hemming up but never came back."

Alex's mouth thinned into a hard line. "Thanks."

He had no choice but to wait for the elevator that took him to the penthouse though he itched to burst through the stairwell door and take them two at a time. Seventy-four stories and double that many flights of stairs were impossible on foot and definitely wouldn't be faster than the elevator. He swiped his keycard that allowed unrestricted access to his penthouse.

The floors that usually whizzed by seemed to take forever, and he cursed as the elevator stopped on the 52nd floor and an old lady, carrying a purse with one of those unrecognizable hybrid dog breeds sticking out of it, hobbled on.

"Hello, young man," she said pleasantly.

Alex tried to smile, but his guts were twisting into knots. "Good evening." He nodded and smoothed down the front of his jacket impatiently. *Fuck!* He closed his eyes as she rambled on about a bridge game on sixty-seven.

The car stopped again to let the woman off, and Alex prayed he'd have no more interruptions. He sighed as the elevator opened with nothing between him and the door to his place. He quickly walked to it, swiped the card again, and opened the door.

"Angel?" he called before he'd even gotten through it. "Angel!" The apartment was dimly lit with no sound coming from anywhere. Alex walked briskly from the empty kitchen into the living room, past the open door to his study, and down the hall.

"Angel!" he hollered again, panic seizing his chest. "Fucking answer me!"

He opened his phone and pushed her speed dial number, running up the stairs toward the bedrooms. Her phone began ringing then and he heard it in the other room. He moved toward the sound and his bedroom as it continued to register, the sound echoing strangely in his ear and the room around him. The door to his room was ajar and he pushed through it, eyes darting toward the ringing phone. His bed was strewn with clothes, a red file folder sitting in the center.

His heart fell and his steps slowed as realization hit him, and he flipped open the folder. Inside, there was nothing but the ringing phone he'd given to her. He sank down to sit on the edge of the large bed, his hand running through his hair, and heat infusing like poison beneath his skin. "Son-of-a-bitch! Un-fucking-believable." He rummaged through his contacts searching for the number to Angel's other cell phone and frantically waited for her to answer. It went straight to voicemail.

"This number will change so please call my office tomorrow, and if you're on the list I'll be giving to my assistant, she'll give you my new contact information. If this is Alex…" her voice cracked on the pause, and she cleared it. *"Please, just leave me alone. We're over."*

Alex's mind reeled and his heart raced with anger. How could I be so fucking stupid not to get rid of that fucking file folder?

"I never even looked at the goddamn thing, for Christ's sake! Aaarrrgggggghhhh!" he yelled and flung his own phone at the wall with such force it shattered into a hundred pieces. "Fuck!"

15

Hear Me

"ALEX! ARE YOU listening?" Allison's shrill question made Alex jump and brought him out of his reverie. His concentration was lost outside the glass windows at the back of his parents' large estate, past the deck to the large, manicured lawn, to the flock of geese swimming around in the lake.

His fingers scratched along his chin in introspection until her screeching caused his brow to furrow, and he sat up more into a sitting position with a grunt. His head pounded and his eyes burned from lack of sleep.

The house smelled of roast pork, spiced apples and the faint lingering aroma of expensive cigars. He wondered how in the hell his dad got away with smoking in the house because his mother had never allowed it during the time he was growing up.

"Alex!" she demanded again.

"Stop that infernal squawking, Allison," he said flatly, shooting her a bored expression. "You're giving my migraine a headache."

"I've been speaking to you for ten minutes or more!" she began but was interrupted.

"Yeah, that's the problem. I'm not in the mood."

Allison frowned and pursed her lips. She adored Alex, and the closeness she felt with him made her well aware he was not himself and far from his best form. She snorted shortly.

"I don't know what your problem is, but you're being rude!" Her eyes skated over her brother, and while he was immaculately dressed and his hair perfectly combed, he hadn't shaved, and there were suspicious purple shadows beneath his bloodshot eyes.

"You asked me to be here. I'm here. I only came to shut you up and yet there is still more of your endless screeching." He stood up and walked to the built-in bar on the far side of the great room. It was salvaged from an 18ᵗʰ century mansion and fit in well with the stone fireplace and dark olive walls. The house was built twenty years earlier, and his mother had taken great care to create Old World elegance from two centuries past. The ceilings, painted a light eggshell, and the plush carpeting added the only modern touches. He loved the surrounding grounds, but he preferred the contemporary minimalist décor of his place… or *Angel's*, he thought, disgust making him grunt.

Can't she leave my head for five fucking minutes? Would a five-min-ute reprieve be too much to ask? His hand closed over the decanter of amber liquid, and he splashed three fingers into a glass before loudly replacing the stopper and shoving the crystal back from the edge roughly. "Shouldn't you be helping Mom frost a cake or something?" he asked casually.

Allison scowled at him. "You're being a dick."

He stopped and turned around, shoving one hand deeply into the pocket of his slate grey dress slacks. Jeans weren't the attire his mother preferred at her Sunday dinners, but on this occasion, he had forgone the tie and left his dark blue dress shirt untucked and rolled the sleeves up beyond his elbows. His brow shot up. Allison never used profanity with such casualness. He only knew one woman who did. He took a big swallow from the glass and grimaced as the liquid burned its way down into his stomach as he willed his mind to shut off, yet he couldn't help but ask. "Been spending time with Angel, I see."

He watched his sister's expression change from anger to surprise. "Um, well…" she stuttered.

"Enough said."

"What's that supposed to mean?"

Alex leaned against the bar, facing her, his bland expression said he knew what she was hiding. "Don't fuck with me. What'd she tell you? About us, I mean."

Allison's features softened at Alex's subdued distress. If he was suffering, it wasn't showing other than his excessive drinking and pissy attitude. He'd always been moody when something bothered him. She shook her head sadly and walked toward him to lean on the bar beside him. Her lips thinned and her shoulders lifted in a slight shrug. "Nothing. Other than she didn't want to talk about it."

He swirled the liquid in his glass, watching it as if it kept him in rapt attention. "Yeah."

Allison reached out and laid a hand on his strong forearm. "Do *you* want to talk about it?" When he hesitated, she continued. "What's it about?"

"Misunderstanding." He pulled away as if her touch burned him and walked back toward the chair he'd just vacated. "It's ridiculous, really."

Allison pushed for more. "What did you do, Alex?"

"Nothing I don't always do. I did a background check."

Allison's mouth formed a small 'o', yet no sound came out. She was aware Alex made it a habit to find out about anyone he got involved with in advance, from business partners to relationships. But, after getting to know Angel, Allison understood that it wouldn't go over well with her.

"Hell," he said, exasperated, "it isn't like I singled her out!"

A slow, sad smile spread across Allison's delicate features. "Of course you have, Alex. Anyone that you sick Bancroft on has been singled out."

He could hardly argue with her. She was right. "When did you see her last?"

"Yesterday. She's helping with the last minute details of the benefit. She's extremely resourceful." The unspoken question lingered in his eyes with an unbidden hunger to know every detail of the time the women spent together, every word of their conversation. "Have you tried to talk to her yourself?"

Alex shook his head. "No." His answer was harsh and simple, but Allison knew that tone. He was not just hurt, he was mad as hell.

"I can see that you're upset, Alex, but doing nothing will not get the result you want. Call her."

His face twisted, and he swallowed more of the liquor he was holding. "No, Allison! Since we met, all I've done is chase after her, and that's not me. She made it plain she wasn't interested in my perspective when she left without giving me a chance to explain. Begging has never been in my repertoire."

"Pride is a funny thing. You've always had it too easy with women. Whitney still calls daily asking me to get the two of you together."

"Yeah, and Angel doesn't give a fuck, so can we please change the subject?" he asked angrily and started to walk from the room.

"You're wrong. She's upset too. She seems—"

Alex stopped and turned back around. "What?" His exasperated and anxious attitude evaporated as a small ray of hope bloomed in his chest. "How does she seem, Allison?"

Allison sighed, her eyes soft and concerned. "Sad. Just, very, very sad." She watched her brother raise a hand and rub the back of his neck wearily. She wasn't used to seeing him so... lackluster and broken. "You're coming to the benefit, aren't you?"

Alex raised his head to look into Allison's face, his own sadness too much to hide. He'd been planning on taking Angel, but now he had no interest in attending. "I'll write you another check, but no."

"But Avery is a major sponsor; you *have* to come, Alex! I have five tables reserved! The board members are attending as well as all the VPs! It's not black tie, so—"

Alex interrupted her in his irritation. Allison had a penchant for being overly dramatic.

"I'm not in the mood, okay? I don't have to do a goddamn thing, except run the business! I certainly don't have to keep up appearances and socialize with people I can barely tolerate when I feel like shit! I'm not going, Allison."

Allison's chin jutted out. "You know, Alex, someone might be trying to do you a favor! Go to the damn benefit!"

"Alex! Allison! Josh and Cole are back! Time for dinner," their mother called from the other room.

"Cole?" A new anxiety gripped Alex's chest. Josh had made a grocery run for their mother, but he had no idea his brother would be at the dinner. He quickly walked into the other room to come face to face with Cole as he unloaded a grocery bag next to their mother. "What are you doing here? Why aren't you with her?" he asked angrily.

"It's good to see you, too," Cole shot back blandly. "Angel is fine, Alex."

Cora looked up, confusion settling on her features. "Angel? When are we going to meet her, Alex? And why was Cole with her when she's dating you?"

Alex ignored his mother's question and concentrated on Cole. "I asked *why* aren't you with her?"

Cole smirked and set the last of the groceries on the counter as Allison began to help her mother put them away. All of them took note of Alex's agitation but only Allison and Cole understood.

"She doesn't need babysitting, and she told me she'd have me arrested for stalking if I didn't leave her alone."

"No, she won't. She's aware of the situation."

"Yep, and she told me to get lost. She's agreed to let me check in with her, but that's it."

Alex's face clouded in anger, and he clenched his teeth. He felt like acid was eating away at the skin of his neck and face. He'd been furious with Cole the night Angel left and still wasn't in a forgiving mood. "*I* didn't agree!"

"No offense, little brother, but right now, that doesn't seem to be a factor. She just wants some space. She agreed to call me when she's coming and going, and so far she has. I trust her. She just doesn't want me following her around. The um... *problem* is being monitored, instead." Cole's eyebrow shot up and the look on his face communicated what was needed. Alex visibly relaxed. "Since the recent disownment, well—" Cole's eyes darted to his mother to see if she was listening, "—let's just say the situation is under control. Chill out."

"You can't protect her if you aren't with her!"

"Bancroft assured me she's not in any danger. Swanson's *family* cut him loose, remember?"

Alex's lungs constricted, and Allison's hand closed around his forearm. She met his smoldering green eyes. "Go to the benefit, Alex."

"Is this your backward way of informing me that Angel will be in attendance? If she knows I'm going, she'll probably skip it despite her do-gooder nature."

"She'll be there, Alex," Allison reassured him with a nod. "Trust me."

Alex was already walking to Cora to place a soft kiss on her cheek. "Forgive me, Mother, but I won't be able to stay for dinner. I'll deal with you later," he shot at Cole, but he was already on his way out.

Cora's glance darted between her other two children's faces. "Is someone going to tell me what the hell is going on?"

*****

"This is Angel After Dark. What would you like to talk about tonight?"

Angel's hands trembled every time she pushed the button that connected her with a new call. She was a little stunned Alex hadn't called or tried to see her, and she was disappointed though she'd never admit it out loud. She still held her breath until she heard the voice on the other end of every call. He wasn't one to give up easily. However, she hadn't heard a peep from him, not once in the month since she'd burned the contents of the folder.

Becca admonished her for not giving Alex the opportunity to explain, but Angel had been too angry and hurt to confront him the night it happened. She was doing okay and would continue to put on a brave face, as long as she could maintain enough distance. After all, how could she give advice if she couldn't practice what she preached?

The problem was she missed him so much. The piercing pain of betrayal she felt had been replaced with an aching sadness, that seemed to be getting worse, and followed her through everything she did. She was haunted with memories; his presence lingered in so many places.

She put on a brave face, letting burning tears fall only when she was alone, sometimes in slow silence and only once in body-shaking spasms that she couldn't control. It happened when a week had passed without one attempt from Alex to contact her, and she was forced to face the fact that there was a chance he never would. Now, he still had the power to reach in and pull her heart from her chest; she silently chastised herself for falling in love with him in the first place. She knew it would all fall apart, yet she ignored her longstanding convictions. It was difficult to counsel other women on heartbreaking situations when her heart was no less broken.

Angel glanced through the glass at Christine as the call ended, grateful she had a three and a half minute break while the commercials rolled. Darian was sitting across from her for the first time in weeks, and she felt his eyes bore into her like a knife. He'd been there for two hours, and the situation hung like a wrecking ball over her head. Finally, she couldn't stand another second of it and her head popped up.

"What?" Her elbows were on the edge of the desk, and she raised both hands in exasperation, letting them land with a thud as she glared at him. "Why are you here? Go have boy-time with Alex! You're bothering the shit out of me!"

Darian sat back in the chair, his unhurried actions irritating Angel even further. "I'm the producer of this show, Angel. It's my right to be here." He studied her as she fidgeted in her chair and fiddled with a pen on the desk in front of her. She pretended to read over some paperwork that Christina had given her, but her eyes finally shot up to meet his. "Alex didn't want to have *boy-time,* as you put it."

Angel had the grace to flush and pushed back from the desk. Her discomfort was apparent to Darian as he studied her. She was flustered, some tendrils escaping from the messy bun she had on the top of her head, and her face was tense. "Just say it and leave."

"Say what? That it's unfair you didn't give him a chance to explain anything? Okay. It was unfair." His voice was devoid of emotion, but his mouth lifted in the start of a sardonic smile. "Happy now?" He wasn't sure whom he felt sorrier for: Alex or Angel. They both clearly cared about the other, and now they were both letting pride screw things up.

Angel sighed heavily. "No, I'm not happy at all," she answered in a quiet tone. "It's so great that he ran to you with his problems like a whiney little girl."

Darian laughed at the absurdity of the statement. "Hardly. I'm his best friend, and, despite popular belief, Alex is only human. It came out after half a bottle of scotch."

"Yes, I should have talked to him, but I felt violated!" Suddenly, Angel felt defensive. "I was so goddamned mad! We had such a beautiful evening planned and it all turned to shit. It felt like a lie to me, and it ripped me open. He doesn't trust me at all."

"I'd be mad, too, but he feels the trust is lacking on both sides. Understand that Alex is someone people want to get close to and not always for the right reasons. He's made a habit of protecting himself, his family, and his company. It wasn't personal. You were no different from anyone else."

"Yes, well, that's the problem. No different and not personal. It sure felt fucking personal!" Her voice rose as hysteria threatened to grip her chest. Her closed fist flew to press between her eyebrows, her eyes squeezed tightly shut as she fought the emotions down.

"That isn't what I meant, Angel. I shouldn't be the one telling you this. You should call Alex."

She walked across the room with her back to Darian. She didn't want him to see the trembling of her chin or the glistening tears building, despite all of her efforts to keep them at bay. "I'll think about it. Maybe he doesn't want to talk to me."

"You're correct. Maybe he doesn't, but you'll never know unless you call."

Let me just get through tomorrow night, she thought. "Okay, maybe I will next week." She couldn't be an emotional mess on stage; she was a professional. "Now, will you get the hell out of my studio? I need to finish this show." Her voice wavered slightly, and Darian got up and placed his hands on her shoulders and squeezed gently.

"Call sooner than later, Angel."

Angel closed her eyes, a lone tear falling from one eye tumbled down her soft cheek. She quickly whisked it away with her hand as Darian's hands released her, and he silently walked out of the studio.

"Angel, you're on the air in ten seconds," Christine called through the intercom.

Angel sucked in air, filling her lungs to capacity, and ran both hands through her hair, letting them stop to fist and tug on the silky strands. She took her place in front of the microphone and shoved the headphones back on her head as she watched Christine use her fingers to silently count down; three, two, one...

She went back to work, looking forward to the Ambien that would grant eight hours of relief later when she went home.

"This is Angeline Hemming; we're going into the last hour of the show, and it's time for our next caller." She pushed a call button. "Go ahead, you're on the air. What's your name?"

"Dr. Hemming! It's Whitney! I called you a few months back, and you gave me advice about my boyfriend. Do you remember me?"

The cold rush of apprehension raced over the surface of Angel's skin as the voice and name registered. Her heart started pounding sickeningly in her chest, and the desk and room blurred while the room began to spin. *Oh, my God!*

She swallowed hard and found her voice; her eyes flashed angrily in Christine's direction, who looked as horrified as Angel felt. *How in the hell did this call get through?* Angel mouthed silently.

I didn't know! Christine mouthed back.

"Yes. Of course. How are you, Whitney?"

"I'm amazing!" the other woman gushed on the other end of the line. "I took your advice! I kicked my man to the curb, and he came crawling back to me about two weeks ago! Things are better than ever! He appreciates me now. I just wanted to thank you for your help."

Angel felt sick to her stomach, and the chill on her skin was immediately replaced with raging fire seeping up from her neck to flush her face. Her breath rushed out, and her fingers curled into fists as unshed tears burned at the back of her eyes. She blinked them back hastily, praying for the strength she'd need to hide the turmoil she felt.

"Congratulations, Whitney," she said in a steady voice. "Good for you. Just stay strong, and don't let him use you again."

Angel reached a hand forward to end the call. It was visibly shaking violently, and she struggled to control it, curling her fingers into her palm. Apparently, Alex had moved on in a hurry, straight back to the arms of a woman he'd told Angel wasn't his equal. Though her heart burned like it would consume her and she wanted to scream out loud, she straightened her back in defiance, her jaw jutting out as she clenched her teeth, steeling herself to face the fucking facts. Alex wasn't going to call. He wasn't going to apologize, and he sure as hell wasn't as miserable as she was. If the intensity of their time together had been a lie then she was better off! She was strong, untouchable... and it was time she remembered that. She told herself she wouldn't let more tears fall for Alexander Avery. *Not one fucking tear.* And, she'd be damned if she'd ask Ally anything about her brother. Hell would freeze over first.

*****

Alex glanced around at the hundreds of people crammed into the venue. It wasn't like most of Allison's functions. This one was more casual, teeming with more activity and enthusiasm, more youth, and people from all walks of life. It was also apparent that it had been much more heavily promoted. A satellite truck from KKIS FM was parked outside, the jock broadcasting live from the event.

He only hoped that the alcohol flowed and the music was good enough to distract him until he could graciously escape without too much disdain from his little sister or his mother. His eyes searched for Allison. His parents, Cole, and Allison's husband, Josh, were sitting at the table reserved for them as Alex walked up. He grimaced when he saw Whitney sitting next to Josh. *What the hell is she doing here?* he wondered. He stopped and seriously considered leaving but hesitated too long. His mother spotted him.

"Alex!" she called and patted the chair beside her that had been saved for him. He reluctantly moved forward and leaned down to kiss her cheek. His father met his eyes and the two exchanged a knowing look. Charles was aware that Alex would not welcome the presence of his ex-girlfriend at an event that he'd already tried to get out of attending.

"Hi, Mom. Dad."

"I'm glad you're here, Alex," Charles stated and raised a hand to signal one of the waitresses to come over.

"I'm not," he muttered as he pulled out the chair and sat down after shaking Josh's hand and raising an eyebrow at Cole. Again, who was watching Angel? Bancroft had assured him that they were watching Swanson like a hawk, and he had confirmation that the Chicago mob was cutting ties with him. Alex was surprised that Swanson hadn't met with an unexpected accident since he held no value to the organization and he knew too much. Top it off that he'd been accused of rape by the niece of one of the most respected members of the organization, and Alex didn't hold out much hope for him. Part of him was glad. In his mind, no one deserved death more than that bastard.

The round tables for ten were arranged in a circular pattern around the dance floor and covered in dark blue linen, but that was where high society ended. Drinks were being served in plastic cups, and the staff was dressed in jeans and blood red T-shirts with the Leukemia and Lymphoma Society logo on the back in white. The lights were low, like a nightclub environment, with votive candles in clusters on the tables. The number of people milling around and crowding the dance floor and stage made it seem more like a concert than an organized benefit. Alex had been less reluctant to make an appearance when Allison mentioned the dress was casual.

Alex could physically feel Whitney's hungry eyes on him and had no choice but to speak with her. Obviously, Allison had invited her friend, but it would have been nice to be warned.

"Hello, Whitney; you look well." She was wearing a somewhat loose-fitting dress in mauve that made her look younger and softer than he remembered. It was a nice compliment to her complexion, the one-shoulder style baring some tanned skin.

"Thank you, Alex. I've missed you," Whitney said as she moved to the empty chair on his right, and, although Alex could guess what was coming and didn't particularly want to deal with it, he was nonplussed and distracted, his green eyes roaming the room, scanning the faces for Angel.

"Where's Allison?" he asked his mother, hoping the answer would also bring news of Angel.

"She's backstage, darling."

"Yeah, I can't wait to see this!" Josh put in. Alex's brother-in-law wore a happy grin. "She's so excited."

Alex's face took on a mocking expression. "About what? She does ten of these damn things a year. This one does look less stuffy, though."

"Allison is playing with the band!" Excitement danced in Cora's eyes.

Both of Alex's eyebrows shot up and his lips lifted slightly in surprised amusement. "What? Is it a band or a string ensemble? Shit, I was hoping the music would be somewhat tolerable."

"Alexander!" Cora admonished, but she was teasing as much as Alex was. She watched her middle child with careful consideration. Allison and Cole had spilled the whole story in her kitchen last weekend, and she finally understood the soulful mood haunting Alex the past few weeks. It also explained why she and Charles had seen so little of him in the past few months. It was clear that, finally, someone had touched his heart, and deeply. Cora heard about Angel from her other children but not much from Alex, which was perplexing. She was dying to meet her and know more, but the blonde sitting next to her son prevented her from asking any questions. She'd never liked Whitney, and she was relieved that Alex had moved on from her. "Are you okay, honey?"

Alex's green eyes met hers, and she sensed his quiet sadness. "Yes. I'm fine, Mother."

"Really?" she asked knowingly.

"I'm reeling, to be honest. I feel like I'm in a goddamn cage and someone is sitting on my chest. I just want to forget it ever happened."

"You never forget the good stuff," she said quietly.

"Yes, well, then I'm pretty much screwed for life."

The din of the band testing out the sound system and a room full of voices allowed for their conversation to be kept between the two of them.

"What's Whitney doing here?" his mother almost whispered, not wanting the woman to hear.

"Beats the hell out of me." He shrugged slightly and shook his head. "She didn't come with me. She probably wants to see Allison in *the band*. I wish to hell she wasn't sitting next to me, though. I don't need to deal with her bullshit tonight."

The waitress came and took their drink orders as the lights dimmed further and a screaming riff of rock music split the air. Then it softened into a quiet harmony between an acoustic guitar and piano as a spotlight came up to reveal Allison dressed in tight black jeans and a sleeveless top covered in silver sequins. The two large fans positioned at the sides of the stage blew her hair and the fabric of the blouse around her body.

"Good evening! I'm Allison Avery-Franklin, chairperson of this evening's event. Thank you all for coming and showing your support for the Leukemia and Lymphoma Society. It is my pleasure to present tonight's entertainment, one of Chicago's most renowned musical acts: Archangel!" The crowd erupted in applause and shouts and a bright smile split across Allison's face; her happiness was like a living thing. "Please give generously and enjoy the evening!"

The guitar faded away and the piano took over in a basic repetitive chord run of a song Alex recognized from his collection. The spotlight hit one of the guitar players as he began to sing and his instrument began to whine as the drums joined in with the strings. The crowd quieted, and Alex couldn't argue that the music was good. It wasn't long until the chorus hit and the background was filled with a female voice he'd heard before. His head snapped toward his brother, and even in the darkness, he could see Cole's eyes on him. He got up and walked quickly around the table to where Cole stood.

"Is Angel on that stage?" Alex asked emphatically. He was filled with emotions he couldn't define. Cole only nodded. He leaned in but had to raise his voice over the music. "Why the fuck didn't I know about this?"

"At first, she wanted to surprise you, but after you guys broke-up," he shrugged. "Well, she just didn't want you to know," Cole shouted back. "At least you know I didn't leave her unprotected. I've been watching her the entire time."

Alex couldn't help the twinge of pain and regret that shifted through him. "This is her band then? The one from college?"

"Yeah! They're awesome! I mean *really great!*"

Alex nodded but already his eyes were straining toward the stage, his ears picking out her voice from the harmonies. She sounded strong. Good. Amazing. His chest filled with pride.

"Wait until you see her. She's really in her element. Gorgeous!"

Most of the stage was in darkness, the spotlight on the one guitar player singing lead. He was lean and tough looking, the dark

T-shirt he had on had the sleeves cut out, exposing a few tattoos on his arms. The distance and Alex's preoccupation with locating Angel made it impossible to determine what they were.

The music was loud and the crowd boisterous, the dance floor filling with people actually dancing and more gathering at the front of the stage like groupies. Overall, the crowd was younger than expected, though Alex had seen some of the more prominent Chicago philanthropists when he'd first arrived.

"Do you know where she is?"

"Playing keyboards," Cole answered. "I didn't realize she was so good."

"There isn't much she does half-assed, is there?" Alex asked with a grin. He was filled with an anxious need to speak to her, to see her, to make things right between them.

Cole just smiled and shook his head. He didn't understand why his brother didn't pull his head out of his ass and talk to her.

As the song ended, the lights came up slightly, illuminating the rest of the instruments, and Alex's eyes darted to the keyboards, but a tall, gangly man was taking his place behind them. Angel walked up to the microphone, and Alex lost his breath. Her hair was a wild mass of waves, her eyes heavily made-up, and her lips a dark shade of red. Against her alabaster skin, it was a striking contrast. The breeze from the fans blew the sparkling black mesh dress to hug the lush curves of her body. The material was transparent, sleeveless, and low cut, hanging loosely over a small, black skirt that hugged her low on the hips, and a tight strip of matching black fabric across her breasts emphasized the swells of her breasts. Her legs looked like they went on forever, her knee-high platform stiletto boots were sexy as hell. Alex's gaze moved up over her firm, bare thighs, the dress sparkling as it blew around her body, and the heavy curtain of her hair moving in unison around her beautiful features. The hands wrapped around the microphone were encased in fingerless gloves up to her elbows. She looked tough, untouchable, but hotter than hell. His body reacted even as his heart ached. His eyes barely registered the other band members; the huge Hispanic man on drums, a blonde woman in a tight black dress standing at a microphone on Angel's left, along with two more men with guitars on either side of the stage, and Allison behind her. It all faded into nothingness around her.

Angel smiled brightly as the band began to play softly, her eyes scanning the room. Alex couldn't tell if she saw him, but she paused briefly before speaking. Her voice was warm and rich as it traveled from the speakers out over the room.

"Good evening!" Applause broke out and she waited for it to die down. "Thanks for coming out and helping in the fight against blood cancers! Everyone here is donating their time, which is a true testament to the people of this city! Even the servers and bartenders are giving all their tips to the cause, so if they do a good job, please give generously!" More applause, whistles, and yells followed.

"It's good to see you back with the band, Angel!" A man yelled from three tables away, and she smiled wider.

"Yes, it feels good to be back! What'd ya say we rock this bitch?"

Alex's face split into a grin and the room erupted at the same time as the beating drums and wail of guitar amped up for the start of the next song.

Alex didn't know how long he watched her, and though he didn't realize how, he'd ended up away from his table and closer to the stage. He was fascinated. She had such a commanding presence as she moved across the stage, interacting with other members of the band and the audience, as naturally as if she'd been performing forever. Alex didn't know a moment that he'd ever felt more proud; all the billion dollar deals paled in comparison. Even his acceptance to Julliard didn't come close to the fullness in his chest. She was mesmerizing, and he couldn't take his eyes off of her. She was sex personified, made worse because he had first-hand knowledge of the delights of her body, and how it reacted to his.

"Alex," Whitney said from beside him, her voice elevated to compensate for the music. "I'd like to talk to you, please. Can we go outside for a minute?"

He'd seen her out of the corner of his eye a few times trying to get his attention, but he had no desire to engage in any type of conversation. "Not now," he answered shortly.

Whitney's hand shot out to wrap around his forearm, forcing Alex to rip his eyes away from Angel and look at her. Despite the darkness, Alex could see the tears swimming in her eyes when the lights from the stage flashed across her features. "Please," she pleaded.

Alex turned to her. The pain he'd felt these past weeks making him more empathetic than he might otherwise have been. His hands closed around her shoulders. "This isn't a good time."

"Just for a minute." Her face twisted in pain. "Please," she said again.

Alex sighed. The band was announcing a break, and all he wanted to do was go backstage and get a chance to talk to Angel. He'd never been good at groveling, but he loved her and he realized he'd do whatever he had to do to get her back. The hundreds of male eyes trained on her for the past hour and a half convinced him not to waste any time. He wasn't sure yet how he'd get her to listen, but he was damn straight going to try.

"Whitney, I'm sorry you're upset. Really, I am, but I can't right now."

Alex left her and found the stairs that led up to the stage and pushed through the curtain. His eyes scanned the dim light as several of the band members moved off in the other direction. Angel had her back to him as the arms of the male lead wrapped around her small form. She hugged the man back as he lifted her off the floor, and Alex's lungs were paralyzed as if caught in a steel vice.

He clawed at the front of his shirt, trying to ease the tightness in his chest; the enthusiasm of a moment before exploded in shards of red light behind his eyes. This was surely Kyle; the familiarity between the two of them was eating away at Alex's guts.

What the fuck am I doing? Running to her with my tail between my legs while she runs into the arms of another man? Alex's mind raced, conjuring all sorts of sickening possibilities he didn't want to consider.

Each second felt like a year as he watched the embrace in slow motion, fingers gliding down her back to the bare skin of her midriff barely covered by the sheer mesh. As far as Alex was concerned, Angel belonged to him, goddamn it! So what was she doing cavorting with someone else? Kyle, still holding Angel, caught his gaze and leaned in to say something to her and touched her face with his hand before he walked away. Finally, Alex was able to read the tattoo on his shoulder and jealousy rushed over him in an angry wave.

Angel turned, a surprised look on her face that started to turn into a smile as her features softened

"Alex, I wanted to…" she began and took two steps toward him.

"What the fuck do you think you're doing?" he thundered at her, not hearing her words as his face twisted in jealous rage. "Prancing around like a peacock and letting men put their hands all over you!"

Angel was startled for a second before her face clouded and she railed back at him. "It's none of your damn business! Oh, I know! Why don't you just have Bancroft investigate me again? I thought you knew all about me, tracked my every! Fucking! Move! That was Kyle!" she said, as if that explained everything.

"I know who the hell he is!" Alex moved forward like lightning and grabbed her arm. "What the fuck are you wearing?"

"Clothes." Angel rolled her eyes and grabbed a water bottle that was sitting on one of the oversized speakers, trying to ignore

Alex's aggression. "You know *clothes*? The things you put on when you're not screwing someone's brains out?" she snarked.

Alex yanked her back a few feet in an attempt to speak to her out of the others' earshot. "Every goddamned man here wants to fuck you!"

"Really? Wow. That's original! I bet you worked on that one all goddamned day!" she scoffed back, yanking her arm free and stomping off to the very back of the stage away from Allison and Crystal, who stood there agape.

"Damn it! Don't you walk away from me!" Alex stormed.

She turned, abruptly, facing him, her arms flying into the air. "What are you doing here? Did you come just to screw me up so I can't do the job I'm here to do? Well, fuck you!" Her chest was rising and falling rapidly, her face becoming flushed and her eyes flashed furiously as she resumed her retreat.

Alex caught up to her in four strides and flipped her around by her shoulder. "I told you in the beginning, honey, all you have to do is ask! Anytime, anywhere, any way you want it." Emotion clouded his objectivity and shook him to the core, and loosening his hold on control of his actions and words.

"Oh, for God's sake! Shut up and leave! You're making a scene and asses out of us both!" She stumbled backward, the heels of her boots catching on some of the cables of the electric instruments and she started to fall. Alex's arms closed around her as her hand pulled back and slapped his left cheek as hard as she could. Frustration brought angry tears to her eyes as a sob rose up in her chest. "Don't touch me!" she panted, her brown eyes shooting daggers. "Let go!"

Alex's own pulse was pounding, his breathing labored as his eyes met his sister's pained look behind Angel. Allison shook her head and put her hand to her mouth. Alex stopped dead; his green eyes searching Angel's brown ones for something other than anger and hatred. Her jaw was pushed out defiantly, and her eyes glistening with unshed tears, as her breath huffed from between her open lips. Even though he was furious, the last thing he wanted was to hurt the woman he loved more than his own life.

Alex's hand unwrapped from around her gloved forearm, consciously making the choice to release her. He was mad as hell and his chest ached, but he was who he was and he sure as hell didn't let his emotions make an ass of himself. He was lucky the scene took place behind the side curtain and only a few people were there to witness it.

Angel moved to the keyboard on shaky legs and took her place behind it, longing to put something solid between them. She'd never seen him angrier, and still, he stood there glaring at her, his chest heaving with effort, his hands clenched into fists at his sides. He was so fucking beautiful, even then.

Her head fell to rest on tented hands as she struggled to control the quaking. She still had another hour and a half to get through, ten more songs to sing without a fucking crack in her voice. If he wouldn't leave, she'd make it impossible for him to talk to her in the only way she had left. Her fingers slid over the keys, despite her bandmates not being in position; she played and raised her head, the tears glistening in her eyes.

What she saw next almost broke her resolve, and her fingers faltered, if only for a note or two. A blonde woman was standing off to one side just behind Alex, her long, red-tipped hand wrapped around his bicep. The woman pulled on his arm and said something Angel couldn't hear, even as his eyes still burned into her soul, sucking away her life like a greedy sponge. She wanted to scream and cry and die. It had to be Whitney. Who else could it be after the phone call the night before?

"Leave!" she mouthed, hatred at his betrayal playing on her features.

She closed her eyes and swallowed the lump in her throat. Jesus, it hurt, but when she opened them again she began to sing in

an aching voice, emotion flowing through it and washing over
Alex. The song she sang, a cover of Kelly Clarkson's *Hear Me*, was
one she could start without the others, one that told Alex what she
needed to say to him.

Whitney's hand slid down to Alex's, and his clamped painfully
around it as he turned abruptly and briskly walked away, pulling her
behind him. The woman shot a smug look over her shoulder as
they disappeared down the stairs and into the throng. The message
was clear.

Angel watched in stunned disbelief as he walked away from
her. It killed her. The pain was worse than she'd ever thought possible as he made his intentions clear. Angel tried to focus on her
hands on the keys, letting her anguish invade her voice as the image
of her man leaving with another woman engulfed her. Torturous
images of the two of them making love flooded her head. She
willed herself not to lose it. She couldn't cry. She couldn't let him
humiliate her more than she already was.

16

Love and War

ANGEL'S ACHING VOICE followed Alex through the
crowd as he made his way down the stairs and past the table where
his family was seated. He briefly met Cole's disapproving gaze, ignoring his mother's stunned expression, and he kept moving with
Whitney toward the bar along the back of the venue.

He needed a drink. Several drinks, in fact. He didn't know
what the fuck he was doing, but watching Angel with Kyle and
seeing her name inked on his fucking shoulder had set his heart on
fire. His insides burned with jealousy. She owned the other man
just as she'd staked her claim on him, and the knowledge anyone
else would be as connected to her made him insane. He'd even
named the goddamned band after her!

"Scotch, neat," he commanded and threw a hundred dollar
bill on the bar. "Leave the bottle, and please get the lady anything
she wants." He turned, his eyes trained on the stage, his breathing
shallow, and a soft sheen of perspiration breaking out on his brow
and upper lip. He was far enough away that Angel wouldn't be able
to see him through the throng and the bright lights trained on her,
but he could see her, still at the piano, her voice strong as she

waded through the notes. His gaze darted to Kyle, who became the bane of his existence; the focus of his hatred from the minute Alex had seen him holding her when he'd run backstage like a lovesick teenager to beg her forgiveness! He huffed out loud and threw back the burning liquid. "Again," he muttered at the faceless bartender as he shoved his glass forward to be filled.

"Alex," Whitney began, but his hard glare effectively silenced her, and she took a seat to his left and quietly sipped on her piña colada. Alex grimaced. *A fucking piña colada! How fitting!* Convoluted, milky, cloyingly sweet and predictable. What a contrast to the rich earthiness, depth of color, and complexity of flavor of the various wines Angel preferred, each one with individual nuances, a surprise each and every time.

Alex shook his head and a bitter laugh burst forth as the parallels between the two women and their drinks of choice hit him right between the eyes. Whitney eyed him warily, her finely manicured brows lifting in question. She was clearly wondering at his crazed outburst. He laughed so hard half the scotch in his glass slopped over before he raised it to his mouth and downed the rest.

"Could this be any more goddamned ironic?" he asked to no one in particular. "I mean, seriously? Fucking hilarious!"

His shoulder was shoved back violently and he sobered, registering his brother's large presence. "What in the hell do you think you're doing?" Cole's eyes skittered over the woman sitting beside Alex, her hand on his arm even as Alex ignored her. It was obvious Alex was furious, but he clearly wasn't thinking straight. Despite the ridiculous laughter when he approached, Cole knew Alex well and he sure as hell wasn't one to drink excessively or let emotions dictate his actions. To do so would mean a loss of that precious control.

Alex glared at Cole and reached for the bottle of liquor behind him on the bar and started pouring another drink. "Getting comfortably numb." He was just barely feeling the effects of the alcohol. Scotch had become somewhat of a friend over the last month when he couldn't sleep, couldn't keep from turning on the radio, and couldn't forget. Whitney's hand tightened on his arm and, for the first time, he noticed she was touching him. "Maybe some much-needed recreation," he said to Cole, taking a long pull from the glass, his eyes unavoidably drawn to the stage and the woman at the center of it. His chest tightened painfully. His mind was made up. He needed to purge the demon that possessed him.

The triumphant look on Whitney's face disgusted Cole. He, who used to pick up chicks and fuck their brains out for no other reason than they were in front of him, found Alex's actions abhorrent.

"Think about what you're doing, Alex. You're pissed off right now and out of your mind."

"Pissed? Is that what I am?" He emptied his glass and began pouring again. "I'm tired of thinking," Alex said. "It's time I did something other than feel like shit."

"You'll work things out with Ang—"

Alex threw up his hand and stopped Cole. "Don't say that name to me. Ever again! How can I trust you, anyway? You lied to me about staying with her."

Everything began to blur—the room, the music, and his intentions—as the large quantity of scotch finally buzzed his mind slightly, but he was still way too lucid for his own comfort. He closed his eyes and still he saw large, liquid brown eyes, flowing dark auburn hair, and he swore to God he could smell the sweet and musky scent of her perfume mixed with sex, feel the luscious curves pressed warmly against the hardness of his body, and hear her voice breathing out his name when he made her come.

"Jesus Christ!" Alex muttered, shaking his head in disgust.

He threw back the drink and stood up from the chair, taking Whitney's hand in his again as Angel's voice blended with Kyle's in a softer song. He was determined to do whatever he needed to forget, even if it ripped his heart out in the process. "Let's get out of here."

*****

Alex followed Whitney into the apartment and the door closed behind him. His eyes didn't recognize his surroundings; the alcohol and his pounding head blurred his vision. The events of the night still in effect, he clawed at the pain in his chest. It hurt and he was hot, despite the drop in temperature. Sweat broke out on his upper lip, and he wiped the back of his hand across his forehead and then his mouth.

"Do you want a drink, sweetie?" Whitney cooed.

His stomach turned, and he tried to swallow the tightness in his throat, bile rising until the sour taste laced his mouth. Alex shook his head, stumbling into the living room and falling into a large chair. It was fluffy and over-exaggerated—not his taste at all.

"Uh-uh. No more. I shouldn't even be here," he mumbled, more to himself than to her.

Whitney's low laughter fell around him in the small space. For the first time, he registered that this was not the apartment he'd paid for, though some of the furnishings were familiar.

"Of course you should, silly. I'll take care of you. Just like before." She dropped to her knees in front of him, her fingers closing around his thighs and raking upward toward his hips and groin.

Alex cringed. She never took care of him. She'd only slaked his lust. These were not the hands he wanted. His eyes closed, head dropping back as he remembered Angel on that damn stage with Kyle. She was so beautiful, ethereal, and untouchable... by him at least. *Kyle has no problem touching her.* Heat seared in his gut and pain pierced his heart. *Just forget her. She's killing you. Forget her any way you can.*

His head snapped up as he forced his eyes open, trying to bring Whitney's face into focus. Her lips were too red, her voice too shrill, her body too skinny, and those plastic, out-of-proportion tits poked toward him as if in some absurd 3-D film. Alex's lips lifted in a sardonic smirk and he almost laughed out loud. He should just let her suck him off and try to forget his world had been reduced to a series of torturous lifetimes punctuated by a few blissful, mind-blowing moments.

He reached out and wrapped some of her blonde hair around his fist. She sighed, her eyes victorious. Her hands moved up his thighs toward the closure on his jeans and he let her, telling himself to just close his eyes and be a man. He should just fuck her sense-less and get back to his life. Back to unfeeling, uncomplicated... *unbeautiful*. Easy, controlled, and empty.

Whitney's hands rubbed over his cock beneath the denim, and he willed it to get hard. He pulled her onto his lap, his hands rough as her wet mouth found his. His cock responded as he imagined a different woman in his arms.

"Oh, Alex, I missed you."

Please, stop talking, his mind screamed. *That's not the voice I need.*

His lips took hers roughly, his tongue pushing into her mouth and his moved, searching for something, *anything* to make this hap-pen, but after a minute or two of frantic groping and her grinding on his crotch, his heart ached more and more. It seized even more when his cock twitched unwillingly under her continued kneading. He could fuck her, his traitor body would respond, but he didn't want to. It fucking killed him that it was even possible.

He turned his head away in disgust. Her mouth was too sloppy, too loose, and not Angel's. Whitney was making loud mewling noises, frantically panting and still clutching at his hair, trying to turn his head back.

"Alex, please," she begged. "I want you."

"I... I'm..." Alex shook his head to clear some of the alcohol-induced haze. "I can't do this, Whitney. It isn't going to happen." His hands found her upper arms to stop her body from rocking into his. "Stop," he said as he tried to still her.

She continued to pull on him, trying to kiss him even as he turned away, desperate to have him back, desperate to get him away from the other woman.

"I said stop it!" He commanded as his hands closed around her wrists and held them between them.

She stopped moving and looked at him, unable to deny the truth she found in his eyes and his hard expression.

"I'm in no condition to do this, even if I wanted to."

"But, you don't want to," Whitney stated simply, her eyes filled with tears as her face fell.

Alex pulled in a breath as he pushed her from his lap and stood, beginning to straighten his clothes and doing up his jeans quickly. "No. I'm sorry."

Whitney sat on the ottoman where he'd deposited her and didn't bother to pull down her skirt or replace the strap on her shoulders as silent tears rolled down her cheeks. Her breasts were grotesque to him now when he used to find her beautiful. Now, no one was beautiful. Except *Angel.*

"It was wrong of me to come here. Wrong to let you think there could ever be anything between us again. I have no excuse and I'm an asshole. I'm sorry, Whitney."

"Why don't you want me?" she asked quietly, though her tone was bitter. "Why didn't you *ever* want me? Why am I not good enough?"

Alex ran both hands through his hair and cringed at the differences as he turned way. Angel would never cower and cry at his feet, begging like this. There were times when she'd begged him to fuck her, sure, but it always felt more like a demand or a siren's song he couldn't resist. He wanted to go to her. Even with another woman sobbing in front of him, Angel was all he could think about, the hurt on her face when he left her up on that stage, her voice singing to him as he left with Whitney, was ripping at his guts like acid. There was a woman in pain in front of him, yet all he could think about were the soulful brown eyes, hardening in determination to get through her set even as her voice audibly cracked. He knew he'd hurt her like hell and it disgusted him. He felt claustrophobic, the walls closing in around him. He had to get the hell out of there.

Alex rubbed his hand over his mouth, trying to lose the feeling of the kisses that he'd just been party to. He felt guilty, dirty... and deeply sad. "It wasn't your fault. It was always me," he murmured, turning back to her with a slight shrug.

She cried harder, and Alex moved toward her, pushing the straps of her dress up over her shoulder again then pulling her to her feet, before turning away.

"But, why her and not me? This is because of *her*!" Whitney yelled after him.

"I can't tell you something I don't even know myself. We were over before Angel and I met. I never meant to hurt you."

He turned again and began to walk toward the door.

"But why *her*?" she screamed after him.

Alex stopped and turned. "It's beyond me. I can't control what she does to me. She... *creates needs*... only she can ease."

"Well, you won't find it so easy this time, Alex! After Allison told me... Let's just say that seeing is believing."

"Goddammit! What did you do?" Alex demanded.

"Thanked her for her advice. But, it was enough. She got my point. I made sure of it tonight! It will serve you right when she tells you to fuck off, and you get what you give. Finally."

*****

Her heart was breaking, falling in shards, ripping and tearing her flesh as they fell. Angel buried her face in Kyle's shirt and sobbed uncontrollably. How fucking ironic was this? Sobbing her eyes out in the arms of her ex-lover was certainly the last thing she ever thought she'd do. She never thought she'd cry like this over a man. *Ever.*

"Shhh, honey. Angel, it'll be okay."

She shook her head without moving away. "No, it won't," she said simply. "I feel like I'm dying, Kyle. I'm—fucking dying!" Her shoulders shook softly as she continued to cry, soaking his shirt. "How could he do this to me?" Her lungs wouldn't pull in the air she needed. "How could he leave with her?"

Kyle rubbed her back over and over, hushing her and doing his best to soothe her hurt. "He's a guy and he was pissed, Angel. Alex looked like he wanted to kill something. He was crazy with jealousy. He obviously cares about you."

"The hell he does! He's only upset because, for once in his life, he isn't getting what he wants. He doesn't care about me. If he did, he would be here with *me*, not fucking *her*!" She knew she sounded crazed, and her heart protested at her lack of control. He'd shown he cared before, but it was such a contradiction to his actions now.

"You don't know that's what he's doing. Stop doing this to yourself." Kyles voice took on a soothing tone.

Angel pushed back and looked up. Her eyes were swollen, and her tears left tracks of mascara and smeared make-up down her face. "He was holding her hand! That was his way of making sure I'd know his intentions. How could he be such a bastard?" Her face crumpled again and a quiet sob broke free of her chest. "He knew what it would do to me!"

Kyle's arms wound around her as she burst into a new fit of tears. "Angel, you're going to make yourself sick. You have to calm down. You were amazing tonight, and he had to have seen it."

"So what? He's more interested in convincing me he doesn't give a shit and that he never loses his precious control!"

Kyle sighed. He had to admit, if positions were reversed, he might have done the same thing. "He doesn't want to seem vulnerable, Angel. But, he is. That's easy to see."

"Uh-uh," she cried. "He's fucking *fuh—fine!*"

They were sitting on the floor in front of her couch. She'd fallen apart the minute her door closed, somehow managing to hold it together through the last set. Allison and the boys, even Crystal, hadn't said much when Kyle had offered to take her home. Allison had pulled her phone from her pocket and began texting furiously. Even Cole let her leave without stopping or following her. Angel didn't protest about leaving her car behind or Kyle putting her into his, a sure sign of her fragility. Maybe it was an attempt to get back at Alex, unsure if she wanted him to know he was killing her or that she didn't give a damn either way.

A few minutes later, Angel quieted, and Kyle nudged her chin up with his thumb. "Do you want some wine or something? I saw a bottle of red on the counter. It might help calm you down."

Angel nodded wearily, pushing her tear-dampened hair off her face. She could smell the hairspray and she wrinkled her nose. "The glasses are hanging there." Her hand waved in the direction of the kitchen as she scrambled onto the couch and curled up in a ball on her side. Her nose was stuffy and she sniffed then wiped at her eyes.

Drawers opened and a hollow rattle of metal on metal echoed as Kyle dug around in the drawer for a corkscrew. Angel's damp eyes were tired and refused to focus. The Chicago skyline blurred in the frame of her great room window, becoming nothing more than a multicolored smudge, a blurry rainbow of dark and light.

Her heart squeezed inside her chest, and she felt sick to her stomach. *How could I let this happen? How can I love him this much?* Her eyes stung again, but she bit her lip hard, hoping the pain would stem the tears from falling.

"This place is yowza, Angel. Really nice. I guess psychology pays better than singing."

"Thanks, but you guys should have a record deal. You're more than good enough."

"If it's meant to be, it'll happen. Maybe if you were still fronting us, then, yeah."

"You don't need me. You're all amazing." She sniffed and wiped at her nose with the back of her hand. "Won't Crystal be upset that you're here?"

He reappeared with two wine glasses filled halfway with the deep garnet liquid. "She saw what went down with Alex. You and I are friends now." The words sounded weird to Angel in light of the song and the scene Alex had witnessed.

"Really?" she asked hesitantly.

Kyle shrugged. "It's what I'm left with. If I have to live with it, Crystal does, too."

"Easier said than done," Angel murmured, feeling suddenly sorry for the other woman. "See how well I'm handling Alex and Whitney."

"That's because that bitch wants him. You're clearly over me; even Crystal could see that tonight."

When Kyle handed her a glass and then sank down next to her again, her eyes fell to his left shoulder. The tattoo was glaring proof of their past relationship. She flushed, realizing Alex must have seen it. She touched the outline of it with her finger.

"This was so dumb."

"It didn't make a difference anyway," he said quietly with a shrug. "I was such a dick."

Angel leaned up on the arm of the couch and took a swallow of wine. "Shit happens. It's in the past."

"But, I'm sorry. Angel. I'm not sure if I'm sorrier for you or me."

Angel's expression softened and gentle fingers traced Kyle's jaw.

"I've never seen you like this. Were you this hurt... when we, I mean, by me?"

Angel inhaled deeply, meeting his brown eyes with hers. "Sure, it hurt. I think most of it was that Crystal was so different and not like me at all. I thought you could do better and, honestly, I'm shocked you're still with her. Really, Kyle, I want you to be happy, but Crystal is not the one for you."

He shrugged. "I let *the one* get away. Hopefully, Alex is smarter than me."

Angel's chin jutted out. "Obviously not. He did the same thing; chose someone else."

Kyle studied her face and watched as her chin began to tremble. "No, he didn't. You don't know he's cheating."

Angel closed her eyes and swallowed hard as visions of Alex making love to Whitney filled her mind. "God, I wish I could shut off my brain."

"What is it about him? His money? His family or the company?"

She shook her head thoughtfully. "No. When I look at him, I don't see any of that. It's how he makes me feel. I've never felt so desperate or so... *beautiful*. It's like when he's with me, I'm a better version of myself. When he touches me, I come alive. Does that make sense?"

Kyle's face fell slightly, but he nodded. Angel could see the regret in his eyes and knew her words pained him. "I'm sorry, Kyle."

"It doesn't hurt that he's loaded, though," he muttered.

"He doesn't buy me things because he knows I wouldn't want it. His money doesn't factor into it. He's just... *Alex*. I've known all along he'd gut me. And I... let it happen. I have no one to blame but myself. He told me going in he didn't fall in love."

Angel laid her head on her folded arms that rested on the edge of the couch, and the two of them sat quietly, listening to music. It calmed her down, and eventually, her eyes started to droop.

"I probably should get going, Angel. Crystal is probably ready to kill me by now." He touched her knee and shook it gently. She got up sleepily and walked with him to the door, rubbing her eyes and smearing her mascara and tears into a black mess. Her nasal passages were swollen from her tears, which made her voice sound funny.

Kyle was hugging her goodbye when someone banged the door loudly five times. Angel started in his arms with a gasp.

"What the hell? It's three in the morning!" Kyle mumbled, turning to open the newly replaced door.

"No, Kyle. Don't open it," she whispered, her heart dropped like a stone. "Just be quiet."

"Open up, Angel! I know that son-of-a-bitch is in there with you! Open the fucking door! Now!" Alex's voice roared from the hall. More pounding followed. "*Angel!*"

Kyle's eyebrows shot up as he watched Angel come forward slowly; he could see her trembling. Her hand reached out tentatively and touched the wood. She jumped again when Alex resumed the pounding.

"Goddamn it! I said open this door right now!" The handle rattled as he shook it violently from the other side.

"Go away, Alex," she said quietly, knowing she wouldn't be strong enough to turn him away if she looked him in the face. "I can't right now."

"If he's touched you, I will fucking rip him limb from limb! Now open the goddamned door!" He pounded one more time with such force that it made the walls shake.

"Just go away, Alex." There was defeat in her voice as she leaned her forehead against the door as Kyle waited beside her silently. "What do you care if he touched me after what you've done tonight?"

Seconds ticked by, and Angel was scared of what was next… scared he'd walked away or what he'd say.

"Angel," Alex's tone was calmer but clearly strained. "We need to talk."

She leaned her head on the door, eyes closed, fingers grazing the wood. "You said it all when you left with Whitney."

The door banged loudly enough to shake the art on the walls and make Angel jump again. One single hit. "Uuugggghhh! We both know I can break this fucking door down, Angel! Now, let me in!"

"Angel, we have to open the door. Your neighbors will call the cops," Kyle said as he pulled Angel behind him and then opened the door a crack.

"Don't, Kyle!" She tried to stop him, but it was too late.

"Look, man…" he began and was then hurled backward into Angel, sending her slight form tumbling to the floor as Alex pushed forcefully through and into the room.

"You! Get out!" he yelled angrily at Kyle, pointing a finger at him, his eyes on fire. He was livid as he let a right hook fly that hit Kyle squarely in the jaw. The other man stumbled backward as pain shot through Alex's hand. When Alex saw Angel on the floor, his expression changed and filled with worry as he moved toward her. Kyle's hand closed over Alex's shoulder and whirled him around, putting his hand up between them.

"She's not in any condition to talk. Give her some time."

Alex's focus was totally on Angel as he turned back to her. He bent to help her up but she scrambled out of his reach.

"Get bored fucking Whitney? She's not me, you bastard!" Angry tears fell on her cheeks, and Alex took it all in, despite the alcohol he'd consumed. She was a disaster. Broken and furious, her hair a wild mess, tears leaving make-up tracks down her face. "She'll never be *me*!"

"I know, sweetheart..." He reached for her.

"No!"

Alex felt ill as Angel stumbled away as if his touch would burn her. When she reached the sanctity of her room the door slammed, leaving the two men where they stood. Alex started after her, but Kyle's words stopped him.

"You fucked her up bad, man. She doesn't need this right now."

Alex's fists clenched and the muscle in his jaw worked overtime. "Don't tell me what she needs! I know her better than you will ever dream of. This doesn't concern you." His voice was quiet, but deadly.

"I've known her longer than you—"

Alex's nostrils flared angrily and his chest heaved. "That's irrelevant, trust me," he shot back.

"Look, I still care about her." Kyle could see the misery in Alex's expression, and it stopped him from full-on assault. He put up both hands in front of him to silently ask Alex to calm down. "If I were you, I'd hope to hell I didn't fuck that other bitch tonight. Take it from someone who knows. She forgives me now, but only because she doesn't give a damn anymore. Having Angel not care is something you'll never recover from."

Alex paused and looked at the other man, his eyes narrowing before his anger faded. He nodded in understanding before striding down the hall to her room, thankful when he found it unlocked. His heart felt ready to explode, his throat was tight, his eyes on fire. He opened the door slowly. He had to make her understand.

"Baby?" The room was in darkness. "Angel?" He could hear her crying softly, but couldn't see her.

"Please don't call me that!" she begged, humiliated. She'd rather die than have him see her so broken. She cleared her throat and hardened her voice. "It feels like a lie. It's over."

"The fuck it is," he said quietly.

"Well, sloppy seconds aren't my style." Her voice was hoarse and thick with her tears.

Alex walked to the other side of the room and found her huddled in the corner behind the bed, a dark ball of shadows.

Alex's heart broke. "You say that to me when I find you in here alone with *him*?"

She slid up the wall until she was standing and folded her arms across her chest. "Fuck you! You made me watch you leave with her knowing I had to keep singing! Do you know how fucking hard that was?" He heard the pain; he could see it on her face as her brow crinkled and she closed her eyes.

"Goddamned right, I did!" he railed. "I wanted you to suffer like you've made me suffer! You're dragging me through hell!"

"How? By forcing you to be honest? Did you have files on all of your women? Investigations of us all?"

"Yes! So what?" Alex barely hesitated. He sighed and ran a hand over the lower half of his face. "It means nothing."

"From what I saw, you had every day of my life documented," she spat out.

"That's what I did! I found out about women before I got involved. Think about it! I have my family and business to protect. But with you... none of it mattered."

"Right. I guess I imagined that file in your drawer next to my panties," she said sarcastically. "I bet it bored the shit out of you."

"I didn't read it, Angel!" he yelled at her. "After I met you, I put it in that drawer and haven't touched it since."

"Why should I believe you? You lied about Mark Swanson, too. You had me tailed without telling me!"

"*I lied* about that bastard? *You* lied to *me*! You didn't tell me the whole story and wouldn't let me protect you! If you were honest with me in the beginning, I could have been, too. What the fuck was I supposed to do?"

"Nothing! You were supposed to do *nothing!*"

"Like hell! I'd go back and kill that motherfucker if I could get away with it!"

"It wasn't your problem until we agreed on the plan!"

Alex laughed, sarcasm dripping. "Everything to do with you is my problem, Angel!"

"I can take care of myself! I don't need you!"

Her words hurt and he visibly recoiled, but then turned and railed at her. "And we see how well that went, right? Stop trying to change what this is about! You're killing me—maybe both of us—and, for *what?* What does this prove?" He moved closer, and she turned her head, unable to bear the pain in the green depths, trying to block out the voice that filled all of her fantasies, afraid to believe anything he said. "It was a stupid file. It means nothing!" Alex insisted again.

His hand closed around her arm above her elbow and pulled her closer, his other arm going around her waist, dragging her roughly into his arms. Angel resisted, pushing roughly against his chest in protest, but he had her against a wall, and she was trapped by his body.

"It means I can't trust you!"

"No, it doesn't! It means I'm not used to trusting *anyone.* I had it compiled before we'd even met. Are you trying to convince me you don't need me? Fine. But, *talk* to me. Yes, I fucked up, but don't push me away." His lips rested against her forehead as he spoke, and he breathed in her scent, fingers kneading the soft flesh of her arm. As always, the need to touch her overwhelmed him.

"I need distance. I can't function like this, Alex! Please. I can't think straight when you touch me." She didn't have the strength to push him away but willed herself to maintain control and not melt into him.

"No. Just once, I can't give you what you ask. I can't breathe when you're in front of me and I can't touch you. All night, I was suffocating."

"Then tell me you didn't fuck her," she commanded miserably. The other woman's perfume was a sickening assault on her nostrils, and she wanted to vomit, her heart plummeting to the pit of her stomach. She already knew the answer.

Alex froze. He had to come clean and he knew it. How would she ever trust him if he didn't tell her the truth? From here on in, he would tell her absolutely everything, even if it meant he'd lose her. His eyes closed and he prepared himself, turning his face into her hair as he inhaled deeply. The wetness of her tears smeared across his cheek.

"I didn't fuck her, Angel."

"But you touched her."

He steeled himself and pushed on. "Yes, but…"

Instantly, Angel's voice caught on a sob and her arms shoved at him violently. "Uuuuuhhhhhggg! Don't touch me after her! Don't!" She cried hard, her body shaking with her sorrow as she fought to push him away. Alex's heart dropped.

Her reaction only made his arms close around her more tightly as she kicked and clawed, angry tears streaming down her face as she beat at his chest; anguish threatening to choke her. The palm of her hand connected in a sharp slap that stung his cheek. "Don't touch me!" she cried brokenly.

"Angel! For Christ's sake!" Fire ignited across his face.

"No! Nooooooo! Arrahhhhhh!" Her scream pierced his ears, and her struggles caused him to fall with her onto the bed. "How could you? I fucking hate you!" she cried and cried, her heart breaking, fighting against his steel arms and hard chest with all she had, yet sucking in his scent with each gasp. "Don't ever touch me again! I can't bear to have you touch me!"

Alex let her hit him over and over, steeling his muscles against her blows. Ignoring the pain, he held her tighter, his voice trying to calm her down, his fingers stroking her hair while his other arm wrapped around her as tightly as he could. It was unbelievable that this hysterical reaction was coming from this woman.

"Baby, it wasn't like you think. I couldn't... Shhhh..."

"I hate you!" she cried again. "Are you happy? Seeing me so broken and out of control? Did you make fun of me with your whore? Did you kiss her? Was this what you wanted from the beginning? Is this your revenge for that fucking phone call? Tell me, Alex!"

Alex rolled over on top of her and held both hands above her head, his own heart aching as he caged her in with his body. He was burning, his skin crawling until he wanted to rip it off. Somehow, he had to make her understand. His very life depended on it.

"Angel, listen to me!"

She closed her eyes and struggled against his iron hold, her body shaking with the force of her sobs.

"Do you think you're the only one affected? I can't work; I think of little else, keeping myself sane only by talking to Allison and Cole, working with Gant to make sure Swanson gets put away, but even that is about *you*. I thought we were in a good place, until you found the file. I should have gotten rid of the damn thing, but I didn't think twice about it! I haven't touched it since the night we met."

"There are too many lies between us." She turned her face away, tears still dripping from her eyes, and her chest heaving. Her heart was broken, yet he was here, close, and even if it was screwed up, she needed him to take it all away, to rewind the world and erase all that went wrong between them. He was the only one that could ease the ache, and Angel was desperate for it to go away.

"I watched you tonight, looking so fucking amazing, so magnificent, and was so proud of you. Then it all fell apart when I came backstage and Kyle was touching you, your name tattooed on his shoulder like a brand! I felt like I was having a goddamned heart attack! Do you think I'm not suffering? That I haven't *been* suffering? The way you tease me, taunt me... staying just out of my reach! You suck me in closer, and then pull away again! You're sending me to hell and I've had enough!"

"No, I wasn't! I've... missed you." She shook her head violently and gasped as the admission ripped from her. "I would have told you after my last set, if it all didn't go to hell. You fucking destroyed me when you left with her!"

He rested his forehead against hers and tried to steady his breathing. Angel had stopped struggling, but tears still dripped from her eyes. Those eyes, so deep he could lose his soul in them.

"I know. I knew it would." He sighed heavily and prepared for what came next. "Yes, I went to Whitney's tonight. I was drunk off my ass, and I *wanted* to fuck her." Angel heaved beneath him, once again trying to be free as another sob broke from her throat. "But, not because I wanted *her*! I wanted to get you out of my head!" he said urgently. "I *couldn't do it*, Angel! I don't want anyone else!" Alex's chest heaved with the exertion of her struggles and his emotions. His heart thudded heavily in his chest and his breathing was shallow. "I'm—" He paused as he struggled with himself. "—*in love*!" he almost shouted. "Jesus! Can't you see it?"

She stopped struggling as her eyes snapped open, and his mouth found her cheek in a slow, gentle caress, the salty wetness of her tears found purchase on his tongue. His own eyes welled, and his voice thickened. "Agony and ecstasy all rolled up into one. *You* are *everything to me*."

Alex's chest was heavy as he struggled for breath, his heart constricting, throat aching. He waited for words that never came. Fresh tears squeezed out of her eyes as she gasped for her own breath.

"I went crazy seeing you in his arms. I don't want to see another man's hands on you again. Never. Again. Is that clear?" His hot breath fanned her temple as his lips moved against her skin.

"You don't own me."

"*We own each other.* We both know what this is, so just… fucking… *stop denying it!* You belong with me. Admit it."

"If that's true, then why are you acting so damn insane right now?" she breathed.

Alex's knee moved between her legs and he pressed his thigh on her sex, letting go of her wrists and lowering his body to hers, the fingers of one hand gently entwining with hers as his other ran down her body, over the soft swell of her breast. His eyes never left hers as she gasped.

"Because you drive me to it. Because this is mine," he whispered against her cheekbone, "and this…." He squeezed her breast gently, bushing his thumb over the nipple as it hardened. His thigh pressed against her heat, making her body open and moisten against her will. She moaned softly in protest.

Instantly, his body sprang to life, filling so fast it hurt as his cock rubbed painfully against the constricting denim and Angel's thigh. His hand moved further down between them to cup her, his fingers pressing into her soft, hot flesh until she arched up into him. "And this…" he whispered, "every inch… all of you. *Mine.*" Finally, he let his mouth take hers in a deep kiss. Angel cried into his mouth, trying to resist until she gave in, opening fully, her tongue sliding against his in ravenous hunger, both of them forgetting everything else as their bodies melted together, and he settled against her.

Jesus, it hurts so bad, her heart cried, tears falling even as she surrendered to the inevitability of his ownership and her love.

Angel pulled her hand free of his and pulled him closer, her hands going to his hair and then the side of his face as the kiss gentled, his mouth seeking and lightly sucking on hers.

"I hate that you make me so weak," she said brokenly.

"I'm just as weak. I can't stay away from you."

"How could you touch her? Didn't you know what that would do to me?" She curled into him, her arms tightening around him, holding on for dear life as she let go of everything she'd held in and sobbed her heart out. "I di-didn't... wa-want to fe-feel like this."

Alex's heart swelled with hope, yet screamed in pain at the same time. He gathered her shaking body closer still, and her arms and legs encircled him, her hot tears soaking into the shoulder of his shirt. They both fought to get closer even though they were tangled up together. Alex wanted to take her pain away, to soothe her and make sure she knew how much she meant to him. For her to be this upset, surely she must love him in return. He stopped and looked down into her sad eyes, his fingers gentle as his knuckles brushed the side of her face, pushing the hair back.

"Yes, I knew, but I needed you to admit your feelings. I was out of my mind with jealousy. Angel: I'm so sorry. I have no other excuse," he said, his tone like velvet. His nose nuzzled hers until she responded, and finally, he placed a series of soft, open kisses to her now willing mouth as her breathing evened out and deepened. She was calmer now, and Alex needed to finish the conversation. She still hadn't said she loved him, and it ate at his insides. He never thought three simple words would have come to mean so much to him.

Alex forced himself to pull away, rolling off her and sitting on the edge of the bed. Angel was surprised, her skin cold from the sudden loss of his body heat. She turned onto her side toward him, her eyes wide in confusion as they glittered in the half-light, a little crinkle appearing above her nose. Even in all of this mess of emotions, she was the most beautiful thing he'd ever seen.

The tears still glistening in her eyes ripped at his insides, but he needed this to be her choice. He knew he could weaken her resolve, make her give in and probably never leave this room, but he ached for her to come to him of her own free will. Only then would he know for sure she belonged to him.

"I never thought I'd feel anything for anyone, let alone this consuming burn. I hate it, and I'd die for it at the same time. It was inconceivable to me, but, Angel... you... enchant me. Maybe that matters, maybe it doesn't, but I'm to the breaking point. I can't take any more of this push and pull bullshit. I know the game. I used to play it, but it's done. I'm leaving now, and it's up to you. You will come to me," he commanded softly. "Tonight, Angel... or, I'm out. I'll tell Brody to expect you. If you come, we're together and committed. If you don't, then I'm done. I can't live like this." He took her hand and kissed the inside of her wrist, then her palm. He studied her face, her lower lip trembling as she looked up at their entwined hands, then up into his eyes. "I love you. I would give you anything... *everything*. Let me."

With a touch of his index finger to her chin, he was gone.

17

Strength in Weakness

WAITING... FOR THE beginning... or the end.

The minutes ticked by, dropping like nuclear bombs. The more time that passed, the more certain Alex became that Angel wouldn't show. He didn't know how long he'd waited, sitting alone in the darkness in the luxurious big chair, nursing a bottle of Chivas without a glass. The liquid burned on the way down and Alex welcomed the pain. It helped him concentrate on something other than the tightness that refused to let his lungs expand, but the alcohol had yet to numb his mind.

His eyes blurred. Regretting his choice to give her the decision, he told himself he should have stayed and made love to Angel until she had to admit she loved him. She *had* to love him. He sucked in a painful breath. He couldn't stand the consequences if she didn't. He'd be completely lost for the first time in his life.

He laughed bitterly at the irony of the situation. The sound harsh against the background of soft jazz he had playing. Alex—fucking—Avery brought to his knees by a beautiful face, a sultry voice, and a brilliant mind. The responsive body with its lush delights was a bonus. His laughter soon died as the unfamiliar thickness in his throat threatened again. His eyes stung.

"Ughhhh!" he yelled, violently flinging the bottle of expensive scotch at the fireplace. It shattered and splattered against the stones, the alcohol feeding the flames and turning them blue as they crackled and flared up.

He closed his eyes and leaned his head back, willing the blissful peace of unconsciousness to overtake him. Maybe the scotch and his exhaustion would grant his wish. He'd left the door unlocked in an unspoken plea, even though Angel still had his key.

How his life had changed. How *he* had changed. Just months earlier, there was no way in hell he would've given a woman full access to his life. It would have been utterly ridiculous to even consider, yet now, his methodically plotted existence was in shambles, and emotions, he never knew existed, ruled his every move.

He ran a hand through his hair with a big sigh, wondering if he'd ruined any chance he had with her. His heart began to burn. Somehow, he'd gathered the strength to walk from Angel's apartment and slam out the door before he'd given into his need to stay. He probably owed Kyle his gratitude and an apology, but he wasn't ready for that. Images of the other man touching Angel, possibly making love to her, were more than Alex could contemplate without wanting to fucking kill something… or rip his heart out. Either would be preferable to the pain he was experiencing.

Alex's skin crawled at the memory of leaving her alone with the other man, who had openly admitted he still cared for her, but Kyle had still been waiting on Angel's couch when Alex had walked out of her apartment.

What the hell was I thinking? What if she was in Kyle's arms right now? What if he was kissing her, possessing her? He is obviously still in love with her and would no doubt jump at the chance to comfort her. His mind tortured him. He didn't know what he was trying to accomplish; the only thing he was conscious of was the all-consuming feelings that ate away at him. Jealousy, love, desire, protectiveness, fear, pain... he couldn't even get his head around it. His heart was ready to explode and the sick feeling inside his body, coupled with the helplessness he felt, was debilitating.

His emotions made his tight control slip, and he'd done and said things he regretted. He'd wanted to prove to Angel, and to himself, that he could take back control of his life... of his own fucking mind. Backstage, he couldn't stand by and quietly watch her with Kyle's hands on her body and do nothing. He'd snapped. Of course, he'd known how much it would hurt her when he left the benefit with Whitney, but in that moment, all he could focus on was his own agony. He wanted her to hurt like he was hurting.

"Jesus," he groaned softly. "What have I done?"

His fine, white cotton shirt was unbuttoned and the sleeves rolled up on his forearms, his fingers digging into the expensive leather arms of the chair until his well-manicured nails left marks.

The door opening startled him from his thoughts and made his head snap up. He'd turned the chair to face the entryway so he'd see her come in. His breathing stopped as the light from the corridor spread across the floor and she stepped inside, her willowy shadow blocking out most of it. His heart thudded so hard he thought it might burst, unsure if she was real or just a figment of his imagination.

Neither spoke as she slowly moved closer, drawn to him like a reluctant moth until she was standing right in front of him. She made no mention of the change in the chair's position and sank to her knees, weeping silently at her inability to stay away and hating the weakness she couldn't deny. Maybe she was unwilling to lose him completely, no matter how he'd hurt her, no matter the cost to her pride. He realized he didn't want to see her broken. He wanted her love. More than he'd ever wanted anything.

She was dressed in black leggings and an over-sized black sweater, and Alex's gaze lifted to her face only to find her head bowed. Angel would see this as surrender—something she never did willingly and he was well aware of what it cost her. His own heart suffered with it, but he was so damn grateful she was in front of him.

Unable to help himself, Alex shot forward and pulled her to him, wrapping his arms tightly around her, his hand cupping the back of her head as he exhaled in relieved sigh. When her arms slid up around his neck, clutching in desperation as she softly cried into him, he turned his face into the curve of her neck and shoulder in relief. She was here; in his arms… they were going to be okay.

Her hair was damp and freshly shampooed, and he sucked in the aroma thankfully but his rigid lungs protested painfully. He pressed her closer, hands splaying out on her back and hips as his own emotions overwhelming.

"Angel, shhh. Don't cry, my love. Oh, baby," he breathed. "It's gonna be okay. I'm so glad you're here."

"Why does it have to hurt so much? It hurts like I've never hurt before." Her voice was thick and broken.

"It means you love me. Doesn't it?" The seconds of her hesitation felt like years.

The response ripped out of her. "You know I do." Alex closed his eyes at the much-needed words. "I love you *too much*."

Her pain soaked through his skin, and soon he wasn't sure if it was her ache or his that was suffocating him. He longed to take it from her as his mouth found hers in a frantic quest for solace. The kisses were a passionate building and ebbing as each accepted the inevitability of their own defeat.

His hands cradled her face, and his tender worshiping left her breathless. Alex pulled his mouth from hers reluctantly; anxious to speak to her, to hear her words.

"Angel, I was wrong about so many things. I'm sorry. I know how bad it hurts, but that's over now."

"Shhh, just hold me. Don't ever let me go."

He held onto her for dear life as he lifted her onto his lap, kissing the side of her face. They couldn't get close enough to each other. Angel brought her knees up, and she curled into him in the big chair, her head coming to rest on his strong shoulder, forehead meeting the pulse in his neck. The steady beat reinforced his presence, and she relaxed in his arms; her hand fell through his open shirt onto his bare chest, inhaling the familiar scent of his skin and cologne.

Alex's chest rose, his lungs finally filling for what felt like the first time in weeks. The sensation left him unsure if this new pain was good or bad. "God, I've missed you. I love you so much it's killing me, Angel."

She closed her eyes, praying he spoke the truth. Touching his face, she pressed her lips to his jaw once, twice, and left them there, open and longing for him to turn his mouth back to hers.

There was so much she wanted to talk to him about, but this was too magnificent to ruin with questions that could crack her open. Maybe she didn't even want to know the answers.

Alex had admitted he loved her and she needed the peace his words afforded more than anything else. After a while, he slid his arm under her knees and lifted her in silence, carrying her up the stairs and into the master bedroom.

The hour left the room pitch dark as he placed her gently on the bed. Angel's arms tightened in protest as he began to move away. "Stay with me."

The ache in Alex's heart began to ease. "It's almost dawn, sweetheart. I'm just going to close the blinds so we can sleep in." Exhaustion laced his voice as his fingers brushed the side of her face. "My girl can't sleep with the sun streaming in."

She smiled into the darkness. There was a soft whir in the blackness as the electronic shades moved over the windows, followed by the soft sounds of him shedding his clothes.

As she lay in the dark, listening, her heart pounded and her body throbbed, missing him even in the mere seconds that passed.

She felt desperate to have his arms around her; his closeness had become the greatest need of her life.

Alex sat next to her, his fingers gentle and unhurried as he removed her clothes, which soon littered the floor with his.

The second he was beside her, Angel rolled into him, and his arms enveloped her, their legs tangling together.

"I was so worried you wouldn't come."

"How could I not come?" she murmured softly into his chest as his lips fell to the top of her head, and he sighed. "You said it. You own me."

"It's both of us. I'm a slave to whatever this is. I never believed feeling like this was possible, but I never want it to end. I never want you out of my sight again."

Alex's mouth claimed hers hotly as passion flared between them. It was glorious and desperate, hands seeking and finding inch upon inch of smooth flesh, bodies sliding, rubbing, and arousing each other to madness.

Angel's fingers clawed at Alex's back and the side of his neck, her body strained against his, silently begging for his possession. Her breathing was sporadic, washing over his skin like it was the most precious gold, her soft moans music to his ears. His heart swelled and then tightened, tears burning the back of his eyes.

"Baby. Angel… I want to take this slow. Make love with me."

She stopped, her hand coming up to push back his hair and linger along the side of his face.

"We always make love. It's always felt like love to me. Even when I didn't want it to be," she whispered against his mouth, taking his lower lip between both of hers to nudge and nibble, and Alex let out a low groan as his mouth crashed into hers in response to her words, his tongue invading the warm recesses of her mouth to worship hers.

He'd be happy just to kiss her forever, to have her arms around him and know she belonged to him was enough. His hands slid down her flesh, over the soft swells of her breasts, and her already hard nipples tightened even more. Her back arched, and her arms tightened around him when the warmth of his mouth closed around one rosy peak.

"Ohhh... Alex," she breathed as he suckled and gently rolled it between his teeth, softly tugging until she was writhing. His hands slid further as he moved his mouth to the other breast, finding the flesh that called for his attention with the rise of her hips.

Angel was hot and slick, and his dick, already fully engorged, ached as his desire became unbearable. He wanted to bury himself inside this woman and never separate. His fingers probed softly, exciting her more when he pushed his middle finger inside her.

She groaned aloud. "Mmmmm..."

"God, Angel," he groaned against her breast. "I want you. Every day until forever." Alex's thumb found the bundle of nerves and he began to work his magic on her body. Angel bucked beneath him with a throaty moan. The hunger in that sound made him crazy, and he had to fight to keep the urgency out of his actions.

Her small hand closed around his length, and his breath caught. She longed to feel the fullness of him pushing inside her, but she wanted to tease and taunt him the way he was doing to her. She moved up and down, pulling and pushing until his hips moved with her hand, and her thumb caught the drop of pre-cum leaking from his thick head and she swirled it around his throbbing flesh.

"Please, Alex..." she begged, kissing his temple and winding her fingers into his sweat-dampened hair. "Please... now. I can't take anymore."

"I wanted to make you come."

"I'll come with you. Please don't make me wait to have you inside me."

Alex's hands slid up her body and curled into the flesh of her waist as he rolled over, positioning her above him, his hands kneading her firm thighs beside his hips as she straddled him.

Alex watched her face, needing her to be left in no doubt about how he felt. "This time, when my body slides into yours, know I love you." She slid along his hardness, pressing her clit against him until they were both panting. Angel's eyes closed and her mouth parted. "Ohhh, mmmm," she whimpered as he finally slid inside. It had been so long—too long—and her body craved his. "I love you, too."

"*Jesus*. Angel, you're so perfect. Your body is perfect. So sexy. Nothing on earth is better than this." His hands reached up to trace the outline of her breasts with tender touches as she began to move on him, long, slow strokes as both of them savored the connection and the slow building of sensation. He sat up and cupped both sides of her face in his hands, and his mouth took hers in a series of long deep kisses... So hot, each one more than the last. He wanted to communicate how much he loved her, his desperation for her body, and how he couldn't exist without her.

Her body was hot and tight around his, and in combitation with the love and lust on her face, Alex was convinced he wouldn't last long. Already, his body was tightening, the orgasm building in strength. His heart tightened and he couldn't breathe.

Suddenly, one arm wrapped around her waist to yank her body closer to his as he thrust upward, deeper, grinding her clit into his pelvis. His arms wrapped around her, tightly controlling the movements as he pumped into her harder and faster. He could tell she was getting close too, her body clenching and milking at his, her arms tightening around his shoulders, nails raking his skin.

"Angel." Her name was like a prayer on his lips. He slowed down, but still pushed in to the hilt, their bodies as close as they could get with every thrust. "I want this to last, but you turn me on so much."

"Don't think. Just love me. Ummmm…" She moaned softly, and he wanted to show her how much. She felt her body stretch to accommodate him and her muscles clenched around him.

The seated position allowed for a deeper connection, Alex's body reaching deeply into hers, and his mouth taking and giving, sucking and worshiping hers like he couldn't get enough.

He rolled her over onto her back, his hands lovingly stroking back the hair on both sides of her head as he moved in her, pinning her to the mattress with the deliberate force of his thrusts. He raised his head to look into her face, his eyes burning in the darkness. His body was on the brink and he slowed down, pushing into her in long, strong strokes.

"Hey," he said softly, and she opened her eyes. "You're everything. Do you hear me? Never doubt me. I can't imagine being without you now."

"Yes." Her face lifted, wanting his mouth again, even as her body began to unravel around his. She trembled from head to toe with the force of her orgasm, her back arching of its own volition as her body spiraled out of control. "Oh, Alex…" Her voice was low and sensual, the words slow and breathy. She shuddered around him, her body falling into pleasure made more by the emotions overwhelming her heart. Being with Alex like this was a miracle, hearing him say he loved her filled her up, but still there was fear of the incredible pain she would suffer if she lost him. "Don't break my heart… I love you, so much. You'll destroy me."

His green eyes glowed and finally closed, his heart both heavy and full at the ache in her voice. Hurting her was the last thing he ever wanted to do. She was the most precious thing and he'd spend as much time as necessary to ease her fears.

Finally, the emotion and the pleasure became too much and he came inside her in a series of powerful spurts, embedded as deeply as possible, while her body still jerked and squeezed his. Alex held Angel tight and found her mouth again, still moving inside her and on her. Even as their bodies came down, they kissed again and again, unable to get enough of each other—kissing as if they were only starting to make love rather than finishing. Finally, he rested his cheek against her temple, her hair clinging damply to both of them, their breathing still heavy and hard.

"I fucking love you so much. I never want to be anywhere but where you are." He pushed into her again to prove his point. "*I love you, babe.* Please believe me. Trust in me."

Angel's hand lifted and her fingers traced along his jaw, now slightly scruffy and her eyes locked with his. She nodded and he kissed her once more.

Alex rolled away just enough to slip out of her gently, but never letting her out of his arms. His fingers stroked her back and hair as she lay draped over him, each of them needing to soak up the closeness. Angel lifted her head and kissed his chest, her lips moving in a reverent path of open lips and slight sucking. Alex's heart tightened when he felt her hot tears drip onto his skin. "I'm scared," she whispered.

"You don't need to be. I'm here and I'm not going anywhere. Ever."

"Promise?"

"I want to marry you and make babies. What does that tell you?"

She gasped in surprise, her head lifting so her chin rested on him and she could look up into his face. "Are you serious?"

"Babe, seeing you with Jillian, being with you, the insatiable desire and the protectiveness I feel, the desperation when we're fighting with each other, the *jealousy*... Are you fucking kidding me?" He shook his head incredulously. "I know it's only been a few months, but you've wrecked me."

Her arms tightened around him, and she closed her eyes, laying her head back on his chest. "I love you more than I can take."

"I know. It hurts, but in a good way."

Angel felt compelled to tell him everything. "Alex, it was me. I was with you. You weren't dreaming that night."

His gentle fingers touched the velvet softness of her cheek. "I know. I could smell you on the sheets afterward, but it was so breathtaking; at first I thought it was my imagination. I realized I was in love with you that night." Her arms tightened around him, but she remained silent. "What made you come to me?"

"I was scared, worried for both of us. I needed you. I just... I wanted to be close to you, to feel you, to be safe and know you were, too. Plus, I was miserable... missing you."

"Knowing now what you went through that night, I realize I could have hurt you. I'm sorry if I did. I've never hated anyone as much as I do Mark Swanson. I could kill him for what he's done to you. My methods were probably wrong because you were so stubborn, but my intention was only to take care of you. Can you forgive me?"

"It's over now and I know why you did it. There's nothing to forgive."

They lay together in silence, soaking each other in, until Alex couldn't help himself.

"Angel..." His fingers wound into the hair at the back of her head. "Tell me about Kyle's tattoo."

She sighed, one shoulder lifting in a slight shrug. Part of her thrilled that he was jealous and she could tease him, but she sensed he was hurting. "It's nothing. He got it after we split up. It was his way of showing he cared, and he was trying to get me back. Sheer stupidity on his part."

"What did he do to make you leave him?"

"He cheated. With that air-head, Crystal."

"He'd choose her over you? No wonder you were so upset tonight. I'm an insensitive ass."

Angel snuggled into his arms, understanding, but choosing not to address the issue of Whitney again.

"Kyle and I wanted different things. He wanted to continue with the band, and I wanted to go to grad school. We were drifting apart, and I suppose he turned to her when I wasn't there for him anymore."

He digested what she said, continuing to stroke her hair. It eased the ache in his heart knowing she wasn't heartsick over Kyle, even when she left him. It was somehow unbearable that she would feel this deeply for anyone else, ever.

As if reading his mind, Angel reinforced his thoughts with her words. "It wasn't like it was tonight. Tonight... I was dying, Alex."

Alex rolled her over onto her back again and settled into the cradle of her body in one fluid motion. His fingers were tender as they brushed against her face, first her cheekbone and then her chin. He needed to make her understand the depth of how he felt.

"Angel, listen to me. Look at me," he commanded.

Her eyes met his, and even in the darkness, she could see the shimmer in his eyes. "I was overwrought with jealousy. I have no excuse for how I acted, but I couldn't breathe; I couldn't see straight. When I saw him touch you... Well, I wasn't prepared for how I felt." His voice was low, urgent. "My world imploded."

"I understand..."

"No, let me finish. For the first time, I didn't think; I just re-acted. The whole time, you're all I thought about... how much I wanted you and how much it hurt. I was beside myself to find a way to stop the pain."

"Don't tell me you thought about me when you were with her." The sorrow in her eyes made Alex even more determined.

"Understand what I'm saying. It wasn't like that. I... *love you.*" Alex insisted with a smile and then huffed with a small shake of his head, his eyes burning into hers. "You're always with me, even when I don't want you to be. It's not a choice. It's just how it is."

Angel returned his smile and nudged his jaw with her nose, wanting nothing more than to touch him and to be held in his arms. "Better get used to it," she whispered.

Alex's breath rushed out in amusement, and he smiled down at her. Her lips lifted in the start of a smile, her finger running down the side of his face as they stared into each other's eyes. Alex's face sobered as his body found hers and she surged up to take him inside.

"With pleasure," he groaned. "So much pleasure." His mouth closed hungrily over hers.

Coming soon, Alex and Angel's story concludes in

~Promises After Dark~

If you'd like to receive the first chapter of Promises After Dark, sign up here: http://eepurl.com/Q-KCH

CPSIA information can be obtained at www.ICGtesting.com
Printed in the USA
LVOW09s0615221114

415023LV00001B/18/P